CREW ELEVEN

Robert Bartron

DEDICATION

To all the military spouses and families
that must serve by staying behind.
It is always harder than going.

ACKNOWLEDGMENTS

The author wishes to acknowledge and express his deepest
gratitude to his wife who over four decades has
accommodated her life and dreams to his often times erratic
and eccentric choices and projects. She is the epitome of the
perfect "Navy Wife" who has three wonderful (now grown)
children to evidence it. She is simply the best.

Books by Robert Bartron

Crew Eleven

*The Autobiography of
Terry Ryan, A Shooter*
(with Pat Bartron)

You Can't Give Up On Love

My Life as a Sailor

River People

The Jake Riley Military Crime Series
To Steal a Million

To Murder a Ghost

To Clear Datum

To Steal a Nuke

To Drown a Fish

Young Adult Books
Nearcus Versus the Gods

Amelia Takes on Cancer

Merrilee & the Pirates

Children's Books
Wylie Finds His Special Place

Simone Saves the Day

All titles available at Amazon.com
and other on-line book sellers.

PRELUDE

In the United States Navy all sailors know a "sea story" when they hear one. There are two basic classes of sea stories. A normal sea story, by definition, has, at most, 80% truth in it. If it did not include at least 20% of "elaboration" (after all, sailors never lie) then it is merely a retelling of an actual event. The relationship between a sea story and the retelling of a true event is inversely proportional to the listener's interest. The more truth, the less interest. In other words, a normal sea story recognizes that it often times is necessary to add some detail or attitude to the telling just for the sake of the listener, less the poor fellow be forced to endure a dry recitation of boring, un-enhanced facts.

But there is another, special class of sea story. It is sometimes referred to as a "November Sierra" tale. It can always be recognized by the use of two words in the first line of the story. If the teller utters the couplet "no s---!" placed anywhere in the story introduction, then it most definitely qualifies as a "November Sierra" tale. Again, by definition, this special class of stories cannot include more than 25% of truth. Some might call them "whoppers" or "B.S." or, in land lubber terminology, "fish stories," but for those of us long-serving sailors we just refer to them as the best tales.

I have a long sea story to share with you, and "no s---, it is all true." It could of taken place during the height of the Cold War and while I was serving in Japan. *"And trust me, it is all true."*

CHAPTER ONE

His teeth hurt. With every bounce Petty Officer Thomas's teeth clatter together and sharp pain races up his jaw. His body is exhausted. He is nearly limp in his seat; only the shoulder harness keeps him from falling out. The heavy helmet makes it difficult to keep his head upright. He feels like a fighter in round fifteen. Beat upon, bruised, tired. Only the smell is worse. The odor of rotten, twisted Philippine cigars and puke.

The P-3C Orion is the Navy's version of the Lockheed Electra airliner of the 1950's. It is now 1985 and this airframe went into service before Thomas was born. It is a four-engine turboprop that rides like a flat-bottomed boat in a choppy sea and every bounce rattles his teeth. Piece of junk. Sturdy and reliable, with long legs and okay speed; but still a piece of junk in bad weather. And why would the Navy spend millions on these planes and not invest another $9,000 in a weather radar? Can't even see around the strong cells to avoid the worst weather. Piece of junk.

Petty Officer Second Class Rick Thomas has flown with Crew Eleven for the entire deployment. He is convinced that it is a good crew with at least one competent pilot. His teeth may hurt and he may hate flying right at this moment, but usually the job is all right. It is better than what he left in Watervliet, New York. High school seems a century ago. Could it have been just five years? Thomas forces himself to grin as he considers the different path he chose. His good buddies in high school are still looking for something to do on Friday nights; still living in a world defined by $5.50 per hour and being bossed by petty managers. Their lives remain just big talk and no action. Here he is, making good money, strapped in a seat, facing backwards in the dark with no windows nearby, defying death and gravity in the air over Misawa, Japan after a long mission. He is finishing another twelve full hours of rotten weather, flying all night trying to locate a Russian submarine in the Sea of Japan while putting up with the smoke from those cheap cigars his senior AQA-7 sensor operator, Petty Officer First Class Ambrose Jones, smokes just to make him airsick. Thomas groans to himself, "Jones knows I don't handle foul weather good and he smokes those things just to watch me puke. A-hole."

The airplane takes an especially heavy jolt. Thomas involuntarily flexes his tired body to fight against it. Then he lifts his left leg so he can hurriedly reach into the flight suit calf pocket for a fresh airsickness bag. He pukes again. Jones, who is sitting behind Thomas in their landing positions, gives a hearty laugh that can be heard over the engine noise and through Thomas's helmet ear protection.

Between wretches, Thomas recites his immediate mantra, "A-hole. Piece of junk."

In the cockpit, the fatigue factor is even higher. Lieutenant Commander Jim Keene, the Patrol Plane Commander, is in the right seat. This is his third tour in P-3s. His experience and skill level have made his reactions to the situation automatic. But his body feels like it is hanging from his skeleton. For twelve hours one tune has been replaying itself in his mind. No, one line from one tune has haunted him the entire flight. The line from the Eagles, "Lying Eyes," that goes, "another night, it's gonna be a long one". He has pulled a couple hundred of these all-nighters in his career and they only grow harder. At thirty-three he feels like an old man. He no longer has the desire to "hit the beach" when the crew lands in a new liberty port after one of these flights. He now realizes the truth in the adage: "military flying is a young man's game." Every part of his body and brain desires nothing more than to climb between

2

clean sheets in his BOQ rack and sleep forever. Fatigue weighs heaviest on the "old."

Now Keene's impatience with his Second Pilot bubbles to the surface. He must continuously remind himself that George McKay is only a lieutenant j.g. and still learning to lead a combat aircrew. But Keene questions whether McKay will ever learn the most important attributes that cannot be taught: self-confidence, decisiveness, command judgment. Whatever you call it, McKay is in short supply. He has good hand-eye skills and enough judgment to make safe decisions. Basically he is an okay stick. But the crew does not trust him. Maybe distrust is too harsh a judgment. The crew lacks confidence—*respect*—for him.

Keene watches McKay in the left seat. He is flying a good precision approach in really rotten weather, yet on his face he wears a worried look. His voice is weak when he speaks. Keene is tired, so he lets doubt in McKay's ability taint his thoughts. It is not enough, he thinks, to be able to wrestle this fifty tons of twisted steel and sex appeal down an imaginary slide in the sky to a precise landing on any one-hundred foot patch of concrete you desire; you have to look confident doing it.

Keene keys the microphone with the thumb switch on the yoke, "Misawa control, this is delta-sierra-four-two-five on I-L-S final for runway one-three. Say again latest ceiling and winds."

"Delta-sierra-four-two-five, Misawa control. Ceiling is one hundred feet. Winds are one-four-five at fifteen. Be advised your two squadron sister planes had to divert to Atsugi after multiple approaches earlier this evening." The Japanese accent in the controller's voice reminds Keene of previous problems he has experienced in this northern sector. He prefers to fly near Tokyo and Okinawa despite the heavier traffic there because most of the controllers are American ex-patriots. You can understand them better. Keene is convinced that the Japanese at the bottom of the controllers training class, those with the worst English, are sent to the northern sector.

From his high center seat in the cockpit the flight engineer has the best view looking forward. But there is nothing to see except darkness, rain smashing against the windshield, and the reflection of the landing lights' glow illuminating the dense clouds. Chief Petty Officer Ronald Smithers reaches to the overhead panel and lowers the lights to keep them from blinding the pilots when, that is if, it is necessary to transition to outside visual references. At nearly six foot six inches, he is one of the tallest and strongest flight engineers in the fleet. A gentle giant, he has enjoyed the seat with the best view for over seven thousand hours in the air. He is experienced; a good sailor you can trust with your life.

"That must've been Marlin Four and Seven," says Smithers, referring to other Patrol Squadron Forty crews that were also on patrol this night. Smithers feels that the "Fighting Marlins" of VP-40 is a good squadron. He has been in others that were better and a few that were worse. It is a good squadron.

Keene continues to watch McKay as well as the instruments, "How are you doing, Mr. McKay? I have you right of centerline and on glide slope. Two-hundred feet to decision height."

Just then the plane pitches downward in rough air. McKay immediately corrects to the right glide path.

"I didn't see that pothole coming," Keene says as he drops his scan from the window screen to his instruments.

"It were a big one alright." Smithers doesn't speak much, so getting seven syllables from him means the situation is tense.

Keene goes through the mechanics of multi-place cockpit landings, "One hundred feet to decision height. Missed approach procedures are reviewed. Gear down and locked. Landing checklist reviewed complete. Now all we have to do is breakout and find this place."

"Flight engineer, set seven hundred shaft horsepower." McKay says as his eyes dance between instruments as he struggles to finish the approach.

"Seven hundred, aye sir." Smithers leans forward and carefully adjusts the four power levers on the right side of the center console.

Keene and McKay look for the runway through the rain. The sound of the water hitting the airplane is hollow and monotonous. The windshield wipers are loud. The rain comes so fast at 160 mph the wipers prove under effective.

"Go to high on the wipers, Chief." Keene's voice is an octave lower and much calmer than McKay's.

Without taking his eyes off the front engine instrument panel, Smithers reaches above the windshield and turns a knob. The beat of the windshield wipers doubles. Keene regrets the unconscious raising of the tension in the cockpit this causes, but it must be done to give the best chance to see the runway.

Sitting behind McKay, perched on the forward radar cabinet is Ensign Fred Glenn, the third pilot. Having joined the squadron and Crew Eleven just before the deployment commenced four months ago, this is his first actual night, foul weather approach down to precision minimums. Glenn opens his mouth to share a bit of humor to try and ease the tension. He notices the white-knuckle grip McKay's left hand has on the yoke and thinks better of saying anything. He looks at Keene and notices how much older he appears at the end of the flight. He can tell by the slight bounce in Keene's head that he is singing to himself. Glenn thinks, "I wonder what song is in his head?" as he gives a slight grin at the contrast between the two pilots.

Keene breaks the silence stating firmly, "Decision height. I have nothing over here. You have anything over there?"

"I think I have the approach lights," McKay answers tentatively.

"Either you have the runway environment in sight or you don't." Keene snaps at him, "Which is it? Take us around or land us—now!"

McKay strains to make out the running rabbit of strobe lights that will lead to the runway threshold. Just to his left he makes out what he thinks are the approach lights. Or are they? The weight of the decision is enormous. Get it wrong and twelve good men will die. McKay's thoughts weigh heavily on him, "Why did I put myself in this situation? Am I crazy to be here? Don't over think it. Just react."

"It's the lights...yeah, I'm sure, we're going down."

Keene sees nothing but blackness and rain outside his wind shield. He could override the copilot's decision, but that isn't his style. He will trust McKay's judgment, but ride the controls to try and pull it out at the last minute if it is a mistake. His left hand squeezes the base of his four power levers, having it strategically placed under the flight engineers hand. Smithers notices this slight reaction, and smiles to himself, "Keene is okay. He won't bury us." But he wonders about McKay. This should be a good test.

"Misawa control, four-two-five has field in sight." Keene's voice is smooth and deep. What military aviators call their "Chuck Yeager" voice.

The entire crew aft hears Keene's transmission. His voice over the radio brings a quiet confidence to nine men sitting in the dark, refusing to consider just how truly perilous their real situation is. Knowing they are close to the ground, there is a small panic buried deep in the back of their subconscious screaming "Death! Death is in charge and you have no control, only death dictates!" All refuse to listen. All dull the cries with thoughts of the future. Yet as fatigue grows, the strength to keep that voice locked in the subconscious weakens. But now Keene's voice has driven it back into its hole. Pilots and flight engineers refer to these non-cockpit personnel as "tube rats". Most pilots have trouble understanding how they can trust control to others.

In a flash the end could come and if it does then you have to sit there and take it. Like Christians to the lions. No chance to fight. No chance to hit the homerun and save the game. Yeah, tube rats are special. They have a really perverse courage.

The plane takes a sharp twist to the left. Jones isn't laughing anymore. His whole body tenses. Now the right wing dips. Jones' jaw clamps tight. The plane yaws like a car on a sheet of ice.

"Feels like the commander is having to dig his spurs in hard and hold on tight to get this ol' Brahma back in the barn." Jones pretends to speak to Thomas, but he doesn't care who, if anyone, hears. He just needs to say something.

Thomas can sense his back grow stiff as he feels the nose come up. The landing flare is smooth but too high. He can feel the pilot searching for the deck. Any second now the main mounts should touch down. Any second now. Please.

The touchdown is firm. No airline squeaker, it is a good firm Navy landing. Smack it on the deck and hold it there, the Navy way. The tube rats are thrown against the back of their seats as the propellers' pitch reverse, grabbing, then throwing masses of air forward to slow down this huge tricycle. A shallow skid to the left, and then this piece of junk slows to exit the runway. Once on the taxi way, the crew is released from landing stations.

McKay's worried look has been replaced by one of amazement and pride. It passes quickly and he again furrows his brow as he squints to see in the driving rain. His left hand is on the small ground steering wheel by his left knee. His right hand manipulates the four power levers on the left side of the center console. Keene has gotten taxi clearance to the Patrol Squadron Forty ramp. He now attempts radio contact with squadron maintenance control to arrange a lineman for parking.

Jones and Petty Officer Tom Ford, the In-Flight Technician, crowd into the cockpit. Jones gently taps Keene on the shoulder, "Great job Commander! I'm glad we don't have to follow those other guys to Atsugi, it's steak night at the club tonight, don't cha know."

"Yeah! Screw those prima donnas in Crew Seven. We got in when no one else could!" Ford says, smiling ear to ear. "Good driving Commander Keene!"

"Why are you slapping my back? I didn't do anything. It was Lieutenant McKay that got us in."

There is a moment of silence as Ford and Jones look at McKay with astonishment and new respect.

Jones is the first to recover, "Well, Mr. McKay, good on ya, sir. Maybe it'll be okay if you do get your papers soon."

"If you can fly like that, there might be hope for you yet...sir," Ford adds, his honest feelings being expressed in an awkward manner.

Keene is too tired to smile at his good fortune. McKay sets the parking brake and the lineman signals to shutdown the engines. Ford and Jones exit the cockpit.

Keene leans forward to look around Smithers and make eye contact with both McKay and Glenn, then he speaks, "Chief, you can't hear this."

"My ears are closed, sir."

Keene goes into his senior flight instructor mode and says, "George, in case you missed it, that was the ultimate compliment you just received. Always remember that those guys in the back are betting their lives every time they climb up the aircraft ladder that you can do your job and bring this beast home safely. They gotta believe you can do it or you'll never have a true crew."

McKay wants to say something, but he doesn't know what. He smiles and looks into Keene's eyes for a moment. He thinks, "I wonder when he got so old? He looks rung out." McKay's chest swells a little as he contemplates the message. It feels good to have the crew's respect. It feels even better to have Keene's trust.

* * * * *

Keene is loaded down with his Life Preserver Apparatus, a large metal clipboard, a helmet bag loaded with charts in the side pockets, and his flight jacket. He is soaking wet from the walk to the hangar after parking the aircraft. He crosses the hangar and enters the maintenance control office. Behind the counter, balanced on two rickety stools, are Chief Cressman and Senior Chief Howard. They truly enjoy being in charge of the night shift. They work well as a team. Howard knows avionics better than anyone in Westpac. Cressman is an airframes whiz. And they can bum cigarettes off each other. It is uncharacteristically quiet in maintenance control. In just another hour the day shift will report and the other 150 maintainers will "turn-to and commence squadron work." The chiefs enjoy the respite and unspoken brotherhood of the shadow time before the dawn.

"Morning, Commander. Well done on getting in. Crew Eleven turns out to be our only customers tonight," Howard says with an easy Tennessee drawl. Keene is the Maintenance Officer of the squadron and Howard respects his approach to these department head duties. Howard bristled under the smothering direction of Keene's predecessor who was so worried about getting promoted that he micro-managed all daily departmental activities. But Howard enjoys the trust that Keene places in the senior enlisted leadership to run maintenance control. Consequently, Howard and Cressman take pride in running a tight shift and actually enjoy the relatively infrequent times they interact with the "M.O.," which is what every aviation maintenance department head is called.

"Yeah. Been pretty quiet around here except for the rain on the tin roof. Bad weather the whole flight?" asks Cressman.

Keene nods with a small grin to acknowledge the interest of these professionals.

Howard takes a long pull on his cigarette, slides off his stool and snuffs out the butt in the Government Issue glass ashtray on the counter. "'Fraid I've good news and bad news for you, M.O."

Keene looks up from the metal clipboard he has opened on the counter. He appears puzzled.

Howard continues, "The good news is that you came home with Q-E 06. We needed her back. She is scheduled for a 45-day inspection today. The bad news is that you got back when Crew Seven didn't."

Petty Officer Second Class Peters, the Crew Eleven Second Mechanic, enters Maintenance Control and lifts a heavy flight bag containing reference publications onto the counter. He removes his Mickey Mouse ear protectors and shakes the water from his hair. He throws the airplane key, fastened to a large hunk of metal shaped like a marlin, at Cressman who nearly falls from his stool to catch it.

"Here ya go, Chief! Six is all buttoned-up. She has a ramp load and the belly is empty of buoys." It is obvious that Peters is becoming more familiar with the routine. This is his first Westpac deployment, but he joined the squadron four months before they left. A smart boy, his mother was shocked when he said he had enlisted before graduating from high school. Just days after getting his diploma he got his head shaved and was yelled at by his Boot Camp company commander. After a tour in a helicopter squadron as a hydraulics technician his application for aircrew duty was accepted. A good shipmate, always willing to do his share, he suffers from a serious personality flaw that even he is unaware of just yet.

Jones stomps into Maintenance Control and grabs Peters by the elbow. "Come on, Tommy. We're holding up the van for you. If you don't want to walk to the Q in the rain, let's look lively sailor."

Keene makes eye contact with Howard and continues their previous conversation, "Let me guess. We get Crew Seven's tactical. Right?"

Howard nods. "Commander, you should get your boys to crew rest pronto. You guys pulled another one tonight. Preflight at 2330."

"We got what?" Jones is highly agitated. He is a very direct sailor. "Those wouses get to lie around the pool in Atsugi and we gotta do their work for them? That's not fair, Commander. Crew Seven is always pulling this crap. They knew they were on the schedule for tonight. They must've landed in Atsugi four hours ago. Why can't they fly the mission from there? They got an ASWOC down in Atsugi don't they?"

Keene feels the same way, but he just exhales. "We're on the sked now, Petty Officer Jones."

"Yeah, only because Crew Seven is the Skipper's pet. Do you know what kind of mission it is, Commander? It's a rotten PARPRO! The Skipper doesn't want to give them a chance to screw it up again. Wish we were foul-ups so the ol' man would protect us."

Keene stops doing the post-flight paperwork and slowly sets his pen down. He turns his head to look Jones in the eye.

Jones tightens his jaw. "This sucks." He slams the door as he leaves with Peters.

Keene knew Jones was right; but Crew Eleven is now on the flight schedule again. And true professionals fly the flight schedule. He looks at Howard, ""What bird we got tonight, Senior Chief?"

"Q-E 05, Commander. If we can get her back together in time. Otherwise.."

"Let me guess, the hangar queen?"

11

Both Howard and Cressman nod, trying not to smile.

"Don't give me that look. You just have Q-E 05 put back together and the check flight done by 2330. No way I'm going to fly a twelve-hour mission in the hangar queen."

Cressman says, "Come on, M.O., Q-E 09 isn't that bad-- if you don't mind flying on three engines with no pressurization or cabin heat."

"This sucks." Keene says it all.

Howard lights another cigarette and speaks as he exhales the first long drag, "Yes, sir. It sure do suck."

CHAPTER TWO

Not the cheap knockoffs. The real Righteous Brothers. Classic stuff. No one, black or white, can touch him so powerfully. Last week he heard one of those brand new compact discs. Those new CDs are unbelievable, a real break through in technology. He had never heard such clarity in a sound system before. After hearing that quality, the scratches, pops and hiss of an LP really stand out. But what good is CD technology if they don't put the Righteous Brothers on disc? What good is new modern technology if the best of the past is left behind?

Colonel Ronald Milkus, USMC is a traditionalist. He believes in God, the U.S.A., the Corps, and the Righteous Brothers but not necessarily in that order. He moves across the living room of his small townhouse to be near the speakers of a sound system that covers the entire wall. He leans forward to hear Bobby Hatfield speak those tender words, "Baby, I can't make it without you, and, I'm tellin' ya Honey, you're my reason for laughin', for cryin', for livin' and for dyin'". When Bill Medley belts out the next line, goose bumps literally climb up Milkus's arm. He wants to finish the song, but duty calls. So he carefully lifts the arm on his turn table and removes his precious album. With delicate care he wipes the dust from it, slides it into the jacket and replaces it, alphabetically, back on the shelf. He hums "You're My Soul and Inspiration" as he picks up his hat from the end table near the door. In a motion that is totally second nature to him after repeating it for twenty-six years, he places the hat squarely on his short-cropped head. He doesn't notice the picture of his ex-wife and two daughters on the same table. He stops, turns and stands in the door and looks back. All squared-away; okay to depart.

It is only four stops and fifteen minutes on the Metro Yellow Line for Milkus to reach the Pentagon. He stands to the right on the long, long escalator to let those who fail to plan properly run past. Milkus is proud of his organization, in everything, including his time management. Pentagon duty is not bad, except for certain civilians. Why must they always arrive late for scheduled meetings? Civilians and Army officers can never seem to make it on time. Air Force and most Naval officers understand the efficiency of punctuality. And God help any Marine who arrives late to a Colonel Milkus meeting. Luckily, this meeting is with Navy and Air Force officers and only one civilian. Want to bet who is late?

The Pentagon is busy even on Sunday nights. Milkus passes through security at the Metro entrance. Up the ramp, down two halls and he reaches the bulletproof glass guard station for entrance to the Joint Chiefs of Staff area. Another security pass, and Milkus goes to the end of the hall, turns right and reaches the office of J-2. He checks his watch. It is 1825. Five minutes early. There is no secretary at the desk in the front office, but the door to the small conference room is open. Milkus is the first there. Two minutes later Captain Frank Carter, U.S.N. and Lieutenant Commander Francine Denton, U.S.N join him. Exactly at 1830, Lieutenant General Augustus Adams, U.S.A.F and his aide, Major John Griffith, U.S.A.F, stride into the room. The Marine and Naval officers stand and come to attention. Officers of other services often grow lax during the familiarity of Pentagon duty, but professional courtesy is inbred in the naval service and absolutely second nature to these officers.

"Please be seated." Adams is still amazed by the formality of the Navy and Marines. "Who are we waiting on? Anyone?"

"Mr. Bordon has yet to arrive, General," says Milkus. He isn't making a point about unprofessionalism of civilians; he is simply stating fact.

The General looks at Major Griffith. "John, could you see what's keeping him? It is bad enough we all have to assemble on a weekend. We don't want it to take any longer than is necessary."

Griffith nods and exits. There is an odd silence in the conference room. It passes when Carter speaks, "I believe there is coffee on the sideboard, General, if you'd like a cup?"

Adams, who is short and square and gives a grandfatherly impression except for his stern eyes, shakes his head. He is deep in thought as he looks at his watch. Then he breaks his concentration and looks up. "Not for me, Captain, but please help yourself."

Carter gets a cup. Black. Just like on the mid-watch. He wishes he was back on the bridge of a ship watching the sun set over a red horizon and not at this meeting. Four years of "Puzzle Palace" duty was supposed to be career enhancing. But Carter knew the score like every O-6 in the Navy. Only three or four of every hundred captains ever get to put on stars. There is a very steep slope at the top of the promotion pyramid. He was a hot runner when he came to this assignment from a deep draft command in the fleet. He had made the playoffs. But it was a long way to the championship, and even that game only yields one winner. He had given it his best shot and there was hope he could pull it out. Twenty-seven years is a long season. To make it to the playoffs after so long and so much effort and then to be eliminated short of the Super Bowl is heartbreaking. It didn't have to be that way. Except for Black Jewel. He thinks, "If Bordon brings the news I expect, then I'm sunk...unless I can redeem my career with another stroke of fortune. And fortune favors the brave, right? This Navy Cross has taken me as far as it can. I need to do something else, something to break me out again. Admiral Carter sounds right. It should be Admiral Carter. I must get back to sea to break out again. And I could if I can get this Black Jewel crap from around my neck. Let's just bury this thing and let me go back to sea."

* * * * *

In Atsugi, Japan, Rear Admiral Frederick Evans can hear morning colors being executed outside his office window. Each morning at 8 o-clock sharp the trumpet sounds, the national anthem of the United States is played, and then the stringy, off-key Japanese anthem is played. As is his habit, Evans has been at his desk for an hour and a half. His early arrivals had generated anxiety in his staff initially. Some wondered if the new admiral expected them to be in the office before him. Normal working hours commenced at 0800 weekdays. After all, this was staff, not fleet work. His 0630 arrivals were in direct contrast to his predecessor who knew assignment as Commander, Fleet Air, Western Pacific was a twilight tour. Promotion was possible, but not probable from this assignment. Consequently, arrival at 0900 and departure at 1600 were the norm. Now Admiral Evans assumes the post and the flag's working hours are 0630 to 1830. Seventy- to eighty-hour work weeks are very common in the Navy, just not on staff duty, at least not in the relative backwater of Atsugi, Japan. Not in an administrative command. Maybe in an operational command that controls the movements of ships and planes and subs. But COMFAIRWESTPAC is administrative. It controls parts and paper and people. Over the past three weeks, since the change-of-command, the staff has adapted to Evans and no longer feels concern about the admiral's work habits. He had made it clear that he expects all to work to get the job done. If it can be done in 30 or 40 or 50 hours a week, then do it and take-off.

Evans feels he needs to work the long hours because he is new to WESTPAC. Except for two cruises fifteen years earlier when he launched out of the South China Sea to hit targets in North Viet Nam, his entire career has been on the East Coast. It truly is two separate navies. If the truth be known, Evans is afraid his ignorance of the way things are done in the Pacific navy and the rust from years of Pentagon duty will show. So he attacks the challenge like he does everything else in his life. He feels sweat can overcome most deficiencies. Besides, what else did he have to do? His love, his lover, his wife stayed behind in D.C. But he will think of her at another time. Right now there is more to read about this job. There is always more to read in this job.

Evans's office is large. Thick blue carpet with an inch of pad beneath lets all that enter know they are in a "special" office. This is the boss man. The CEO. The top dog. Stand erect and mind your manners. You have entered "the admiral's" office. Evans keeps a clean desk. It is not the normal Navy steel gray, but rich wood, five feet wide and three feet across. On the credenza behind him is a hand carved model of an F-8 and a gold framed picture of his wife. He married late and there are no children. His in-box has ten inches of reports and computer printouts. Evans keeps his door open, but the distance across the massive office means he cannot hear conversations in his secretary's outer office. He smiles whenever he recalls the tiny shoebox his one star rated at the Pentagon. Then he sighs. Great office now and all the trappings of power, but no real power.

Captain William Brownell, Chief Staff Officer, appears at the door. Brownell has four years to go to finish his thirty. A Naval Flight Officer with thick glasses, he hasn't seen the inside of an operational airplane in twelve years. An excellent staff officer, he lacks the personality to fill a room with command presence. Brownell knocks to get Evans's attention. As soon as Evans looks up, Brownell enters the room. In his hand is a metal clipboard filled with messages.

"Excuse me, Admiral, I brought the latest status reports on all special mission flights scheduled for the next twenty-four hours. It looks like the VQ-1 Det will have to can-x the afternoon PARPRO off Vlad."

Evans keeps a stone face in response to Brownell's apparent concern and responds, "Thank you, Bill. Now maybe you can translate what you just said and tell me why I should care?"

Brownell takes a good look at the papers piled in the admiral's in-box and the computer report unfolded on the desk. He gives a slight smile and says, "I guess we have piled it on pretty thick since the change-of-command."

"I thought I was a fair paper shuffler at the Pentagon, but you guys have shown me to be an amateur at it. All I've done is read into this job since I assumed command and you bring me more every day. I can't catch up. Granted, I haven't been in the Pacific since Viet Nam, but I thought I was coming out here to command aircraft and flyers, not paper and computers."

Brownell's eyes widen a little as he responds. Surely this one-star wasn't that naive about this command? "We are an administrative command, sir. We push around parts and policies. The operational commands get to fight any fights."

Evans needed this break from paper just to talk to someone. Brownell is a good officer, if unimaginative. This small talk will vent some of the frustration and give some human interaction. Whoever said it was lonely at the top was right. Especially if your true love is 7,000 miles away. Evans reaches for the lukewarm coffee in "The Admiral's" mug on his desk as he speaks, "I know, but I thought I was returning to the fleet, not transferring to Pentagon, Far East. Good grief, CSO, I haven't been airborne since I assumed this job."

"It's not exactly a flying billet, Admiral. Your predecessor didn't touch a stick during his entire tour."

Evans grunts. Brownell just doesn't seem to catch-on why they're talking. Even an admiral is allowed to have a gripe session now and then. But then Brownell's face lights with an idea as he looks at the clipboard in his hand.

"Admiral, do you know what a PARPRO mission is?" It was a rather bold question and Brownell regretted the phrasing as soon as it passed his lips. He thinks, "That's why my career never had a chance of going any higher. I say the obvious without much, no, without any consideration for the other's feelings. Even when the other person is flag rank."

Evans shakes his head.

Brownell tries not to sound as if he is teaching, only informing. "Peace Time Aerial Reconnaissance Program, PARPRO, flights are special JCS Priority Two missions flown off the coasts of China, North Korea, and the Soviet Union. They monitor shipping and electronic transmissions from these countries."

"We still send planes to do that?"

Brownell wonders how they get this information on the East Coast. Maybe those guys in the Pentagon really don't know what goes on out here. "Yes, sir. Even with all the sophisticated spy in space technology, nothing is better than the mark-one, mod-zero eyeball. They usually confirm what is already suspected, but sometimes they turn up the unusual. It's operational stuff, but we must support them. Perhaps it would be beneficial if you gained an understanding of the sensitivity the squadrons have on completing these missions. They are always throwing the need to complete these flights in our face when they are screaming for parts or bodies."

Evans leans forward in his chair. He is on the edge of it now as he anticipates the next suggestion by his chief staff officer.

"You should see first hand what PARPROs are about. Patrol Squadron Forty up in Misawa is scheduled for one early tomorrow morning."

Evans surveys his desk, then jumps to his feet, grabs his hat and heads for the door. As he passes Brownell, Evans places his hand on the CSO's shoulder and makes eye contact with him. "I like your thinking, CSO. I'm going to the Q and get a flight suit on. Get me transport to Misawa."

A warming fills Brownell's chest. It feels good to get a compliment from your boss no matter how senior you may be. He grins and says, "Aye, aye, sir."

* * * * *

Keene should have been in bed two hours ago, but as always, he found a pile of paperwork on his desk when he stopped by his office on the way to the BOQ. Being the kind of officer that feels a burden to keep current in all his tasks, he stayed in his office to get much of it done. Now he looks at his watch and notes that the morning Maintenance Control meeting should be finishing soon so he grabs his hat and pushes back from his desk. He will stop by Maintenance Control on his way to start his crew rest for the next flight.

Behind the counter is Master Chief Petty Officer Frank Strait. A big man, standing over six feet four with paw like hands and giant wrists. He has a flat top that can never stay up, so most of the time he has more of a Caesar look. This is appropriate, for as Maintenance Master Chief he is the emperor of the hangar. A very light skinned Black man with his white father's hair, he has risen to the top enlisted rating through pure dedication and raw, natural, forceful leadership. His favorite saying is, "You can step on my newly shined shoes, spit upwind of me, kick my dog, and even try to date my wife and it will roll off my back. But I will never, ever, be ignored!" When the master chief speaks, you listen. Fiercely loyal to those he respects, he never lets little things like Navy regs get in the way of him getting the job done for his "boys". He hates whiners, wimps, and wouses. Officer, enlisted, or civilian, he measures all by the same standards:

do you love the Navy? Will you give all you have to help a shipmate? Do you love the Four Tops? Answer "no" to any of these questions and you become, by definition, a whiner, wimp, or wouse.

Strait has a stern, angry look on his face. The ten shop supervisors assembled in front of the counter are all silent when Keene slips in the door to their backs. The tension is so thick that Keene knows the Master Chief had just laid down the law to everyone. Slowly, Strait pulls a Zippo from his shirt pocket and lights a large stogy that looks small in his massive hand. He puffs it to get it going.

"Now you know how I feel this morning. Go forth and change it," Strait says in a low, angry voice.

Each of the shop supervisors turns to leave, with some mumbling an acknowledgement such as "Okay, Master Chief," but with most just hanging their heads and exiting as quickly as they can. A couple nod to the M.O. and one even says good morning to him.

Strait thinks Keene is a solid officer, an officer who cares, works hard, and, most importantly, listens to the chiefs. And Keene is a good stick. But Strait does not acknowledge Keene. He turns and strides into his office adjacent to maintenance control. Strait knows Keene will follow in a moment and they will talk then. Once inside the office he slips a cassette in the boom box by his desk. He turns the volume up. He waits until Levi Stubbs reaches the soulful line, "I'll be there to love and comfort you" before he turns the volume to max. It has the desired effect on the maintenance control personnel. Each shakes his head and gives a knowing smile. An airman enters with paperwork to turn-in and bobs his head to the beat and slaps his hands on the counter in sync with the driving pulse. It is okay now. The emperor is back into the Four Tops.

As Keene enters Strait's office he flops down into a worn Government Issue Naugahide, stuffed chair. Strait remains seated behind the desk and holds his hand up for a second. The song comes to an end and the master chief turns off the boom box.

"Didn't expect you this morning, M.O. Thought you'd be crew resting." The master chief is not apologizing, just explaining. "Had to kick a few asses this morning. It was getting lax around here. Some of the shops had gripes over twenty-four hours old with not even an inspection done yet."

"Got the sense you tore 'em down pretty good, Master Chief," Keene says, leading through suggestion.

"Don't worry, Commander, I'll build 'em back up before dinner."

"I know." Keene pauses, not for dramatic effect but because he is so tired the words are starting to come slowly. "Is QE-05 gonna be ready for our PARPRO tonight, or do I have to wrestle the hangar queen into the air?"

"You drag your tired butt up to bed, M.O., and lay your head softly on a cool, clean pillow. You dream of home and your wife and kids." Then with a purposeful dramatic pause Strait continues, "QE-05 will be back together, signed off, and polished, ready for you a half hour before preflight."

With a quiet voice and sincerity, Keene says, "Thank you, Master Chief." An unspoken compliment is passed between two proud men. Strait promises and Keene believes unquestionably. Keene may doubt, but he will never, ever insult the maintenance master chief by voicing or displaying any uncertainty.

Strait rises from his chair and moves to the doorway. He shouts, "Tommy, get the duty truck at my back door and have Commander Keene driven to the BOQ."

* * * * *

Joshua Bordon is only 32. A George Mason Law School graduate, he has never practiced law. After passing the Virginia Bar, he joined the staff of Congressman Henderson. Henderson represented the fourth district of Michigan.

Bordon has never been to Michigan. But he is smart and political and he was readily hired in an attempt to salvage the dying career of a poor representative. It was good experience for Bordon, but in the end, Henderson was defeated four years later. Bordon, however, had connections by that time. His only moral code is ambition. A perfect fit for Washington. Now he is assistant to the President's personal counsel. It is one of the few jobs in D.C. where the title suggests less power than the office actually possesses. More than just a staff member buried in the White House, everyone in the Pentagon knows that it may be Bordon's lips moving, but the words carry the full force of the oval office. Bordon knows it too, and has yet to gain the maturity to learn humility. Dressed in overpriced suits, with a perpetually smooth shave on a pale face, he is the ultimate arrogant, self-important politico. Maybe he has no real world experience, but he is smart, very smart.

It is 1845 when Bordon enters the conference room in the JCS J-2 offices. Colonel Milkus stands out of proper protocol and duty. However, his only greeting is to glare at Bordon and to think that by being fifteen minutes late, this politician has wasted over a full man-hour. Milkus just hates inefficiency. Lieutenant Commander Denton follows the colonel's lead and comes to attention. Major Griffith is already standing, against the wall behind the seated General Adams. Captain Carter makes no movement to rise from his seat. His sense of protocol and duty are not so great as to offer deference or honor to a young man who has done nothing or faced anything important in life, yet is so full of himself. Carter stirs his coffee and remains seated. Bordon struts to the vacant seat at the head of the table and sits down. He offers no apology for being late and making a general officer wait. He is unaware of the slight intended by Carter.

"I hate these Sunday evening meetings, but I have a conference in Atlanta that starts early tomorrow and we need to resolve this by Wednesday. I came tonight to let you know that Black Jewel has received additional funding for the next quarter." Bordon's voice is high and matches his pale complexion and hollow facial features. "I have less than thirty minutes before I must leave for my flight, but before we finish this meeting we must determine the disbursement of the funds."

Colonel Milkus feels his toes curl in his Corfam shoes. His jaw clinches. Bordon can drain a good mood from Milkus so quickly and completely that even the Righteous Brothers are helpless to sustain a positive mental attitude. He ponders, "If Bordon had gone to The Basic School after college graduation instead of law school, he would be what? Maybe a senior captain in the Corps by now? So here I sit being addressed like a waiter at a poor pasta joint by some non-combat-tested young captain. And he came to the meeting late. I gotta get back to the Fleet Marine Force. Soon."

General Adams is an old, Air Force beltway warrior. The young Bordons have come and gone with each administration, but Adams is still here. He looks past the petty, playing-at-having-power-and-importance rudeness, and concentrates on what information is being supplied.

"Mr. Bordon, depending on how large the additional authorization is, this meeting can be done in five minutes."

"Adams, I mean General Adams, it is another eighteen million. It will be funneled through four company fronts starting next week. We expect this to buy enough information to enable a conclusive timeline about future deployment."

Carter carefully sets his coffee spoon on the saucer. The anticipation that had kept his hopes high now drains from him. He feels like a balloon losing air. His body is shrinking; shoulders dropping, chin and eyes lowered to stare into the coffee. He sighs quietly as he thinks, "If it is deployed I will be transferred with the project. Buried in black operations for the rest of my career; too important to be released and too secret to be noticed. It wouldn't be such a sacrifice if Black Jewel were vital to winning the Cold War. But it is contingency crap for crying out loud! My career thrown away on something that will never be used and will never be known. Over a quarter century in uniform and I end up here. I gotta laugh or I'll cry." A sly smile comes over his face, but his hazel eyes are sad and heavy.

"Is there something funny in this course of action, Carter?" Bordon interrupts the captain's thoughts.

"That's *Captain* Carter, Mr. Bordon. And the only thing I find funny about this situation is the varying priority it seems to generate. It is on life support for the past four months, on its way to a slow but sure death, and then we're called in here this evening and told to prepare to deploy it." There is an edge in Carter's voice he has no real control over.

Adams chuckles to himself as he considers the bluntness of Carter. He must have run a good ship. Probably hated by some of his crew, but respected by all. It must be hard on fleet officers to understand and accept D.C. ways.

Bordon won't back down and retains eye contact with Carter. "Black Jewel has remained a priority of this administration. Maybe you should stay current in your job, *Captain* Carter."

Adams sees nothing coming from this exchange, so he exercises a general officer's privilege and interrupts, "The clock is ticking. Eighteen million is not enough to get exercised over. Colonel, your group needs, what, about four million to get the field deployment study done? And Captain Carter, can you get the peripheral damage and collateral risk controls study completed with another two million?"

Milkus responds immediately, displaying that he is right on top of every facet of his project, "Four million will be sufficient if we don't have to rush it. The faster they want to go on this, the more expensive it will get."

Adams responds, "Colonel, four million is all you can get, regardless of how fast they want it. It will take at least

25

another twelve million to get the final answer on delivery options."

Bordon checks his watch before he speaks, "Colonel Milkus, we expect answers soon. There has been too much feet dragging on this project already. We expected faster results when you replaced the admiral."

Milkus's toes curl again. He feels he must answer that slap not only about him but a disparaging comment about a good officer who escaped this millstone of a project by getting promoted. Before Milkus can open his mouth to stumble through a response, Adams takes control again.

"Mr. Bordon, we don't want to keep you from making your flight. I believe you have your answer in macro numbers. Colonel Milkus and Captain Carter will have a detailed breakout of the numbers on your desk by Wednesday."

"I want them by Tuesday C.O.B." Bordon rises quickly and exits.

Carter and Milkus exchange amazed glances. Milkus starts to mumble a funny string of curses under his breath, but then notices Francine Denton and bites his lip. She starts to laugh.

Adams starts for the door with his aide in tow. He throws some words over his shoulder as he departs, "Can't believe I missed dinner with my wife on a Sunday night for this. You all have a good weekend, what's left of it."

* * * * *

Keene struggles to get his flight boots untied and off his feet. He drops then to the floor next to his BOQ bed. Next his flight suit falls around his ankles and he steps out of it. He sheds his blue jeans and two pairs of white cotton socks. He pulls back the covers and climbs between the thin sheets wearing only his skivvies and a light blue VP-40 Crew Eleven t-shirt. Keene looks at the picture of his family that sits on the night stand next to the phone as he reaches to turn out the light. It was taken at Monterey Bay a year ago. Foggy and cold, but all five were smiling brightly. Joyce, holding little four-year old Sammy on her knee, with twelve-year old Peter and seven-year old Meredith standing in front. Keene thinks even he looks good standing in the back. It is so hard to get a good picture of everyone. It is a good memory that he dwells on before he falls to sleep when on deployment. He turns out the light and shuts his eyes.

Immediately the telephone rings. He reaches for the receiver on the nightstand.

"Lieutenant Commander Keene here"

"Commander, this is Petty Officer Mazurak," the captain's yeoman identifies himself. "The Skipper wants to see you at 1300 in his office."

"Can't we make it around 1700? I've got another late night preflight tonight with Crew Eleven. I'd like to get a little crew rest before that."

"Commander, I know. I told him that, but he said he wants to see you anyway."

"Yeah, yeah," Keene responds with the only words that he can muster when faced with stupidity and arrogance.

Mazurak is a savvy first class yeoman. Yeomen serve as officer secretaries and consequently know all the secrets the officers try to keep from enlisted men. Mazurak sometimes pushes this special relationship a little too far. Such as now, "You know, M.O., this sucks. The skipper is a real S.O.B., plus you know he just doesn't like Crew Eleven."

"I'll be there at 1300."

"M.O. I'll be finishing lunch about then. I've got the Chief's car while he is on that boondoggle to Cubi. I'll swing by and pick you up in front of the Q at 1255 so you don't have to walk down in the rain."

"Thanks, Petty Officer Mazurak. Thanks a lot."

"My pleasure, Commander Keene. Sometimes good things do happen to good officers." Mazurak was usually not

27

that complimentary. That comment just slipped out. He hung up and reflected on the statement. It wasn't true all the time and he knew it. But it felt good to say it to one of the good ones. He's glad he did.

CHAPTER THREE

"Welcome, Billy-san!" sings out the wide smiling young Japanese woman. She had been waiting at the dirty window, watching through the old lace curtain. She had seen LT (JG) Billy Warbuck pay the cab and jog through the light rain and narrow alley leading to the faded gray door. The Crew Eleven Tactical Coordinator, as always, has found pleasures of the flesh even in the small town of Misawa. Miko is twenty, but looks younger. A school drop-out at age twelve with dreams of becoming someone special, she is still dreaming. Others may think of her as a prostitute, but she never does. She might be friendly with those few men she finds fun and attractive, but that is her choice and not a profession. And a single girl has to eat and have a place to stay. So if these friends care to share some of their good fortune to assist her, well, that is their choice and not payment for services.

Warbuck does not answer Miko's greeting verbally. Rather, he pushes the door open and roughly grabs her. Pulling her tight against himself, he tries to force his lips onto hers, but Miko turns her face and pushes him away.

"Billy, no! You are all wet and too rough." Even when she says no, her voice is tender and pleasant.

"Then what should I do, My Soft Blossom?" Warbuck and Miko both know the next step, but there is an unacknowledged propriety in the execution of ritual. It gives simple or dark things an element of grace and beauty. Like the tea ceremony, this accepted proper order of back alley sex is necessary to elevate the common to a fulfilling experience.

Miko takes Warbuck's hand and leads him down a dimly lit and narrow hallway. Miko slides the third door open to reveal a sunken hot tub. The steam floats six inches above the dark water. The room is candle lit and smells of roses mixed with chlorine. Robes and towels are hung on hooks near a wooden bench. Miko slides the door shut behind them. She sits Warbuck on the bench and pulls his heavy shoes and wet socks off. Next she loosens his belt and pants, removing them as he stares at her. Miko muses to herself, "Billy is a sweet man. Although my robe has come open, he does not stare at my nearly exposed breasts. Billy looks at my hair and eyes. I can feel him crawling into my heart through my eyes. He is such a wonderful and deep soul. Am I his dream? Can I please him sufficiently to draw him into my life and world? Or can he carry me into his?" She feels that nothing is impossible while they are in this room. The world ends at the closed, flimsy door.

Billy is soon naked and immersed in the hot, relaxing water. Miko sits at the edge and gently massages his scalp. Warbuck's eyes are closed and peace flows over him like the warm water. Thoughts of ex-wife Brandee, the bitter divorce before he left on this deployment and his recent previous poor choices that put a strain on his friendship with his Plane Commander, Keene, start to enter the room, but he quickly slams the door to keep them out. There is no future; no tonight or tomorrow; no past, just present. No clocks or heaven or hell. Just now.

Miko kisses his forehead. Billy is her whole world, at least for these few hours. She draws a sponge from the wooden bucket and rubs his shoulders with it. She rocks him forward and bends his chin to his chest. Slowly, with experienced hands she manipulates his spine with one hand and scrubs his back using the sponge with the other.

The low beat of a heavy-metal song starts to bleed through the thin wall leading to the next room. This whore house is popular even on a weekday morning. Warbuck starts to slightly bounce his head to the bass rhythm. He only vaguely notices Miko's massage has stopped. He raises his head and opens his eyes just in time to see her naked body slip beneath the water. She is not beautiful. Some would say she is a little too round. Maybe fifteen pounds away from being a true beauty. But her skin is flawless and taut.

He shuts his eyes again to return to the moment's paradise. He feels her hands take his foot and lift it to her waist. With his heel resting on her knees, she rolls every muscle of his foot between her strong fingers. Starting at the ankle and working towards the toes, this creates a wave of flesh between her fingers that repeats and repeats. With each repetition Warbuck becomes more and more lost in the now. This ritual is full of immense immediate satisfaction along with the anticipation of what happens next. The experience is cheated if care is not taken with each step. Nothing can be omitted or shortened. There is joy in the satisfaction of completing the ritual regardless of the participants. This mixture of current satisfaction and future ecstasy is a balm that soothes Warbuck's broken life. He feels the urge to mumble the three words he knows are true for the moment, and this moment only. Miko wants to hear the words, but she, too, is afraid he might give in and say them. So there is silence, uncomfortable yet secure. And the ritual continues.

* * * * *

Milkus figures the night is shot, so he might as well get some work done since he is here. He unlocks his office and flips on the lights. A secure space, it has no windows. He shares it with two 0-5s, one Air Force and one Army and a couple enlisted administrative support personnel. But the corner space, the "lucky" desk, is now his. Two previous heads of this section were promoted to 0-7. One is now an Air Force brigadier and the most recent is now a Navy rear admiral. Granted, they were the only two of the five who have held the responsibility for this top secret project since its inception in the early 1970s to be promoted. Milkus is too "hard corps" to have any personal ambition that is separate from protecting the Constitution and advancing the United States Marine Corps. But sometimes, when he is alone in front of the mirror at night as he removes his uniform, he pauses and imagines how it would feel to see a star on his collar.

Milkus unlocks the tall safe near his desk. He initials the form taped to the inside of the door, noting what time he opened it and his name. Before reaching in to get his files he turns the paper sign on the safe front door from "Locked" to "Open". Attention to detail. It marks a professional Marine. How many times did his TBS instructors repeat that phrase? Milkus takes a thick file to his desk. From the inside cover he removes a floppy disk. He boots up the personal computer on his desk and loads the disk. It still amazes him how swiftly the military has moved from paper and typewriters to computers and word processing. When he started in the fifties it was carbon paper and three typos allowed per page. Then it was magnetic cards and now in 1985 this PC has the capacity to calculate with the same power of big mainframes from only a few years ago. This computing power is what has made Black Jewel a viable subject for advanced research. It would be impossible even to attempt it without modern computers.

Field deployment of Black Jewel sounds easy to do when using the computers and their artificial modeling world. However, he knows in his heart that he won't change. He will continue only to trust his life to a grunt Marine with a rifle. Computers know nothing about esprit d'corps and tradition. No computer model can account for the heroics individual Marines will evidence to save their buddy or the mission.

Milkus lets his mind drift to an earlier time as the computer slowly brings up the complicated program. He recalls Foxtrot Company's fire fight on a moonless night fifteen years ago. His entire company's survival depended on second squad, second platoon repelling a savage assault by the NVA. No re-enforcements were available. No air support. No evacuation. No way to redeploy the company. If that squad's remaining ten men did not hold, the thin perimeter would be violated and what little mutual support the platoons provided each other would be lost. The company would be destroyed piece meal. It didn't matter what errors had led to this situation. It didn't matter that Milkus had two previous in-country tours and was the most experienced and senior company commander in the battalion. It didn't matter that every Marine knew the war was already lost by the politicians. What mattered was that second squad, second platoon, Foxtrot Company was elected by destiny to receive the ultimate test of courage and fidelity. In a War College computer model, the skirmish would be over in minutes and the post action critique would commence to point out what errors had resulted in the company's destruction. But computers were not in that tree line on that night. No, not a computer but grunt Marines with M-16s who chose to do their duty. And when morning came and with it air support, Foxtrot Company was still there to be evacuated. Sixty seven dead NVA surrounded second squad's position. Those bodies closest to the Marines were dead of stab wounds. Another five Marines in second squad were dead, two more wounded. One would die later that day of multiple wounds. For three solid hours this squad had refused to retreat an inch. They used automatic weapons, grenades, side arms and finally hand-to-hand combat; anything and everything to protect their buddies.

Milkus shakes his head to clear it of a memory he usually keeps locked away in a very special, secret garden of his mind. He normally visits that walled remembrance only in his dreams or when he has had two beers too many. He is bothered by questions in his mind, "What were the names of those four who lived? What did they look like? What was the name of that rifleman I nominated for the Navy Cross? Why can't I pull up their names and faces anymore?"

The computer program finally springs to life and Milkus stops his memories. He enters his password, "2SQ.2PLA.FOX". Every time he enters it he chuckles about the little irony in his choice. Computers will always have limitations. True Marines know no limits. He pages through multiple screens until he reaches one dealing with cost estimates. It is a large spreadsheet and as Milkus moves the cursor around it, he hears a knock at the office door. He turns the screen off and goes to the door. There is a cipher lock on the outside so whoever is there does not have regular access to this office. Upon opening the door he sees Carter.

"Excuse me Ron, I thought I might still find you around. I've got something I could use your input on, if you have just a minute?" asks Carter, his eyes quite serious behind his regulation glasses.

Milkus answers, "Sure, come on in."

Carter ensures the door is tightly closed behind him then sits on the edge of a desk opposite Milkus's. Then he speaks, "Ron, I'm seriously concerned that we are being led down a purely political path in a very thorny rose garden." He waits for Milkus to show any response, but when he gets none, he continues, "That little pin-head Bordon is not sharing all he knows about the future of Black Jewel. Look at these."

Carter pulls a set of papers from his inside coat pocket. He unfolds them and sets them on the desk in front of Milkus. Milkus examines them, at first casually, and then he notes an item that draws his complete attention. Leaning forward in his chair, hunched over the papers he lets a sense of urgency crawl into his voice as he speaks, "Where did you get these?"

"White House communications."

"How?" Milkus is caught flat footed by the revelations in the papers and his voice shows it. "Why would they give you this?"

Carter is serious, not purposely evasive, in his answers, "They didn't. They gave them to the White House staff associated with Black Jewel. But those jerks can never keep a secret and this actually was given to me by an Army major, a White House social aide. He knew I was working on special projects and suspected I might know of Black Jewel."

"How did he get it?"

"He is on the alternate list as a social aide and got a call that he would be needed last night. He said he was bored having to escort the 17 year-old daughter of the Costa Rican Minister of Trade, or some such crap, so he decided to take a break. He walked into one of the ante rooms between dances and saw this on the floor next to a sofa. There were overcoats on the sofa so he thinks it might have fallen from someone's pocket. He only attends functions at the White House infrequently and did not know who to turn it into. His full-time assignment is over in J-4 and after reading the contents he knew it was not anything you throw away. So he gave it to me."

Milkus re-reads the second paragraph as he throws obvious questions at the Navy captain, "You mean to tell me, Frank, that this major just put these in his pocket and walked out of the White House?"

Carter nods.

Milkus asks, "Did he even think what would happen to him if they searched him on departure?"

"He is a bit of a cowboy. He's never impressed me with his forethought. He just reacts."

"When did he give it to you?" Milkus asks.

"He saw me in the passageway after our meeting. I got it about five minutes ago. I wanted to talk with you before I went to the General with it. Or do we just shred it without showing it to him?"

Milkus looks up and makes eye contact with Carter. That was an option Milkus had not yet considered. Pretend we don't know and just move forward. Interesting option. No, just screw the politicians. What is best for the country? What is the best way to protect and defend the Constitution?

* * * * *

Mazurak snaps his gum as he bombs through the rain in an old Mazda. The windshield wipers do not work well so the short ride from the BOQ to the patrol squadron administration building is an adventure. Keene is still tired. Four hours sleep was not enough. Especially four hours of fitful sleep. Mazurak is a compulsive talker and must fill every silence.

"M.O., I almost got lunch can-x'd today because the C.O. is going hyper over an unexpected visitor. Some TACAIR-puke one-star who took over COMFAIRWESTPAC a little while ago. He and his aide arrived about a half hour ago."

Keene feels his anxiety over having to see the commanding officer grow slightly. He speaks, "That's all I need today. Any idea why he's here?"

"Nope."

"Come on, Petty Officer Mazurak, you know everything. What's really up?

"I just know his CSO calls this morning and the skipper takes it personally. A little later the ol' man comes out of his office with that stupid panicked look he gets, and says to hold a field day and clean all spaces and to be sure you were in his office at 1300. I got nothin' else." Mazurak parks the car and they enter the building.

Keene sees Lieutenant Joy Steward using the telephone on Mazurak's desk just outside the C.O.'s closed door. She is in Service Dress Blues with the gold epaulette showing her current assignment as the admiral's aide. She has dark, long hair swept back in a professional, regulation bun. She wears moderate make-up that minimizes her ethnic nose and highlights her best facial feature, her full lips. At 5'8" she creates a robust image. And like most aides, she has already become quite adept at "wearing her admiral's stars". She will not take "no" for an answer and will readily insist that her way must be done because it is "what the admiral wants."

Keene approaches, dressed in his flight suit. He looks at his watch. It is exactly 1300. He shows Steward his watch and motions his intention to enter the skipper's office. Steward smiles and nods her head as she continues her telephone conversation. Keene hastily rubs his flight boot toes on the back of his calves and checks to ensure all zippers on his pockets are closed. He knocks, hesitates, and then opens the door.

Inside, Commander Richard Morse, a Naval Flight Officer and Patrol Squadron Forty commanding officer, is sitting behind his big desk. The office is long and narrow. Evans is seated on the Navy regulation fake-leather sofa along the near wall. He is dressed in a flight suit and flight boots. Keene mentally notes that a flight suit is an odd choice for a visiting flag officer. Evans and Morse have coffee cups and saucers in their hands. Keene enters and remains standing, not at attention, but with excellent formal military demeanor.

Keene speaks, "Excuse me, Cap'n, Admiral, I was told to report at 1300."

Morse remains seated, but Evans shows courtesy to his junior and sets down his coffee and climbs out of the deep sofa. As he does so, Morse says very dryly, with almost a touch of disdain, "This is our Maintenance Officer, Lieutenant Commander Keene."

Evans reaches across the coffee table and extends his hand to greet Keene. "Nice to meet you, Commander. Frederick Evans. I'm the new FAIRWESTPAC," Evans says as he shakes hands with Keene. On doing so, he notices the academy ring on Keene's hand. "What class?"

"Seventy-three, sir," Keene replies with pride and a big smile. He sees Evans ring and asks, "And you, sir?"

"Sixty-one," says Evans with even greater swagger.

Morse watches the easy exchange between two strangers that have immediately bonded and he resents it. Those ring knockers have been a thorn in his side for his entire career. Sixty officers in a patrol squadron and never more than five or six are ring knockers, yet they always steal some of the top ranking spots. Think they know it all. Treat the rest of the officers like outsiders. It makes him sick.

Morse speaks with cold words, "Keene here is the plane commander on Crew Eleven. It is not our best PARPRO crew, that would be Crew Seven, but they had to divert to Atsugi due to the weather this morning. Keene's crew, I'm sure, will be able to adequately demonstrate the general purpose of the mission, Admiral."

Evans is shocked by any commanding officer actually condemning through faint praise subordinates in front of a flag officer. He takes mental notes, "Doesn't Morse know that all his crews are a reflection of his leadership? Is this man so inept not to understand that basic tenant of command? I've got to learn more about these P-3 types. I hope this isn't typical for the community. If it is, then they are surely one of the weakest in Naval Aviation."

Keene's jaw tightens and his face becomes a little flushed. On other days this kind of needling by a superior officer he doesn't respect would just roll off Keene's back. But the ground job work load and the fatigue from flying an unfair schedule combine to elicit a response from him. "That's right, Cap'n, it was Crew Eleven that made it back when Crew Seven could not. And, might I add, sir, that Crew Eleven has never been late on a PARPRO departure or returned before the complete track was accomplished."

Morse stands up. He wants to put this officer in his place. They both know that Keene is referring to the troubles Crew Seven has had this deployment with PARPROs. Morse has his own opinion about Crews Seven and Eleven. He thinks, "Every crew goes through rough spots. Keene should get off his high academy horse and realize that the personnel on Crew Seven are just better aircrew men. Better pilots, better NFOs, better sensor operators. Just better. And none are academy men. If the admiral wasn't here right now, Keene would be at attention and be strictly in a receiving mode."

"Keene, the Admiral desires to see how a PARPRO mission is flown. He will be accompanying you on tonight's hop. Your preflight is at 2330 with a 0330 take-off." Morse almost spits the words out. "Admiral, we can have a driver pick you up at 0245 for the planeside brief. Keene will be starting engines at 0305."

Keene interrupts and it is Morse's turn to tighten his jaw, "Unless, Admiral, you desire to attend the tactical brief which will give you a good overview of what the mission is about. It goes down at 2330."

"Commander Keene," Evans answers, "I would like that. I have purposely not brought along any paperwork to keep me busy. I came here to get airborne again and to learn how you P-3 guys spend all that per diem!"

Keene smiles at the gentle ribbing by a TACAIR pilot, but Morse just squeezes his jaw tighter. Keene says, "We usually spend it on lousy Air Force box lunches. You can get hungry on a twelve hour flight."

"Twelve hours? It's going to be a twelve hour hop?" Evans interrupts.

Keene replies, "Yes, sir. Do you want ham and cheese or 'chef's choice'?"

"Chef's choice?"

Keene continues, "It's a late night preflight, Admiral. Better stick with the ham and cheese. The night chef might be bored and try to get creative with horsemeat. And, sir, should we plan on your aide coming along?"

Evans says, "You take women on your combat planes?"

"We're shore based, Admiral. We have women in the squadron, but none are aircrew. We transport them often however and can accommodate your aide if you think you will need her," answers Keene.

"I flew F-8s, Commander. I don't need anyone along when I fly."

Morse joins the conversation, "Roger that, sir. I'll make sure BOQ accommodations are made for Lieutenant Steward and for you, Admiral, in case you want to grab some crew rest before the preflight." Then to Keene, "Keene, you're dismissed."

Keene glares at Morse. Even enlisted sailors are addressed by their rank in the "New Navy." He has taken about all the insults he can take this day from that man. However, Keene just comes to attention and says, "Aye, aye, sir."

* * * * *

"Do you want it in your safe?" asks Carter. He hopes Milkus says yes. It is getting late this Sunday evening and Carter's ultimate motive in bringing the paper to Milkus was to drop this hot potato on the marine before Carter's hands were burnt. But it is taking longer to cut and run than he had planned.

Milkus sets the paper on his desk and crosses to a coffee maker on a small table. He hits the power button to heat up Friday's left over coffee in the pot. With his back still to Carter he says, "Frank, let's take a couple more minutes and think this out before we do anything. We're a couple of 0-6's in a world of stars. I don't want to get squashed when the elephants start dancing. Any ideas?"

Carter thinks to himself, "Yeah, I have an idea. I dump this on you, Mr. Tried and True Ramrod Straight Marine, and then I run for cover. But you don't seem to be buying that option."

Carter speaks, "We can, one, take it to General Adams. Or, two, shred the thing and pretend we never saw it. Or, three, or....I guess I don't have a third option."

"Or, three, we take it to someone other than Adams."

Carter answers, "You're not suggesting the press are you?"

Milkus shakes his head vigorously. "No, no. Some other elephant. Someone with enough stars and political pull to see that the right thing is done. Someone connected so well within the beltway that he cannot be ignored or be flanked by the end run of some pinheaded politician."

Carter adds, "And a straight arrow who can keep us from becoming elephant toe jam. Any ideas?"

"Admiral Bella," says Milkus. Carter goes silent in thought. Milkus touches the coffeepot to see if it is hot yet. It is not, so he returns to his desk. Carter absentmindedly walks to the coffeepot and repeats the action of touching the pot.

Milkus continues, "Do you know Admiral Bella?"

Carter shakes his head and says, "Not personally. I know what his title is, but I never see him around the spaces. Do you?"

"Not since I've been here. Although I did meet him once when he gave a speech to a battalion I commanded. We had coffee and donuts before the event," answers Milkus.

"Why Bella then?"

"Technically he is the Deputy Chairman with offices here in the JCS. But I hear he spends more time in the White House basement and over at NSA in Maryland. He has black project clearance. Hell, word is he even runs the really deep stuff for the White House. He is a fleet officer who can be

41

trusted. And he knows the beltway tango better than most," Milkus says while sitting erect in his desk chair.

Carter responds, "Why would he care about Black Jewel? About this paper?"

"I will never forget his speech to the battalion," says Milkus. "He made Marine grunts from private to lieutenant colonel understand clearly and simply how the Constitution not only requires the military to serve those civilians placed in authority over us, but it also requires the civilians to use that authority solely to support and defend the Constitution. Honestly, Frank, I don't think any of us had ever considered the requirements on how to use the military that the Constitution places on our civilian leaders. Misuse of the military can occur in many subtle forms. It is not just coup d'états that violate the Constitution. There are instances when we perceive violations of rights protected in the Constitution and we complain, but ultimately accept it because the violations are by the hands of 'our elected civilian leaders.' Bella laid it on the line with my battalion. Our oath to support and defend the Constitution against all enemies, foreign and domestic, might require us to stand up and say no to unconstitutional orders. We, the military, and especially the officer corps, must be ready to sacrifice more than our lives in our duty to the Constitution. We must risk careers and reputations and pensions if necessary to protect the guarantor of our freedom. Does he sound like the guy to go to?"

Carter goes to the coffee again. It is warm enough now. Milkus's words ring in his head, "Risk careers and reputation and pensions if necessary. Damn! Why did I ever have to get connected to Black Jewel? Bella may have some power around this town, but he is a military officer, and the ultimate power belongs to others who are not so keen on abiding by their oath to follow orders. Crap. Kiss stars goodbye, Frank. You'll be lucky to come out of this with your retirement."

Carter sips the lukewarm coffee then speaks, "Sold me. I don't see any better choice. Do we cut Adams in on this, or just shoot it right by him?"

"What do you think?"

"Adams has always been square with me. I think we should show him and tell him we are going to Bella with it," says Carter.

"What if he orders us to drop it?" asks Milkus.

"Look, you're the one who was quoting our Constitutional sworn oath. We do what is right," shoots back Carter, irritated more by the possibility than at Milkus for voicing it.

Milkus takes a cup of coffee. He takes a big gulp, and then speaks, "Enough said. Let's do it."

Milkus puts the report into a large manila envelope and seals it. Carter and he leave the office and walk shoulder to shoulder down the corridor to General Adams office. It is locked.

Carter says, "Do we bother him at home or wait until tomorrow morning?"

"I'll lock this in my safe. On Mondays Adams is at the White House in the morning. We should be able to see him right after lunch," answers Milkus. "See you here at 1300."

* * * * *

Mazurak sits in the duty truck parked in front of the VIP quarters and pulls a long drag on his filtered cigarette. He checks his watch. It is 2315. He decides to wait another five minutes before going to the lobby to retrieve Admiral Evans. Being assigned as a flag chauffer has made it a very long day for him. But on deployment there are no normal working hours and no weekends. The Tactical Support Center is only a couple of minutes from VIP quarters, so there is plenty of time to finish this butt.

The Tactical Support Center is always referred to as

"TSC" by aircrew new to the community. Those with salt on their bars often refer to it by its old name, "ASWOC," a typical Navy acronym for Anti-Submarine Warfare Operations Center. In Misawa this ops center is a group of six double-wide trailers connected to form a maze of prefab rooms. It is anchored to the earth with large cables and surrounded by a ten-foot chain link fence with razor wire on top. The same model is used in other P-3 overseas deployment sites. In war they can be moved easily and follow the action.

Each TSC consists of three main sections. One tracks Soviet activity and plans operations to include giving aircrews detailed pre- and post-flight briefings. Another area is a communications center. It bristles with various sophisticated equipment and the noise they generate. The third section houses the acoustic analysis section. The tracks generated by each crew that forces contact with interesting surface and subsurface vessels are dissected and the information passed to the central depository for all acoustic information in Monterey. The acoustics section is crammed with computers and acoustic processors that have much greater capabilities than the airborne equipment used by the crews.

The TSC is staffed, for the most part, by aircrew on shore duty. Their function is to pull the most information possible out of crews to get the best available fix on communist activity around the world. However, a peculiarity of the P-3 community is that every tactical flight is analyzed with the scrutiny of a prosecutor drilling a hostile witness. Unlike carrier based TACAIR squadrons which grade traps, in the patrol community every detail of a tactical flight is graded. Although the de-briefers are shore based aircrew, at times they seem to forget the challenges of finding and tracking evasive submarines, or the discomfort in being beat up by bad weather for twelve hours. Normally, when necessary, the mission commander takes the flak and poor grade with nothing more than a sailor's griping. Very rarely, a mission commander has refused to sign the grade sheet and tossed it back to the grader and told him to "pend it", then gathered his tactical crew and marched out of the TSC. To "pend it" means the crew's performance and grade will be reviewed by the TSC Officer-in-Charge and the squadron commanding officer. If they cannot reach a fair grade, then the commodore becomes involved. Keene is one of an exceedingly small number of mission commanders who have said "pend it" three times in his career. He cannot abide unfairness and he won't let his crew be treated that way.

Mazurak checks his watch again. It is now 2320. He takes one long, slow last drag on his cigarette, and then flips it out the window. He starts to exit the car when he notices Evans striding up the sidewalk. The admiral is in the duty truck passenger seat before Mazurak can greet him.

Evans speaks, "This gonna take me to an airplane?"

"Yes, sir." Mazurak says as he returns Evans' smile and starts the truck. "May I say, Admiral, that all you pilots are alike. Can't wait to get airborne."

Evans chuckles and replies, "I guess you're right. I once had a master chief tell me that he had figured out that for naval aviators everything in life is motivated by one of two desires: sex or flying. I think he may have hit upon one of life's truths. Don't you?"

Mazurak likes this senior officer already. It appears the admiral has his head screwed on right. He answers, "I'd say that's been my observation with pilots. Although I think some of the NFOs don't always fall into that category."

"Oh, I've known some seagull pilots, too," says Evans.

"Seagull?"

Evans answers, "Yeah. They're like seagulls. You gotta throw rocks at 'em to get 'em to fly."

Mazurak smiles at first, then starts to laugh as he pictures the C.O. with a seagull body. Morse surely matches that description. He would rather bark orders from behind

45

his desk than be on the flight schedule, or even spend time in the hangar talking with his troops.

As the truck pulls through the unguarded gate by the flight line, Mazurak fills the silence, "Admiral, you'll be flying with a good crew tonight. The M.O. is okay. At the barracks he's known as a good stick. I know he's a good officer."

Evans answers with just a nod. He knows what the YN1 is saying. This petty officer knows what goes on in the squadron's front office and he probably types the officers' fitness reports. This has been an interesting visit already.

The truck stops by the entrance to the TSC. Evans exits carrying his helmet bag.

"Thanks for the lift," says Evans.

"You're welcome, Admiral. Just ring the bell by the door, sir, and they will buzz you in. And, Admiral, have a safe one tonight," Mazurak says while maintaining eye contact.

The petty officer assigned front desk duty stands when the admiral enters the TSC. The large heavy door reminds Evans of entering a meat locker. He smiles at the petty officer who is at attention. A special VIP pass is at the ready and Evans accepts it in exchange for his ID card. He is escorted through a small corridor and into the briefing room. The room is actually larger than it feels. The low overhead of the trailer complex makes any sailor over six-foot walk in a natural, unconscious but unnecessary, crouch. Evans does the same. As he enters the room Morse calls "Attention on deck" and everyone stops their conversations and comes to attention. The tactical members of Crew Eleven are nearly all assembled in the briefing room. The plane commander, second pilot, navigator, sensor operators one, two and three are present. However, the most important tactical crewmember is still absent. Keene checks his watch and looks towards the entrance, hoping Warbuck is following behind the admiral. But he sees only Lieutenant Shelly Rosseau, the Air Intelligence Officer.

Evans calls "As you were" and everyone immediately resumes their conversations. The sensor operators are reviewing Soviet and Chinese surface and subsurface vessel parameters. AW1 Jones is deeply concentrating on the results of the most recent flights and has only minimal interest in Evans's arrival. He is not impressed with a free-riding admiral. Evans is ushered to the middle seat in the front row of folding chairs. There are fifteen chairs total, all facing a white board and film screen. Behind the chairs is a projection system that shows slides as well as very basic computer generated presentations. On the white board is information concerning the next three launches written in a surprisingly feminine hand. Next to the wall, by the entrance doorway is the duty officer's desk. It is cluttered with messages and files. In a small bookcase by it are binders full of instructions and guidelines. The duty officer is dressed in khakis. He is on a 24-hour shift and hasn't seen the outdoors since he reported at 0700. A lieutenant, he is one of the squadron NFOs who has pulled TSC watch officer duty for the week. This is his first WESTPAC deployment and only his second week of TSC watch standing. He is nervous about making a possible error, especially with an admiral in the area.

Lieutenant Shelly Rosseau is the squadron Air Intelligence Officer. Only one of three female officers in the squadron, she is better looking than the flight surgeon and Maintenance Material Control Officer. Rosseau is medium height with a standout figure and auburn hair with green eyes. But she doesn't smile too much. An extremely hard working junior officer, she takes great pains always to present herself in an attractive fashion; hair done, make-up in place, uniforms tailored tightly with sharp creases. But she is all business. She never relaxes, even at wardroom functions. The aircrews refer to her as the "Ice Queen". But never to her face. After all, a guy has to keep all roads open in case she might start to thaw and he just might get lucky. Deployments become very long after the first four months. Patience and politeness may yet yield a victory. It is a war of the sexes, not a battle.

"Good evening, Admiral and Skipper. Could I get everyone to take a seat and we'll get underway," says Rosseau in her high, breathless voice that immediately captures the attention of every man in the room. It is flat out sexy. "Commander Keene, is your crew all here?"

Keene looks over her shoulder into the passageway. No sight of Warbuck yet. Keene's thoughts are rushed as he feels the unnecessary pressure the situation has caused, "I am going to lay into him but good. I sent word to that whorehouse about the admiral being on the flight. How could Warbuck be so...such a...such a sailor? Relax, Jim, Evans seems like an okay TACAIR puke. Tell him your TACCO is late because of sex and he will probably nod and chuckle." In Naval Aviation, sex is a valid excuse for about any infraction. Rather, perhaps it is an understood motivator, not necessarily an accepted excuse.

Rosseau sees the apprehension in the Mission Commander's eyes and does something the Ice Queen never gets credit for. She says, "Oh, excuse me Admiral, Skipper, but I just noticed there is another intelligence report we could use. I left it in the comm center. I'll be right back."

Rosseau makes eye contact, pretty but cold, with Keene as she turns and exits the room. The conversations between the aircrew and TSC personnel resume. Keene scans the room and seeing Morse engage Evans in small talk, he slips out of the briefing room. He proceeds to the Officer-In-Charge's empty office and dials 8 to get an off-base line. He pulls his wallet from his chest pocket and finds a slip of paper. He dials the number on the paper. As the line is connecting he turns and looks across the hallway. Leaning against the copier is Rosseau nursing a Styrofoam cup of coffee. She actually gives a small smile as their eyes meet. Keene's smile grows very wide as her selfless act in support of the aircrew, and him particularly, becomes clear to him. He mouths "Thank you". She nods in return, then points to her watch. Keene responds by holding up five fingers. Rosseau nods again as she takes another sip.

The phone connection is finally made and Keene listens to the ringing at the other end. Before anyone can answer, Keene hears heavy, booted steps bounding down the hall, reverberating on the false floor of the trailer complex. Sticking his head out of the office, Keene sees Warbuck hurrying down the passageway. Warbuck is a mess. Hair still wet from the rain and uncombed. Ripped T-shirt under the flight suit. Boots untied and unshaven wearing a heavy five o'clock shadow. Keene's glare is burning a hole through Warbuck's eyes right to the back of the TACCO's skull. Warbuck stops suddenly when he sees Keene. Warbuck comes to attention. He wants to say something. He wants to apologize for his weakness, that professionally embarrasses a mentor he admires; but he cannot find the words. He is back in the real world now and expelled from the safe, accepting womb of Miko's arms. And he doesn't like it. And he doesn't know how exactly to make the transition. He seems lost in the cold reality of duty and responsibilities he had so easily shed just hours before. Rosseau disrupts this momentary still life by brushing past the two men towards the briefing room.

She says, "I suggest you both wait until I turn off the lights to start the brief, then slip in as I shut the door." Both men nod and follow a few paces behind her to the briefing room.

Lieutenant Rosseau squints into the green light from the projection system. Her shadow covers most of the Pacific Ocean. Whenever she turns to make eye contact with the admiral and commanding officer, she shades her eyes from the high powered green beam of light with her left hand while using the pointer in her right hand to identify ship positions on the projected display. She points to a rectangular shape that encompasses most of the Sea of Japan. Inside this rectangle is another line that forms the designated track of Tango Bravo One Four Niner, Crew Eleven's tactical call sign for the night's flight. The navigator and TACCO write "TB149" on their left hands in magic marker. Each crewman has a detailed brief with track point latitudes and longitudes identified, communication frequencies, emergency procedures, divert fields, acoustic and R-F parameters of potential contacts, required sonobuoy load, and a host of other detailed and necessary information. One page, however, is highlighted in red ink. It is entitled "PARPRO CONDITIONS". Rosseau quickly runs through the standard information found on most of the other nine sheets of the brief, but she slows when reaching the red page.

"Admiral," she says, "please note the PARPRO CONDITIONS page. As the senior officer aboard the flight, it will be very important for you to be aware of the possible condition commands the aircraft could receive from the Fifth Air Force in Yokota. Commander Keene, you are to have two men on the HICOM frequency at all times. If, at anytime, you are unable to monitor an Air Force HICOM frequency you are to abort and attempt to re-establish receipt of HICOM. Do not break EMCON Alpha while within the PARPRO boundaries with the exception of your hourly position report in the blind over HICOM. You can resume the mission if HICOM monitoring is regained."

Keene turns his head to see the admiral. Evans is following Rosseau's reading of the brief sheet as she goes through it. Normally, this is the only part of the brief read verbatim from the sheet. Keene has been briefed by other AIOs who would read all nine pages. But the Ice Queen is better than that. Keene wonders if Evans is truly a novice on PARPROs or is just being polite for the lieutenant briefer.

Rosseau continues, "You will receive all condition calls via a call-sign Tuna King broadcast. During this flight all Tuna King broadcasts will be directed at you. A review of the conditions follows. Condition One: this signifies that forces have launched on your mission with hostile intent. Condition Two: this signifies that forces have launched to intercept you with no hostile intent. Condition Three: you are departing the PARPRO boundaries, check your navigation. Condition Four: abort immediately. Condition Five: break EMCON Alpha and contact Fifth Air Force immediately. In the event of Condition One take immediate evasive maneuvers. For Conditions Two, Three and Five turn away from the Communist coastline and proceed out to sea until the situation is resolved, then you may resume your track. When in receipt of Condition Four climb to best cruise altitude and return to Misawa. Once in receipt of a Condition Four you have departed the PARPRO system and you may not resume your track."

"Excuse me, Lieutenant," Evans interrupts. "I've just got to ask. How can Fifth Air Force know if the interceptors have hostile intent or not?"

"That's easy, Admiral!" pops-up Jones. "The CIA has some guy working as a janitor in the Commies' hangar and when the jets take-off he hustles over to the pay phone and whispers to Langley, 'I heard two MIG pilots saying "Let's go kick some American butt" just before they took off. Tell that P-3 to watch out 'cause these guys are pissed off'.

Everyone chuckles at the good Russian dialect Jones effects; everyone except Morse. Rosseau waits for the laughter to subside and then says, "I really don't know how they determine that, sir."

"Okay," Evans says, "I guess the real important question is what can a P-3 do about it?"

"Run away," responds Keene in a serious tone. "We drop low enough to suck salt spray into the intakes and push the power levers to pop four bingo lights then we try to make it far enough out into the Sea of Japan so our pursuers run out of gas before they catch us."

Evans gives a slight grin in response to the simplicity of the maneuver and asks, "No way to fight back?"

Morse speaks for the first time, "We hunt submarines, Admiral. We have no air defenses."

Rosseau adds, "Fifth Air Force will coordinate fighter protection in the event of a Condition One."

"But on some parts of our track it will take over forty-five minutes for the fighters to reach us, Admiral," Warbuck says with cynicism, "and we will be only fifty to one hundred miles off the Commie coast when they launch on us. That's about fifteen minutes for a MIG to splash us. Best case, the cavalry shows up a half hour late to the dance."

Rosseau tries to regain control of the briefing, "The North Koreans and Chinese do not have look down, shoot down capabilities according to our most recent estimates. So hugging the deck and opening the range should be an effective countermeasure."

Evans and Keene make eye contact. Keene gives a shrug of the shoulders as if to say, "You can't live forever". Evans breaks into a smile that shows he understands the pilot's message loud and clear.

CHAPTER FOUR

Crew Eleven assembles by the main cabin door of QE-05. The three and one-half hour preflight has been completed. All sensors, engines, radios, fuel, and provisions check. It is 0300 and the rain has stopped. Evans, McKay, and Smithers buckle their LPAs as the crew finishes squeezing into the only open space in the fuselage. A P-3C is built on the air frame of a 1950s airliner, but it is filled with tactical equipment. The inside of the fuselage has a dinette area with two beds in the tail, just aft of the main cabin door. Forward of the door on the port side are two acoustic sensor stations facing sideways where complex stylus-pen displays are operated. On the right side is a radar operator's station. Moving forward, there are multiple computer equipment bays and immediately behind the cockpit, one on each side, the Tactical Coordinator's and Navigator's stations. Both are filled with computer screens and keyboards. The only open area is near the main cabin door, just forward of the dinette area, near the internal sonobuoy chutes.

Keene speaks and everyone quiets. The joking and casual interaction of the brief and preflight give way to professional faces. It is now time to get down to the real work, time to focus. Keene says, "Attention to the plane-side brief. I want to formally welcome Admiral Evans, COMFAIRWESTPAC, on tonight's flight."

Evans nods and says, "Great to be along, crew. I'm just here to see what it is you guys do. I've heard some pretty impressive stuff about P-3s and I'm here to see for myself." His words are well chosen, and every member of the crew

53

unconsciously puffs their chests out a little with the pride of recognition.

Keene continues, "Then you picked the right crew, Admiral. We'll show you how it's done. Today's mission is to find and identify all shipping over one hundred gross tons within twenty-five miles of our track. We will be under the PARPRO system which means once we're on-station, either Petty Officer Ford or Airman Fiedler must monitor HF-2 in addition to the Nav and one cockpit person. Let's review emergencies quickly." Keene's voice now drops into a remote, robotic pace. He has given this portion of the planeside brief hundreds of times and it never changes. "In the event of an emergency on the ground necessitating evacuation of the aircraft, everyone is to exit via the over-the-wing hatches, slide off the wing and run aft like a big dog. In the event of an emergency in the air, we will either bailout or ditch. Review your placards on procedures and what to take into the rafts in the event of a ditch. Remember, in this crew I use the ankle-knee method of ditching. Any questions, comments, suggestions, deletions, additions or requests? Okay then, let's get this beast in the air." Keene usually gets a chuckle from crewmembers when they hear his personalization of this mandatory, dry brief. It was his brief that hung the handle, "Big Dog", on him years ago. He turns and heads for the cockpit, and as he does, he says to Jones, "Be sure the Admiral knows his ditching station and how to use one of our backpack chutes."

"Aye, aye, sir."

Evans bites on the bait put out by Keene during the brief and asks Jones, "Okay, I'm curious. What did he mean, 'the ankle-knee method of ditching'?"

Jones smiles as he answers, "The M.O. told us when he joined this crew that if we ditch and he is wading his way from the cockpit back to the over-the-wing hatches where we launch the rafts, if he sees one of us slumped over in our seats, what he does next is determined by the level of water in the aircraft. If the water is around his ankles he will stop to see if we are dead or just unconscious. But if the water is around his knees, well then, he says screw you, he's rushing to the raft—he don't pretend to be no hero!" Evans joins Jones in the laugh.

At 0318, Crew Eleven, call sign TB149, is cleared to take position-and-hold on runway 32. PARPRO flights are monitored by JCS in the National Military Command Center and have a precise window in which to take-off. Departures must be no earlier than ten minutes of the scheduled time and no more than ten minutes after. Depart too early or too late and the plane commander, crew, squadron, and air wing are all embarrassed at the highest level. That is why the pucker factor for these flights is so high.

McKay is in the left seat, Keene in the right, and Smithers in the center. Evans is perched on the radar cabinet behind McKay. A final check is made of all instrument readings in the dark cockpit. It will be another hour before the sun peaks over the eastern horizon. At precisely 0320, TB149 is cleared for take-off.

"Chief, set maximum power," says McKay.

Smithers advances the power levers. The engine noise increases dramatically and the nose lowers, compressing the nose wheel strut. Over seventy tons of shaped aluminum strain to race down the dark stretch of asphalt rolled out before it. McKay taps the top of both rudder pedals and releases the brakes. The aircraft lurches forward. Evans is thrown back against the aft cockpit bulkhead. He is surprised by the jackrabbit start. No where near the jolt of a carrier cat shot, but unexpectedly rapid and powerful, especially for such a large machine.

Smithers is hunched over the center console, his hands manipulating the copilot-side power levels. He scans the sixteen engine instruments. McKay does a little dance on the rudder pedals to insure he has gained directional control with his feet and then slides his left hand from the nose wheel steering control to the yoke. His right hand rests on the pilot-side power levers. McKay shoots quick glances at the second row of four engine instruments on the center console, the shaft horsepower gauges. His focus is the far end of the runway, interrupted by fast glances at the airspeed indicator and engine instruments. Keene backs up McKay on the yoke with his right hand and Smithers at the base of the co-pilot power levers with his left hand. Keene watches the airspeed indicator.

"Eighty knots," Keene says above the din of the straining engines. Smithers raises his free hand and gives a thumbs-up gesture to signify that his take-off roll power check is good and all engines are operating normally.

As the acceleration passes through 121 knots, Keene says, "Refusal." McKay takes his right hand off his power levers and places it firmly on the yoke so that he now has the yoke with both hands.

"We're goin' flyin' now," says McKay.

At 131 knots, Keene says, "Rotate." McKay pulls back on the yoke and the aircraft slowly becomes airborne. As he does so, Keene's attention is on the third column of engine gages.

"Chief, how does number three look?" Keene asks Smithers.

Before Smithers can answer, McKay interrupts and calls for the landing gear to be raised. Evans, whose entire flying life has been piloting single seat aircraft, watches a team of professionals carry out a well-rehearsed drill with precision. Although it is foreign, new and interesting to the admiral, none of the cockpit crew gives any notice or importance to the smooth, automatic flow of the events. In answer to McKay's call for gear up, Keene raises a large white lever by his left knee and responds verbally. Then the flaps are raised, followed by the completion of the seven item climb checklist. Very smooth, very rehearsed. Like a pro team, Tinkers-to-Evers-to-Chance. A thing of beauty so natural all the drill and practice necessary to achieve such professionalism is often overlooked. Layered over top of this conversation is an exchange between Keene and Smithers.

"Number three is a little wobbly on acceleration, but the RPM settles out after a bit. I think she'll be okay," answers Smithers. Keene just furrows his brow in reply and calls Misawa Departure Control and gets clearance to proceed enroute.

Passing through 1,000 feet, McKay says, "Set normal rated power, Chief."

"Aye-aye, sir," replies Smithers as he pulls back on the power levers. The noise decreases. As it does, Keene snaps his head sharply to look at the center console.

"There it is again, Chief, and I heard it this time," says Keene. "That prop control on number three sucks. Did you see a gripe on it in the book?"

Smithers reaches over his head and manipulates the switches on the prop control panel as he answers, "The last one was over seven flights ago. No reported problems since then. I'll use number two as the master and sync them up. I think two can control it okay."

Keene watches the RPM gage on the front panel. He is concerned.

Evans has been watching and admiring the cockpit crew. Now he senses a real edge in Keene's voice he had not noticed previously. He peers around Smithers and speaks to Keene, "Something the matter with number three?"

"Not yet, Admiral," Keene says while keeping his eyes on the number three RPM gage. "There is some prop RPM fluctuation when we move the power level, but it is still within limits."

"You looked a little concerned."

Keene feels fatigued and it is only the start of this long flight. He needs to grab something to eat to recharge his energy level before he is in the mood to teach this admiral the inner workings and hidden magic of the Lockheed Orion and the Hamilton Standard propeller specifically. He sums up the situation with minimal effort for now, "When you've got four engines like we do, not much concerns you. However, there are only two things a P-3 pilot really fears; a fire we can't put out and a runaway prop we can't control. I always keep a close eye on the props."

* * * * *

Over an hour into the flight the sun is starting to appear on this Tuesday morning, a normal start to this very unusual day that will change the lives of Crew Eleven forever.

The morning twilight in the cloud tops creates dramatic canyons of brightness and shadow. The P-3 has the early morning sky over the northern Sea of Japan to itself. Another thirty minutes to the descent point and departing air traffic control. Then the PARPRO track begins in earnest. Not much happens at the top of the track, so the next hour will be a quiet time in the flight. Keene nods at McKay to slip out of the pilot's seat. After first returning the gesture with a quizzical look, McKay widens his eyes in understanding and slides his seat back. He climbs out of the seat and past Smithers. He smiles at Evans who is looking out the side window.

"Admiral would you like some stick time?" asks Keene.

Evans jerks his head towards Keene and a big smile lights his face. It is in his eyes, too. "You bet I would!" he says, then slides into the vacant left seat.

"Ever flown P-3s before?" inquires Keene as Evans slides his seat forward and fastens his harness.

"No. I was an F-8 jock."

"Well, my only recommendation is to think of this as a bus, not your ol' F-8 hot rod. It's all yours," Keene says with a grin. He lifts his hands from the yoke. Evans turns the yoke just slightly, but very rapidly and coffee cups resting on the circuit breaker panel ledge start to spill. Smithers reacts quickly and catches the cups before they fall.

"I see what you mean. Where are we headed?" says Evans as he immediately slows and smoothes out his movements.

"In about a half hour we'll be at the start point and go into a modified EMCON Alpha. Then the fun starts. We get to drop below this layer and start buzzing ships," shares Keene.

"I could go for that. How low do we go?"

Smithers adds his first input to the conversation, "Depends who's flying, Admiral."

Keene chuckles a bit. Smithers never says much, but when he does, his tone reveals more than his words. Keene is aware of the sarcasm in the comment, but he knows Evans is in the dark. In the Pacific Fleet P-3 community most experienced aircrew men know of the VP-1 crew that had a hot dog for a pilot. Keene is the only one onboard today's flight aware that Smithers was on that VP-1 crew years ago. Smithers was a second mech when his PPC thought the authorized minimum altitude was for wimps. Keene thinks, "I wonder if Smithers voiced any objection back then? I bet he was wilder then and went along for the ride. A cowboy's attitude can be infectious. A whole crew can get the 'we're supermen and cannot die' attitude from the plane commander." That flying error is notorious in the community because not only did that pilot violate the minimum altitude, he did it on the overhead pass. They landed with pieces of a Soviet AGI's antenna in the plane's belly. If he had been just a few feet either side of his course he would have hit with the props and then VP-1's little known error could've become a fatal international incident.

"We are limited to taking this airliner-sized crate down to two-hundred feet in daylight, or three hundred feet at night or in bad weather," Keene tells Evans.

"That's low enough?" asks Evans.

To answer, Keene squeezes a button on the right handle of his yoke. There is an audible click as the autopilot disengages and with it the altitude hold feature. Immediately the plane noses down. Evans pulls up, but does so with too much movement and he over-corrects. Loud shouts and moans are heard coming from aft of the cockpit. Evans is all over the sky trying to fly an airliner like a fighter.

Keene says, "This handles a little heavier and is a bit more to push around the sky, Admiral. Two hundred feet will feel plenty low enough when we get down there. The first time I made a 45-degree angle-of-bank turn away from my side of the cockpit I swore we were low enough that the wing was going to catch the surface of the water."

Evans answers while he concentrates on smoothing out the ride, "I hope the crew recovers okay. But I'm having a super time. This is something I've always wondered about. Slamming fighters around the sky, with only me to consider, hasn't quite prepared me for this world. But I had always wondered what it was like."

"When I was in Safety Officer School, I had an instructor who said the F-8 was called the 'widow maker' because over half the flights its first year in the fleet ended in mishaps of some sort. I always found that hard to believe. Was it true?" Keene inquires.

"I don't know about half. But I do know we lost a few in my first squadron tour. It was a bear to bring back aboard the boat," Evans says as he finally gets the P-3 straight and level again. He continues, "I guess that is one of the differences in our communities. With every bad crash we would scratch a name from the flight schedule. You guys have a bad one and a dozen or more are removed."

Keene is impressed that this fighter jock, an admiral even, would acknowledge that patrol aviation could have its dangers. Most young jet pilots spend too much time strutting and not enough on reflection. Evans is okay. In Safety Officer School Keene had seen numbers that fighter and attack squadrons might lose a plane each year. A very hazardous profession indeed. Patrol squadrons might lose a plane once every dozen years. But the death toll per year averages out about the same. The worst hit the patrol community has ever taken in peacetime is the mid-air collision of two planes from the same squadron when changing stations over Southern California waters. Two crews lost, two dozen men not returning to their families. It was all due to one mistake; all dead in less than a minute.

Keene pauses as he looks out the window. This is his home, really. He is good at this. He understands the tactical utilization of this weapons systems platform. He knows the properties of sound in water and the tactics of Soviet submarine commanders. He can identify Communist bloc ships, subs, and aircraft in less than two seconds thanks to intensive recce training. He can flight plan the fuel and weather and navigate to fly in the Arctic Circle or around distant, forgotten tropical isles. But more than all of these, he can fly the airplane. Most anyone can be taught to fly. But only a few are born to it. There are natural-born flyers like there are natural-born ball players. Keene is one. He's a natural. He has made mistakes, but he has always been able through skill and natural abilities to overcome them.

Keene takes a deep breath and then exhales slowly. Then he says, "They won't be taking any names off the crew list today, Admiral. We'll just get it done and get home."

* * * * *

Milkus is drumming his fingers on the envelope centered squarely on his blotter. At the Pentagon it is 1255, Monday. The buzzer rings at the locked office door. The sergeant by the door opens it and admits a naval captain. Carter enters and makes immediate eye contact with Milkus. The naval officer is in his service dress blues which are crisp with razor sharp creases and his ribbons are brand new; his Corfam shoes are like mirrors and stiff with newness. Carter is ready for inspection, his wedding, or court-martial. His posture is ramrod straight. His eyes are intense and cold, like clear marbles. He nods very slightly at Milkus. These two serious officers exit the space, the envelope tucked firmly under Milkus's left arm.

At Adams's office the secretary greets them and says Adams has yet to return. He is expected any minute and they can have just a couple minutes of his time before his 1315 appointment. Milkus and Carter acknowledge the information but, uncommonly, do not smile or sit on the straight back chairs available in the outer office. Carter turns his back to Milkus and pretends to examine the print of a turn-of-the-century racehorse decorating the bulkhead by the door. Milkus retains his grip on the envelope and starts to click his heels together. It is an old habit he has not exercised since he was a major at the Marine Corps Recruit Depot, San Diego. He rocks from side-to-side and a loud bang is heard as first one foot and then his other swings and pops the stationary heel. Milkus is lost in his thoughts and is unaware of his swaying and popping. Carter is oblivious to it as well. The secretary catches the seriousness in the room and stares at Milkus's feet, but refrains from saying anything.

General Adams slowly enters the outer office. He never seems to hurry any place, and yet never seems to be tardy. Milkus and Carter turn to face him and come to rigid attention. Except for rookies or visitors, this is unusual in the Pentagon. Formal behavior is forfeited for casual efficiency. Adams smiles at the two officers. He immediately senses that something unexpected and quite serious is about to change his day.

"Come into my office, gentlemen," says Adams, taking charge of a situation of which he knows nothing yet. It is what he gets paid to do. "We can talk in my office."

Adams goes to the chair behind his desk and sits down. Carter closes the door then moves to Milkus's side, the

Marine standing at parade rest in front of the desk. The two
0-6's exchange a short glance. Carter takes a breath and
proceeds.

"General, I came into some rather disturbing information
yesterday. It concerns a possible violation of law and ethics
by senior members of the administration. It affects the
national security."

Adams adjusts his position in his chair and motions for
the two to take a seat. Milkus looks behind him and sits on
the sofa along the wall. Carter remains standing. He pauses
and considers how to tell Adams of their intent to go to
Admiral Bella. Adams takes the pause as a request for a
response or direction.

"What is the subject of this violation?"

Milkus jumps from the sofa and hands Adams the
envelope. Adams opens it and quickly scans the material as
the two officers observe him. Then Milkus says, "As you
can tell, it outlines sharing crucial information with the
Chinese. It reflects either total idiocy or treachery."

Milkus stops and chooses his next words very carefully.
He ponders, "Should I say it or should I let him come to the
same conclusion? You have nothing to lose now anyway.
Might as well belt it out like Bobby Hatfield chasing the ebb
tide." He blurts out, "I think it is treachery. It is treason."

Adams looks up from his reading and stares into
Milkus's eyes. They are hard and determined. Adams
moves his glare to Carter. The two retain the non-verbal
connection of warriors deciding their personal fate. Adams is
seeking Carter's opinion. The sailor hesitates just for a
second and then commits, "Treason, sir."

Adams reaches for his phone. He pushes one button.
"Melinda, reschedule my afternoon appointments. I won't be
available the rest of the day. And Melinda, see if you can
reach Admiral Bella. I need to speak with him as soon as
possible. And I do mean ASAP."

Carter and Milkus look at each other with disbelief and relief. Adams speaks, "I feel we need him in on this discussion and decision. He can be trusted. You tell anyone else about this?"

"No, sir," they answer in unison.

"Good. Grab some coffee or a coke from the side bar and take a seat. We've got some work ahead of us."

* * * * *

The coffee is percolating on the stove. Like her husband, Joyce Keene does not drink it, so she has never invested in a coffee maker. Maybe three times a year does the coffeepot come out from the cupboard above the refrigerator. It now will be a more frequent occurrence. Every fifth week has become Joyce's turn to host the Monday evening Moffett Field base wives' Bible study. Since moving into officer housing last spring, Joyce has been presently surprised by the support network available. She has been even more pleased to discover how many of the families share her emphasis on the spiritual element of life. A Navy wife since Jim and she wed immediately after his Academy graduation, this is the first time she has lived on base. Housing is so hard to get for junior officers' families; it wasn't until this tour as a lieutenant commander that the option became available. She reflects on how real estate costs are ridiculous in Silicon Valley. She thinks, "Our first tour here we were able to find a nice home to buy, but, poor Jim, the commute was so long it nearly killed him. Now, we have security and friendliness and low rent and the commissary and base movie theater right here and his commute is only five minutes to the hangar." And she ponders a bigger, more important benefit to her. Unlike their previous home in East San Jose, here there are no bars on the windows and children without supervision. Her thoughts elicit a small prayer, "Thank you, Lord, for providing such a unique and wonderful opportunity for our kids. Thank you."

The doorbell rings. Joyce turns the burner down underneath the coffeepot, checks the correctness of the silver laid out on the dining table and goes to the door. The quarters are small, only three-bedroom townhouses, but they are pure 1940 California architecture. Many windows create an easy inside-to-outside flow. It has a large living room off the dining area with sliding glass doors to the patio. Joyce opens the front door and three chatting ladies enter. One has a sleeping two-year old in her arms. Joyce beds the infant on the sofa in the small family room. Looking at the child she smiles in appreciation of the joy in having her youngest, Sammy, being old enough to attend kindergarten. Joyce enjoys the couple hours of freedom each day after the last fourteen years of at least one child home all day. The doorbell rings again and Joyce admits two more ladies.

Refreshments are served and all settle into chairs that circle the living room.

Helen, the study leader, opens by saying, "Ladies, let's start with any prayer requests."

"I think we should pray for Joyce and Freda and their husbands who are on deployment," says the quiet wife of a senior enlisted man, normally never one to initiate conversation but today eager to speak. Her words pour out almost faster than she can articulate, "I had a bad dream last night that has bothered me all day. In it I saw a P-3 fly into a cloud and then come out the other side. It flew into another cloud and came out the other side of it. Then it flew into another cloud and it never came out. Then I awoke gasping for air. I couldn't breath. I felt this coldness over my face, then it felt like an ice cold hand grabbed my heart and squeezed. I started to cry uncontrollably. I have been up since 4 AM, unable to shake this horrible dream. I have been praying since dawn that this fear would leave me. My Bill is no longer aircrew, so I am not upset for him. I am probably just feeling the effects of too much pizza last night, but I can't help thinking we should remember in prayer all who are flying, today especially."

Joyce looks at Freda. Her husband is due to come home in two weeks from Adak, Alaska. Freda smiles and sips her coffee, showing a polite face that appears not to be touched by the premonition. But Joyce doesn't smile. She nods in agreement. Deep in her, for just a flash, she sees the figure of her worst fear come out of its dark shadows, but then quickly retreats, its form vanishing. Her thoughts race, "What if Jim did crash and die? What would happen to this wonderful life? What would we do? Don't think of that. It can't happen. Look, Helen is out of coffee."

"Would you like more coffee, Helen?"

"In a minute, Joyce, after we pray."

"Yes, let's pray first," whispers Joyce.

CHAPTER FIVE

"It should be on the nose at about three miles," barks AW3 Lane Bricker into his headset. As "Sensor Three" his job on the P-3 is to operate non-acoustical detectors. His primary instrument is the AN/APS-115B radar. He takes three quick sweeps then stops transmitting, waits a couple minutes and repeats the procedure. He is good at it. Last cruise he earned the handle "Spots" because of his rapid learning curve in mastering how the radar picture changes between sweeps. He can spot the next target location before it appears on the scope. By "hooking" the contact with his cursor and inputting the position, course and speed into the computer, the pilots can see the target displayed on their cockpit screen and drive to intercept it. The ability to accurately determine a course and speed in just a couple sweeps gives Bricker status within his professional community.

"Radar, Flight, we still have nothing. Spots, you sure there's something out here? All I got is rain right now," says Glenn as he shifts his scan from the instrument panel to outside the windshield to search for the contact. It is now 1415, eight hours into the patrol. Glenn has been in the left seat for the past 90 minutes. A half-hour ago, Keene relieved McKay in the right seat. The patrol started slowly, with just a few contacts worth photographing, or "rigging" as the aircrew call it, in the Northern area of the Sea of Japan, or "SOJ." The PARPRO track is taking the crew on a giant, clockwise orbit around the SOJ, starting at the two o'clock position. The action really picked up three hours ago as the patrol entered the shipping lanes by the Korea Strait. Now the patrol has worked its way to the seven o'clock position. They are approaching the crazies in North Korea. The track will take a swing to the east very shortly to give North Korea a wider berth.

The weather is the typically ragged, low gray overcast found in the SOJ in September. It is like flying under a stainless steel saucepan lid. Over the entire East Sea it is nothing but gray under wet clouds. Zooming low beside merchant ships and snapping their picture sounds fun, and it is in clear blue skies. Flying the same track through thick squalls and variable ceilings is just plain tiring.

The crew is organized for every mission. For surface vessel rigging, the pilot at the controls positions the plane to run past the ship from stern to bow, while the flight engineer, or FE, focuses on nothing but the instrument panel. The FE monitors the 16 engine instruments, the two hydraulic panels, the pressurization panel, twenty warning lights, the fuel control panel and fuel pumps, the hundreds of circuit breakers, the propeller synchronization system panel, and adjusts the four power levers at the pilot's command. It is an extremely demanding and responsible position on the crew. And the pressures to be the systems expert on a very complex aircraft can trip up even those sailors with excellent talent. Sailors like Tommy Peters, who slipped into the center seat an hour ago. As Second Mechanic—or "second mech"—he is under training to become fully FE qualified. Another four months and he should be ready. But the crew will soon discover that a good personality and smarts are only two-thirds of the recipe for a good FE.

In the right seat, Keene is responsible for the safety-of-flight back-up of the pilot. Airspeed, altitude, angle-of-bank limits can be easily forgotten by a pilot intent on yanking and banking the plane to reach a specific point in space. Keene easily slips into the role of watchdog. He could care less about the success of this pass. His current job is to keep this beast airborne. When he is at the flight controls he will worry about tactical junk. Not now.

Sitting behind the pilot, perched on the radar cabinet, is the In-Flight Tech. His job is to capture the first half of the ship's name as the plane streaks by. Billy Warbuck looks out his window at his TACCO station and reads the last half of the name. He also uses the computer to insert fly-to points which appear on the pilot's screen to direct them where to go next. In the rear of the aircraft, peering out the aft lookout window is the ordnance man, Fiedler. He tries to see the whole name.

Glenn is developing into a good stick. He can anticipate where he should be next in a tactical problem. This is a skill many good hand-eye jockeys never develop. And it is what separates the good warriors from the kids with toys. Glenn flies out of the rain and nods at Peters to stop the windshield wipers. As the windshield clears, Glenn sees his target, a small ship laboring to make five knots.

"Radar, Flight, Tally-ho on your target," Glenn says into his microphone, using a flat monotone, the repetitiveness of the flight beginning to wear on his young enthusiasm. "Good pick-up, Spots, this guy has a low signature. Crew, Flight, we'll take him on the port side in one minute."

Glenn takes the P-3 down from 500 to 200 feet over the water. He swings a long, wide turn to the left to approach from the rear. He establishes a slight crab to compensate for the left-to-right crosswind. The Navy invested in different camera sights and systems over the years to help pilots get sharp intel pictures that fill the frame with nothing missed. Like most others in the fleet, Crew Eleven keeps those sights stowed. During preflight, Keene places a single grease pencil dot on the pilot's side window, about three inches below the top of his shoulder and abeam of it. Once that mark is in place, Keene merely advises Glenn and McKay to drive that dot over the target. It is very low tech, but very accurate in the hands of a professional.

At thirty seconds out, Keene gives another stand-by to the crew over the PA system. Once astern of the target, Keene verifies the course and speed to the navigator. The closer the aircraft approaches the ship, the great disparity in relative speed becomes very noticeable. The P-3 zooms up the butt of the small cargo ship at 200 knots ground speed. When directly abeam of the target, the pilot must complete three actions which equate to patting your stomach and rubbing your head simultaneously. It takes a few passes before a pilot can press and hold the camera button just aft of the left communications panel by his left thigh, call, "Mark on top, now-now-now", note the ship's name, and then release the camera button, all the while maintaining positive control of this militarized airliner with his right hand and feet.

During the three seconds this takes place, the other crewmembers must perform similar tasks, all connected to the pilot's call of "mark on top". Many rookie pilots return to base with hundreds of photographic frames of blank ocean because they forget to release the shutter. Most embarrassing however, is to return without pictures of the last half of the flight's contacts because you ran out of nose camera film. Keene knows that in some crews, the copilot operates the shutter to prevent these errors.

Keene has a reputation as one of the best airborne photographers in the fleet, being the only pilot to win the WESTPAC Silver Shutter Award three times and the EASTPAC Golden Lens Award twice. And he feels he can teach his pilots how to grab complete shots of the target with minimal film waste. If taught right, you don't need to develop procedures to compensate for less than the highest standards of professionalism.

Immediately upon passing the bow of the small freighter, Glenn releases the shutter button with his left hand and uses it to grab the yoke. He moves his right hand to the power levers and adds power to the three operating engines.

Number one engine was shut down hours ago to conserve fuel. It is normal procedure on long missions for the P-3 to fly most of the tactical mission with "one in the bag." If the mission can be conducted above 1,000 feet, often number four engine is also shut down to stretch time aloft even more.

"Set 2500 shaft horsepower," says Glenn as the plane climbs through three hundred feet. Peters learns forward and adjusts the three power levers as Glenn looks down to view the computer screen on the front panel. He turns west towards the next point on the track.

Keene looks at the fuel totalizer gauge on the center panel. Then he asks Peters, "We light enough to shut down four yet? And more to the question, will it save us any gas?"

Peters pulls out a laminated chart, does a series of calculations, then responds, "Yes, M.O., we're about 2,000 pounds under. And I figure it could extend our time on-station maybe another hour if need be."

"Okay. Fred, take us up to 1,500 feet. Once there, we'll put number four to sleep," Keene says to Glenn. Then he keys his ICS and says, "Ordnance, Flight. Airman Fiedler come forward with your telescopic lens." Keene plans ahead. He is one of the few PPCs who will shut down two engines on a PARPRO flight. If you must constantly dive to two-hundred feet to rig a contact, then you must constantly restart number four engine when you go below 1,000 feet. A minimum of three engines must be running when below 1,000 feet. Keene avoids most of this by using a telescopic lens on a hand-held 35mm camera to get pictures of non-sensitive targets. Keene re-starts his number four engine and dives only when there is an interesting ship to rig. He calls Fiedler to the cockpit because the crew ordnance man is the designated hand-held cameraman.

The checklist is completed just as Fiedler enters the cockpit. The admiral squeezes in right after Fiedler. Keene orders Peters to feather number four. Evans is unaware of what is happening and is startled by the Christmas tree light display that appears on the warning panels as Peters pushes in the feather button over his head.

"We got trouble?" Evans asks in a flat, calm voice.

"No, sir," replies Keene, who continues with the checklist before explaining.

Once the shutdown checklist is complete, Keene gives the post shutdown brief to the pilot and flight engineer, "We have number one and four shut down for fuel conservation. Our hard deck is 1,000 feet with two engines shut down. In the event of an emergency, we will restart number four first, starting the checklist at item number eight, P.C.O. Once number four is up and running, we will then handle the emergency. Are there any questions?"

Glenn and Peters shake their heads. They have heard this brief many times.

"Roger, then," says Keene. "Shut down is complete." Now Keene strains his neck to make eye contact with Evans who is behind him to the left. "Admiral, you never know what we might find on the last half of the track, so we've shut down two to be sure to have enough gas to use on station should we need to."

"This big gal flies okay on just two?"

"If we're light enough, it does okay."

Keene and the admiral make eye contact. Keene can see some concern deep in Evans's eyes. Not obvious when he smiles, but there just before the admiral pushed it deeper.

Evans responds with a smile, "It just seems very odd to me, Commander, to shut down perfectly good engines. There is something a little strange in that. Normally, we try to keep our engines running and the enemy is trying to stop them. Yes, sir, just a little strange indeed."

* * * * *

Major Julie McWalters, USAF, looks at her watch upon seeing the line at the Pentagon cafeteria. She is frustrated

72

that there are so many people wanting to eat now. It is just after 0300, lunchtime for the graveyard shift at the puzzle palace. Julie is irritated that only one cafeteria is kept open for the night shift. It just creates crowds that decrease efficiency. She just wants a quick sandwich and to return to work. Ever since her mother's comment last week about how slim she looked, McWalters made a resolution not to skip meals. But it looks like she will miss a meal today. She has just too much work sitting at her desk to waste time in line. As she turns, however, she sees Lieutenant Bradley Dewalker, USN, leaving the cash register. He crosses the crowded dining room and sits at a table being vacated by two civil servants. Julie fights her way between tables and takes a seat next to him as he returns from placing his tray on a nearby stand.

"Julie! What a scrumptious surprise!" says Dewalker. His comment could have been taken as a slimy pick-up line, except anyone who knows Dewalker knows that nearly every statement or description he gives is connected to food. And this Surface Warfare Officer has the build to show it. His Service Dress Blue uniform coat fit him as a j.g. but now has become so tight he avoids buttoning the double-breasted front whenever possible. McWalters knew when she saw him that he would have enough food on his tray to feed three.

"Bradley, you're a life saver again," says McWalters as she lifts one of the three sandwiches on the table and opens the plastic wrap on it. "I've got to return to the center in five minutes and I really need the nourishment. You don't mind, do you?"

Dewalker doesn't over eat because he is lonely, depressed, or has a low self-image. He eats because he truly enjoys the taste, texture, smell, and warm filling feeling of the food. Yes, he does mind that his planned meal has been altered. He minds whenever his plans are redirected or changed. But Julie has such almond shaped, Sophia Loren sexy brown eyes, and she is so well proportioned, with all parts of her svelte body complimenting the others, that the sandwich theft is not a crisis. He muses to himself, "A hard working, dedicated Air Force officer with beautiful eyes and such alluring perfume. What is ham and cheese compared to alabaster skin and perky, short hair?"

"I don't mind, help yourself," he forces out with as much pleasantness as possible.

"You're a good—what do you call it in the Navy? A good shipmate, Bradley."

"What are you working on in that glass castle that is so important you can't take time for a real lunch?" Dewalker asks.

McWalters sits next to him and munches the sandwich with large bites. She works in the action room of the National Military Command Center. Dewalker is assigned to the general section in the main bay. Nothing much different happens in the action room than in the main bay, but because it is separate and requires entry through another cipher lock, an air of mystery and exclusiveness hovers over those assigned behind the glass wall in the elevated room. Dewalker has the same level of security clearance as McWalters, but he doesn't know he does. All information is on a strict need-to-know basis to maintain security through isolation and compartmentalization. Dewalker's question is not a suspicious inquiry. It is a dig at one of the "glass castle dwellers" by one of the peasants in the main bay.

"Bradley, you know we play pinochle up in the castle. Once you get your playing abilities up to standard, maybe you can join us," answers McWalters, her mouth full of ham, cheese and bread.

"I would love to join the game. It is totally dead in West Africa. I'm having trouble staying awake," Dewalker mumbles as he pops open a chocolate Jell-O cup and begins to slurp the contents. He is the staff watch officer for the area. McWalters has North and South Korea, and this assignment rates duty in the glass castle.

"I know what you mean. Not much happening in my area either. It's earned me a special assignment from the Admiral."

"Lucky you."

"Yeah. I've got to get back to work on it right now. Thanks for the sandwich, Bradley. I owe you one," says McWalters as she rises to leave.

"You owe me more than that. I'd just like to know when you will start forking over the cupcakes in payment."

McWalters sees something more than a reference to food in Dewalker's eyes. She hesitates a moment and starts to speak. But she stops herself and smiles broadly and turns and leaves. She is surprised to find herself slightly attracted to the overweight, but nice junior officer. She shakes her head and smiles again as she rushes across the dining room and out into the wide Pentagon hallway. She is still smiling as she fumbles to get out the first of her two ID cards to gain access to the JCS section, then the NMCC.

* * * * *

"It is just a mother ship for the fishers to the east," Glenn tells Warbuck over the intercom as he pulls the P-3 into a climbing left turn. He is climbing from 1,000 feet, back to the search altitude of 1,500 feet, heading west, and back on the track.

Warbuck smashes six buttons on his computer console and "F2" appears on his and the pilot's scopes. He speaks into his headset, "Okay, then head to fly-two and we'll cover the westerly edge of the track."

Keene, still in the right seat as the patrol enters its ninth hour, comes on line, "Billy, put a line on the track border. I don't want to bust the area, and one square mile of ocean looks the same as another up here."

"You should already have it. I put it up an hour ago."

"Wait a minute," Keene responds. He reaches over to the computer keyboard on the central console and pushes the scale button twice. He pushes it again and a vertical line appears on the left side of the scope. He calls the TACCO, "Billy, it is too long. I can only see it on the largest scale. Make it smaller so I can see it on a 32-mile scale."

The conversation is abruptly interrupted by HF radio traffic heard in the headsets, "Tuna King. Tuna King. Do not answer. Message follows: Yankee Delta Tango Romeo--I say again--Yankee Delta Tango Romeo. Tuna King. Tuna King. This is Yokota Radio. Do not answer. Out."

Keene grabs his grease pencil from his left upper arm flight suit pocket and quickly writes Y-D-T-R on his side window. He keys the intercom, "You guys get that back there?"

Smoltz, sitting at his navigator station just aft of the cockpit answers, "Yes, M.O., I got yankee delta tango romeo."

"I got the same thing, Bobby," responds Keene. "Decode it and let me know what they are saying."

Evans was lying in the aft rack, eyes shut, but listening over the PA to the intercom conversation. He was marveling at the professionalism of the crew in keeping such sharp focus on a mission that becomes repetitious and tiring hour after fatiguing hour, when he hears the tuna king call. He slips out of the rack and makes his way forward, arriving just as Smoltz enters the cockpit.

Smoltz reports to Keene by leaning over Peters lap and raising his voice to be heard, "It's a condition three! Check our navigation!"

"Well, did you Bobby?" asks Keene in a dry tone to counterbalance the excitable, inexperienced ensign.

"The Air Force must be screwed up. I am sure we are well within the PARPRO boundaries," says Smoltz with only a hint of uncertainty.

Warbuck now squeezes into the cockpit. His voice is as rough as he looks, "Bobby, did you screw up encoding our last position report?"

"No!—I mean I don't think so."

Keene is ignoring Evans as he stands to the side in the crowded cockpit. This is internal crew stuff and he wishes the admiral wasn't onboard to see it. But screw him. It is more important to get this right than try to hide any confusion from the brass.

He speaks to Warbuck, "Billy, take the ensign back to his station and check his last position report. I'm going to break off this run on the next target and climb to the east to move away from the coast. And, Navigator, you better pray we haven't busted the PARPRO boundary."

Keene places his right hand on the yoke and left hand on the power levers. He nods at Glenn to tell him he is taking control of the aircraft and simultaneously pushes the power forward and rolls into a shallow right turn. "Flight Engineer, set 3,500 shaft horsepower."

Peters advances the power levers. Smoltz and Warbuck exit the cockpit. Evans takes a seat on the radar console. Nothing is said. A tint of anger, laced with fatigue begins to shade Keene's face as he thinks, "A Tuna King call. With an admiral aboard. We'll let's wait and see what the true situation is. Don't rush to judgment just yet."

It starts as a low wobble. Like a flock of sheep being herded toward you, but still around the bend in the road, out of sight. Slowly the wobble begins to steady into a repetitious wah-wah-wah. Soon the sound rises from muffled sheep to a distinct, screeching cry of death's goblins converging on the aircraft from all compass points. In just a matter of half-seconds, fear reaches critical mass in the cockpit. Three sets of knowledgeable eyes focus on a single gauge on the vertical central console.

Peters yells first, "Prop fluctuation number three!"

"Syncs off." Keene is surprised at how automatically the correct procedure flows from his lips. Practice, practice, drill, drill, saves lives. Keene stops his climb and turn. He instinctively shoves the nose over to accelerate from climb to cruise speed.

Peters reaches over his head and flips two switches on the prop electronic control panel and answers, "Syncs are off."

The wobble decreases slightly, but does not disappear.

Keene is still on automatic as he directs the next steps, "She is still fluctuating. Let's restart number four and then try and shut her down. Flight Engineer, restart number four starting at Pressure Cutout Over-ride on the restart checklist."

Glenn reaches across the cockpit and grabs the laminated page of checklists from its location stuffed underneath the copilot's instrument glare shield. He starts reading, "Airspeed."

"I'm too slow—continue the checklist. I'll get the nose over more and get enough airspeed to restart," Keene says as he maneuvers the airliner without conscious thought. Years of practice have made the aluminum and wires and steel an extension of his body.

Glenn continues, "Pressure cutout override"

Peters reaches overhead and pushes a small black button next to the large round feather button which is covered with a clear, plastic box guard. "I'm pressing it now--" His worried voice breaks as he shouts the rest of his sentence, "—there she goes! Run away prop on number three!"

The noise level in the cockpit instantly becomes deafening. The rpm gauge on number three races from fluctuating around 100% to its maximum limit of 120%. In reality, the RPM of the large four-bladed propeller has accelerated to where the tips are nearly supersonic. The noise is so loud in the cockpit Glenn expects blood to be rushing from his ears as he stuffs his palms over them. The four blades have pancaked to such a flat angle-of-attack the drag on the right side is equivalent to a barn door being fixed to the wing. The plane starts an immediate, drastic yaw to the right. Keene instinctively fights it with left rudder and twisting the yoke to lower the left wing. His corrections have minimal effect. Evans looks for a handhold to secure his perch on the radar cabinet. He finds nothing but the top of the cabinet to hold onto and uses his balance to try and survive Mr. Toad's Wild Ride without injury. Evans wants to grab his ears, but he cannot free his hands from grasping the surface of the radar cabinet.

"Go ahead and feather number 3!" Keene shouts as loudly as he can. He knows pulling the large feather handle will probably have no effect on a runaway prop, but he thinks there is no harm in trying now that the worst has happened.

Peters pulls the feather handle. Nothing changes.

Keene is not conscious of the noise. He funnels his full attention to keeping airborne on one engine. He shouts with all the air in his lungs, "Get number four running now! The drag from the dead prop will kill us. We'll never stay airborne on one engine!"

Glenn does what he is trained to do. He continues with the checklist, yelling in the calmest voice he can muster, "Restart checklist continues—"

"Screw the checklist!" Keene snaps. "Peters, just light off number four *now*!" He pushes his intercom switch forward, "Nav, Flight, get off a mayday now!"

Peters begins to panic. He grabs the feather button on number four and pulls it down. He has unfeathered and started dozens of engines in his training, but it has not yet become automatic. He must think about what he is doing. Yet he cannot think with the noise and the pressure of the rapidly moving events pressing him harder and harder. He tries to force himself to focus on the engine instruments for number four. He wants desperately to see the rpm climb off zero and the turbine inlet temperature gauge wind wildly in a clockwise manner. He realizes that he has been holding out on the button long enough. He frantically thinks, "But where is the light off? Where is it? Oh, please God let it light off! Please!" Peters shouts, "Number four won't light off—it won't light off!"

Keene knows that the next few seconds, not minutes, will decide the fate of Crew Eleven. He must get more power now. He is trading altitude for airspeed. He is diving to keep sufficient speed to maintain control. If he slows, the drag from number three will cause the aircraft to stop flying.

Glenn shouts, "Passing through 1,000 feet!"

Keene wants to look over his left shoulder and see what Peters is doing, but he cannot take his attention off his immediate task. He must wrestle this beast and force it to stay in the air. He also knows if he looks at Peters he would scare himself. Keene can hear Peters crying even with all the noise. Keene plays the hand he has been dealt the best he can, "Try number one—Now! Now! Now!" He keys the PA system and continues shouting, "Crew, set Condition One for ditching—Prepare to ditch! Prepare to ditch!"

Peters releases the number four feather button and wipes his eyes. He pushes the protective cover aft with his thumb and pulls down on the number one feather button. He remembers to look out the left photo window and watch the prop start to turn slowly, then he looks at the front instrument panel. Oh God! No light off again! He reports in a crying panic, "Number one won't light off either!"

Glenn looks directly over his head at Peters's hands, "Peters! You stupid jackass! The fuel and ignition switch—you forgot the fuel and ignition switch!"

Peters immediately remembers his procedures. The engines cannot light off unless there is fuel flow and a spark to fire it. This is done by the fuel and ignition switch located immediately in front of the feather button for each engine.

Sometimes there comes a time in a sailor's life when his actions can save or take the lives of his shipmates. Peters doesn't realize it, but such a moment has come to him. He will shift his vision just a nanosecond too early and men will die as a result.

Peters looks up and sees the outboard fuel and ignition switches for engines one and four in the rear position, and the two inboard switches for engines two and three in the forward position. While still holding out on the number one feather button, Peters reaches for the number one fuel and ignition switch with his other hand. He looks down before he reaches it. In the noise and his confusion and fear, his right hand is one and one-half inches off the mark. He grabs the number two engine fuel and ignition switch by error. He tries to move it forward, but when it doesn't move, he performs an act natural to most western men, an act that takes no conscious will. He flips the switch the opposite direction. As soon as the switch reaches the aft position six electrical connections are made and number two's fuel and oil are cut-off. Number two quits running immediately and starts to wind down. With it goes the last remaining engine-driven generator. No electrical power means no engine can be restarted.

Even with the unholy din of the supersonic blade tips of number three propeller, Keene's experienced ear can hear number two engine wind down. Immediately his controls freeze. With the loss of electrical power the hydraulic pumps cease operation and flight controls in a P-3 are hydraulically assisted. The power steering just went out on the largest Buick ever made. Keene can ignore the Christmas tree of warning lights popping to life on the instrument panels, but he must regain control now. The nose is low, speed low, heading veering irresistibly to the right.

"You shut down number two!" is all Keene can shout.

Before a blubbering Peters can answer, a giant paw grabs his left shoulder and hurls him from the center seat. Chief Smithers has arrived in the cockpit like John Wayne and the 7th Calvary. He reaches to the front firewall and yanks out the long, yellow and black stripped emergency shutdown handle for number two. This drives the pin-wheeling prop to the feather position. Simultaneously, he flips the in-flight arming and start switches on the Auxiliary Power Unit panel directly over his head.

"APU coming on sir. Keep us airborne for another two minutes and I'll have number four running." Smithers pushes these words through his tense lips with force, but with so much control that a new optimism floods the cockpit.

"Boost out!—Go boost out, Chief! I'm gust locked!" shouts Keene as he wrestles to pull the aircraft out of the shallow dive.

Smithers mumbles a curse to himself and flips a small compartment cover up with his left foot, then reaches down and carefully pulls three long handles straight up, one at a time. These handles disconnect the hydraulic assist to the rudders, ailerons, and elevators. Even though his PPC cannot hear him, Smithers shares an admission of his self-perceived lack of total professionalism, "Sorry, sir. I forgot."

By using all his upper body strength, Keene can now influence the plane's flight. He motions with his head for Glenn to help him level the wings. Slowly, the right wing is lifted towards level. Now Keene does the most difficult and important curl he has ever performed. His biceps burn from the inside out as he pulls back with all the strength he has on the yoke. The rate of descent slows and then, near six hundred feet, it stops. QE-05 is now level, in a slow right turn, with airspeed falling off rapidly. Passing through 190 knots, Keene must let the nose lower slightly. The big, wide wings on this airliner-sized aircraft mean it can glide better than some smaller, high performance planes.

Keene does the rapid calculation in his head that only desperate professionals have ever experienced, "It looks like I can maintain a four hundred foot-per-minute descent by holding the nose up above normal and letting the airspeed slowly bleed down to 160."

"Chief, we'll be in the water in less than two minutes. Get your harness on. We're gonna get wet."

"APU is up," the Chief says as he flips another overhead switch. "Here's electrical power."

Smithers immediately moves his right hand to the right. Out comes the number four feather button. He is concentrating on getting power to an engine before hitting the water. No time for a harness now.

"Chief, if we have hydraulics, give me boost-in. I'll need the control when we ditch," shouts Keene in almost a matter-of-fact voice which is loud, but not screaming.

Smithers continues to pull down on the feather button overhead with his right hand, and still manages to slowly reset the long boost handles at his left foot using his left hand. Today there is an advantage to being one of the tallest flight engineers in the Pacific Fleet. His condor-like span means he is only one of a very few who can perform these functions simultaneously. As the last handle reaches home, Smithers takes his left hand and moves the number four fuel and ignition switch forward.

Smithers picks-up the matter-of-fact tone, "Number four fuel and ignition on—no light off—"

"Passing through two hundred feet," Glenn interrupts.

Keene speaks, "Give me approach flaps before we stall and fall out of the sky."

Smithers continues, "Checking circuit breakers." He turns to his right and quickly scans four of the hundred black and red buttons on the cockpit distribution bus panels.

"Tell the crew to prepare to ditch. One minute to impact," Keene says, reverting to a drill he has performed and instructed and graded hundreds of times at 6,000 feet. Now it's for real. For real. Who would've thought? Really.

Glenn shouts into his headset and the tube rats hear the worst, "Crew, standby for water impact in less than a minute. We're gonna hit hard."

Evans rushes aft towards his assigned ditching station. He dons a Mae West passenger life preserver. He slides into the aft-facing dinette seat in the tail. He puts on his lap belt. He cinches it as tightly as he can pull.. The admiral has reverted to his combat flying mentality. He thinks of what is to follow, "What did they say during the safety briefing? Once we stop, go forward to the starboard over-the-wing exit. Right." As he thinks he prepares himself for impact. Evans has no idea when he was trained to zip up all his flight suit pockets before ditching. It is one of those learned behaviors that just come to the surface when needed. He slides on his fighter jock helmet. He comments to himself, "To think, I was hesitant to bring it along. Who needs helmets on P-3s?

Fear is no longer present in the cockpit. Work, hard work, has replaced it. Smithers's eyes grow wide as he spies his target. A circuit breaker on the start bus has popped due to the rapid electrical power shifting.

"Fuel shut-off valve circuit breaker in, number four,…light off number four!" Immediately the dials on the right side of the front panel take-off in a beautiful clockwise rotation. T.I.T. rising rapidly. RPM spooling up nicely. Fuel flow jumping up. Shaft horsepower climbing to 700.

Keene feels a slight pull to the left as number four powers up on the starboard side. That big Ham-Stan prop is rotating those four massive blades forward and grabbing great gobs of air and shoving it back over the wing. Thrust. The feel of it excites Keene and Smithers, the old salts fighting to save the bird. But he can read the altimeter and it tells the end of this flight. Passing through 100 feet. Now the water is close and cold.

"Fred, what's my ditching speed?" Keene asks Glenn.

Glenn stretches his neck to see a placard over Keene's head. "I think it's about 120 knots—passing 135 knots now."

Smithers is adjusting the number four power lever with his right hand and holding out on the number one feather button overhead with his left. As he advances the power lever on the only operating engine it creates a momentary surge of hope in the cockpit. Keene takes control of the power lever from Smithers and pushes it all the way forward. A red warning light illuminates on the T.I.T. gauge. Keene ignores it. He has no concern now about over-temping the engine. He lowers the left wing ten degrees to try and regain heading control. No luck. But the rate of decent has dropped to 150 feet-per-minute. Questions race through his mind, "Can I keep the airspeed above stall and nurse us to level flight? Can I keep it right on the ragged edge of being airborne? Are we light enough? 130 knots now. What effect will that big old flat prop on number three have on stall speed? At this weight....stall around 117?...125 now.....will the descent stop here?....will it?....NO! Lower the nose quickly! Accelerate before we stall and all die!"

Smithers is completely absorbed in getting number one engine restarted, yet he can sense what Keene is trying to do. Good PPC, Commander Keene. He doesn't give up. Good officer. Smithers speaks, "Number one is about to come back on line. Can you keep us airborne?"

"I only got one card left, Chief." Keene stops talking to look at his hole card to see if it is an ace or a deuce. He has traded altitude for airspeed and now he has squeezed out 130 knots and is less than 30 feet off the water. More questions race through Keene's thoughts, "Where is that ground effect? We should be low enough now to get another 150 feet-per-minute boost from that lousy cushion of air....it was always there when trying to land on a short field and would make us float forever...where are you now, baby? ...trap that air between the wing and the surface.. .ride the cushion...ride the cushion."

"One's on-line, sir," Smithers says as he runs the left power lever forward. The right drift increases with the added thrust on the left wing. Keene dances on the rudders, unconsciously making adjustments. Smithers continues, "We gotta go in, sir?"

"Bingo lights on one and four, Chief."

"Aye, sir. Max power set."

"I'm trying to keep us airborne in the ground effect. Maybe we can burn off fuel and get light enough eventually to climb out of the ground effect. Look, we're steady at 140 knots. But I can't hold a heading. The drag from number three keeps forcing us in a circle. And I've no idea where we are?"

"We're still 30 feet above the Sea of Japan. I'd say that's all that matters right now." Once again, when Smithers makes a point, it is usually a good one.

Glenn adds, "The gyros and inertials went down when we lost power. According to the magnetic compass you're heading westerly now."

"Keep the crew advised, Fred. Tell them we'll try to stay airborne until we can figure some way out of this mess and get home. But keep them ready for an immediate ditch at any time."

As Glenn shouts into his headset, Keene shouts just as loudly to Smithers, "Chief, can you get number two started? We'll never get home without it."

"Sorry, M.O., it's freewheeling out there. When he fuel chopped it, the thing decoupled. There's no restarting it now. We're screwed."

Glenn takes his eyes off the water screaming below the nose of the aircraft and looks up for the first time in minutes. Through the gray and drizzle he squints to make out a shape. Is it a ship out here? Maybe we can ditch by it? No, no, it is not the shape of a ship...what is that? Right on the nose...what is that?

Suddenly Glenn screams, "Land ho! Land ho! Look! At eleven o'clock—land! And it's close!"

Disbelief and near panic immediately flood the cockpit. With a flash, these three aviators become aware that the emotions and possibilities of the last few minutes were just a bad, cruel joke. Hope, in fact, was a still born.

Keene states the obvious, "No, Chief, now we're screwed. That's North Korea."

* * * * *

Joyce had gone to bed early. There is a darkness in her heart. She is restless and tosses in bed for hours. She becomes fully awake when she hears the whimper of Sammy in his bed. She notes the digital clock as she slips on her robe. It is 1:30 A.M. It had been a slow Monday. They are all slow when Jim is away. She crosses the hall and gently opens Sammy's bedroom door.

* * * * *

Major McWalters quickly flips the page of an exceedingly boring report. She muses, "No wonder the admiral asked me to review this. The boob who wrote this analysis had better find a real job because he sure knows nothing about the future of North Korea's economy." She stands and stretches. For someplace that is supposed to be the hub of communication and control for the entire free world, it sure can get deadly quiet here at 0430 on a Tuesday morning.

* * * * *

Milkus slides his earphones off. He is a good neighbor who does unto others as he desires done to him. Townhouse living requires wearing the earphones when riding the groove at 4:30 A.M. It is his habit to get mentally up for his 0500 daily work-out session. He rises from his easy chair and carefully flips the "Best of the Righteous Brothers" over and manually places the needle in the groove. Back in his chair, earphones on, and lost in an Unchained Melody he can squeeze out another three motivating songs before he starts the outbound two miles of his morning run.

It is a lonely existence, but it is his life now. He thinks, "Relax, Ron, relax. No one can touch you right now. In the past, yes, and most assuredly in the future when Black Jewel is wrestled to the ground. But right now, nothing, no one can touch you. Safe. How many times in the jungle did you beg silently just to be safe for five minutes? And here you have it. Now relax, Ron, Relax."

* * * * *

Master Chief Frank Strait grabs his cover as he struts out of his office in the Misawa hangar at 1530. He missed lunch earlier, and now he is going to the gedunk in the admin building to grab three hot dogs; one with chili, one with mustard and relish, and one with onions and sauerkraut. A bag of plain potato chips and a red cream soda will make it a fit meal. He eats the same lunch six days a week. The gedunk is closed on Sundays. He squints in the momentary sunshine flooding the flight line. It has been days since the sun shone in Misawa. Like a birthday card from home, the sunshine can give a quick little lift. But he won't let the moment get his hopes up because he knows it is just a single hole in the overcast. He is still on deployment. Yet again. But now he is a master chief on deployment. And the Maintenance Master Chief is greeted with respect by all who pass him. The junior officers nearly salute him first. Well, the good ones do anyway. Man! This is a great job!

* * * * *

No one can believe all that can happen and all that can be thought in just thirteen minutes. Thirteen minutes later and now this proud, solid aircraft is riding a ground effect cushion of air at thirty feet over gray seas, unable to maintain heading and barely able to stay faster than a quick stall to sudden death.

"TACCO, Flight," Keene says with absolute authority over the intercom system, "destroy all classified equipment and papers now! We're going in the water. Hurry, Billy! I won't be able to keep us airborne much longer."

Warbuck releases his harness and pulls off his helmet, throwing it to the deck. He crosses the aisle and pulls two long electronics boxes from the overhead panel above the navigator. Smoltz is looking out his window at how near the water is. He forgot to connect the pigtail on the back of his helmet to the intercom system when he donned it. Consequently, he did not hear Keene's directive to the TACCO. But once he sees Warbuck pulling the KY-7 and KW-30 from their slots he knows what is being done. Smoltz cracks open his navigator's bag and pulls out three code books. He shoves them into Warbuck's hands. They make eye contact and pause for just a half second. The communication is clear. We are in deep kimchi. This is it. No chance left. The real thing. Please, God, don't let me screw it up.

Warbuck, his arms full, rushes to the aft end of the aircraft. The other crewmen stay secured in their seats. They know he will ask for help if he needs it. They should stay strapped in for what, even in the windowless tube they know, is imminent. Warbuck drops his load by the freefall chute opening. Just opposite the main cabin door are four chutes for launching sonobuoys. Three use a small explosive charge to drive the sonobuoy from the fuselage, just as is done from the 48 externally loaded chutes in the belly. The fourth chute however is just a hole in the floor to slide buoys out freely. The aircraft was depressurized automatically upon reaching 1200 feet, so Warbuck has no problem pulling the cover off the chute. He pulls and tears at the non-bound code books, shredding them the best he can. Then he stuffs the pieces down the chute.

Next he grabs the crypto box by its handles and feverishly, as quickly as possible, raises it over his head and smashes it against the deck. Crash after crash, with all his might, but it seems to have little effect. Warbuck sweats more and smashes even harder. Eventually one piece falls off it, then another and another. One last excited effort and the KY-7 pops into four pieces. Warbuck pushes the pieces out the hole.

Warbuck starts on the KW-30. He hits the deck with it and on the first slam it comes apart like a toy crash car. Warbuck is throwing the pieces to the ocean bottom when he hears Keene's authoritative voice over the PA, "Billy, brace yourself! We're going in!"

Warbuck jumps from his knees to wobbly legs and lunges for the nearby dinette area. He falls into the seat opposite Evans. Warbuck fumbles for the seatbelt and pulls it snug. He looks up. He thinks, "Evans looks young for an admiral." His thought is interrupted by the nose pitching up and then down, which tosses the tail in a wild arc. Evans and Warbuck grab the table, their hands touching as they search for a good hold to grasp. The pitching is repeated three times, then it steadies for just a moment. Everyone in the tube can feel it. Keene must be searching for the surface just before touchdown. It is only a matter of seconds now; time only for a quick prayer and to review, one more time, what to do when we hit. Wait for the movement to stop, release my harness, grab my designated survival gear and head for the assigned raft at the over-the-wing exits. Don't think, just do. Dear God, let me live through this.

Time has run out. No more willing the beast to stay in the air. Airspeed is down to 122. The rate of descent is 100 feet per minute. The aircraft is still in an uncontrollable right turn. For just a quick moment, Keene mentally steps out of the situation. For just a flash, it is an analytical thing with him. He thinks, "Will you look at that? I am flying this thing now the same as I was just a minute ago, but she has decided it is time to end this tantalizing dance. Independent of my input or wishes we are slowly descending. Like an elevator. Smooth and steady. The water will come up and gently touch our butt in just a few seconds. And I have no way to influence or delay the spectacular crash we are about to experience. So this is what a real ditching is like, eh? I've often wondered."

QE-05 is a majestic, but stiff machine. She keeps her proud chin up, but allows her belly to test the water. Then she skips back into the air in one last attempt to not go gently into the night. But her last great act of defiance is fleeting. She settles once more from her twenty foot perch. It starts as a good, flat skid on a bumpy country road. Then the small waves combine to make one big one located right in front of her graceful snoot. The gentle, controlled water landing ceases with a tremendous bang. The wall of cold sea water slams into the nose and there is a sudden, shocking brake applied that twists the aluminum fuselage. The giant airplane skids to the right as if attempting to deflect the massive blow to the snout. The right side scrunches accordion-style. This queen of three-dimensional space is now imprisoned in a two dimensional world. It has become a train wreck at sea. The caboose nearly uncouples from the cattle cars and swings to the right. A large tear in the skin develops on the port side just aft of the main cabin door. The engine of this train is buried under water and starts to pull the coaler and mail car to the bottom. QE-05 hit hard on the second bounce. She is no longer an airplane, a warrior in gray paint. She has become a large, silver coffin.

Water is blasting into the cockpit around the lifeless body of Chief Smithers, which is now jammed in the hole where the center windshield had been. Keene feels a dozen fire hoses hitting him with such force he cannot raise his chest enough to draw breath. But he does not panic. How long was I unconscious? A second? Minutes? Open your eyes and find a way out. Open your eyes and look.

The water rushing into the cockpit through the center windshield slows as the small front cabin is filled. Keene, eyes open now, releases his harness and floats to the cockpit ceiling. Calmly, so calmly it amazes him, he rocks his head back and sucks in a giant lung full of the air trapped at the top of the cockpit. He slips below the surface and pulls himself to the cockpit exit hatch on the port side. It is now completely submerged and opens easily. Keene is focused on only one mission—to get to the surface. He can feel the pressure on his ears increasing. The plane is sinking now. He needs a secure hand hold to pull him through the hatch and free of the tangled cockpit. As he reaches for the side of the hatch he is surprised by the swift image of a man streaking before him. However, Keene doesn't hesitate for even a heartbeat. He follows the image through the hatch and into the open ocean.

Aft, in the tube, water is only a few inches deep, but rising swiftly. The tear in the aft port side is providing the sea a quick path to snare its prey. Evans immediately unfastens his harness when the motion stops. He has an easy exit with plenty of room to slide from the dinette seat and scramble forward to the escape hatches. The water is pouring in the big split, but it is only to his knees and he is just a few feet from the hatch. But over a quarter century of training and caring for sailors and cockpit awareness and, well, just some sixth sense breaks his concentration and concern for his own escape. Evans turns and looks back. There, in the dinette seat, Warbuck is trapped by the dinette table. The second bounce had broken the table free from its legs and jammed it into Warbuck's belly. Warbuck is sitting in water and coughing up blood; ribs are broken, organs bruised and bleeding. The pain is so intense that Warbuck rolls his eyes back into his head in an uncontrollable last-rites maneuver.

Evans doesn't hesitate. He wades back to the dinette and pries the table free of Warbuck. Evans grabs Warbuck by the collar of his LPA vest and heads for the emergency hatches. The water is to his waist now. Evans changes grip and gets semi-conscious Warbuck higher and able to breathe a little better. Everyone else who is departing, has departed. Water is now to the admiral's shoulder. It is filling faster. The deck is developing a steep slant towards the sinking nose. Things are moving very quickly now. Evans slaps Warbuck. No response. He slaps him again. Water is above his chin now.

"TACCO! Breathe! Breathe now or be left behind! Breathe!"

Warbuck takes a small breath. Good enough for Evans. He sucks in the biggest bucket of air he can and slides beneath the water. Holding to Warbuck's LPA, Evans wiggles through the small hatch. He pulls a limp Warbuck after him. Evans struggles, but Warbuck is jammed in the hatch. Evans's lungs are on fire. The aircraft is sinking rapidly now. Evans doesn't know if it is growing darker because they are sinking or if he is passing out, his air finally gone. He gives himself stern mental direction, "Can't quit now! Never quit! Pull, Frederick, pull!" Suddenly, with one quick jerk Warbuck's body pops through. Evans kicks and pulls towards the light. When he is just two feet from the surface and life, Evans' grip on Warbuck slips. Can't stop now! Must get air! AIR! Evans breaks the surface and inhales completely. Just once. Then he dives to retrieve Warbuck. No joy. Where is he? Evans pulls for the surface. More air. He dives again. His foot hits an object in the murky water. There he is! Grab him!

Evans explodes through the surface, sucking all the air he can swallow. He pulls his right arm up and the head of Warbuck bobs to the surface. Evans has his eyes closed as he repeatedly fills and refills his lungs with sweet, sweet air. Suddenly, he feels multiple hands grab his Mae West and pull him from the water. He slides into a 12-man orange life raft, and lays spread eagle on his back, still breathing heavily. Just a moment passes, and then Warbuck is thrown on top of Evans. Petty Officer Bricker rolls a blue Warbuck onto his side. He slaps his back and pulls his mouth open. As soon as he gets his fingers into Warbuck's mouth, the TACCO goes into convulsions, which lead to mini-eruptions of salt water and blood. The air passage is cleared and Warbuck inhales and coughs simultaneously. His mucus and blood land on Evans who tries to get from under Warbuck, but with little success. He stops his struggling and marvels at how resilient the human body and spirit are, thinking, "This man on top of me was dead and now he is alive. His family did not know it, but they had lost him and now he has returned. The best is yet to come for this young officer. He has been chosen to have more."

* * * * *

"You're too young to remember," Master Chief Strait says as he lights up an after lunch cigar. The young sailors take pleasure in sitting with him when he is in a quiet, reflective mood. They will scramble to get away from the master chief when he is in a sour mood, but they enjoy nibbling wisdom from the old salt when he cares to dispense it. "You only know because your momma probably told you. I know exactly where I was when Kennedy was shot. I was changing a flap actuator motor on a P-5M on the seawall at Sangley Naval Air Station, in the Philippines. We were working tropical hours, 0600 to 1400 with no lunch hour. I had just got started when the branch chief come up and asked me about the job, then as he left he says, 'Oh, yeah, the president was shot while you were twisting those wrenches.' I remember it well. Like it was yesterday. Ever since then, I often wonder what is going on right now—at this very instant—in the states and all over the world. While we're beating our gums, right now, something great or terrific could be happening to those we know. Yet, here we are, oblivious to it. Weird, eh?"

* * * * *

Sammy was having a bad dream, so Joyce cradles his head in her lap and rocks him. Soon his breathing is regular and deep. Innocence shines from his angelic face. But then a coldness suddenly seems to touch her in the back of her neck. It startles her. Methodically the cold touch slides down her spine. When it reaches bottom, it transforms into a hot flash of panic. Joyce sits with a start. Something is wrong, terribly wrong.

* * * * *

Evans gets to his knees. Warbuck props his head upright against the raft side but tries not to move any other part of his body. Even breathing is painful. With each breath sharp, very sharp, stabs of screaming pain rocket from his left chest to his toes and back.

Evans looks into Warbuck's eyes. He wants to know his condition. He sees that the TACCO is scared and in pain. But he wants to live. Good. He can wait until we take stock of the rest of the crew.

Evans identifies the others in his raft. Peters, Bricker, and Ford. Bricker is standing and stretching his neck. It is a large octagonal raft with high sides. Evans stands next to Bricker, who he uses to keep his balance.

"What do you have, sailor?" asks Evans.

"I catch a glimpse of the other raft when we ride up on top of one of these crests," answers Bricker with the ease of talking to a peer not an admiral. Right now he is focused on the job at hand. "There! See it?"

Evans shouts to the other raft and waves his hands over his head. Jones yells back.

It takes nearly fifteen minutes for the crews to paddle the thirty yards between the rafts. When ten feet apart, Jones yells a report to Evans that he has Ensign Smoltz, Lieutenant McKay, and his fellow acoustic operator Thomas on board. Jones is a natural leader and despite the presence of two officers, he has effectively assumed command of the raft. The two officers are confused on what their roles should be. Shock has already become evident in some of the survivors.

"You got the M.O. and the Chief and Glenn in your raft?" Jones shouts.

Bricker answers before the admiral can draw breath, "We haven't seen any cockpit guys. We hoped you had picked them up."

Immediately, all peer out over the ocean looking for their shipmates. Even Warbuck struggles to see over the raft wall, concerned and in near panic at the thought of losing his friend, Keene. A minute passes. Then two, very long minutes. No one speaks. Everyone hopes.

"Listen!" Ford says, breaking the silence. All cup their ears or turn their heads, straining to hear. Faintly, from the west, comes the sound of a whistle. They hear multiple blasts on a whistle. With the three ineffective paddles in each raft and their own hands, all feverishly stroke the rafts to close the noise. Progress is slow. Thomas, Jones, and Smoltz slide out of their smaller seven-man raft and swim to the west, towing their raft as they go.

After what seems an exhausting hour, but in reality is only ten minutes, McKay points and shouts, "There! Someone in the water over there! About twenty yards more! Let's go! Paddle!"

As the smaller raft draws closer, the helmet markings on the man in the water give his identity. It is Keene and he has yet to inflate his life preserver. In fact, he is swimming away from the rafts, heading west doing a breast stroke and blowing his whistle. As the rafts finally close him, Keene is almost spent and points to the west, excitedly urging the crew to quickly continue in that direction. Jones gets to Keene first and they climb into the cramped seven-man raft.

"Fred is out there! Don't stop! I saw him. He's out there," Keene gasps while breathing heavily. "He popped his preserver and couldn't swim with it inflated. I tried to reach him, but he just floated away. To the west, I think. Gotta find him. He's still alive."

All hands scan the sea and yell for Glenn. Nothing is seen or heard. Evans's raft is now next to the smaller raft. Without being told, Bricker is lashing the two rafts together. Evans and Jones make eye contact and shake their heads. They both know that Glenn will have to fare for himself and find the rafts. There is no way two awkward rafts can search for one man in three-foot seas. It will be dark in another two hours and if the current moves both the rafts and Glenn with the same force and direction, there is a small chance that a light on his life preserver could be spotted in the dark. But the seas will have to quiet considerably.

Peters is sullen with tear soaked eyes. A great depression has engulfed him as he realizes the errors he made. For the first time he looks at the others in the raft. A black hole opens in the pit of his stomach and fear races up from it as he realizes that some are absent. He speaks in a high, scared tone, "Commander, where are the others? Where's the chief?"

Keene, still out of breath, answers, "The chief never made it out of the cockpit."

Jones' glare passes from one tube rat to another as he speaks, "Anyone see if Fiedler made it out?"

There is complete silence as all shake their heads. But just a moment passes before Keene speaks, "Bobby, did you get the mayday out?"

"Yes, sir. Multiple times, but there was no acknowledgment."

Warbuck, in great pain, almost hisses as he speaks, "What frequency did you send it on?"

With great confidence, like he has the correct answer on a check-ride question, Smoltz says, "Two-forty-three point zero."

Warbuck, with great disbelief shoots back, "You sent it UHF?"

Smoltz's voice trembles as the reality of his error shocks him, "Oh dear God—what have I done?—we were too far for UHF—no one heard me!"

The remnants of Crew Eleven sit in silence, the only sound coming from the waves slapping the rubber raft walls. Evans is thinking of a plan for the future, while all the others are focused on the past.

Keene speaks softly and almost fatherly, "Don't get down on yourself, Bobby. There were a lot of mistakes made to get us in these rafts. And it wouldn't have made a difference if you had used HF. We saw land just before we ditched which meant we were too close for the Air Force to send anyone anyway."

Peters sobs again. He speaks, "The Chief's dead. I screwed up and now the Chief is dead. I didn't mean to kill him. I didn't know what to do—I tried—but I killed them—I killed—"

"Shut up, Peters!" Keene interrupts. "I killed them. I killed the Chief and Fiedler and lost Fred. I was flying. I was the Plane Commander."

Evans now hears the conversation he had been ignoring. Enough of this crap. "There will be plenty of time later to review how we got here. Right now we must get organized. Let's start by getting an inventory of what we saved. From the look of these seas, we're going to be pushed towards the Korean coast. We very well could be guests of the North Koreans by lunch tomorrow."

CHAPTER SIX

Major McWalters read the short report with minimal interest. To her it was just another screw-up by a Navy flight crew. Air Force crews were much easier to track. They flew a pre-determined course and hit their planned checkpoints within one or two minutes every time. But the Navy had a different mission and there is no precise track for their surface surveillance PARPRO flights. Now here is a crew that has obviously pushed the PARPRO boundary and drifted off the reservation. They are late with a position report as well. She reasons, "Bet they're delaying their report so they don't have to lie. Probably figure they can race back within the boundary then give an honest position. They should report within the next ten minutes. I bet if I check the satellite I can catch them."

McWalters rises from her seat and makes a bee-line for a monitor on the opposite wall. One of eight screens mounted on the wall, she clicks a couple of buttons to pull-up the Sea of Japan. The photo bird shows nothing but solid clouds. Infrared shows land and water, but is useless to track a single moving aircraft. She mumbles to herself, "I bet they report within the next five minutes. I bet."

Julie paces the glass castle twice in succession then gives in to her need to know more. She cannot wait another five minutes. She takes a seat in front of a secure teletype set and pounds out a short message requesting an update on the Tuna King flight directly from the staff watch officer at Fifth Air Force headquarters.

* * * * *

The alarm had gone off at 4 A.M. and it had taken Carter two hits of the snooze button before he was able to drag himself from his warm bed. He hates getting up this early just to make it to work at a normal hour. Living on five acres just south of Quantico is fantastic for his family. He can afford twice the house and it's safe. The only price to be paid for this family lifestyle is collected twice a day, his commute in some of the worst traffic he has ever experienced. He must leave the house by 4:50 A.M. Every five minutes after that time will result in arriving at the Pentagon fifteen minutes later. Unbelievably, even at that hour it will be bumper-to-bumper. He can be at his desk by 5:40 A.M. and get over an hour's work done before the storm of the day hits. If he left his house at 7 A.M. like a "normal" person might, he would arrive at the office after 9 A.M. Maybe senior admirals could get away with those hours, but not a Navy captain. In the fleet a captain might, but this is Washington D.C. and commanders get the coffee here.

Carter didn't sleep well, and now he is angry as he keeps his position in the conga line of cars "racing" at 40 M.P.H up I-395. Black Jewel is crushing his attitude. At first he was regretful that it had to cross his path. But now his thoughts are, "Of all the officers in all the services in all the offices at the Pentagon, Black Jewel had to come my way." Then regret grows to anger. "How dare they manipulate the American people this way? Who do they think they are? My shipmates and I are out there defending freedom by risking our lives and denying our families, and these bozos think it is a game for them to make money. You can't lie to your citizens and retain your moral right to lead and serve. If the admiral doesn't do right by this insult to our citizens, then I am going to the press. Woodward still works on the Post, doesn't he? I wonder how he would like another Watergate? Yeah, like he would even take a call from you! But one thing is for sure. No more going along to keep my career going along. If I go out with a blaze of futility, so be it. But I'm not going to let the S.O.B.'s get away with it."

He arrives at the Pentagon north parking lot and treks the half-mile to the entrance. He makes his way to the JCS spaces.

As he walks down the corridor, trying not to spill the coffee he picked-up at the snack bar, Carter is surprised to see a light from under General Adams outer office. He is even more startled when the door opens and Adams nearly runs him over as he hurries down the hall. Carter's coffee sloshes over the top as he maneuvers to get out of Adams' path.

"Sorry!" Adams says over his shoulder. "In a hurry to make my morning deposit. Man, I hate these early hours!" He rushes through the men's room door.

Carter arrives at his office down the hall and unlocks it. He is finishing placing his brief case under his desk and booting up his computer when Adams sticks his head in the door.

"Glad to see you're an early bird, Frank. I was finally able to get on Admiral Bella's calendar. Are you available to meet with the admiral at seven this morning? I was hoping Ron would be here to join us."

"I believe he gets in around 0630, General. I'll grab him and meet you at the admiral's office. Is there anything we should bring or prepare?"

Adams actually gives a small grin as he answers, "Oh, I think we have all the presents Admiral Bella will ever want to see. See you there."

* * * * *

Just as a senior duty officer should, McWalters has followed the missing aircraft checklist with cool professionalism. She has not given one thought to the men represented by the name "Tuna King" or by call sign "Tango

101

Bravo one-four-niner". To her it is merely a list of "to do's" and nothing personal. And besides, it is a Navy flight and she asks herself, "What do I know about the lives of sailors?" She records the time of each action. Item number six is to call the beeper number of the senior watch officer. She checks her notes and rehearses her report before dialing. This will be a general or admiral who responds and she wants to make the right impression. Check the list again. Everything done? Make sure nothing is missed before you call.

* * * * *

Glenn is surprised by the sound of the wind. It is almost noisy floating in the ocean. It has grown dark and fear left him some time ago. He is tired now. Just tired and sick to his stomach from the mouth full of JP-5 jet fuel he swallowed just after the crash. He has floated surrounded by the fuel slick for more than an hour. Now he is very tired. The first twenty minutes he was convinced that sharks were circling his feet in the unseen waters below him. Now he doesn't care anymore if there are sharks or not. He is cold. And tired. And alone. He has never been so alone in his entire life. He is almost afraid of engaging in a conversation with himself because the answers he could receive might depress him. One stream of thought keeps forcing its way into his brain, "What a horrible way to die. Alone, without hope. Waiting for the end. Powerless to save yourself. All that training I received in deep water survival seems a waste now." He is right. There is no raft and no search teams to signal and, well, no hope of making it through. Now he is absolutely alone in the sea. Waiting for the end. And so very tired.

* * * * *

Milkus and Carter follow Adams into the walnut paneled conference room. Admiral Norm Bella is sitting at the head of the long table. He is a robust looking man with a squatty, but solid build and deep tan. Blue eyes are hidden under bushy eyebrows of dark hair speckled with gray. His Service Dress Blue uniform is freshly pressed and his black necktie is tied to the best Naval Academy standard with a perfectly centered crease. The tie's knot is especially sharp against the stiffly starched white shirt.

On his own time Bella wears stained blue jeans and a ripped T-shirt to K-mart to shop. But he learned years ago that a perfectly tailored uniform, eternally fresh haircut, a manicure, and always having what appears to be a new set of ribbons gleaming on your chest can sway arguments without speaking a word. The uniform, correctly worn, has that much power by itself. He has trouble understanding why fellow officers fail to see that. If you are going to wear the uniform, don't lose its tremendous power by only meeting the minimum standards, especially here in D.C. And naval officers have the greatest advantage and opportunity to use it well. The Army and Air Force have pedestrian uniforms for daily wear, and when they don their full service attire they have too much junk hanging all over it. It hides the cut and style. Marines don't have the same power as a sailor because a Marine is expected always to look sharp. But when a naval officer wears a perfectly tailored, properly rigged, complete uniform, it draws attention, always. Nothing can ever hope to compete with the black double-breasted, modestly adorned, classically styled suit worn by naval officers. Bella is one officer that truly enjoys the tradition and formality of the Navy's heritage.

"Good morning, Gus," says Bella looking up from the thick folder opened in front of him.

"Good morning, Norm. Let me introduce Captain Carter and Colonel Milkus. They are the reason I got on your calendar so early."

"Good morning, Ron. And it is Frank, correct?" Carter nods and Bella notes how his knowledge of their first names causes the two career officers to stand a little taller. It is amazing how the little things often register with more force than the flowery citations and medals.

Milkus is impressed. He knows that Admiral Bella is a definite mover and shaker in the White House basement and Pentagon. Milkus now sees that the admiral's reputation is well earned. This confirms the Marine's confidence that they came to the right guy after all.

"Thank you for seeing us this morning," Adams continues, "we are quite concerned about a report that came to our attention. It's Black Jewel, Norm. The captain here received this report from a social aide who found it lying around while attending a White House function. It is very disturbing. Frank and Ron work in my section and brought it to me. It is so sensitive that I asked for this meeting to help decide the best next steps."

"Black Jewel?" Bella questions as he reaches for the report. There is a heavy silence in the room as he reads it quickly. Finally he mutters an expletive under his breath. He flips back to the second paragraph and re-reads it. He directs his question to Carter, "You say this was found unattended at the White House?"

"Yes sir, in an ante room by the North entrance. It had fallen next to a sofa and was just visible to a novice White House social aide. He thought it important and turned it over to me."

Bella shifts his glare to Adams, "Gus, do you think it's on the level? Who else has seen this?"

"I think it is legit. I believe the social aide and we are the only ones not on White House staff to know."

"Where do you stand on Black Jewel development, now?" asks Bella, his words spitting out like bullets.

"We were told on Sunday to proceed with deployment preparations. We have the green light to move forward," answers Adams.

"Can somebody set me straight on this? Black Jewel is supposed to stay ahead of Red Chinese biological and chemical weapons systems, right? Over ten years and millions and millions of dollars have been invested in B and C countermeasures. Justification for these millions spent on Black Jewel has been the perceived Chinese threat to be able to eventually develop a sophisticated, effective virus and a viable delivery system to deploy this weapon. If I read these papers right, it appears that the only reason the CHICOMS have been successful in achieving these goals is because we are selling them the know-how. That is flaming ridiculous! We make their threat viable so contractors have a reason to make millions more?" says Bella with a low growl. As he hears his own words, his anger grows.

"I think you summarized it pretty well, Admiral," Carter responds in a voice just above a whisper.

"The big, immediate question is 'who?' And how long has it been—" Bella is interrupted by the buzz of the beeper on his belt. "Uh-oh. More bad news. This is never good. I have NMCC duty this week." Bella shoves the Black Jewel papers back at Adams and grabs his own folder and steps to the secure phone in the corner of the conference room. "Excuse me, gentlemen. I must do my duty here. Please step outside and we'll get on with this in a minute." Bella picks up the receiver and pushes four numbers.

He hears in his receiver the voice of a woman, "This is Major McWalters, NMCC Staff Duty Officer."

* * * * *

Ensign Glenn can no longer feel his feet or legs. The cold has not only robbed him of easy movement of his extremities, it has also made breathing a concentrated chore. His lungs feel as if they are pushing against heavy weights to inhale shallow breaths. "I wish I could make it until daylight. I would like to feel the sun on my face when I die," he forces himself to say out loud. The past hour he has cried, laughed and shouted. Glenn has accepted his death and had all the thoughts of home and how his single mom would feel when she learned how he died. He does not like it, but he has accepted it. An only child raised by a singe mom, his entire family was his mother. And her entire family was him. This will leave her so alone. So alone. Again he forces himself to whisper, "I wish the sun would come up." But Glenn closes his eyes and falls to sleep under a dimly lighted, overcast Sea of Japan sky. His is a gentle death. He stops breathing in his sleep. A short life completed.

* * * * *

Hours later it is the same hope miles away. The sun can't rise soon enough. Looking down sun, the sailors see nothing but dark. To the east a very slight hint of a horizon can be imagined. But in the western darkness there is a frightening sound. It is nearly 0400 and the Crew Eleven survivors have been adrift for nearly twelve hours. The rain and swells breaking over the raft have kept everyone soaked. Not a light was seen throughout the night. Talk stopped hours ago. What appeared to be a futile struggle with an inoperable, hand-cranked emergency HF transmitter drained every one's energy and hope. Shock and fatigue now rule in their miserable tiny orange prison. And now fear is added to the emotional cocktail. The sound of crashing surf in the night will do that.

Warbuck is breathing irregularly. With each breath his broken ribs send a sharp complaint to his brain. It has been the longest and most miserable night of his entire life. And it isn't over yet. He slips in and out of consciousness and sleep, his mouth and nose barely above the water sloshing around the floor of the raft. First he dreams of his ex-wife Brandee, the Brandee of their courtship. Then her face becomes Miko's and the cold sea water becomes a warm bath. Then the pain returns, very near to his heart.

Evans has watched Keene most of the night. He is a good officer, but it is hard to tell how the loss of his men is really affecting him. He has not tried to exercise any authority since it became dark. Is he burnt out? Overloaded? This will be the big test. Can he see something worth living for? Can he beat the siren's call to give up and die? Evans has heard the call before and he knows it sounds sweet for just a moment. But now, well, now since Margie, the siren is mute.

Evans stops his musing and speaks, "Commander, with a little luck I think we might not hit the surf until morning. We'll need the light to see what we are up against."

Keene looks to the west, and then nods.

Evans says, "You pretty sure it's North Korea? We couldn't be south of the DMZ?"

Keene remains silent and looks at Smoltz. The Navigator looks up and speaks, "No, Admiral. We would've had to drift near a hundred miles to be south of the DMZ." He looks at his watch and continues, "We crashed about twelve hours ago. I don't see how we could've drifted at nine knots."

"If it is North Korea," Jones joins the conversation, "what do you think they'll do if they capture us?"

McKay raises his head and speaks, "What do you mean 'if', Jonesy?"

"Well, I'm not gonna let them take me without a chase," Jones says defiantly.

"Let's just take one problem at a time, shall we gentlemen?" Evans says to limit the conversation about "what ifs". He knows that is one path ten men in rafts in the dark and stormy sea should not go down. Besides, he is

107

aware that capture would be far riskier than the others might think.

* * * * *

Adams accompanies Bella through the maze of Pentagon corridors to the NMCC entrance. Adams has the Black Jewel papers in his brief case. Bella asked him to tag along while he checked the current status of the missing PARPRO flight. Milkus and Carter were sent to their offices to stand-by in case they could supply any further assistance. Now late in the afternoon, Bella's tracking of the missing P-3 has risen steadily until it has become the most urgent priority on his plate. It is typical for Bella to handle two very high priority and urgent problems in real time. He thrives on these situations. But the nuisance of this pressing, immediate situation in the SOJ is irritating because he cannot give his full attention to the more serious problem. Throughout the day he has kept current concerning the search efforts and he had visited the NMCC for an initial brief in the morning. His hectic day has been filled with exploring Black Jewel options while keeping an eye on efforts to locate the missing aircraft. Now he is concerned that the PARPRO plane or crew or wreckage has not been found. He feels it is time for a more in-depth face-to-face briefing. It has become serious enough that it is time for his four-stars to assume control of the problem from the duty watch officer and in-theater units.

As both officers enter the upper deck of the watch coordinator's room, McWalters is standing with briefing papers at the ready. She recognizes the senior officers and greets them by name. The presence of Adams who is assigned to J-2 raises a question in her mind. The general also pulls NMCC duty, but he is not on the schedule for another week. She notes that Bella is in an apparent rush to put this problem to bed very quickly if possible. So McWalters steps to the lectern by the head of the briefing table and immediately launches into her synopsis. On the screen she flashes a map of the Sea of Japan. Tuna King's track is marked on it as well as the last position report and satellite fix.

"Admiral, General, good afternoon. It has now been over twelve hours since the last contact with the Navy PARPRO track 23B, with system call sign Tuna King. Nothing has been heard from or about the flight since they sent a position report just before disappearing. What we do know is very little. The Fifth Air Force PARPRO monitoring team noted via satellite that the flight was approaching the outside PARPRO boundary near Wonson, North Korea. The monitoring team broadcast a Condition Three. Approximately five minutes later satellite coverage was lost for twenty minutes."

Adams interrupts, his voice even, without emotion, "Why?"

"Ever since the delay in launching a replacement for the Eyewatch Nine that fell from orbit last year, we lose satellite coverage for twenty to forty minutes over the Sea of Japan three times a day," McWalters says then pauses for a response from the senior officers. With none forthcoming, she continues her short brief, "When satellite coverage was resumed, Tuna King was missing."

Bella speaks in sentences that come out sounding like one long word, "That's it? That's all we know?"

McWalters stands her ground confidently. She now has been on duty for nearly twenty hours, but she gives back respectfully, "Fifth Air Force notified NMCC and commenced a communication search. No joy on any frequency. In addition to the gaps due to Eyewatch Nine, cloud cover has hampered satellite searches. Tuna King's squadron has launched a search effort and has had two aircraft conducting patterns using low-light level nose mounted cameras. It will be dawn soon in Japan and they can mount a more efficient daylight search in another hour.

The Fifth Air Force has been able to assign two additional aircraft to assist, but so far no joy by any of them."

Adams asks, "Any detection of North Korean interceptor activity last night?"

"None whatsoever, General."

"Any Mayday from the crew?" inquires Bella.

"None reported, sir."

"Have the North Koreans responded in any way? Increased flights or radio activity?" Bella says as he leans forward in his seat, a perplexed and concerned expression on his handsome face.

"No, sir."

Bella looks at Adams as he asks the next question, "Has or did Fifth Air Force launch fighter protection?"

McWalters opens her mouth to answer, but the senior Air Force officer beats her to it, "To protect what, Norm? We don't know where they are."

Bella just glares at Adams. He has a deep-seated reservation about the Air Force. They play politics and hide behind their rules too much. Give him the Navy's "can do!" attitude any day. He believes the Air Force can keep their procedures, just give him results.

McWalters recaptures the conversation, "The search continues in the SOJ, Admiral. However..." She pauses, letting her sentence trail off into silence. She is hesitant to share her opinion on the matter.

"However what, Julie?" Bella asks.

"Sir, the search planes are hoping for blind luck. They cannot search at the last estimated position because it would take them too close to the North Korean coast." She takes a long breath before venturing another opinion. "And I do not recommend they try it due to the decoy problem."

Bella scrunches his forehead and asks, "Decoy problem?"

"Yes, sir. I've been a Far East duty officer for nearly three years now. In that time I have seen three instances where North Koreans have used bogus emergency locator beacons to lure search planes within their claimed airspace. They even tried to fire on one aircraft. My point, Admiral, is that our crews will not and should not bust the PARPRO boundaries even if they do detect an ELT."

Bella speaks in a soft, fatherly voice, "So they could be bouncing out there on the ocean waiting for us to get to them before the North Koreans and we won't try because of a line somewhere on a map?"

If McWalters was not so fatigued, she probably would not have risen to the bait. But she does and says, "We shouldn't try it, Admiral. The risks outweigh the gains."

Bella expected such a textbook answer from an Air Force officer. He maintains eye contact with McWalters and softly responds in the same fatherly voice, "Unless it was you or your husband in the raft."

"Norm...." Adams gently scolds Bella.

"I know, Gus. I know."

McWalters wants to take offense to Bella's inference, but she is interrupted by a sergeant who enters the room and delivers her a note. She reads it while the senior officers wait patiently, lost in their own thoughts.

Adams speaks just as McWalters finishes the note, "Any sign they ditched or..?"

"No, sir. We have no evidence they ditched, were shot down, or defected to North Korea." McWalters now starts almost to read the note out loud, "General, I was just informed that Commander, Fleet Air Westpac was onboard Tuna King."

Adams asks, "Who is that?"

McWalters looks at the note and reads aloud, "Rear Admiral Evans, sir."

"Frederick Evans?" Bella and Adams say in unison in urgent and louder than usual voices.

McWalters looks at the note again and answers softly, "Yes, sir."

McWalters is confused by the reaction of these senior officers. Adams and Bella both grow very tense and stare at each other. Bella is the first to speak, mumbling under his breath, "Just like that cowboy. Now we're in deep kimchi that is over our heads."

Adams responds with the unthinkable, "Maybe he is dead and there is no problem."

Bella hears Adams' words and is shocked at how cold they sound. But he is even more ashamed that he was thinking the exact same thought. Now he rights his skewed perspective and says, "I know Margie Evans. She and Fred are good people. She deserves to get him back."

Adams holds up the brief case he has kept by his feet and says, "Norm, this impacts what we have here."

Bella nods and rises. He walks over to the telephone by the computer console and pushes four numbers. "This is Admiral Bella. I need to see the Secretary immediately... Okay, thank you." He turns to Adams and speaks, "Let's keep the memo out of it for now, but we must tell SECDEF about Frederick and then we can take on the White House. And before we go there, I want to get to Margie before she finds out Frederick is missing from some other source."

Adams starts to object, then thinks twice about it. He reasons, "After all, I did bring Bella in on this problem because of his ability to play the game well. Now this new development means his involvement is even a better idea. I hope."

* * * * *

Instant gloom and dread replace the bright sunshine that floods the cul-de-sac of officer housing on Moffett Naval Air Station in California. It is a neighborhood caught in a time warp. It could be 1955 rather than 1985. Two parent families are the norm, and many women are full-time housewives. Children can play in the street and they obey the adult neighbors because they are anxious about any shame reaching their fathers' ears. It is a safe place to live, in no small part because it is isolated from the civilian community. Muggers and burglars must get past armed Marine guards to get on base. The neat and tidy yards are full of color with annual flower gardens reflecting the California sun. But now a dark cloud covers the hearts of wives tending to typical Monday business in the neighborhood. A gray Navy sedan slowly cruises up the street. Mothers grab their children and take them in-doors. A chill shakes their very being as they close the shades in hopes of protecting themselves from bad news. But then they peek through the blinds to see the street, a morbid irresistibility drawing them to face what might be coming. Each is near tears and prays, some out loud, that the car doesn't stop in front of their town home. "Please, dear Father, not my Tony." "Please, O God, not Sid." "Please, please, dear Baby Jesus, not my daddy." It is the unspoken nightmare of every air station family come to life. As the sedan passes each home, a sigh of true relief escapes from tense lips. But the relief is momentary and then followed immediately by an honest concern for whom the bell tolls.

The sedan reaches the end of the dead-end street and retraces its route. This causes the fear to grab the throats of those who thought they had escaped. It is not a designed torture, but merely the by-product of the driver not being familiar with the house numbering system. He is lost. He needs to find 8A. On his second pass, he locates it.

The sedan parks by the curb. Like all the homes in officer housing, it is a small, two-story duplex, with one family occupying each side. A carport serves as the front porch and garage. Through the drawn shades a set of very nervous eyes watches as two officers exit the car. When they approach the other half of the duplex she nearly collapses with relief. She goes to the phone and starts the jungle drums beating the news of her neighbor's misfortune. Not to gossip, but to rally support. It's going to be needed.

Commander Frank Billings is a pilot and currently the Operations Officer on COMPATWINGSPAC staff. This is his second time having to make the "death watch trip". Last time it was for a single person, a pilot killed flying an Air Club plane on a pleasure flight. Today is different. He is doing personal next-of-kin notification for the three officers on Crew Eleven with local ties. The Master Chief and a lieutenant drew the duty to notify the enlisted crewmen's families. The whole base will be emotionally affected by the loss of a 12-man crew. Wives will be nice to their husbands for days and will stare at them in appreciation of them just being alive. But a dozen homes will be hanging black wreaths, and everyone in the close knit community will mourn.

Billings had to go home and change from khakis into his Service Dress Blue uniform this morning when he was selected for this duty. Now, he is nervously approaching the front door of Quarters 8A, accompanied by the duty chaplain. He makes one last check on the address. He absolutely cannot screw this up. His concerns and memories flood his mind, "Man, I hate having to do this. This time I know these people. Last spring, we sat together at the Base Housing block party and talked for an hour. This is harder than a night approach in snow at Adak." He can almost feel the eyes of all the wives watching from their windows.

On the placard above the carport it reads, "LCDR James Keene, USN". They have the right house. There is no car in the car port. They approach the door and ring the bell. No answer. They ring again. No answer. They are confused on what to do next. Do they go on to the next notification? But it is off-base and if they leave now, Mrs. Keene could hear from the grapevine before they do their duty.

The dilemma is solved when a mini-van pulls around the corner. It parks in the carport. Just seconds ago Joyce Keene was preoccupied with thoughts of afternoon chores. Then she saw the sedan and two officers in dress uniform at her front door. A wave of fear crashed over her. But then it just as quickly subsided. She forces herself to be composed and in control. Joyce can be as hard as steel when necessary. She parks, releases her seat belt and exits the van. Billings watches as the petite woman in her early thirties with short, blond hair and well proportioned figure stares right through him. She holds her hand up to stop Billings from speaking and goes to the other side of the van. She slides open the passenger door and lifts Sammy out of his car seat.

"Sammy, get the bags out of the back and go into the house. Hurry! Sesame Street is about to come on!" she directs her son. Once Sammy is in the house and Joyce hears the TV, she turns to Billings, "Frank, is he dead, injured, or missing?"

"Missing, Joyce."

"Presumed dead?"

"Well,...actually...we just don't know."

There is a long pause as Joyce searches Billings' eyes for the truth. She comes to the conclusion that he really doesn't know.

The chaplain speaks, "Mrs. Keene, his plane went down in the Sea of Japan very early this morning our time. No emergency transmissions were received. A massive search is currently underway, but nothing has been found yet."

Joyce moves her glare to the chaplain and asks, "Nothing? No wreckage or rafts?"

Billings gives a direct answer, "Nothing."

Joyce exhales for the first time since she saw the sedan. "That's hopeful. There is still hope then."

"There is always hope," adds the Chaplain.

The steel in Joyce starts to bend just a little. She has trouble controlling her voice as she asks, "How many were with him?"

Billings answers, "It was an entire Crew Eleven tactical flight."

"Have the other wives been notified?"

"No," Billings says. "We're headed there now."

"Oh,...okay...well...eh...let me know if...if...I can do anything for them," Joyce says, her voice breaking and tears forming in her eyes.

* * * * *

Warbuck opens his eyes to see the others in his raft paddling furiously and shouting loudly. They are straddling the outer tube of the raft and stroking with all their might using paddles and helmets. The salt water flooding the floor of the raft sloshes in his eyes, stinging them and blurring his vision. The rough ride and commotion stirred him from unconsciousness. He notes it is now light out and he can make out the knees and flight boots of his shipmates near his face. Warbuck tries to lift his head but the ride is too bumpy and his ribs, chest, and stomach hurt too much to improve his view. So he listens. Jones and Evans and Thomas are the loudest. The others are mumbling and breathing heavily. Suddenly, he feels the raft lift rapidly like an elevator, straight up. For a split second the rafts float in the air, and then it crashes back to the surface. Water pours in over a submerged raft wall. Warbuck can't breath. The crash has forced all air from his one good lung. Now the water has covered his face. He feels the raft tilt and he tumbles. He shuts his eyes to keep the salt water out. His nose fills with water. His lung burns and he is consumed with the desire to open his mouth and suck in a full breath of air. But he doesn't. He can't. The forces now in control of his body are immense and overpowering. Warbuck feels totally helpless. A rag doll in a clothes dryer. Much to his surprise he is thinking calmly, "So this is it? This is how a guy drowns. I have wiped out on a surf board before, but nothing like this."

Light, then dark, then light—the speed of the movement is incredible. The weight of the water and the force of the waves feel as if they will crush him. Then it all goes black.

* * * * *

It is a narrow beach, only fifty yards of sand between the high tide and the cliffs. The sand terminates at a solid wall of stone, maybe one hundred feet high, with outcroppings of boulders clustered at the base. The rain has started again. Spread over the wet sand are bodies dressed in flight suits and life preservers. Only two of the eight are moving. Evans and Smoltz stagger from one body to another. Evans reaches Keene and rolls him over. Keene rises to one elbow, the surging surf still splashing against his feet. Keene waves for Evans to continue as he sucks in air and adjusts to the lack of movement of the sand. After so many hours being tossed about by the sea, his inner ear needs some time to adjust to the stillness. But his primary difficulty is shock. His eyes are dilated and breathing shallow. Thoughts are fuzzy and there is no continuity to his logic.

Smoltz moves from Jones to Peters to McKay. They are dazed, but okay. Evans reaches Thomas who is breathing but not moving. Evans shakes Thomas and the petty officer stirs almost immediately. Thomas lies in the sand and lets the rain drizzle on his face. He is dizzy and is waiting for the earth to stop moving. There is one thought in the center of the twirling nausea that fills his mind, "I'd rather be at my favorite table at the Purple Pub in Watervliet. Really."

Evans looks to the ocean, and sees Warbuck face down in shallow surf. He rushes to him, rolls him over, and crouches to check for breathing. As Evans places his ear near Warbuck's mouth the TACCO once again regains life by spewing over the admiral. He erupts with a cough that shakes his whole body. Salt water and blood fly from his mouth. He gasps and hacks. More salt water and blood.

117

Finally, he is able to draw in a full breath and hold it. Evans waves towards Jones who is weakly regaining his feet. They pull Warbuck onto the beach.

Keene sits up and forces himself to concentrate. Slowly the fog in his mind clears. He counts the sailors and takes a mental muster of the crew. Eight. Only eight! He jumps to his feet. Who is missing? Bricker and Ford! Keene runs into the surf shouting their names. Jones and McKay chase after him and join the search. Keene is frantic. He wades into waist-deep water and jumps into the crashing waves. Jones and McKay rush to stop him from going back out to sea. Keene spies something floating just beyond the small breakers near shore. He reaches it. It is Ford's body floating face down. Keene drags the lifeless form to the edge of the water, drops the body to the sand and then slaps Ford's chest and face, screaming for him to breathe. But Ford is dead. Keene lets his tears fall and cradles Ford's head in his lap. Just before Jones and McKay reach him, Keene jumps up and runs into the surf again, shouting "Bricker! Bricker!" His shipmates chase after him and pull him back to shore.

* * * * *

The telephone rings only once before he grabs the receiver, "Captain Carter."

"Frank, this is Ron. I just got a call from Admiral Bella. He shared some important news you will want to know. Can you come down to my spaces?"

Carter answers in the affirmative and is soon knocking on the secure door to Milkus' office. Milkus answers the door himself and Carter joins him at his desk.

Milkus speaks to the other three occupants of the room, "Gentlemen, clear the space." There is no need to be polite. These are all military men used to getting the job done with efficiency and find the niceties to be unnecessary. They know it is an unusual demand and respect the colonel's needs with no explanation needed. They all exit.

Milkus ensures the door locks behind them, and then turns to Carter. "Frederick Evans has crashed in a P-3 off the coast of North Korea."

Carter feels the air leave his lungs and he sinks into a nearby chair. For the last two years Captain Evans was his peer and held Milkus' job as the operational boss of Black Jewel. Evans had defied all odds by making rear admiral while buried in black ops. Now when he has just made flag rank he ends up dead! Carter quickly composes himself and asks, "Will the body be okay for the memorial service? When is it gonna be? It'll be back here at Arlington, I presume?"

"That's the sticky part of the situation. Admiral Bella says there is no trace of the plane or Frederick. They're not sure if he is alive or dead. And if alive, he already may be in the hands of the North Koreans."

"That would be like giving the entire Black Jewel project to the Chinese on a platter!"

"Yeah," responds Milkus pensively. He thinks about how his old boss looked when he sat in the desk he now occupies. A superior officer, everyone was pleased when he got his one star. Now this. Milkus forces the news from the personal to the business compartment in his brain and speaks, "They can learn from him that we're close to deploying countermeasures for the Gamma Three virus. Do you think he knows we're going ahead? When he left everything was really dormant."

"I don't know," Carter says as he stands and starts to pace. "It is conceivable—no probable—that he doesn't. I bet he still thinks it will be at least another three years before it is ready for full deployment."

"So the Chinese get him and he gives up the effectiveness of Black Jewel and then what do they do?" wonders Milkus.

"The Chinese scrap the Gamma Three virus and go full blast in development of something twisted and evil, the likes of which we can only guess. Years of research and success flushed because they know what they have now can be neutralized," Carter spits out with disgust. Not only has this project ruined his career, it will now turn out to be useless. Both men sit in silence. Then Carter speaks, "Just suppose the Chinese do get their hands on Frederick. Do you think they will know who they have?" The questions are coming faster and faster to Carter as the full impact of the situation sinks in. "Do you think the traitor on the White House staff will let them know?"

"That would be rich. The traitor who sold the Chinese the virus and delivery details would get the last laugh. He would pocket the blood money and then wipe it clean. He could ensure no direct harm would occur as a result of his treachery because the Chinese would never use the stuff. If the Chinese knew we could counter their weapons effectively, where's the advantage in having them?" Milkus pauses, and then re-states the obvious, "Frederick cannot fall into the North Koreans' hands."

Carter is still catching up with Milkus' thoughts. "So you think the traitor will rat him out?"

"Will that be even necessary? If we caught a Soviet admiral and could deny we had him, don't you think we would research his last assignments? Heaven knows how easy it will be to learn of Evans background. I bet it will be published in detail in the Washington Post obituaries," says Milkus.

"Or they can call the Naval Academy Alumni Association or read of his entire life and assignments on the last pages of Shipmate magazine. Right now they could be torturing him and his country will just pretend he is dead. Or some traitor working for a buck will sell him out to clean their hands and he will suffer for what?" Carter's bitterness is coming to the surface again.

Milkus is two thoughts ahead of Carter. He feels a pang of déjà vu and suddenly remembers the names Dickens, Silverson, Edwards, and Grayston, the survivors of second squad, second platoon, Foxtrot Company. Good Marines who, along with their dead brothers, were placed in a position where sacrifice was necessary. Yet, in the end we pulled out of Vietnam and it was all for nothing. Milkus blinks away yesterday and speaks, "What is Bella going to do about the treason? What is he doing now?"

* * * * *

Julie McWalters was stung by Admiral Bella's chiding over her advice not to violate the PARPRO boundaries to search for American sailors who could need help. As much as she tries, she cannot put his words out of her mind. What bothers her most is that what he said was partially true. She was not thinking of the crew as real persons with real families, but rather as a job that had to be done. They were just part of a checklist that had to be completed.

Julie is not an officer who lacks initiative. So she contacted the squadron directly and got the names of all members of Crew Eleven. She is now writing them on a large grease board located just to the right of the Korean map mounted on the wall in the command center glass perch. She steps back and takes a moment to read each name slowly. Then she thinks about what a crash at sea must be like. She shivers at the thought. Slowly these names are becoming real, breathing persons who are suffering and it is her job to save them.

* * * *

The parking lot is full this early evening at Pattie Elementary School in Montclair, Virginia. It is the start of "back to school" night and parents and students are assembling in classrooms to meet teachers and administrators. Pulling into the school's circular driveway is a black sedan with "U.S. Navy" stenciled in small gold letters on the door. Admiral Bella opens the passenger door and slowly gets out. His aide scurries around the front of the car to fall-in one pace behind and to the right. Bella is in no hurry to carry out this duty. The aide steps in front to open the glass door for the admiral and then he moves ahead again to be the first to reach the administrative counter. The aide acquires the correct room number and directions, but before the two military officers can move away, the principal appears. An older lady, nearing retirement but still a powerful authority figure, she offers to escort the officers to their destination.

Down the hall and a right turn, and the trio is standing in front of a door marked, "Third Grade—Mrs. Evans." Silently, the principal leaves the men in the hall and enters the classroom. In what is really less than a minute, but seems like forever to Bella, Margie Evans comes through the door. She is a short woman in her mid-forties. The typical elementary school teacher, she is wearing a mid-calf, solid blue cotton skirt and plain, buttoned-up white blouse. She is trim, but not sensuous with chestnut hair, green eyes and flawless skin. She is a very controlled woman with plans, order, and structure being hallmarks of her class and life.

Upon seeing the officers in their dress uniforms, Margie is initially confused, and then terrified. She is able to squeeze out a short question without her voice breaking, "Good day, Norm. What brings you here?"

Bella feels 100-years old and his voice is uncharacteristically slow and low as he responds, "I'm afraid it's not good news, Margie."

"I assumed that, if you made the effort to track me down this evening and come personally. What is wrong?" Margie says with surprising control. Her entire body is both numb and tingly. Her adrenaline pumping, she is totally alert to all that is happening, yet her stomach and heart seem dulled and empty.

"Margie," Bella says as he takes her arm and moves a couple steps away from his aide, "Frederick was on a P-3 flight over the Sea of Japan that disappeared this morning." He pauses to watch her reaction. His eyes bore into her green pupils. He sees the ice start to crack, so he continues while she can still listen, "We don't know what happened. You won't hear about it on the news because we believe he was very close to the North Korean coast when he went down."

"Was he shot down?"

Bella shakes his head in reply. He continues to shake his head as Margie shoots more questions at him, "Was he captured? Were there any survivors? What was he doing on a..ah...what did you call it? A P-3? What's a P-3 anyway? Are you sure he was on it—he doesn't fly P-3s—he doesn't fly at all anymore—"

Bella interrupts, "Margie, Margie, we don't know what happened. I presume he took a ride on a P-3 tactical mission to see what they do and the flight disappeared. I know this is terrible news and poor information, but I am going to the White House from here and it is all I can tell the President. And it is all I can tell you because that is all we know right now."

Margie had started to break down and bawl, but now she composes herself and quickly turns steely cold. "Sometimes I truly hate the Navy. I hate what you do to Frederick." Bella stands erect and takes this explosion, not with understanding or sympathy, but with rigid military bearing as she continues, "You make him think that he has to be involved in everything—to know everything about his command...his command! You give him a wife and I become the mistress. Why is he like that, Norm? Why are you all like that?"

Bella does something foreign to his nature. He reaches out and holds Margie. She buries her face on his perfectly pressed uniform shoulder and sobs. Bella whispers, "I guess it's a character flaw, a character flaw that makes you love him. He was born to care, to be a leader, to be in the game. He can't sit on the sidelines. He's a player."

Margie pushes away from Bella and wipes her eyes. She says, "You say you don't know if he's dead. Then I choose to believe he is alive." Margie straightens her blouse and smoothes out the wrinkles in her skirt. She pulls a handkerchief from her pocket and wipes her eyes and nose. Standing to her full height, she exhales and then looks at the classroom door. "I guess I better get in there and do my duty to my students and their parents."

Bella asks, "Have you someone to stay with you tonight? Melissa can come over so you don't have to be alone."

"No, thank you. I'll call my sister in Culpepper. You just keep me informed better than the President."

Bella nods and gives a small smile. Margie throws her head back, swings the door open, and strides into the classroom. Bella looks at his aide and shakes his head. Bella is broken hearted, yet inspired by another strong Navy wife.

"She is going back to work?" asks the aide.

"She has her job to do. And we have ours." The sound of the officers' heels clicking on the tile echoes through the school as they march down the hall in a quick step.

CHAPTER SEVEN

It is 10 A.M and still raining. Eight survivors are huddled around a mound of sand, a couple dozen yards from the surf. Over the roar of the waves, Keene finishes saying a short prayer for their dead shipmate. Silence follows, broken only by Warbuck's hacking cough. He is the first to turn away from the grave and after a few steps, he gently lowers himself to the sand, holding his side as he does. Jones and Thomas follow, and then take seats by Warbuck. Smoltz and McKay are next to move away, then Peters opens his eyes and seeing the others assembling a few yards away, moves to join them. Admiral Evans watches Keene stare at the grave. A long minute later, Keene slaps his hip in disgust then turns towards the group. Evans takes a deep breath, stretches to his full height, stands tall with all his full military bearing, and then he joins the others. He remains standing, as do Keene and McKay.

Evans, his voice with the edge of authority, speaks, "I'm a little surprised the North Koreans haven't arrived yet. When they do I want all of you to be absolutely clear on how we are to behave with them. We will tell them the truth, because a lie is too hard to remember and keep straight. We are from a patrol plane that had serious engine trouble and crashed into the sea off shore yesterday. Some of us died. We drifted ashore in life rafts. We expect to be repatriated to our homes immediately. No other information is to be given except the big four required by the Geneva Convention—name, rank, serial number, and date of birth. Any questions?"

After an extended pause, Jones picks up a clump of wet sand and tosses it six inches. Then he looks up, squinting to keep the light rain from his eyes, and peers into Evans' face. He speaks, "Should we turn ourselves in like that, Admiral, or should we evade and make our way back home without their help?"

Evans has given this option much thought, but it irritates him that Jones hasn't given him enough credit to think of it. Evans snaps back, "Look around, Petty Officer Jones. We have Lieutenant Warbuck there with a couple of busted ribs and maybe more. He needs medical attention and we are all exhausted and spent. We are not in open hostilities with North Korea. I expect they might use us for propaganda reasons for a week or two, but then when that dies down, we'll be sent home." He said the last sentence with all the convincing forcefulness he could muster. But the truth be told, Evans was not sure just what the crazies of North Korea might do.

McKay verbalizes what others are thinking, "Took a lot more than a couple of weeks for the Pueblo crew."

"They were a spy ship," Evans responds. "We're just a patrol crew that wrecked."

Jones jumps to his feet in a surprising challenge to the Admiral's authority and spits out, "NO! *We* are the patrol crew, *you* are an admiral. I think they might feel there is more to our mission than harmless patrolling once they discover you. Why did you have to come along? Who invited you?" Then with pointed disdain he adds, "Sir."

Evans and Jones are locked in a tense confrontation, two strong men testing each other. Each is determined not to bow to the other's force of personality. Rank is forgotten by these two, if not by the others. Jones has overstepped his position and forced this clash and now the others are anxious to see just how big is this man wearing the stars.

McKay steps nearly between the two bulls facing each other. He edges his left foot in front of Jones, then slides his hip forward to force Jones to fall back. McKay speaks, "You know, Admiral, Jonesy may have a point regarding surrender. We weren't taught to give-up. We should survive, evade, and escape."

Smoltz stands and joins the somewhat quieter conversation now, "Yeah, Admiral. I vote for escaping. The DMZ can't be too far south from here. What do you say, Boss?"

Every crewmember turns to Keene. He hears them, but he cannot acknowledge their request. He is staring at the mound of sand that has covered the dead body of a crewmember he failed. He failed to bring the crew back safely. His thoughts are defeatist and confused, "How can they ask me what to do next? What makes them think that my next decision won't result in the same failure? Listen to me and you can all end up dead? Why, God, why?"

Evans speaks loudly to ensure all hear him over the crashing surf and he speaks slowly to let his words sink in with the full effect he desires, "Listen gentlemen. If this was a democracy, maybe your vote would mean something. But I'm in command right here, right now. I'll make the decisions. I'll give the orders."

The tone and delivery of Evans declarations brought those standing to attention. This happened unconsciously. Evans had pulled out his "admiral's" voice and these sailors immediately reverted emotionally to boot camp. All had the same instantaneous response in their minds, "Aye, aye, sir."

Evans continues, "You have had survival and POW training, but has anyone besides me been in combat?" No one nods, all remain still, listening intently. "I spent three nights in the jungle before a Seawolf helo pulled me up to safety when I was surrounded by Viet Cong. There is a time and place to evade and a time and place to play the game and get home. We need food, water, shelter, warmth, and medical attention. The North Koreans have it. We'll play the game and be home in a few days. Keep the faith, sailors. I'll see you through this."

Jones watches Evans eyes closely as the admiral makes his bold statement. Jones is mulling over the situation and his course of action to himself, "This admiral can talk the talk, but can he walk the walk? Can this flag be trusted? Is he a desk officer or an operator? Look at those eyes. He believes what he is preaching. Maybe, just maybe he got to where he is by talent. I'll buy another card."

Jones then responds, "Aye, aye, sir. But you had better be right. I'm not going to end up like Ford there, dead and buried in some filthy, forgotten country. I'll go along, but get us home...sir."

Evans steps slightly towards Jones. He can understand the sailor's apprehension and anxiety, but it doesn't have to like the way it is manifested. He has Jones locked in a stern glare. Jones stands his ground for just a split-second then backs up a foot. Maintaining eye contact, the instantaneous rage quickly drains from the admiral and he speaks more softly, "Petty Officer Jones, I promise you that no one will be burying you in this country. Now let's make contact with our hosts. Lieutenant McKay, you take Petty Officers Peters and Thomas north, up the beach and see if you can find a path to the top of these cliffs. Navigator, you stay here with the TACCO, and Commander, how about you and Petty Officer Jones coming with me and we'll check south. We'll all meet back here in two hours to report on what we find."

As the two groups head off, Smoltz helps Warbuck to the shelter of the boulders at the foot of the cliff face. The constant drizzle continues. It is cold and gray. So is Crew Eleven.

* * * * *

It is after 10 P.M. in Washington D.C. Tom Verbel is Secretary of Defense and has been for three months. He is just learning the job, having never been in government service previously. A successful industrialist in his early sixties, he got the appointment because he had rebuilt a string of steel plants into the number four producer in the world. Over serious objections by a choir of senior politicos, the president chose the person he thought best for the job over many others who gave much more in money and service to the party. The DOD was in shambles when the president took office and now as his second term is about to begin, the president had accepted with real regret the resignation of Verbel's predecessor. The president expected Verbel to have the toughness to continue to rebuild and strengthen the nation's defense. However, Verbel has so far been ineffective because the wall of bureaucrats has been nearly impenetrable. But he hasn't given up and he is determined to make a difference. Eventually. Verbel has yet to identify his allies. Those who can advance his agenda and can be trusted. If he were more experienced he would know that he could demand the president's assistant counsel come to the Pentagon. However, Admiral Bella, General Adams, and Verbel have trekked to the White House and are meeting in the small conference room near the Oval office. Joshua Bordon is already seated at the head of the table as the trio enters.

Bordon asks the question before any greetings can be exchanged, "So what was he doing on that flight anyway?"

Verbel looks to Bella. The admiral responds as he takes a seat, "I don't know. He's the type that needs to lead from the front."

"What front? We're not at war. There's no front!" Bordon says, putting his youth on display.

Adams doesn't miss an opportunity to put this young man who is constantly full of his own perfection and importance in his place, "Actually, we are still at war in Korea. There is only a truce and not a peace."

Verbel smiles at Bordon's ignorance being highlighted a little, but then he adds his opening observation, "You know, Norm, this really sucks. Really, really sucks. It is a truly rotten situation."

"That's a real understatement, Mr. Secretary," Bordon continues in his attempt to bully the military officers. He says, "We stand to lose a lot if he is alive and the North Koreans get hold of him?"

Bella baths his response in sarcasm, "Gee, maybe with a little luck the Koreans can accommodate you and they've killed him already."

Verbel takes control of the meeting, "Shut-up, Norm. We don't need your sarcasm. If they get him we will have to assume Black Jewel is compromised. Then it will be years of research and nearly a billion dollars probably wasted. All because this hot dog wants to play operational. What idiot sent him to the Pacific after working on Black Jewel? We couldn't send him to Europe? No, we send him to the Orient. Doesn't anybody think around here?"

Bella is not defensive, just explanatory in his response, "It was an administrative command. After four years of cloak and dagger B.S. in the puzzle palace, he earned a break back with real sailors. It seemed a safe job."

"Well, one thing is for sure." Verbel's voice is gravelly and echoes confidence in its judgment. "Whatever it takes, we have got to know what happened to him. If he's alive we must get him. If he is dead, we verify it with a body."

"And if the North Koreans have him?" Bordon asks in almost a threatening manner.

"What are you suggesting?" Bella asks with alarm.

Bordon cleans his spotless glasses as he responds, "I'm not suggesting anything. It is just my job to make sure the president is aware of all his options."

Bella is combative, in speech and physical presence as he leans towards Bordon and says through clinched teeth,

"You mean political options. I'm not going to let you play politics with the lives of these sailors."

"If they are alive you mean." Bordon replaces his glasses and leans back in the chair. "We first need to determine the situation. Then military, diplomatic, and political considerations can be examined."

Verbel nods towards the door in a motion that invites Bella and Adams to exit. The officers stand and begin to leave. Bella has kept the knowledge about Black Jewel gained from the White House memo from the SECDEF. Bella is still not certain that now or here is the right opportunity to play that card. He hesitates at the door, then turns and speaks, "Mr. Secretary I have some other matters I believe you should be aware of. May I have a couple moments of your time when you are done here?"

"Can we discuss it in the car on the way back to the Pentagon?"

"Yes, sir. I'll wait to ride back with you." Bella has Adams shove off with their driver and he goes to the gate to wait on the SECDEF. He leans against the car and lights a big cigar. He is oblivious to the light drizzle coming down, being deep in thought trying to piece together the Black Jewel puzzle.

* * * * *

It took nearly twenty minutes of hard climbing on a narrow rock and sand path to reach the top of the cliff. McKay now leads his small band through tall grass and squatty trees. The rain has slowed to a faint drizzle, but the day remains overcast and gloomy. The trail leads the three sailors to a single lane dirt road that runs north and south, paralleling the shore line. Just as they step from the bushes, an old rusted coupe approaches from the north. McKay motions for Peters and Thomas to take cover, and then he steps to the middle of the road. McKay's raised hand brings the vehicle to a sudden stop. Behind the wheel is a middle-aged Korean, who becomes very excited at seeing McKay. Peters and Thomas watch from the tall grass. They see McKay lean into the driver's window and motion with his hands towards the sea. The driver nods repeatedly. McKay steps back from the car and stretches his arms to simulate an airplane. He leans into the window again, slaps the Korean on the shoulder, and then steps back from the car, smiles and waves. The driver backs and fills three times to execute a U-turn, and then departs to the north at a very fast speed.

McKay watches the car disappear, splashing through the puddles in the dirt road. He steps down the path to join Peters and Thomas.

"Well, looks like the Admiral might be right. I don't think that Korean knew what to make of me, but he sure got excited when I tried to tell him there were more of us. I told him we would wait here for him to go get help."

Peters is nervous about the contact and asks for clarification, "Gee, Mr. McKay, I didn't know you could speak Korean."

"I don't, and he didn't know English. But you can be sure that there are not too many round eyes around here dressed in flight suits, so I figure he will be back with help very shortly."

"Should we go back and tell the others we made contact?" asks Thomas in a dry, steady voice. He thinks McKay is being a little too bold and cavalier about the encounter. Thomas would have preferred checking out the situation more before acting. But McKay does these things sometimes trying to prove he can make decisions and be "officer-like." Thomas is beginning to wish he had gone with the other group, with the more experienced Admiral and the M.O. In truth, once more he is wishing he was back in Watervliet working a $5.50 an hour job and drinking beer with his loser high school friends.

McKay is confident he is following the admiral's orders and desires and will be appropriately recognized for gaining contact. He is anxious to let the admiral know of his success, so he answers Thomas by saying, "Yeah. That's a good idea. But that was a long climb. Let's take five and then you can go back and tell them."

Thomas has a gut feeling that he needs to get away from this place. He stands and starts towards the cliff saying, "I feel fine. I'll head out now."

But just as Thomas starts to move away, the sound of a truck approaching from the north is heard. Thomas wants to run back to the beach, but McKay speaks before he can decide what to do, "Just a minute, Petty Officer Thomas. Maybe you can deliver more news. Let's see what this is about first."

McKay steps onto the road again. Peters looks at Thomas and softly says, "That was quick."

"Yeah," answers Thomas, "almost too quick."

Rumbling down the rough road, mud splattering from the wheels, is a large flatbed stake truck with military markings. Mounted above the cab is a light machine gun on a swivel. Holding the gun is a sergeant. Three additional soldiers clutch the truck bed railing to keep their balance. All wear olive drab, wool uniforms with black collars buttoned tightly at the neck. They wear matching soft uniform hats with short bills. In the cab is a stern faced officer with the driver. The truck slides to a halt, stopping just two feet in front of McKay who holds his position in the middle of the road with his hands over his head. McKay is smiling and trying to look officer-like. The rain starts to fall harder. McKay lowers his hands to wipe the water from his eyes. He is having trouble seeing due to the water. He finishes clearing his vision with his hands just in time to see the soldiers jump from the truck and rush him. Instinctively he takes a step back. The soldiers lunge for McKay and grab his arms. The sergeant has remained behind the machine gun, providing cover from the truck. The officer walks deliberately to the rear of McKay. The officer kicks the back of McKay's right knee. McKay collapses, falling to both knees, his arms held by the soldiers. No one has said a word. It is all happening too fast. Thomas and Peters see blurred images of the events through the tall grass and heavy rain.

The Korean officer pulls a pistol from his hip holster. It is an old automatic. He pulls back the slide to chamber a round. He points it at the back of McKay's head. Without hesitation, he jerks the trigger and the bullet passes through the back of the American's skull. As it exits McKay's head it spews bits of bone and brain into a wide pattern in the mud, leaving the young lieutenant without a face. The soldiers release McKay's limp arms and let him fall forward into his own parts. The soldiers swing their slinged AK-47s to the firing position and advance towards the path. The officer follows two paces behind.

Upon seeing McKay murdered, Peters knees turn to Jell-O. He loses balance and falls to all fours. His stomach squeezes shut then opens in uncontrollable contractions. Thomas touches his shoulder and whispers, "Come on, Tommy, we gotta get out of here right now. Let's run for it."

Peters cannot get to his feet. Worse, he starts dry heaving. The advancing soldiers hear his retching. Thomas makes the instantaneous decision to leave his shipmate and attempt escape. He starts to run. After only four steps, there is a loud pop of an assault rifle that fires three rounds, ripping through Thomas's flesh. It feels like someone kicked him in the lower back and Thomas knows he is hit really badly. It is getting dark on the outer edges of his vision. The shrinking hole that restricts his view is closing rapidly. His last thoughts before death come quickly, "I should've left earlier. I shouldn't have stayed to see what happens." The pinhole closes and he passes from the struggle.

Peters heard the shots, but he is paralyzed, not with fear, but from shock. He cannot look around. He can only spit-up nothing while suffering terrible stomach contractions. The emotional strain and anxiety of the last twenty hours became too much when he saw the second pilot's brains blown out. He needs time to process the stress before he can continue. But the Koreans have a different timetable. While Peters' vision is limited to the grass inches from his nose, the dead body of Thomas is dumped on him. More stress. Thomas's body rolls off Peters who reacts with an adrenaline panic and hops to the right, remaining on all fours. His convulsions resume, now accompanied by bawling. Tears and rain stream down Peters' cheeks as soldiers each take an arm and drag him towards the truck.

* * * * *

It is nearly midnight when Admiral Bella salutes the SECDEF as he approaches the limousine. They enter the back seat and the car pulls away from the north gate at the White House. Verbel speaks first, "What is it you wanted to discuss, Norm?"

Bella is still hesitant to share all he knows with this rookie. Just how much does this civilian know about how games are played inside the Beltway? He answers in political doublespeak, "Mr. Secretary, I am concerned about the direction of the development and deployment of Black Jewel." Bella pauses to see if Verbel will take the bait.

"Quit the B.S. Norm, and say what's bothering you."

Bella still goes slowly and asks, "How much do you know about the actual progress of Black Jewel? Are you aware of where the funding goes? Have you been brought up to speed on the potential of its effectiveness?"

"It sounds like you think I'm out of the loop. Why don't you tell me what you think I should know?"

Bella is not falling for the straight talking corporate exec bit. He thinks, "When I play poker, you gotta throw some money in the pot to see my hand. But if it is Tin Can poker

Robert Bartron

you want to play, well, I spent enough time on destroyers to understand the game. I'll raise you with nothing showing." Bella says, "Mr. Secretary, how far along do you think the Chinese are in developing an effective virus?"

Suddenly, Verbel's demeanor turns very dark. His eyebrows close together and his nostrils flare. He lowers his chin and with complete seriousness he says in a low voice, "It is obvious, Admiral, that we need to continue this discussion in a more secure environment. You're coming to my office right now."

Bella's back stiffens and he comes to attention in a sitting position in the back seat of the limousine. He has hit a nerve. It looks like he played his hand right. He is going to get a look at the SECDEF's cards.

CHAPTER EIGHT

The rain is continuous now. It varies from pouring to a drizzle and then back to pouring every few minutes. Smoltz and Warbuck are nestled against the base of the beach cliff. Warbuck is on his back, uncomfortable but dry under a rock overhang. Smoltz is outboard of him, sitting with his legs crossed and leaning under the overhang. His back is exposed and if he sits upright the water pouring off the cliff in small streams runs under his collar and down his flight suit. Warbuck is breathing in a very labored fashion. If he lies quietly, the pain subsides and he can get enough air into his one inflated lung to keep him from gasping. He must anticipate any speech in order to consciously draw in enough breath to form words. He speaks in a near whisper, "Bobby, you're not staying very dry."

"I know," answers Smoltz, pleased that the TACCO feels like talking again. Smoltz is worried that Warbuck could die at any minute. It is obvious to him that the TACCO is severely injured and in great pain, but he longs for any companionship that can make this situation more understandable. It's being alone in duress that will make you a coward. Smoltz continues the conversation, "I was just thinking what a day this past twenty-four hours has been."

"Yeah," Warbuck sighs. "They never mentioned this stuff when I talked to my recruiters."

"You know what is bothering me the most, Billy?"

Warbuck shakes his head and carefully repositions his hip, sliding it slightly to his left.

Smoltz continues, "I don't feel anything. I mean about the guys who died during the last day. It's like I don't care, but I do. I mean these guys were on our crew. I'm supposed to feel something. I saw the commander crying and I tell myself I should feel something, but I just don't. I can't even make myself feel guilty for not feeling anything. Why is that? Am I that bad a person?"

Warbuck raises his vision to focus on Smoltz's eyes and responds, "No, you're not bad, Bobby, you're just well trained and under great combat stress, I think. You don't feel anything, because you've been trained to focus on the job at hand. Once this job is over, then you will sit up alone at night and cry for the Chief and Fred and all of them. Trust me. It will hit you about a week or so after we get back...don't think of it now. That's good...don't think of it now."

Smoltz can hear pain not associated with Warbuck's physical condition in his voice. It is in his eyes. Smoltz softly responds, "You say that stuff like you've been through it before."

Warbuck questions whether he should share certain memories with his navigator under these circumstances, then starts to open up without realizing he is speaking.

"Not like this...But my college roommate, Tom, and I joined together and even roomed together during flight school. He died in a training command crash. They were able to recover his and one other body from the Gulf of Mexico. I went to the memorial service at the chapel there in Pensacola. I even escorted the body home to Riverside. Went to the graveside service with his family. Never shed a tear. Went back into a flight status the next day after returning from California. Flew every day for a week on syllabus hops without ever thinking of him. Got a new roommate before the week was over, and life went on.

"Then I was at the gedunk buying some little stuff. I remembered I needed razor blades and as I reached for the blades I grabbed two packs because I thought to myself 'Tom probably needs some more too.' Then right there in the aisle at the gedunk on base I started to bawl like a baby. I ran out of there and drove to the beach to be alone. By the time I was sitting in the sand and watching the surf I had stopped crying. I didn't shed a tear on the beach. I just sat there and for the first time I realized that Tom was gone. Permanently. Not just transferred to another squadron, but gone. That night and for quite a few after, I sat in my room alone and mourned him...with tears."

Both sit in silence, listening to the surf a short distance beyond. Smoltz is beginning to feel the loss as he dwells on Warbuck's comments about his shipmates never returning. He sighs and then breaks the long pause with painful regrets, "I wish I would've known this was going to happen. Maybe I would have acted differently with those guys if I knew they were gonna die so soon."

"Naw,..it's better just to live and do what you do...thinking about dying doesn't get you anywhere."

"Well," Smoltz responds, trying to shake off the onset of melancholy, "when we get back I know I'm going to call my parents and tell them something I haven't said in a long time."

Warbuck nods and winces in pain. Smoltz adjusts his seat and when he does a little river of runoff is ported down his neck. Smoltz shutters and shakes. In a voice laced with disgust he says, "This isn't working at all. If I'm going to get wet, I might as well go out and see if anyone is coming back yet."

Smoltz rolls out from under the small overhang and threads his way around several large boulders which protrude from the sand as if large stone sentries. He steps free from the rocks and takes a couple steps towards the water. Stopping, he scans the beach north and south. He sees nothing. He walks to the center of the beach, halfway from cliff to surf. The rain reduces visibility to a hundred yards. Then, looking northward he makes out the fuzzy images of men advancing towards him. They are emerging from the mist and rain, spread out in a single line from water's edge to the cliff. Instinctively, Smoltz starts to move towards them. After a couple of steps he stops. He can see them more clearly now. They are North Korean soldiers. Each is carrying a rifle, not slung over his shoulder, but at the ready. They spot him and a shout is passed up and down the line. Smoltz hesitates, then raises his hands over his head to signify he is unarmed and not a threat.

In the boulders, Warbuck hears the faint shouts over the constant drone of the rain. With great pain, he eases himself from the small enclave and stumbles towards the beach. Upon reaching the last large rock he leans against it to regain his strength and clear his dizziness. He wipes the rain from his eyes and squints towards the north. He sees Smoltz advancing northward with his hands raised. Warbuck looks father up the beach and the beginnings of shapes start to exit the blanket of rain.

Smoltz is making all movements slow and unthreatening. No need to spook these armed foreigners. Then it happens, quickly and totally unexpectedly. The nearest soldier raises his rifle to his shoulder and points it at the American. Everything immediately flips to slow motion in Smoltz's mind. Everything that happens in the next minute is clear and separate from other events. Smoltz can see every little detail of what happens, much like a NFL halfback who is "in the zone" and sees holes in the defense no one else can. Smoltz sees the flash from the gun barrel before he hears the loud clap of the shot. The bullet kicks up sand one yard in front of him. Smoltz dives to the deck. The soldiers are fifty yards away and now four of them are popping off rounds in quick succession. Smoltz gives a quick look over his left shoulder towards Warbuck's position and his thoughts race, "Should I attempt to reach the safety of the rocks? Or will it just give away the TACCO's location and get us both killed? Why are they shooting at me? This doesn't make sense. I didn't do anything. The surf. Maybe I can swim out far beyond the surf and then come ashore unseen a mile down the beach. They made us do the mile swim in training for a reason. Right?"

The bullets are thudding into the sand all around his position. He jumps to his feet and runs for the water. After only one step he feels a burning in his right calf. He falls. He scrambles to his feet and resumes his dash for the surf. Two steps later, it feels like a sledgehammer hits his left thigh. He tumbles and falls into the wet sand. He is only yards away from the crashing waves. The last little surge of the surf floods over his body. He crawls, trying to go farther into the water, and then his brain bursts with pain reporting that his left heel has exploded. He crawls on two hands and his right leg one more yard. Smoltz's leg gives way and he rolls over in the shallow water. The North Koreans are ten yards away and surrounding him. It is quiet while they reload. Smoltz can now see just beyond the soldiers. There is Peters, his arms tied behind him with a pole jammed between his elbows and his back. Around his neck, like a noose or dog's leash, are two metal wires with two Korean soldiers holding the ends. In his slow-motion world, Smoltz clearly sees Peters beaten face, swollen worse than Rocky in round fifteen. Tears pour from his nearly shut eyes. He watches as Peters jerks back from his handlers and momentarily frees himself from their grasp when they become preoccupied watching Smoltz's efforts. Peters gets five yards towards the surf before his captors reach him and push him face down in the water. Unable to use his hands, Peters kicks wildly trying to get his face out of the water to breathe. The North Koreans press their boots into the back of his head even harder. The kicking becomes frenzied, then slower, and then it stops.

From his vantage point in the rocks, Warbuck sees the events as if he were looking through murky glass. The varying intensity of the rain causes his picture to blur then become clearer and then blur again. He doesn't see it is

Peters who is murdered, but he does recognize the victim as American. Warbuck steps from behind the rocks onto the beach. It is an instinctive reaction. He freezes when he sees the soldiers circle the wounded Smoltz. They laugh as they all point their rifles at the American. It is an impromptu firing squad sans the court-martial and defense attorneys. And they are laughing. In fact, Warbuck hears the laughing before the report of the shots. Smoltz has rolled to his stomach and is crawling towards the waves, like a wounded animal not knowing how to give up or to escape. He goes limp after the first volley. The soldiers reload and fire into his body again. His body slightly twitches as the rounds hit and Smoltz's life runs out the holes.

Warbuck recoils from the sight. He retreats behind the boulder, bends over and sucks air to clear his head. "They will be coming after me next. Dear God, where can I hide?"

The Koreans drag the two bodies out of the water and pile them on the dry sand. The officer in charge disburses the squad across the beach, and they resume their search. Weapons pointed down the beach, they walk deliberately and methodically.

Warbuck goes to the overhang and crawls in. But it provides no cover if anyone searches the rocks. He slides out and, in desperation, scans the area behind the rocks. He cannot climb the cliff and there is no cave or brush to hide in. Warbuck squeezes behind a large rock, wedging himself in a tiny space between boulders. A searcher would have to circumnavigate the great rock to discover him. His only hope is that they are not thorough. A weak hope indeed.

The Koreans approach the boulder area. The one closest to the cliff peers around the first and largest one. He motions for his nearest comrade to join him. They are well trained at small area searches and instinctively provide back up to the other. They move from one area to the next, the only sounds being the crashing surf, the rain bouncing off the rocks and the sand giving way beneath their boots. It is merely a matter of seconds and Warbuck will be discovered. The TACCO holds his breath. Trapped. Doomed. Too scared to even pray. He has no control and now it is going to be over.

A shout stops the Koreans in their tracks. They cock their heads and listen. There is a second shout. The two turn and hustle to the beach. There they join their unit around the unearthed body of Ford. The officer has found his objective. Confident he now has all the Americans, he orders his men to drag Ford's body to the others. The search is over. They take all three corpses back up the beach.

Warbuck remains in the cleft of the cliff, his arm over his face. He still waits. He can't move.

* * * * *

The Secretary of Defense has the top dog's office in the Pentagon. The extremely plush carpet with the DOD seal knitted in the middle, the expensive furnishings and the massive hand-carved wooden desk announce the importance of the occupant to all who enter. Admiral Bella has been in the office on many occasions and the over-the-top décor fails to impress him anymore. Rather than sitting at the mahogany conference table located on one side of the huge office, Secretary Verbel takes his power seat behind the desk. Bella notices that the SECDEF does not offer him a chair. So the four-star admiral stands relaxed off to the side of the desk. He is way too senior to assume the junior position of being at attention in front of the desk. Bella's beltway tours have made him an expert on every subtle power maneuver used in D.C. There is nothing Verbel learned in industry that can top the petty political moves used in this town to gain an edge.

"Well?" Verbel starts the conversation.

"I have the same question, Mr. Secretary," Bella says, bringing the previous conversation's topic back to the center of the meeting. "How far along do you think the Chinese are in developing an effective virus?"

"Why do you ask?"

Bella is still playing "Tin Can poker" with this civilian, so he raises him without throwing any chips into the pot. "Gus Adams was told on Sunday night to push the deployment of Black Jewel ahead ASAP. We were wondering if that might be because new intel has revealed that the Chinese have been successful in isolating the Gamma Three virus."

"I am afraid that answer might be above your pay grade, Admiral," SECDEF responds while pretending to look at papers on his desk. If he had hoped that such an answer would discourage this career officer and send him out the door, then he is disappointed. Bella remains in place, his eyes examining the SECDEF. The memorandum recovered from the White House ante room is burning a hole in his blouse pocket. Bella ponders his next step. But before he has to decide, the SECDEF makes the first move and goes "all in."

"Norm, we are hoping that the Chinese are nearly done testing and are near full-scale development of Gamma Three. Hell, we have done nearly everything we can legally to help them along," Verbel says as he leans back in his chair and throws his reading glasses onto his desk. Now he motions for the admiral to take a seat by the desk as he continues, "My predecessor told me that about four years ago we discovered that they were working on another virus, that they were going a different direction. If they continued along that path, then all the work and money we had invested in Black Jewel would become useless. We would have a defense against a weapon our enemy did not posses. Staffers during the President's first term came up with a plan to save the Black Jewel investment while making it unnecessary to start over to battle a totally different type of virus."

"So we let them think that by stealing secrets from us they can save years and resources in coming up with their own B&C weapons," Bella says, finishing Verbel's thought.

Verbel nods and adds, "It was just a contingency plan until the President's new chief of staff came in a year ago. He put it into play."

"But what if Black Jewel never does pan out? What if we are not successful in development and deployment of countermeasures? Personally, I am not sure the Chinese could have developed a new and rapidly deployable virus in the next decade or even within the next fifteen years. But with our help, they are doing it in under a year. That was a very big risk with American lives," Bella says in an accusing tone.

Verbel nods again. Then he adds, "But four years ago our scientists were saying that Black Jewel would be fully deployed in a matter of months. Then they came across that dissipation and malignant gene transformation problem that was unforeseen. Regardless, our research on and knowledge of Gamma Three was years ahead of any other biological strain. The CHICOMs were hell-bent on getting a virus, so it was best for us if they kept focused on what we knew more about."

"Mr. Secretary, why are you sharing this with me?"

"You know something and it is really bothering you, Norm. I showed you mine, now I want you to show me yours," Verbel said while making intense eye contact with the senior naval officer.

"We've got some very serious problems," Bella says in his controlled, but angry manner. "First, I'm personally not sure that there is anything legal or right about sharing secrets with an enemy. As is usual around this town, it sounds like some seriously ambitious elitist know-it-alls think they have all the right answers, and these answers are overly-cute and dangerous. Secondly, if the American public finds out about this the whole scheme will sound more like it was a plan to line the pockets of big defense contractors. If you sell bullet-proof windows, there is nothing better for business than handing out rifles to the neighbors. Thirdly, this is becoming one of the worst kept secrets inside the beltway."

"Why do you say that? I know of only maybe nine current and former White House staffers who know this plan."

"You really are new to D.C.," Bella says as he shakes his head. "The biggest leaks come from 1600 Pennsylvania Avenue. I know an Army major, a Marine colonel, a Navy captain and an Air Force lieutenant general who know we have been helping the Chinese develop biological weapons and delivery systems."

"But how?"

"White House sloppiness. And now all that cutesy espionage trickery is about to blow up in America's face if the North Koreans get their hands on one person." Bella stands as he finishes his little tirade. The SECDEF stands as well. Neither knows what to say.

Finally, Bella says, "Mr. Secretary if you will work the political problem and try to stop the White House leak, I will work the military side and clamp down the hatches over here."

Verbel nods and Bella sits down again. He starts to brief the SECDEF on how the secrets left the White House, while thinking to himself of the best way to explain to professional, patriotic military officers what the civilians have done. He knows they will not like it.

* * * * *

Master Chief Strait had never lost an airplane in his entire nearly thirty year career in naval aviation. It is his worst nightmare to have a squadron plane fall from the sky due to a maintenance mistake. Now QE-05 is gone. And the Maintenance Master Chief hasn't slept since the aircraft missing report was received yesterday afternoon. The real kick in the butt is the loss of the M.O. with the plane. Ground pounders in maintenance are supposed to look after the aircrew. That's what makes a team. Now the M.O.'s aircraft has disappeared; no, let's face the truth, it has crashed.

If hard work and shear will power can rectify this tragedy, then Strait will set it right. He is running on will and guts. The impossible now has become expected. The hangar queen was launched at first light this morning, having been reassembled from issued and unauthorized "battle spare" parts. There was no shortage of aircrew volunteers to conduct the test hop on the queen and to depart on the twelve-hour search. No pressurization or heat available ceased to be a downing gripe. The crew will merely alter the flight profile to remain below 10,000 feet and they will wear wool socks. No reliable inertials just means the navigator must take more Loran fixes. No computer means the TACCO must plot on charts like it was done in the 1950s. But after unbelievable teamwork and effort all night by all maintenance personnel, the engines run, the flaps and landing gear work. So, a third squadron airplane was launched and joined the search.

Strait is seated at the stool behind the maintenance control desk. It has been his perch since yesterday afternoon. The force of his personality has kept all focused on doing their jobs. No complaints or whines. No excuses or self-pity. No gossip or possible blame laying. Every member of the department comes to the control desk and draws strength from the master chief. They are issued directions in a motivating fashion and they grab confidence from his demeanor and will. Senior Chief Howard walks in to report for night check duty. He looks at Strait and sees a man near collapse, in need of sleep and a shave. Howard hangs his cover on the coat rack behind the counter and speaks in a low voice, "Frank, go get dinner, a shave and a couple minutes of shut-eye. I'll handle the fort here."

Strait shakes his head and swallows another gulp of day old coffee.

Howard responds to the rebuff, "I'll call you if there is any problem or any word. Just a few minutes, Frank, or you will be out on your feet when we need you later."

Strait starts to object, but then he almost spills his coffee by missing the counter as he attempts to set the cup down. He acknowledges to himself, "Okay, maybe Howie is right. I do need a couple hours to recharge." Strait gives Howard a detailed brief on current efforts to get the LLTV birds recovered and ready to launch again to be on station to search at dusk. He then drags his tired body across the hangar and ramp towards the admin building and the gedunk there.

As he approaches the entrance Commander Morse and Lieutenant Steward, the admiral's aide, exit the building. Strait is too tired to notice them and offer a salute. Even the C.O. wouldn't be presumptuous enough to draw it to the maintenance master chief's attention. Especially today.

"We were just on our way over to see you, Master Chief. Will we be able to launch the night birds and another three for tomorrow morning's search?" asks Morse.

"Yes, sir."

Steward is clutching a naval message in her hand and is quite agitated. Her voice is urgent and challenging when she says, "Are you sure? We must locate the admiral."

Nobody addresses the Maintenance Master Chief like that. Nobody questions his "yes" or "no". Especially a female lieutenant who has done nothing to earn her place in this man's Navy, let alone give her the right to address a master chief like that. Strait responds with a glare that causes the lieutenant to back-up a step. Then she stands her ground and rises to her full height. Obviously this enlisted man has no idea what this message says. We must find the admiral before the North Koreans capture him. We must.

148

Morse doesn't do much right. But he does here by stepping between the lieutenant and the master chief. Even he can see that the tone and content of the lieutenant's question have personally and professionally insulted Strait. Morse speaks, "Fine, Master Chief, you have the planes ready and we'll have the crews there. Thank you, Master Chief. Let's go Lieutenant, Maintenance will meet their duties, let's do ours."

Strait breaks his glare and steps around the officers. He proceeds to the admin building, wondering how the hot dogs are going to sit after suffering the insults of dolts.

Steward shows that even though she might wear the uniform, she has yet to truly understand the fleet Navy. She whines to Morse as they approach the operations center complex, "Sir, aren't there nine aircraft in this squadron and eleven crews? Why are only five airplanes assigned to the search? You must do everything possible to save the admiral."

"Look, Lieutenant," Morse comes to a halt and faces Steward to address her bluntly, "First off, we only have eight planes because one is probably in pieces at the bottom of the SOJ. Of those eight, two are in Adak, Alaska supporting the Bear Trapping of the first Pacific patrol of a new Russian Yankee, and one is in Singapore returning from Diego Garcia. Second, have you ever been involved in an open ocean search? We did a lot of it after Viet Nam fell looking for boat people. If you find anything at all, it is pure dumb luck. And lastly, Lieutenant, why don't you let me worry about the search specifics and you concentrate on keeping calendars current and the coffee available."

"But sir," Steward protests. She just doesn't get it. She has never had the opportunity to spend a career immersed in operational matters. The Navy has restricted her to shore duty where there is always someone you can call for assistance and whatever is undone at 1700 on Friday can wait until Monday morning. She just hasn't served where a man's pride is the ultimate driving factor in getting the near impossible accomplished. She is so used to wearing her admiral's shoulder boards that she just doesn't see that a lieutenant, even an admiral's aide, cannot tell a squadron commanding officer what to do. Especially a female lieutenant that wears no warfare insignia. She is not a member of the ruling club. But she just doesn't get it, so she continues her ill-advised protest, "Commander, according to this message you must make every effort to find the admiral. Only three planes searching in daylight hours can hardly be considered 'every' effort."

Morse is a jerk, and a political animal always aware of what can impact his career, but he will not take this kind of berating from some rookie lieutenant, even if she is quite handsome and well built. He answers, "Lieutenant, that message was to me and not you. There is a lot more at stake than your admiral. We have a lost crew and airplane. I'm the task unit commander and I will be the one to decide what 'every effort' means. I am keeping you informed strictly out of courtesy and not because you have any say or authority in what I do. Do you understand that?"

In a reflex action, Steward comes to attention as she responds, "Yes, sir."

Morse reaches for the message in Stewards hand. She gives it to him. He turns and enters the TSC. Steward fights back tears and follows. This is the first time she has been addressed in such a manner. Up to now, she was lead to believe that she was the ideal officer. Nice words in fitreps and constant deference when entering a room of officers. She has not had much interaction in her career with enlisted personnel except the yeomen. It hurts to discover what they really were thinking. She is a pretty face who is not respected beneath the smiles and nice words. She thinks, "But I work hard, don't I? It isn't my fault I cannot get sea duty. So, when push comes to shove, I am nothing more than a second-class officer." What she doesn't acknowledge is that she has earned her status by enjoying all the benefits of being a Naval officer without any of the true hardships; like long deployments away from family, eighty-plus hour work weeks, always putting Navy ahead of family and self, making life and death decisions as normal duty and then living with the results with no whining or regrets. She has been blind to the sacrifices necessary for entry into the club. She remains blind. You never can know the initiation required until you live it and it will be long after her career has ended that a new generation of female officers are given the opportunity to earn club membership.

* * * * *

Warbuck eases out of his hiding place. It has been a half hour since he last heard any noise on the beach except the haunting cries of the seagulls and the crashing surf. He struggles around the boulders and peeks at the beach. He sees no one. The rain has become a mist with intermittent drizzle. Warbuck sees the depression that had been Ford's grave. He stumbles towards it. Upon reaching the shallow indentation he collapses into it. He starts to shake with cold, injury, fear and guilt. Fear of being alone against overwhelming force. Guilt of failing to care for his navigator. Guilt, fear, remorse. It is too much for him. His coughs turn to sobs. Tears flow down his cheeks and he circles his arms around sand and pulls a mound towards his chest. He squeezes it and sways to an old church tune he whispers to himself, "Were you there when he rose up from the grave?...Sometimes it makes me tremble, tremble.."

Slowly he curls into the fetal position. Breath is coming hard due to his collapsed lung, broken ribs, and sobs. But soon he is quiet. He has sent his conscious mind to visit home. He is safe in Mom's arms on the daybed on the screened porch. It is nap time after morning kindergarten. He remembers, "Mom would fix lunch. We'd eat together and then she would lay her arm over me as we lay down to take a nap together. It is so safe in her arms. She loves me and I am safe." Soon, his run from reality is complete and he sleeps in the sand and drizzle.

* * * * *

If the sun was shining, Evans would enjoy the stroll on the beach. It reminds him of the special trips Margie and he had made to Virginia Beach. And the islands. Yeah, the islands when they first met. The sound of crashing surf and the serenity of the rhythmic cycles of ebb then flood then ebb. He loves the ocean. The beach. The shore.

Jones and Keene are quiet and lost in their thoughts as well. The long walk to the south was a dead end. There is no way up the vertical cliffs. Two clicks down the beach a rocky point is flooded with the tide and further passage south is cut-off. The trio is returning with the hope the northern scouting party had better success. Through the mist and drizzle, Keene is the first to see Warbuck in the sand. It looks odd. At first he believes it might be Ford's body. But why is it uncovered? Who dug it up?

Keene sees Warbuck stir. Keene increases his pace. Warbuck stirs again and from fifty yards Keene identifies his TACCO. Keene breaks into a jog and then a sprint. Jones and then Evans chase him. Upon reaching the sleeping J.O., Keene drops to his knees and shakes Warbuck, saying softly, "Billy...Billy"

"What time is the preflight?" are the first, instinctive words Warbuck utters as he stirs from his deep, dreamless sleep. "Did I miss it again?" Warbuck recognizes Keene and is astonished to discover that he is not alone. "Jim! You're alive!"

Keene leans back a little and gives Warbuck a confused look. He thinks, "Of course I'm alive. Why wouldn't I be?"

Keene tries to sort out what the TACCO means by asking, "Billy, where are the others?"

Jones and Evans arrive at the two men in the sand and stand over them. Jones recognizes the spot as the site of Ford's grave. He is upset, very upset and apprehensive of what has happened. "Lieutenant! What are you doing in Ford's grave? This is Ford's grave! What are you doing in Ford's grave! Where's Ford? What happened to Ford!"

Keene looks around him and realizes he is in Ford's grave with Warbuck. He scrambles out of it. Warbuck starts to speak but he must wait to clear his wind pipe. He coughs up blood and then draws a painful breath. His eyes are glazed over and he is nearly incoherent. Having shut down his overloaded brain and emotions and hidden in deep sleep, he has yet to find the handle to permit him to grasp the truth of what he saw. In trying to explain what happened he must fight to regain control of his own sanity. "Dead—they're all dead—killed—shot—they shot Bobby—they shot Peters—they took Ford—dead—all dead."

Evans kneels next to Warbuck and puts his face up close to the TACCO's. He refrains from grabbing his shoulders, knowing that shaking Warbuck could increase his internal injuries. But very deliberately and forcefully he asks the stressed Lieutenant, "Who shot them?"

There is a long pause as the four wet aircrew men search for answers. Jones is speechless. He has gone into temporary shock; his only thoughts are questions, "What has happened? I don't understand. What has happened? What has happened? Wait, tell me. What has happened?"

Keene experiences the exact opposite reaction. The paralyzing melancholy and guilt begins to drain from his consciousness. Now there is an enemy. No longer is it his fault the bad things are happening. There is an enemy causing the hurt. He feels his self-respect and determination to win start to pulsate through his veins. The fog is clearing from his thinking. He is beginning to see a definite path that now must be followed. We fight.

Warbuck responds to Evans because an admiral is asking a direct question. Warbuck is under orders to reply. He pulls his thoughts together out of instinct and years of training. He answers, "Koreans, sir. Uniformed Koreans. I was back in the rocks and Bobby went out to look for you and the Koreans were there. He raised his hands and they started shooting. They murdered him. They had another American with his hands tied behind his back and they pushed his head into the water and drowned him. They came looking for me but left when they found Ford's body."

Keene shoots the next question at his friend who is becoming more alert and recovering his military bearing, "What about Fred and Petty Officer Thomas?"

"M.O., I haven't seen them since you left."

Evans stands and scans the beach to the north. Jones vision remains fixed on the shallow indentation of sand where Warbuck is sitting. Keene stands and also stares to the north as they talk. Evans asks the next important question, "Lieutenant, how long ago did this take place?"

Warbuck looks at his watch and rubs his eyes. After a little hesitation he answers, "Maybe twenty minutes, maybe a half hour ago."

Evans mumbles to himself, "We gotta get off this beach right now."

Jones finally breaks his stare into Ford's grave and grabs Evans's arm, spinning him ninety degrees so they face each other. Jones is angry and scared and in shock. He needs something to hate right now! He lashes out at Evans saying, "Why would they take Ford? I knew we shouldn't have listened to you, Admiral! They murdered our crew! And you helped them do it! You sent them right into their murdering hands!" Jones now directs his glare at Keene. "Why are you letting him do this to us, Boss?"

Keene quickly steps between the admiral and the first class petty officer. He gets right in Jones's face and through clinched teeth snarls, "He's the admiral and I'm not. I'm the one who already killed the crew. We're not back in our soft beds in the Q right now because I screwed-up and not because of him. Get this straight, Jones, he's calling the shots now. So pull yourself together and let's just get off this beach."

Evans knows when to be silent. This is such a time. It has all been said. And right now he wants to get somewhere that is not so exposed. His thoughts are fast and focused, "Only one way to head. South. There must be a way around that rocky point. Come ebb tide maybe there will be a way over the rocks where the waves won't smash us. I hate to think of trying to swim around the point with Warbuck the way he is."

Evans lifts Warbuck to his feet. Keene gives a hand and the three start struggling south, Warbuck coughing up blood. Everyone is beginning to feel the exhaustion and weakness that lack of food brings. Jones stares at the empty grave, kicks the sand and then follows the officers.

* * * * *

Major McWalters is on a mission. She is clutching the left shoulder of Lieutenant DeWalker as he sits at his NMCC work station. McWalters leans over his shoulder and almost whispers in his ear. "Did you get a response back yet from the Canucks?"

"Nothing new. What I gave you is the latest. Do you want me to call again?" Things are so dead in DeWalker's area of responsibility in West Africa he had been delighted to respond positively to Julie's earlier request for aid. She is pretty. She smells good and she reminds him of fresh hot cinnamon rolls on a cold winter morning.

McWalters considers his question and then shakes her head and says, "No, I don't want to draw too much attention to our request. They're pretty thorough up there. We'll just wait for them to respond normally. Just let me know as soon as they do."

DeWalker's voice is full of confusion and a hope that he can glean some in-the-know gossip as he asks, "Why are you so interested in ICAO hits? They never amount to anything. No one much concerns themselves with their complaints unless they are looking for—wait a minute! Are you missing an airplane? Tell me, Major, what's up? Who lost the aircraft? Us or them?"

"Quit the speculating, Bradley. If you had a need-to-know maybe I would tell you about my little project. But since you don't, just shut-up and let me do my job." Even though she said it with a smile, McWalters was still taken aback by her own rudeness. She could see in DeWalker's eyes that he was hurt by the harsh response to his playful comment. She thinks, "It is not like me. It must due to the fatigue and lack of sleep. When was the last time you slept, Julie?"

McWalters smiles at DeWalker again, and he responds with a forced grin. She whispers in a sexy voice into his ear, "I'm sorry Bradley. Bad night." McWalters hesitates just long enough for DeWalker to know she means it and then turns and retreats to the private glass-enclosed operations room. She enters the correct code into the cipher lock and opens the door. Inside, she sits in front of the large computer console in the far corner. She refreshes the screen and stares at the picture it presents. There is the outline of the southern region of the Sea of Japan. Two points labeled 081036Z and 081056Z are shown near the Korean DMZ, the first point being northeast of the second. McWalters has a theory, but two points do not represent sufficient evidence to make the theory even plausible. "Where else can I look? What other information is available? There must be something, somewhere," she mumbles to herself.

The phone next to the computer buzzes. She picks up the handset. It is DeWalker. "They just called me. They are faxing what they have to extension 301, if you want to get it."

"Then they have something? I'll get it. Okay, thanks a million, Bradley. Someday I'll be able to share what's going on. Thanks."

DeWalker's voice is dry and still hurt, "Hope it helps." He hangs up.

McWalters rushes to the central fax machine on the far side of the main, lower room. It seems an eternity for the machine to complete its function. When it does, McWalters has a list of times and locations and durations in seconds. She scans the fifty or so entries until she comes to one that causes her to smile. She rushes to the ops room computer and enters the latitude, longitude, and time into the program. She hits "enter", then "display" and shuts her eyes. She wants so much for this position to fall into place. Slowly she opens her eyes to see whether her theory was right.

McWalters's face lights up upon seeing that her hunch has merit. The third point falls exactly where she expected. It is an extension of the line between the first two points. She doesn't hesitate to grab the secure phone and dial the beeper number for Admiral Bella. After leaving a message to contact her she hangs up. She leaves her hand on the receiver and ponders, "Should I call General Adams too?" After a moment's indecision, she raises the receiver and places the second call.

CHAPTER NINE

The tide has partially ebbed. The surf is still breaking in twenty-foot high explosive squirts as it bangs against the large, sharp boulders guarding the base of the sea cliff. Water is up to Evans's knees as he balances himself on a large submerged rock. Jones and Keene sit beside a spent Warbuck in the sand a few yards away. Evans cannot see any beach on the far side of the crashing surf. He stands on his tip-toes and strains to see what lies to the south beyond the massive, rugged rock formation that juts to a point. Then he hears it. A low muffled diesel sound. Now he sees it. Slowly trolling up the beach, less than half a click off shore is a North Korean gunboat. On the bow and bridge he can see sailors with arms raised to their face as if scanning the beach with binoculars.

Evans quickly jumps off the rock into the waist deep surf. He pushes his exhausted body through the rough waves until he reaches wet sand. Running to the other three he reaches for Warbuck's arms as he speaks through his heavy breathing, "Korean patrol boat coming from the south. We gotta get cover quick."

Keene jumps to his feet and looks south. Then all four look to the base of the cliff. There is no cover there. Without another word, the entire crew realizes their only hope of escaping detection is to hide in the rocks being pounded by the full might of the sea. Jones takes Warbuck's arms from the admiral, and then Keene goes to the navigator to help the petty officer. Keene takes one of the arms of his suffering friend. Evans leads the survivors back into the sea. They wade to waist deep water, the waves crashing just a few feet in front of them. The force of the waves make it nearly impossible to remain standing. They wade parallel to the surf towards the rock formation. The spectacular geysers shoot into the sky with each new set of waves. The sailors edge closer to the rocks jutting from the water. Evans is still in the lead and by timing his lunge with the incoming waves, he is able to jump to a position behind an eight-foot boulder. He slips and slides on the uneven footing, but is finally able to wedge himself against the side of the large rock, sitting in waist-deep water. A wave immediately and entirely submerges him. His head reappears from the brine and foam after it passes. He peers around the rock and sees the gunboat approaching the point. Then he ducks as he sees another wave come crashing over his position. It is obvious to him that his hiding place selection was exceedingly poor.

Keene can hear the gunboat's engines now. He waits for a wave to pass, and then he grabs Warbuck by the collar and lunges for the rocks. Warbuck tries his best to help, however he is having great trouble breathing. He cannot inhale. He gasps for quarter breathes of air. The two friends land in a tide pool within a ring of rocks. It is a good hiding place from the Koreans, but a lousy hiding place from the surf. A wave overwhelms them and fills the pool instantaneously. It quickly drains as the two aircrew men struggle to get their heads above the water. But then another wave hits and the fight goes another round with no rest.

The gunboat is now nearly abeam their position. Evans looks at Jones. Petty Officer Jones has seen the gunboat coming around the point. He knows that in seconds the gunboat will be able to spot his head above the breaking waves. Evans looks at the gunboat from his hiding place and then to Jones and mumbles to himself, "Now what? Do something, man! At least make an attempt to do something!"

Jones makes eye contact with Evans. There is no true communication passed between the admiral and the petty officer. Each is lost in his own thoughts on what is about to happen. Then suddenly, Jones shuts his eyes and takes a deep breath. He disappears beneath the next passing wave. Evans looks for him to appear near shore, but he doesn't. Evans ceases his visual search for the petty officer and hunkers down behind his rock. The Koreans are now right off shore. Out of the corner of his eye, Evans sees something break the surface momentarily beyond the surf. He wonders, "Was it a dolphin or fish? Or Jones? Not that far out, I don't think. There it is again, almost to the end of the rocky point. It was small and quick. Could it be? If it was, then Jones is one strong swimmer." Evans sneaks a peek behind him, around his covering rock. As soon as the gunboat comes into his vision he jerks his head back around into hiding. He can make out the crew sweeping the area with binoculars. Another wave crashes over him. He presses his back against the large rock to hold his position. He is buried in salt water that stings his eyes no matter how tightly he squeezes them shut. Once the water subsides he opens his eyes and looks up. Then he sees it. In the cliff, midway from the rocks to the top, about fifteen feet up the thirty foot cliff. It is a big hole in the cliff wall. Maybe six feet high and twenty-foot wide. A cave. A hideout.

* * * * *

It has taken Admiral Bella over an hour to arrive at the NMCC. His NMCC watch ended yesterday but he decided that this P-3 problem would remain his baby. Although he only lives fifteen minutes away, traffic in D.C. can never be predicted. Road maintenance at 0100 made his response time much longer than he expected. He is not surprised to see General Adams walking up the hall to attend this latest briefing. Soon they are standing behind McWalters looking at the large computer screen. Three points are in a line running southwest from the Sea of Japan into North Korea, just north of the DMZ.

McWalters explains how she developed this line the senior officers are studying, "This morning we received a routine message from the International Civil Aviation Organization headquarters in Canada. The report was a weekly summary of miscellaneous satellite and HF radio hits on the international distress frequencies that were judged to be spurious. The message was a standard request for us to better police our aircrews to prevent the unauthorized use of the emergency frequencies."

Bella grunts as if he is getting bored with the background information and wants McWalters just to get to the point.

She takes a deep breath and continues, "Out of desperation, I entered the report specifics into the computer and filtered all the data looking for anything that might show a possible pattern. I found four from the Far East that were suspect. Of greater importance, these were all received since the last communication with Tuna King. These signals were reported as very weak and uncorroborated and could not be fixed by GPS satellite. However, if we assume they all came from the same source, it narrows down the potential areas of probability to somewhere near Japan. I got lucky when I noticed that two of these very short transmissions were received by three different stations at different times. By entering the locations of the receiving stations and using the time lags between transmission receipts—along with a big leap of faith—the computer was able to estimate four high probability areas of transmission. One of these was over the island of Honshu, one in the middle of the Kuril Island chain, and two in the Sea of Japan. These two SOJ AOPs are the best guess of the source of the emergency transmissions at the times noted. They were both on 243.0."

"I thought P-3 life rafts were equipped with HF emergency beacons, the PRT-5 or something?" Bella says as a question.

"Depends on which rafts might have made it out. The smaller rafts have UHF transceivers on them. Or maybe the PRT-5 doesn't work and only the UHF radios are," McWalters says, displaying her recent homework on how a P-3 is equipped.

Adams has kept his focus on the screen since he arrived, and now he presses his finger against it and asks, "Where is this third point from?"

"I didn't put a lot of credence in just two spurious points, General, but when I got an update about an hour ago it had a solid hit with latitude and longitude on it. And as you can tell, it matches perfectly. Now look at this point," she says as she types in a request to the computer. On the screen appears a small square labeled Tuna King with a time. "Here is Tuna King's last reported position. It falls in general alignment with the other points. They all form nearly a strait line and the times run consecutively from north to south."

There is silence. Then Bella speaks, "So Major, you believe that they were shot down right off the coast of North Korea, just north of the DMZ?"

"Possibly, sir, if the signals came from individual survival vest radios. But my theory is that these signals came from a life raft. I don't know if a P-3 that was shot down could get a raft in the water."

Adams asks, "So you think they ditched?"

McWalters takes a deep breath and says exactly what she feels, not caring how senior the officers are she is addressing, "I've worked over twenty-four straight hours on what happened to Tuna King. This is the best lead I have had on solving the mystery. I based it on the premise that they did ditch and got into rafts. I checked the currents along the North Korea coast, and from this scant evidence, I believe that the crew of Tuna King is, by now, on the beach of North Korea." She reaches toward the screen, points and says, "Right here."

Bella and Adams study the computer screen where she is pointing. Adams finally speaks, "Norm, I think the major is correct. Now the question is: what do we do about it?"

"Major, print out a copy of that screen. Gus, it looks like we're gonna start by waking the SECDEF," says Bella.

McWalters takes a large copy of the screen off the X-Y plotter and gives it to Bella. He rolls it up, turns to leave, then stops and faces McWalters. He speaks in his low, fatherly tone, "Major, you've done good work on this. I'm glad you were on it. I'm glad you didn't give up."

Later, that comment will mean a lot to McWalters, but now she is so tired her response reveals much about her very core, "I couldn't give up, sir. Tuna King was in my area."

Once they are out the door, Bella turns to Adams and says, "First thing tomorrow morning, please be in my office and bring Ron, Frank and that major who found that White House memo. I will get you guys up to speed on the situation."

"0700?"

"Make it 0600."

* * * * *

Jones is truly spent from his swim in the sea, but right now his only focus is to achieve a good foot hold for his right flight boot. His left palm is firmly planted on Warbuck's butt which is located inches above the petty officer's head.

A voice from overhead yells to be heard over the sound of the pounding surf below, "Do you have a good purchase, Jones?"

Jones nods his head and keeps his chin down to prevent the salt water dripping from the TACCO's flight suit from running into his eyes. The voice of Keene continues from above, "Okay then, on the count of three. One. Two. Three—shove!"

Using all his remaining energy and strength, Jones pushes Warbuck higher. At the same time, Keene pulls on Warbuck's arms while Evans holds the pilot's waist to keep him from falling head first out of the cave. This last very tiring maneuver gets Warbuck's torso into the cave. Evans and Keene then pull his legs onto the rocky entrance and roll the wounded man onto his back. Warbuck nearly stops breathing but then gasps twice, coughs up a mouthful of blood and is able, finally, to fill his one good lung with air.

Jones rests from the strain of pushing the TACCO up the side of the cliff, and then slowly climbs the few remaining feet to join what is left of his crew. Upon seeing the great duress that Warbuck is suffering, Jones wonders to himself, for the first time, if the lieutenant might die before this is all over and then asks himself, "I wonder if we all might die?"

Evans is the first to recover from the climb and gets to his feet. He explores the cave. The entrance is wide enough that it lights the interior sufficiently. The first thing the admiral notices is that a few feet from the edge the surface becomes dry. He can't remember the last time he was dry. The depth of the cave is only twenty feet. The height goes down to four feet at the rear wall of the cave. But it has another benefit besides being dry. The floor plan of the cave approximates an hour glass, with the sides squeezing in about six feet each and then widening again towards the rear. The height of the cave above the water and the two small pockets in the back will provide cover to avoid being seen by passing search boats. The rocks and surf below will deter any investigation by soldiers. All in all, Evans decides, this is an excellent place to spend the night and a fine center of operations to decide the next steps.

* * * * *

It is early Wednesday morning in Washington D.C. At 0545, Colonel Milkus is standing in Admiral Bella's outer office absent mindedly clicking his heels. He missed his 0500 daily run and the heel clicking is how he is releasing pent up energy. He is slightly confused on why he was directed to be here so early. General Adams had only told him to report. Milkus assumes the topic will be about the White House memo, but in the Pentagon you learn not to be overly confident in what you know and definitely never in what you assume. At 0550 Carter enters the room. Immediately behind him is Major Winkle, the part-time White House social aide. Milkus notes that Carter, like himself, is decked out in a perfect Class A uniform while the major is in his office working uniform with no tie and short sleeves. Their presence confirms to the colonel what the subject of the meeting will be.

At 0555 General Adams strolls in and nods to the other three officers. He proceeds directly into Bella's office with only a perfunctory knock as he swings open the big wooden door.

Bella rises from his desk and motions for the officers to take seats around the conference table to his right. The admiral has his Service Dress Blue blouse off and his white shirt sleeves rolled up. He gives the impression that he has been at work for hours already. Once his visitors are seated, Bella rises from his desk and goes to the head of the conference table. He remains standing and says, "You must be Major Winkle." The major nods without smiling. His demeanor indicates that he fears he is there to receive both barrels of the admiral's displeasure.

"Hello, I'm Norm Bella," he continues, "And we here in this room have a very difficult situation." He pauses and returns to his desk to retrieve his coffee cup. He takes a sip and then sets it on the conference table. He paces while he talks, "I'm going to give it to you straight. About four years ago, some idiot thought that we could influence the CHICOM's virus research and development to ensure whatever they made, we had a defense for. So he came up with the bright idea to leak key details on how to make Gamma Three and the technology to mass produce it and deliver it over great distances. We all know this, but what you don't know is that the concept was approved by the President, but then put on indefinite hold. As dumb and as potentially treasonous as the act was, it was sanctioned in principle by our elected civilian leader. The President remains the same, but his staff is new this term. The new staff decided to take this proposal off the shelf and put it in action. So for the past year they have been helping our enemies develop weapons that can kill millions of Americans; a weapon we still do not have full defense against. Comments?"

It is quiet around the table. After a lengthy pause, Carter is the first to speak, "Not to be too cynical, Admiral, but helping the Chinese shorten their R and D just happens to guarantee certain DOD contractors funding with a lot of money for a long time."

"Damn right," Bella answers bluntly.

Internally, Milkus has moved beyond the financial and is wrestling with the moral question of what is the right thing to do in this situation. He asks, "What is the plan? What are our options?"

"Gus," Bella turns to the general, "What are your thoughts on plans and options?"

"Well," Adams says and then stops while he reaches into his breast pocket and pulls out a new pack of Juicy Fruit gum. He carefully unwraps the top and slides two sticks out. With practiced care he places the gum into his mouth, and then motions with the pack towards the others. They all shake their heads. He resumes his comment, "I can see two considerations here. First, should the White House be free from consequences for aiding and abetting our enemy? Second, all options are dependent upon one thing, and that is if the Chinese know we have Black Jewel and its deployment status. And right now that question can be boiled down to whether they have Frederick Evans?"

* * * * *

The rain has returned and it goes from a drizzle to pouring instantly. It is typical Korean weather for this time of year. The sailors move Warbuck to the rear of the cave. All four remove their LPAs, which surprisingly they have worn since the crash. The vests have become a natural part of their wardrobe and it wasn't until Jones unzipped his that the officers noticed they were still wearing them. Keene uses his to create a pillow for Warbuck and then takes a small plastic bottle from his vest and throws it to Jones. The plane commander motions to Jones to go to the front and fill it from the small fresh water streams pouring off the side of the cliff. Jones takes a similar bottle from his vest, gives an understanding nod and then goes to the cave entrance to get the water.

Evans pulls the top of his flight suit down and ties the arms around his waist. It is nearing dusk and the temperature is already starting to drop from the mid-sixties. But Evans removes his t-shirt and wrings water from it. As he does this, he gives direction to Keene, "Commander, pull his boots off and lets see if we can get his socks dry." Keene nods and starts to unlace Warbuck's flight boots. Evans then addresses the TACCO, "Lieutenant, what are you wearing under your flight suit?"

"T-shirt and jeans," he whispers in reply.

"Okay, I know it is going to hurt, but let's get that flight suit off and see if we can get it dry, too. If we can, then we'll swap it out with your bingo gear and see if we can get that dry."

Jones returns with the water. Evans asks him, "Did you re-hydrate yet?"

Jones nods. He had drunk his fill while retrieving the water. Jones hands his shipmates the bottles and takes a seat in the opposite rear enclave and starts to undress.

Evans drinks heartily from one bottle while Keene helps Warbuck sip from the other. Warbuck is unable to drink much and waves Keene's hand away. Keene sits back and empties the bottle. Once he has finished drinking, Evans throws the bottle over to Jones and motions for Keene to do like wise. Evans says, "Better refill while the rain is still heavy." Jones is stripped down to his boxer shorts and shivering in the cold. But he just grits his teeth and does as he is directed.

Evans continues to give orders, "Commander, help me get another inventory of what we have here." The admiral empties the compartments of the LPAs into one pile. There is not much to help in evading capture on land. Sea dye markers, whistles, pencil flares, smoke markers, signal mirrors, survival knives, compasses, shroud cutters, and wet matches. Seeing the matches, Keene reaches into the left arm pocket of his flight suit and pulls his non-issue little steel and flint kit. He had gotten it from his oldest son as a birthday gift after Peter had learned about campfire starting techniques in the cub scouts. Keene carries it more as a reminder of how precious fatherhood is than as a practical item. Now he is very grateful for the memento. He fingers it and squints his eyes as if trying to remember something.

Evans notices what he is doing and asks, "You bothered by something?"

"Just remembering home, sir."

"Good. You need to, Commander. You want to go home? You want to put this all in the past?"

The admiral's tone is harsh and upsets the plane commander. Keene feels angry pride well up inside and shifts his glare to Evans's eyes. Evans got the response he wanted. Now in the same harsh voice he hits the younger officer right in the gut with his next question, "Are you going to stop moping around and feeling sorry for yourself and your crew and start focusing on how we're getting through this thing?"

Keene opens his mouth to answer but stops when he realizes that the first word he was about to say was "but". He shuts his lips and nods, maintaining eye contact with the admiral.

Evans continues, "You've been in a shell since we made the rafts. Time to stop looking back. What is done, is done. You got a family, right?"

Keene nods.

"You love them?"

Keene nods again. This was the last place he ever expected to get a butt chewing from an admiral. But he knows he has it coming.

"Well," Evans says, his tone growing softer now, "I have a wife I love, and what I'm going to do is to get back. We're all going to get back. Whatever it takes. We get home. Now start thinking about how to do that and forget what happened before."

Jones returns with the filled water bottles. He can sense the tension between the two officers, so he takes his isolated seat and starts to wring out his flight suit.

Keene now speaks, "So how do we get home, Admiral?"

Evans now addresses all three men, "I believe, gentlemen, that our position is similar to escaped prisoners of war. We are in a hostile country that will kill us if we are captured and we can expect no help from anyone else."

Warbuck gasps for breath and in a muffled voice says, "Oh boy, SERE school for real..."

"Exactly," Evans responds to the unexpected comment from a very hurting sailor. "It is beginning to look like all those tax dollars spent to send us through Deep Water Survival and POW training schools is about to pay off. Let's have one thing clear. We now know what we are up against in the North Koreans. We made a mistake a few hours ago when we naively believed they were a civilized society."

Jones is shivering and angry. He had forced the thoughts of his shipmates being dead from his consciousness, but the admiral's comments bring the pain of their loss to the surface again. He shakes his head and mumbles just loud enough for all to hear, "You made the mistake."

The admiral is in no mood for any feelings or energy to be wasted on anything not directly related to getting home. He blows by the petty officer's bitterness, saying, "Yeah, I did. And I give no guarantee that I won't make more in the future. But be clear about one thing. From here on out we will do whatever it takes to get home. And, gentlemen, we will get home. Believe it."

There is a silence as the admiral's strong words sink deeply into the sailor's belief system. Keene is the first to speak, "Aye, aye, sir. We're all on board now. But what did you mean we can't expect any help? Don't you think Washington will pressure the North Koreans to get us back?"

"I don't think Washington has any clout with the North Koreans. Besides, as far as the public or the administration is concerned, I'm sure we were reported simply as lost at sea. No, shipmates, to get out of this we're going to have to do it by ourselves."

Warbuck joins the conversation again. And again he coughs up blood as he hisses a comment, "Talk about deep kimchi."

Jones provides a one work exclamation to the terse observation, "Exactly."

* * * * *

It is just after 7 AM in Mountain View, California. Quite early for a pastoral visit. Yet Joyce is pleased that Pastor Tom Paine of the Central Nazarene Church is ringing the door bell. He had said he would stop by before his meeting with the district superintendent. Joyce invites the pastor to take a seat at the dining table. Paine agrees to a cup of instant decaf coffee and he stirs it as he waits for Joyce to start the conversation. Listening is a skill he has finely honed during his twenty years of ministry.

She takes a deep breath and starts, "Thank you for coming, pastor. The neighbors have been visiting and very supportive, but we all refuse to consider the possibility that Jim might never return, but that thought has been weighing so heavily on my mind that I must talk about it before I collapse under it."

"Have you heard any more since you called me?" asks the minister.

"No. The plane is missing and that is all we know. Pastor, I am just so confident that he is alive I have trouble even imagining him not coming home this time. What scares me is that I know my confidence is based on nothing more than my emotions, while my brain tells me that he is probably already dead. Sooner or later reality will over take my hopes and I'm afraid I will fall so hard it will break me. It'll just destroy me."

Paine is very slow to answer. He wants to choose just the right words. He is a man who thinks twice and speaks once. He sips his coffee. It is rotten. Then he holds her eyes in his and asks, "Would you rather be mourning him before you know he is dead?"

Tears start to form in Joyce's eyes, but she is able to keep them from falling and answers, "I don't know. I just seem to be denying the whole situation. I'm, well, I'm just lost. I don't know what to feel. I mean, if he were dead I'd know how to feel. If he were hurt or safe, I'd know what to feel, but this. . .this uncertainty is so...so cruel...so confusing."

Paine has insight into the make-up of each of his congregation and he shows it, saying, "It is especially tough

171

for you, Joyce. You have always prided yourself in knowing how to act the perfect Navy wife."

Fourteen year-old Peter has come down stairs to get his lunch bag for school from the refrigerator. He stops in the hallway when he hears voices. He hears his mother respond to the pastor, "I am a good Navy wife! But what does a good Navy wife do when the Navy takes her husband?"

Peter hears his mother sob. The tears and cries come pouring out of her. The pastor reaches across the table and places one hand on her shoulder. Paine knows this is why he is there. She needs this release to keep going. But Peter has never seen his mother cry before. It scares him. Really scares him. He wants to step out of the hallway and go to her, but he doesn't. He is frozen where he is. When he feels the tears start to run down his own cheeks, he quietly retreats to the kitchen, frightened by his mother's emotions.

Pastor Paine now throws a life ring to Joyce. He asks, "How long have I known you and Jim?"

"Three years, I guess," Joyce is able to mumble through her handkerchief. She is starting to compose herself again.

"Right," Paine says. "And in those three years, I have come to know Jim as a fine Christian gentleman. He is a talented aviator and excellent Sunday School teacher, but his greatest strength is his caring heart and love of the Lord. If he is alive, he is in the Lord's protection. If he is dead, he is in the Lord's arms. Is that what you wanted to hear me say, Joyce?"

She sniffles as she speaks, "Yes. Thank you, pastor." She pauses and there is a long silence. After mulling over the pastor's comments, Joyce exhales slowly and says, "Yes. Yes, I can release Jim now. I know he is all right as well as feel it; whatever has or will happen. But it still hurts to be in this situation."

"Hope is a good thing, Joyce. Be at peace with whatever the outcome, but hope for what you desire. You're a strong woman Joyce Keene, but you cannot reach out and pull Jim back. But we can hope. We can pray. We can be at peace."

Joyce loves the words and logic, but she cannot fight back more tears as she answers, "I will hope, pastor. I will trust. I will carry on because...because I can't think of anything else to do."

Peter retrieves his lunch from the refrigerator and then he quietly returns upstairs to his room to wait for the time to depart to catch the bus.

* * * * *

In the Korean cave Jones is fast asleep in his little enclave. He is so exhausted that he can sleep even while his body shakes from the cold. Across from him the Admiral is leaning against the rocks with his eyes shut and appears to be sleeping as well, but his mind is racing, searching for the correct next steps. The TACCO and PPC are near him, Keene very close to Warbuck to keep their conversation from waking their shipmates.

"Billy, it will be time to go in an hour or so. I'm anxious to get started. This doing nothing is driving me crazy. I want to get this over with. Whatever happens. Just get it done." Keene pauses before he turns his attention to his suffering shipmate, "Are you hungry, Billy?"

"Not really. I could use a Big Mac if you happen to come across a Mickey D's while you're out."

"Want fries with that?"

Evans opens his eyes, and Keene notices that he is awake.

"Admiral, how about you?" Keene says.

"Commander, make mine a nice Porterhouse steak, well done."

"Aye, aye, sir."

Evans closes his eyes again and lets a small smile come over his lips. Then he mumbles to himself, "Porterhouse steak...well done..." Then he chuckles. Twice.

* * * * *

Margie Evans lives in a nicely appointed condominium. It is filled with coordinated earth tones with just a splash of color from a selection of bright, fresh flowers scattered around the five rooms. It is a professional space lived in by two professionals. But today Margie is not a well trained professional. A substitute is teaching her class because today she is another Navy wife with a missing aviator husband. She is sitting on the suede, over-stuffed sofa looking intently at the picture album opened on her lap. Her fingers slowly glide over a restaurant menu, a souvenir she has pasted in this memory book. Tears roll down her cheeks, but she is smiling at the memory. Her sister, Ramona Barton enters the living room from the kitchen carrying two cups of tea. Ramona came immediately last night and has stayed. She had to be with her only sibling in her time of crisis. She is five years older than Margie and has always been there for her little sister, and they have grown even closer these last seven years since both live on the East coast and their parents are in California.

"What are you looking at, Margie?" Ramona asks as she sets the tea on the coffee table and takes a seat next to her sister.

Margie doesn't look up as she pours out her memories while caressing the old menu on her lap, "It's a scrapbook of my life with Frederick. Here is probably my most precious memory of our courtship. We met when I was in the Bahamas after I broke up with Tony. I was trying to forget him by eating myself into oblivion. I ordered the largest steak this restaurant could prepare. It was a sixteen-ounce Porterhouse. I hate my steak overcooked, but they brought me this petite steak that was nearly charred black. At the table behind me I heard a gentleman complain that his steak was too large and not cooked enough. I guess the waiter could not believe that I could eat a monster steak, so he had given this impressive looking man my steak, and I had gotten his overdone little Porterhouse. I will always remember turning around to see Frederick for the first time. He was not in uniform, but you could tell he was someone who commanded others. Oh Ramona, I was thirty-eight years old and he instantly made my heart flutter like I was in junior high school. These last seven years have been so precious. I cannot go back to eating alone, to sleeping alone, to being alone. How can I after he has made me whole?"

Ramona places her arm around Margie's shoulder and hands her the cup of tea. Margie takes it, sips, and then sets it back on the coffee table. She suddenly slams the scrapbook shut. She leaps to her feet and rushes to the coat closet near the front door.

Ramona asks, "What is it? What are you doing?"

"Here is your coat. Get your shoes on, Sis," Margie replies. "We're going on a little trip."

"Where to?"

Margie has her coat on and is searching under the coffee table for her shoes as she responds, "Savannah, I believe."

Ramona knows her sister well enough to understand that once she has her mind set, it is hopeless to resist. So Ramona rushes to the spare bedroom and returns with her shoes on and purse in hand. She finds Margie rummaging through papers at the desk in the corner.

"Yes, here it is. Evergreen Nursing Home," Margie says with satisfaction and resolve.

Ramona's confusion shows on her face when she asks, "Who is there?"

Margie answers as she helps Ramona on with her coat and they go through the door, "A little ninety-two year old lady who used to tell sea stories to a ten year old orphan to teach him there is hope in the world no matter how dark the skies. And, sister, right now I need some hope."

CHAPTER TEN

It is 2245 on Wednesday evening in Korea. It is a dark night. A low overcast completely blocks the stars and moon. The rain has stopped and the tide is in. Rolling waves crash onto the rocks below the cave entrance. The salt spray reaches as high as the cave. Keene, Jones and Evans stare at the surf pounding the rocks below.

"How long do you think it will take, Commander?" Evans asks above the noise of the surf.

Keene answers without taking his eyes off the heavy seas, "I figure about five hours, maybe six hours tops."

"I'll let you lead, sir," Jones says as he scans the cliff above the cave entrance.

Keen says, "Always happy to lead, Petty Officer Jones. Follow me."

Keene moves to the edge of the cliff at the right side of the cave entrance. It is only 15 feet to the top of the cliff but one error could result in a quick fall to the rocks below. There, if the rocks don't kill you, the heavy, rough surf will probably drown you. He locates a good hand hold and pulls himself up a foot where he locates a toe hold for his left foot. Keene reaches for another hand hold but the rock he grabs gives way and falls towards the water. Jones and Evans watch the rock fall into the angry ocean.

Keene is not an experienced climber. He has not done anything like this since he was a pre-teen and his family went to a state park. There he had climbed on a collection of large boulders, but it was a nice sunny day and the rocks were dry. On that day, as he started his climb, he fell off those boulders twice before a more experienced climber nearby gave him one piece of advice, which at this moment is all Keene is thinking. "Keep your stomach and pelvis pressed against the surface. If your butt moves back it will take the rest of your body with it. Keep your weight centered over your feet and press against the rock." That was all the training Keene ever has received but he is putting it to great use right now. Slowly he moves upward. In five minutes he is half way to the top. He is exhausted. He rests. Now the rain starts again. As he looks up to his goal, rain fills his eyes.

He tells himself, "Another five feet and I will be able to reach the edge. Move it, Mr. Keene! Do you want to stay here and graduate or be another member of your wouse class that bilges out?" Keene recalls plebe year, the last time he felt his body start to fail him. The mile and a half run that summer at the Academy. He was put on the track just minutes after completing the obstacle course and although he tried to will his body to finish, he soon discovered he was on his knees with one lap to go. An upperclassman jumped in his face and taught him that you can always do more than you think your body can do. Midshipman Keene got back to his feet and finished the course. Lieutenant Commander Keene now lunges for the next hand hold. Using upper body strength he thought had previously left him, he ignores exhaustion and pulls himself to the next foot hold. Two more grabs and pulls and he reaches the top of the cliff. Keene collapses on his back and sucks air and rainwater into his lungs.

After five minutes he has recovered sufficiently to remove the three LPA harnesses he is wearing. He snaps them together to make a linked chain nearly twelve feet long. Keene locates a large rock that should work well to brace him and keep him from sliding over the cliff edge. He pushes his feet against the rock and then lowers the harness assembly to the cave opening. With a boost from the admiral, Jones is able to reach the lowest harness. Using it as a rope ladder he makes his way to the top of the cliff. His exertion has exhausted him as well. Both Keene and Jones lay spread eagle in the rain and gasp for air. It is ten minutes until they can sit up and take stock of their new surroundings.

Keene takes the LPA ladder and hides it beneath a nearby shrub. He scans the dark field and makes out the image of trees to the west and north. He cannot see anything towards the south.

Keene motions to Jones as he speaks, "Let's head inland. There must be people around here somewhere."

The two tired, wet sailors start to slowly trot in a crouched posture. They are not sure if there is any need to make themselves small, but their instinct causes them to present the smaller profile. After 100 yards they come across a single lane dirt road. The road has no traffic. Keene nods towards the south, and they move down the road in that direction. Soon a single light appears in the distance. Keene and Jones move towards the light, trying as they move to keep under cover in brush and shrubs that line both sides of the roadway. After a quarter mile, the lone light is abeam of the road to the west. Jones takes the lead as the duo leaves the road and heads across open fields to discover the source of the light.

Suddenly, Jones falls face first into shallow water as he steps over a small dirt mound. The noise of the splash is not very loud, but it sounds like a thunder clap to these covert explorers. Jones has landed in nine inches of water that cover a recently flooded rice field. He coughs and spits as he tries to clear his mouth and airway.

Keene had dropped to his belly when he heard the splash, and now he peers over the ridge surrounding the rice paddy and whispers, "Jones, you okay?"

"Yeah. Rotten rice field."

Keene crawls over the mound and enters the rice paddy. He motions for Jones to follow him as he half-crawls and half-swims across the field, heading toward the source of the light. After 75 yards, they reach the other side of the paddy. Both ease their heads high enough just to see over the surrounding dike. In front of them is a one room farmer's hut, sitting atop stilts five feet high. The light is coming from underneath a bamboo shade that only partially covers the one window in this hut. Keene and Jones can see erratic movement and shadows inside the hut. They are both wondering what their next step should be. Their mission on this expedition is to seek intelligence on how to best develop an escape plan, and find food if possible. But should they make contact with a local farmer?

As they ponder their options, a chained, sleeping dog under the home raises his head. The dog sniffs the air and immediately jumps to his feet. A loud, vicious bark now fills the still night air. Soon a half-dozen chickens are flapping their wings and clucking wildly. Keene and Jones duck their heads and then make eye contact with each other. No words or orders are necessary. Each turns and retreats on his belly as quickly and quietly as possible. The farmer and his family come out to the front porch to see what has alerted the animals. They squint into the darkness, their eyes sweeping the black horizon. Keene and Jones take deep breaths and submerge as best they can under the rice paddy water. The mother and children return to the house when nothing is seen. But the farmer remains on the porch, intent on finding out what is causing his animals to react. Slowly, Keene rolls over on his back and raises his head to where his face just barely breaks the water's surface. He tries his best to control his rapid breathing while maintaining the lowest possible profile.

Jones continues to hold his breath with his face and body buried in the rice paddy mud. He feels Keene's hand on his shoulder, pressing him down. Soon he must grab some air. He rocks his head back and gulps a partial breath once his mouth is level with the surface. Immediately he smoothly rocks his head forward and again submerges his face in the mud. He repeats this quiet and quick process every 40 seconds. Keene can see the farmer's reflection on the porch in his peripheral vision and keeps his hand on Jones to hold their position.

The Korean farmer stays on his porch. Something is out there, but he doesn't know what. After five minutes he begins to think his dog alerted on nothing. Dogs do that sometimes. The farmer yells at the dog to shut up and then enters his house. A minute later, the light goes out. The farmer and his family have gone to bed for the night.

Keene releases his pressure on Jones's back. He lightly taps his shoulder twice. Jones raises his head and gulps air. Keene rolls over and they both crawl to the far edge of the rice paddy. They scurry over the paddy dike and move under cover of nearby brush.

Keene whispers, "Well, based on our performance so far, I don't think there is any chance we will ever be confused with SEALS."

"Yeah," Jones responds as he wipes mud from his face. "I feel like a whore in Olongapo when the carriers are in port. A real popular attraction everyone wants to get."

Keene smiles at Jones' typical Navy humor that never fails to lighten any situation. He then turns his attention to their objectives of this expedition. They can't be accomplished sitting in these bushes.

"Let's try the road again. It's got to lead somewhere," Keene says as he gets to his feet.

* * * * *

Major Winkle knew he was in over his head when the stars and eagles gathered around the conference table. Following the meeting in Admiral Bella's office early this morning it was very easy for him to take the "advice" to forget the White House memo. The major has been able to pretend that the document never existed with ease and no pangs of conscience. He was sorry he found that paper from the time he picked it up. But the two Department of Navy O-

6s are having greater difficulty with the guidance received from Admiral Bella.

Ten minutes ago Carter poured himself a large cup of coffee from the pot located in Milkus's space, but now it sits on the desk just getting cold, untouched. Carter is starring off into space. His gut is turning. Something is wrong. He is thinking about what really is right and what is wrong. Milkus is lost in the same silence. These two professional officers have a highly developed sense of right and wrong. The gray area in their professional lives is very tiny. Even with D.C. duty, which has the tendency to paint many decisions in gray, this narrow band of indecision has remained small. But this course of action by the White House and their commander-in-chief falls right smack in the middle of the gray. They are not wrestling with whether the White House's decision was wise or not. It was a dumb decision from the start. No, they are wrestling with what is right and wrong. Did the civilians' cross the line from deceptive policy into treason?

Carter finally speaks, "Ron, this sucks. Truly, truly sucks. Damned if we do, damned if we don't."

Milkus is slightly annoyed that this Navy captain would interrupt his thoughts by stating the obvious. He snaps back, "What are our choices? Our choices? We need to decide the best option."

"I know one thing," Carter continues, "Adams is right about the whole affair currently hinging on Frederick's status. The way I see it is this, if he somehow comes back alive, then we have the option of leaving the treachery to the civilians and we go on with our careers. If he is never recovered, then we have another option."

Milkus finishes the thought, "We can blow the whistle on the treason. Whether it was intentional or not, I feel in my core it was treasonous."

"If you put it in those terms, then whatever Frederick's fate, we must blow the whistle."

"Yeah, but.."

"But will it do more harm now than good?" Carter ponders out loud.

* * * * *

Master Chief Strait is putting on a flight suit. He never desired to be aircrew. But he never lost a plane before either. He grabs his fore-and-aft cover and departs his office. Walking through Maintenance Control he nods at Chief Cressman and exits the busy office, striding across the hangar. He passes through the small individual door cut into the very large, heavy sliding hangar door. The light drizzle doesn't faze him. It's as if the rain wouldn't dare fall on the Maintenance Master Chief.

He reaches the ladder to QE-08 and climbs aboard the aircraft. As Strait opens the main cabin door, Crew Seven is assembling. Lieutenant Commander Bill Catrell, squadron Tactics Officer and Crew Seven Mission Commander has delayed the plane side brief waiting for the master chief. Now all are assembled and the flight can commence.

This flight schedule event is another desperate attempt to locate a raft or wreckage. Only this time there is a difference. The plane commander and the TACCO and the master chief know what is planned, but none of the remaining crew is aware. This mission will go directly to the last estimated position, ignoring the artificial boundaries that hindered the previous crews from searching the highest probability area. This time this crew will screw the rules and bust the PARPRO boundaries and give their missing shipmates the best chance possible at being found. It will be a short flight compared to the other searches. In just a couple hours QE-08 will drop below shore radar coverage and run towards North Korea conducting a swift ladder search. They will arrive shortly before dawn and rapidly patrol the high AOP and then run to sea before the sun is fully above the horizon. The master chief is along because he insisted. No officer had balls enough to tell him no.

* * * * *

The Korean coastal road curves back and forth to navigate through a small forest. Obviously it was easier for the engineers to curve the road than to take down the trees. It might have been easier, but it made for a road that limits the speed of vehicles to no more than thirty miles per hour. After fifteen minutes on the road, Jones and Keene have accustomed themselves to the environment and are almost strolling along, Keene leading a few feet ahead of Jones. In fact, Keene's head is bobbing again to a tune stuck in his mind. As usual, it is not a complete song or even a whole refrain. Keene keeps mentally replaying just one line from "Sweet Caroline" by Neil Diamond, "I look at the night and it don't seem so lonely." This current internal mantra makes him smile at the irony of his thoughts.

As he rounds another curve, Keene senses that the constant sound of the surf has grown louder. Then with his next step he fails to find the ground where it should be. His foot drops an extra three inches as the road starts down a very steep hill into the darkness. Suddenly, the tune in Keene's mind is replaced by confusion and panic. He tumbles to the gravely surface and rolls twice. He remains frozen, flat on his back as he takes stock of his body, checking to see if he injured anything seriously. Luckily he had let out a spontaneous, "Whoa!" as he fell. This alerted Jones to stop in his tracks.

"Commander, what is it? Where did you do?"

"I'm down here. Watch your step. The road takes a steep drop."

Jones slides his foot forward until he can ascertain the new terrain angle. Once he has his footing he moves to Keene's side.

"You hurt, sir?"

"Nothing serious. Just scraped my hands. Someday I would like to meet the idiot North Korean who built this unsat, piece of crap road. No wonder there has been no traffic on this road. Would you like to drive this maze at night?" Keene mumbles as he stands.

Even with their vision completely adjusted to the darkness, neither sailor can see anything ahead of them. They are straining to see any light or outline of trees or buildings or towers. But it is as black as a deep cave with no lights. Slowly they move down the steep road. Their concentration is focused on each step as they slide one foot forward and then another. It is extremely difficult to keep on the road.

Jones is worried. He felt comfortable as they weaved their way through the woods. If a vehicle came they had wonderful cover immediately available. Now on this down slope he has no idea what is on either side of the road. His thoughts are full of questions, "What if a car comes? Where can we jump to a safe hiding place? Damn! This just ain't right! Am I the only one with any brains? I wish the M.O. would show better sense than taking this risk."

After two hundred yards navigating by foot-feel in the pitch black, the steepness eases to nearly flat terrain. But it is still too dark to see beyond the next two feet. Suddenly there is a loud metallic "click" in front of them and to their left. The sailors instinctively leap to their right and hit the dirt. They hear a door open and then a light illuminates the dark just twenty yards ahead of them. A lantern, carried by a young boy exits a small front door of a rickety house. Now Keene and Jones can clearly see that they have walked into a small coastal village. It is a group of houses and a couple of businesses lining the road for about two hundred yards.

The boy comes through the door carrying the lantern high in one hand and a roll of toilet paper in the other. He leaves the porch and takes a path by the side of the house leading to the outhouse in the rear of the building.

While Keene observes the boy, Jones uses the temporary light to scan his surroundings. He is lying near the entrance to a small alley that runs between a storehouse and another home. As Keene lies prone in the dirt he wonders to himself why there are no dogs or other animals barking in the night. He then feels Jones tap his foot and when he looks back he sees Jones motion for them to take cover down the alley.

Once in the alley, Keene crouches near the street and watches to see if anyone else is moving about in the black night. Jones explores the alley. He comes across a locked door on the side of the storehouse. The padlock is very old and rusty. Jones gives it a tug and it opens easily. The door squeaks as Jones slowly pushes it open. It is a faint noise, but it sounds like a blaring marching band to these two sailors. Keene turns to see Jones disappear into the storehouse. The officer starts to follow him when he hears a rumble coming from the road in the direction of the steep hill. Keene returns to the alley entrance and sees the headlights of a truck flashing between the trees on the top of the hill. The truck is coming, slowly, towards the village. Keene feels exposed in his current position and falls back to near the storehouse side door. As he arrives, an excited Jones comes quickly through the door.

Jones whispers excitedly, "Commander! We've hit the jackpot! From what it feels like, this place is full of this knarly looking corn. I guess they must feed it to the hogs, which is fine by me 'cause I'm as hungry as a pig!"

Keene looks at his watch and covers it as he pushes the stem to light the face. Then he speaks, "See if you can find a bag or something to carry it in and let's load up quickly. We've got company coming down the road and soon these farmers will be up with the sunrise."

The commander feels his way back to the head of the alley to check on the progress of the truck. It has stopped at the top of the hill. The truck's headlights shine into the sky above the village. To his right, Keene sees the light returning along the pathway by the house down the street. He surmises that the boy must be finished and is going back to bed.

Just when the Americans need the dark night to cover their escape from the village, the low clouds drift out to sea and the half-moon and stars are exposed. This provides enough light for the sailors to navigate the alley better, but it also means they can be seen.

As Keene arrives back at the storeroom door, Jones is exiting with an old, beat-up wicker basket full of corn cobs. Keene takes one handle of the basket and motions towards the back of the alley. Jones sets down his side of the basket and carefully closes the storeroom door and replaces the lock. The duo starts down the alley, unconsciously moving in perfect military marching step. Left, right, left, right, with no verbal cadence needed. The back of the alley opens into a recently raked garden. Keene looks both ways and then starts to enter the garden. Jones pulls back on the basket handle to stop him.

"Mr. Keene, we walk across there and they will see our footprints and know we've been here."

Keene turns and nods. They reverse course and head back to the alley's street entrance. The hole in the clouds closes and the village goes totally dark again. The truck is still parked on the hill above, impersonating a lighthouse in the night. The sailors cross the street and now quickly move to the edge of town, the truck lights providing a new navigational reference to enable them to hurry. Jones thinks that it is counterintuitive to head towards the truck lights, but that is the way to his crew. He figures they will solve the problem of getting by the truck once they are closer.

Suddenly, the lights on the hill start to move, and they are coming down the road toward the escapees. Keene pulls his basket handle to the left to find cover by the road. Simultaneously, Jones pulls his handle to the right for the same purpose. His handle tears loose from the rickety old basket. The basket falls and the corn tumbles onto the road. Jones instinctively starts to pick up the corn.

Keene urgently whispers, "Leave it, Jones. There is cover over here." The officer turns and jumps into a deep irrigation ditch that parallels the road. Jones looks up the road towards the approaching truck. He knows the truck will be upon him in a few seconds, yet he grabs corn cobs and throws them into the ditch. The last four he gathers in his arms and takes two giant steps before he leaps into the cover of the ditch. The truck approaches and passes just a few seconds later. Both sailors have their faces pressed against the ditch wall trying to become one with the earth. They listen for the sounds of the truck stopping, but to their great relief it keeps rumbling along. Keene and Jones look at each other and exhale together. Keene then gives Jones a look of consternation.

"I'm a growing boy and need food. I was too hungry to leave any on the road," the petty officer whispers sheepishly.

The sailors refill the basket with the muddy corn and return to the road. Slowly they move up the hill until another hole in the cloud cover reveals the moon again and with the improved vision they are able to increase their speed to a slow trot. To the east the horizon is beginning to appear as a sliver of light, just a narrow orange line. In another half-hour it will be twilight. Keene looks at the horizon and then his watch. He figures if they keep their current pace they can reach the cave before it is fully light. Keene is tired and begins to doubt that he has enough strength to continue this pace all the way back to the cave. But he pushes those doubts from his thoughts and reverts to his plebe mode of meeting any test that he is given.

Near the top of the hill, Jones looks over his shoulder and his eyes grow large at what he sees. He blurts out, "Commander, we've got trouble."

Keene looks behind them and any doubts about his own stamina are removed as adrenalin jump-starts his energy level. Truck lights are moving through the village and approaching the climb up the hill. The search light mounted on top of its cab is sweeping from side to side. This truck is searching for something or someone. Keene and Jones go from a trot to a hard run. Their breathing is extremely heavy and their legs feel like stones, but they push themselves. A long two minutes later they have reached the top of the hill and good cover. Keene's lungs are on fire and he cannot draw enough breath to continue. He motions for Jones to move to the thick brush a few yards off the road. The truck headlights are at their heels as they dive under cover. Keene curls into a near fetal position to fit totally under a prickly bush. He is convinced that his breathing is so heavy and his heartbeat so loud that those in the truck can follow the sound to his hiding place. He tries to control his breathing, but he cannot. He continues to gasp for air, hold it for a second then exhale in a quick burst before he gasps another breath.

A few yards away, Jones is prone in high grass. Every muscle in his body is tense as he presses himself against the ground. His breathing is slow and deep. He is afraid, very afraid, but the fear is pushed deep within him and his mind is ultra sharp as he calmly controls his body. His thoughts are, "Where did we drop that basket? Is it in sight of the road? What is a search light doing on a truck out here? Should I move to better cover? Can I move without being seen? Is Keene hidden well enough from the sweep of the search light?"

His thoughts come to an end as he hears the truck's brakes squeal. He is tempted to raise his head to see what is happening, but this thought passes as he sees the beam from the search light sweep towards his location. Jones tries to get even lower against the earth and his breathing stops. He shuts his eyes as if that will make him harder to find. Now he swears he can feel the light beam pass over him, so he opens

189

his eyes but his eyelids are the only muscle moving in his body. A few seconds pass and another sweep. A minute passes but another sweep has not slid over him. He thinks, "Should I look to see what is going on? Or are they waiting for me to show myself? Could this be a trap? Who are these guys? Police? Military? A nosey commercial vehicle? Who are these guys?"

Keene can see the light pass through his hiding bush. He thinks that his muddy green flight suit should blend in with the foliage and since his back is towards them, his hands and face are hidden. He listens intently for any sounds of soldiers searching the bushes, but the only sounds are the idling truck engine and, in the distance, the ocean surf crashing ashore. He thinks, "So they are playing a waiting game, eh? First one to move loses. I hope Jones is well hidden and for once in his life, patient. But how long can we play this waiting game? It will be light soon and I have no idea how hidden this position might be in the daytime. Would it be better to chance movement now while we still have darkness to help conceal us? SERE school was good training, but no one can train for these decisions. Keene punctuates the end of his thinking with his 'word of the day.' Crap."

In the far distance a new noise is heard. It grows louder as it nears. Jones and Keene concentrate to make out the sound without looking. In a couple of minutes the source of the sound is known. It is another truck diesel engine. From Keene's position he can see to the north and through the trees he spies a set of headlights approaching.

CHAPTER ELEVEN

Admiral Evans sits at the cave entrance and watches the sun start to rise over the SOJ horizon. He looks at his watch, and then for the hundredth time leans over the edge and looks towards the top of the cliff. He shakes his head. It will be daylight in another 45 minutes. Where are those sailors? Then he rises, stretches, and turns to return to Warbuck's side.

The admiral speaks, "The sun is coming up. I hope they have found a good place to hide. I figure they will hole up during daylight, so I expect them tonight."

"You don't think they got caught, then?" Warbuck asks. This instigates a cough and with it great pain. He winces as his body absorbs another power punch to his ribs.

Evans shakes his head no. Then asks, "How you doing, Billy?"

"About the same, only I'm starting to get hungry now."

"Hunger is always a good sign that your body is starting to heal itself," the admiral comments. "I'm beginning to feel a little weak myself." The senior officer pauses and then tries to change the conversation to get their minds off of the hunger. "So, Billy, what kind of car do you drive back in California? You look like a 'vette man to me."

"Not hardly. Try a 1978 Volare."

Evans laughs as he says, "I don't believe it! No Naval Aviator drives a 1978 Volare!"

"Only those with bad divorce lawyers."

"She got it all, eh?"

"No, not all...I got the Volare." Both aviators chuckle. After a slight pause, Warbuck continues, "You know, the current conditions being what they are, it sort of puts the whole experience into perspective. I haven't let myself laugh about it too much before. Now, in the big panorama of life, it seems pretty small." Warbuck coughs and winces again, in great pain. This causes him to gripe, "Momma's black cats! I wish I would stop doing that. It hurts."

"Momma's black cats?" Evans responds. "I haven't heard that term since I was a boy in Georgia. You a good ol' boy, Lieutenant Warbuck?"

"Not really. My mother was from South Carolina and I guess you can say I was raised in the south...southern California that is. West Covina by L.A."

Evans is pleased that he is getting Warbuck to talk. He figures it might help the lieutenant keep his mind off the pain and help reduce the effects of shock that are still lingering. Evans asks, "Where'd you go to school?"

"Cal State Northridge."

"Major?"

"Mathematics."

Evans grins and asks, "Got a formula to get us out of this?"

Warbuck shakes his head and exhales in pain. Evans stands, looks towards the cave entrance and continues, "I'm not used to this sitting around and waiting. Now I wish I had gone." He pauses and this aggravation passes as he expresses it. The admiral turns to the lieutenant and resumes the conversation, "Why mathematics?"

Warbuck shakes his head as he responds, "My dad is a high school math teacher. I guess I did it to please him."

"Was he pleased with you going into the Navy after graduation?"

"Not really," Warbuck says. "He was in the Army during Korea and did not have a good experience, so he wasn't so hot on my decision to try the military."

"Well, when we get back, now you'll have that in common with him," Evans says with a sly smile. "You aren't having such a good experience in Korea either."

Suddenly the sound of a marine diesel echoes off the cave walls. Evans whips his head around and sees a bright search light beam sweep the inside of their hiding place. The admiral dives for cover behind the outcropping rocks. The beam of light retraces its steps back across the entire cave then moves off to the north. The sound of the boat grows faint. Evans eases his way to the front of the cave and peeks around the rocks to see the silhouette of a patrol boat cruising north, its search light illuminating the shore as it goes. Evans returns to Warbuck.

"That was a little too close," he says.

The navigator makes eye contact with Evans and asks, "Admiral, maybe they did get Jim and Jonesy. Maybe they talked and the Koreans are coming for us now."

"No," Evans replies as he breaks eye contact and shifts his focus to the cave entrance. "I think the Koreans must have just increased their patrols off the coast since they learned of our crash. If they knew where we were they would just come here directly and get us."

Warbuck lays his head back against his LPA pillow and sighs, "My momma's black cats. This sucks."

Evans whispers to himself, "It sure do, shipmate."

* * * * *

Crew Seven's third pilot has been displaced from his normal perch on the radar cabinet behind the pilot in the P-3 cockpit. Master Chief Strait had taken that vantage point at the start of the take-off roll, and no ensign would dare ask him to move. For the past two hours Strait has remained on his perch and scanned the sky the entire transit to the start of their search sector.

Having arrived at the commencement point of their unauthorized search, Lieutenant Commander Cantrell keys his intercom and broadcasts to the crew orders that are rarely heard on a patrol, "Crew, set five aft. I want everyone strapped-in. We are descending to two-hundred feet and increasing speed to the max. It is going to be very rough for the next hour, so get as comfortable as you can. Nav, TACCO, and aft observers be especially alert. Report anything, and I mean anything you see."

Cantrell, sitting in the right pilot seat, leans forward to see around the flight engineer to make eye contact with Strait. "Master Chief, find something to hold onto."

Strait nods and grasps the back of the pilot seat in front of him.

Cantrell now keys his intercom again, "TACCO, you know where I want to go. Give me a fly-to point on my screen. We will start a ladder search heading down-sun from there. Sensor Three, give me only two random radar sweeps per minute. Look for tiny surface targets and give me vectors to anything you find. Be sure that you have your ESM gear in your scan. Let me know if we are painted by anybody."

"Flight, TACCO. Here is your first point," the NFO in the tube says over the ICS as he uses his computer to pass target information to the cockpit display.

Cantrell now addresses those in the cockpit. "Flight engineer set ten-ten T.I.T. on all four." Then to the pilot he says, "Fred, push us over and establish two-hundred feet over the water. Take me to Fly-one."

The P-3 bucks and jumps as it races over the sea surface at nearly 300 knots. Cantrell shares his scan constantly between the radar altimeter, directional gyro, tactical display and a visual search of the ocean surface. The pilot's primary scan is the ocean surface with only frequent glances at his instruments to ensure the autopilot is maintaining altitude. The flight engineer primarily scans his engine, hydraulic and electrical system instruments because the squadron does not need to lose another bird and crew because they ignored safety of flight while being focused on the search. But the FE still manages to sweep the horizon every few seconds in the hopes of spotting Crew Eleven survivors.

Master Chief Strait is focused exclusively on the sea surface. He thinks to himself that it will be pure luck to stumble across something as small as a raft in this wide ocean. But he strains his eyes, squinting into the morning twilight while trying to will the outcome of this long-shot search.

* * * * *

Keene can feel his back muscles starting to cramp. His fetal position in the bush is not comfortable and he has held it without moving for nearly twenty minutes. During that time, the two North Korean army trucks have parked next to each other and shut down their engines. The search lights were turned off and Keene has been listening to the sounds of men in casual conversation. The pilot could smell cheap cigarette smoke as the slight off-shore breeze blew it to his hiding place.

About fifteen minutes after the trucks shut off their engines, Jones surprised himself by falling asleep. Now his head jerked as he snapped to consciousness. It took a couple of seconds for him to remember his predicament. This elicited panicked thoughts, "It is nearly light now. How long was I asleep? Was I snoring? Where's Commander Keene?" Feeling he must get some answers to his questions, Jones decides to lift his head until his vision just clears the tops of the high grass. In less than two seconds he determines the situation and drops his head back under cover. Jones immediately recognized an enlisted man's smoke and meal break. He had counted six soldiers in drab uniforms lounging in a circle. In the center of the group was a two and a half gallon can of some sort of prepared food. He figures that these patrols probably meet here every morning to share breakfast and a smoke. Jones now wonders how long this break normally lasts.

Just then he hears the unmistakable voice of authority bark out orders. A chief's or top sergeant's voice sounds the same in any navy or army. Jones does not need to understand the language to know what was being said. As he hugs the ground, Jones can hear the men gripe playfully, the sound of rifles being slung over shoulders, the can being kicked to the side of the road, the truck engines firing up and soldiers saying so long to the other crew. Soon it is totally quiet. The Koreans have resumed their patrols.

Keene rolls out from under his brush and tries to straighten his body. It hurts. Spasms shoot up his back and down his thighs. His toes are numb. Eventually he is able to sit up and take stock of their location now that it is lighter. As he scans the area, Keene is relieved to see Jones's head appear above the grass. They make eye contact and share a smile of relief. Keene tries to get to his feet but falls back to earth. His body still is not ready to cooperate. Jones sees this and moves quickly to Keene.

Things look much differently to the escaping sailors in the early morning light. The bushes are not nearly as thick and covering as they appeared in the dark. The scrub brush between the trees is insufficient to hide in. Keene cocks his head as he listens to sounds of civilization. Jones stands in an effort to ascertain where the sounds are emanating. Keene gently tugs on Jones flight suit leg for him to lower his profile.

Jones drops to a knee and softly says, "I think it is coming from that way." He points to the south toward the village.

The commander and the sensor operator move quickly to the edge of the tree line that runs along the cliff overlooking the village. Both commando crawl through the high grass to come upon a surprising view. Spread out before them in the morning light is the quiet village, perched on the edge of the shore. Surrounding the eight buildings clustered along the dirt road are neat farm fields, each only about an acre in size.

A couple of rice paddies are flooded but no shoots have sprouted through the surface of the water. Other fields have the residue of a very recent harvest of small corn stocks and potato plant tops. At the southern end of the building row is a community water hand pump centered in a slightly wider portion of the only road; apparently a space that serves the purpose of being a town square.

But the startling discovery this view gives the sailors is what lay just beyond the town square. The road comes to an end at a large chain link gate. Beside the gate is a small one-man guard house. Large, old wooden signs are wired to the fence. These are obviously warnings not to enter. A less than alert guard sits on a stool in front of the security shack, his rifle slung over his shoulder in a careless manner. Behind the fence are two long, clapboard buildings painted white with poorly built red tile roofs that are in need of significant repair. The large patrol truck from the night before is parked between the two buildings.

The Japanese Sea crashes against a man-made breakwater that juts from the very tip of the small peninsula on which the village is situated. Within the small harbor created by the breakwater and peninsula is a pier that is fifty yards long. What Keene and Jones see tied to the pier makes their hearts race. On one side, a fast, 40-foot Korean patrol boat is tied to the pier. Opposite the military craft is a tiny fleet of small fishing boats equipped with single masts. Around the breakwater a second patrol boat is motoring to land on the military side of the pier.

The American servicemen watch as a crew of three leaves the farther building and hustles to the pier. Two of them catch mooring lines tossed by the Korean seamen on the boat. The third soldier stands by a small boarding gangway. The patrol boat docks. A crew of four enlisted and two officers disembarks and wearily walk down the pier to the barracks. What obviously is the senior officer stops and turns to get one more view of the boat. He pulls a long drag on a cigarette as he observes that his boat is properly secured.

Keene's vision moves from the docking patrol boat to two farmers heading towards the warehouse the Americans had visited the night before. He points to the farmers as he says, "Look there, Petty Officer Jones. I think our little midnight raid is about to be discovered."

Jones looks at Keene. "What do we do now?"

"The way I figure it," Keene responds, "We have two bad choices. We can try to find a hiding place until dark. But if those farmers report the break in to the soldiers they might come searching for us. Or we can try to get back to the cave in daylight, which means we could be caught by any passing Korean."

Jones does not hesitate in his answer, "I say we put as much distance as we can between us and that army post. My daddy always said a moving target is harder to hit."

"I agree. Or as John Paul Jones said, 'He who does not risk, cannot win.' Let's move out." Keene actually thinks in these terms, the result of four years at Annapolis where such models were planted deeply in his core mentality.

Jones crawls away from the cliff edge then stands and runs to where the corn basket had been spilled in the dark. Keene takes one last look then follows. Jones scoops up his precious corn once again. He sees the empty food can the Koreans had left after breakfast and grabs it as well. Keene takes a basket handle from Jones and the two scoot across the country side, heading north, their treasure carried between them.

* * * * *

Crew Seven in QE-08 has rattled most every crew member's teeth loose for the past forty-five minutes. So far, search results at the projected Crew Eleven crash site have yielded nothing but empty ocean. They are searching down-sun and down-wind as they close the North Korean coast. Visibility is hampered by low clouds that paint the water surface and windshield with a constant drizzle. Ahead of the searching P-3 is a very dark cloud with a heavy downpour blanketing the ocean for a mile each side of the plane's track. Cantrell gives direction to the pilot with the controls, "Fred, take us up to 300 feet while we punch through this stuff."

"Will do," Fred responds as he squeezes the autopilot button under his left forefinger half way to release the altitude hold function. In a matter of seconds the aircraft is stabilized at the minimum allowed altitude of 300 feet for instrument and night conditions.

As soon as Fred re-engages the altitude hold on the autopilot a loud and excited voice erupts over the ICS, "We've been lit up! ESM contact on an air search radar!"

"Where away?" Cantrell instinctively asks the Sensor Three operator. The use of old school terminology to ask the direction of the radar signal is a conditioned response. None on the crew think it salty or antiquated. Rather, it is just natural.

"Dead on the nose!"

Cantrell now gives quick, authoritative orders to his copilot and flight engineer. "Fred, I've got the aircraft," he says as he puts his right hand on the yoke and left hand on his four power levers. The copilot raises his hands from the controls to indicate that the switch of pilots is complete. "Flight engineer, set maximum military power on all four." The FE slides the pilot's power levers forward until 1049 degrees is read on all four Turbine Inlet Temperature gages. Cantrell continues his orders, "Copilot, I am descending to two hundred feet. Back me up and take the controls if I go below one hundred-fifty." Cantrell turns 180 degrees to his right to put the ESM bearing and the radar directly behind him. He wants to increase the distance between him and the shore as rapidly as possible.

As Cantrell establishes 200 feet altitude above the water, he breaks out of the rain shower and hears what he was hoping for, "Flight, Sensor Three, ESM is quiet again."

* * * * *

Margie and her sister had taken turns driving down Interstate 95 throughout the short fall day. Now as they maneuver through Savannah, Margie is driving because her sister has always been the better navigator.

"It should be your third right ahead," Barton says as she examines the map. Both women are extremely tired and not really sure why they feel driven to complete this undertaking. Margie has had second and third thoughts for the entire nine hour drive. As she turns into the Evergreen Nursing Home parking lot her nerve is almost completely gone.

Being after 7 P.M., the parking lot is nearly empty. They notice the grounds are very well kept. It is a tidy and pleasant place. Beige buildings with dark brown trim; large windows every few feet along the exterior walls.

They enter through the double glass doors. They stop just inside the door and both of them look down to admire the plush carpet. It is a light purple, but it seems to match the off-white walls which are covered in an odd mixture of impressionistic and primitive American copies set in oversized gold frames. Not knowing what to do next, Margie is relieved to see a man dressed in a cheap suit moving quickly towards them.

"Hello. I am Bryan Dillwilliger, the home administrator," he says with a deep southern accent as he extends his hand to Barton and then to Margie. "You are Margie Evans?" Margie nods and Dillwilliger continues, "Then you must be her sister?" He doesn't wait for Barton to respond. "After you called this morning we prepared her for your visit."

Margie smiles, but it is obviously forced, and says, "I know this is really short notice and I apologize for the late hour. When I called it seemed like a good idea, but now I am not so sure."

"On the contrary," Dillwilliger responds as he gently takes Margie by the elbow and leads her down the hall with Barton falling behind and trailing them. "It is nice of you to visit the admiral's great aunt while he is overseas. They are very close, but..." His voice fades as he opens a gray hallway fire door.

"But what, Mr. Dillwilliger?" Barton asks, her curiosity peaked by the incomplete thought.

After a long pause, the administrator replies, "Honestly, in my opinion, the admiral is frightened stiff about her passing. He wants to be in control, and he just can't control her dying. She is doing that without his permission."

Margie stops in her tracks. Extreme fatigue and stress have made this usually composed, confident woman into a shell shocked home-front soldier. She is living with fear that she has never known before. She has trouble forming a sentence, but she is finally able to have words rush out of her mouth, "I didn't know she was dying! Maybe I shouldn't have come! Maybe it isn't the right time to introduce myself? Frederick has kept her a separate part of his life and maybe I should respect that."

Dillwilliger ignores Margie's protestations as he guides her elbow just a few more feet forward. They are now standing before a door marked with the name "Mrs. Sartis."

The administrator says, "Mrs. Evans, you've driven hundreds of miles to get this far. You should go the last two feet. Mrs. Sartis is a tough old lady. You won't cause her any harm. As a matter of fact, maybe she will show you her tattoos!"

Dillwilliger presses the door open and steps back. Barton steps back with him. Margie turns to Barton and they make eye contact. Margie has confusion in her eyes, but

Barton is confident and nods for her little sister to enter the room. Margie shuts her eyes and steps forward. Two steps later the door swings closed behind her.

There is a hospital bed in the corner, but the rest of the room has been made as homey as possible. A brightly flowered upholstered recliner is set in front of a small color television. Fake red flowers are in a plastic vase on the night table by the bed. To the right is a door that is open to a small bathroom equipped with handicapped hand holds and an elevated toilet.

Sartis is reading a large print book, sitting in the recliner with her back to Margie, who is standing silently. After a long fifteen seconds, Sartis raises her head and speaks without turning, "Hello?"

"Hello." Margie's voice cracks due to a suddenly dry mouth and throat. "I'm Frederick's wife and I've come to visit you."

Sartis waves her hand, indicating that Margie should sit in the straight backed chair near the television. "Sit down, Margie."

"You know my name!" Margie blurts out without filtering her surprise.

"Yeah, they told me this morning you were coming. And I remember Freddie talking of you a couple of times. I'm sure he must've said more, but sometimes, well, sometimes I'm not with it these days. Where is Freddie?"

Margie knew this question would be asked, but she has not been able to decide the best answer to give. Should she tell this old, sickly lady that her favorite nephew was missing? She still has doubts as words start to cross her lips, "Eh,..he didn't, I mean couldn't come this time. He is overseas. Assigned to Japan now. He will be back soon I hope." Margie regretted the last two words as soon as she heard herself utter them.

Sartis takes off her reading glasses and looks into Margie's eyes. Sartis hold's her stare even when Margie looks away. The old aunt is quite composed and serious as she says, "Margie, he will come back to you. He will."

Margie can feel the tears welling up in her eyes and she does not want Sartis to see her emotions. She replies with her best controlled voice, "Of course he will. He's been gone before."

"I know he is in trouble right now or you wouldn't be here. But I'm glad you came. Freddie was always an active child, always wanted to do his best so everyone would be proud of him. He'll do his best now too. And he will come back to you."

Margie can feel the burn of a single tear slide down her cheek. She has returned her focus to Sartis and is now lost in the elder lady's eyes; those strong, wise, determined eyes. Margie can feel some of the strength in this old woman, a true survivor, filling her. Margie is beginning to find it very easy to talk with Sartis and she replies, "After his parents died, it was only you two when he was growing up. He always wanted to make you proud."

"There was always more than just the two of us, really. He carried around with him his dreams. Dreams of his mother holding him as he drifted off to sleep, of his daddy coming home and bragging about a B on Freddie's report card. Dreams of his great uncle showing him how to swagger like a sailor. These dreams of his were his best friends when he lived with me. They sustained him. Made him strong. And now, wherever he might be, you are there in his dreams. He is being strong through thoughts of you. Now you be strong for him."

"I will. He is everything to me."

The conversation stops. After a long pause Sartis leans her head back and when she brings it forward, all seriousness is gone and now a twinkle is in her eyes. She is full of vinegar and mischief. She almost snarls the beginning of her reply, "You say he is 'everything' to you. I'll tell you what he is, he is a sailor! I know. I was married to a hard drinking, harlot chasing, sea crossing, land-lubber hating sailor! That sailor of mine could do things for a woman that the wives of the high-hats would pay big money to get a taste of! Why that sailor of mine could out drink, out punch, out belch and out run any soldier, airman, or member of the law enforcement community! Did I ever tell you about the time when we was on our honeymoon and my Tom gets the idea that we should celebrate by getting matching tattoos? Well let me tell you, getting a tattoo can really hurt, especially where he wanted me to get it. Now mind you back then tattoos were rather risqué and..."

Margie listens to Sartis's continuing sea-story but she is thinking, "This is where Frederick gets his strength and now I am drawing a bucket from that well too."

* * * * *

The rain is intermittent, but it is enough to make the ground slippery. But the two evading sailors stay to the forest in hopes they can be less conspicuous. None of what they see looks familiar. Everything looks differently in the daylight. After many false starts and delays, they finally reach the sea cliffs above, they hope, the cave. They search for something familiar.

"Over here, sir!" Jones says loudly. "Here are the LPAs."

Keene ceases his search twenty yards farther south and hustles towards Jones' position.

"Cover!" Jones nearly shouts as he dives into the high grass behind a boulder. Keene immediately drops to the dirt, but there is no cover to hide his location. A few hundred feet off the beach a North Korean patrol boat approaches from the north. Keene and Jones have been dashing from tree to bush and diving to the ground every few yards for the past couple of hours as they made their way back to the sea cliff above the cave. So far, they have escaped detection, but this is the first time Keene has been caught in the open. He holds his breath while he mentally berates himself for getting caught in this position. His hope right now is that the upward sight angle from the boat is too steep for binoculars to make out his form. The pilot listens for the sound of the diesel to close his position. Seconds seem an eternity, but the noise remains at the same level and then, eventually, it fades to the south.

Jones peeks from around the boulder. All is clear. He untangles the LPA ladder as Keene moves to his side.

"You first," says Keene.

Jones nods then stuffs his many pockets and the front of his flight suit with corn. What he can't fit, he hands to Keene who fills his pockets. Jones squeezes the discarded food can between his ankles and slides over the edge, holding the end of the LPA ladder with both hands. Keene lowers the ladder, Jones weight putting a strain on his weakened strength. In just a few seconds Jones feels one hand grab the can and another his ankle. He feels his legs being guided until he touches solid rock and then Evans quickly pulls him into the cave.

"Welcome home, petty officer," Evans says. "Did you bring my Porterhouse?"

"Missed the steak, Admiral, but we brought the trimmings."

Keene yells down to his shipmates, "Pull the ladder in. I got another way down."

Evans grabs the LPA ladder and pulls it in when Keene drops his end. Keene turns to his stomach and pushes his legs over the cliff edge. In daylight he has found a route down the cliff face that offers multiple foot and hand holds. He climbs down the route until he is even with the cave, about five feet to the right of it. Evans motions for Jones to grab his left hand while the admiral reaches his right hand towards Keene. Keene grabs the helping hand and shifts his weight to move closer to the cave. Suddenly, the rain starts. It is coming down in a local down pour. Keene's right foot slides off the now slippery rock he was using to support his weight. He falls towards the rocks below, but Evans's hold is strong and he swings the commander to a hard landing at the cave entrance.

"Welcome back, Jim," Evans says through a relieved smile. "Didn't expect you until tonight."

"It is very hostile out there. No place to be if you can make it to this plush apartment."

The three sailors move to the back of the cave. Keene and Jones empty the corn from their pockets. Evans' eyes widen as he views the loot. He grabs one of the cobs and starts to bite it.

"Please, Admiral, I'm a little better cumshaw artist than that," Jones says as he pulls more corn from his flight suit. After all of the corn is removed he keeps drawing surprises from his pockets and pants legs. Keene is astonished to see Jones produce small wooden branches, twigs and even two foot-long tree limbs the thickness of a man's arm. He hadn't noticed the petty officer gathering it.

Keene asks, "Where did you get the wood?"

"You should know us enlisted men are quite sneaky, Commander. The thought of hot corn on the cob was just too powerful to pass up."

"That's quite impressive Petty Officer Jones," Evans says. "But if you can pull some butter and salt out of those pockets I will personally see to it that you are promoted to chief when we return!"

Jones reaches in a couple of pockets as if searching for something, then says, "Just my luck. They must've fallen out on the way back." The spirits of the survivors are high with the prospect of getting a hot meal.

Jones stacks the wood into a fire pile and takes the can to the cave entrance. He fills it with water dripping off the rocks and washes the tin. Then he fills it half way with fresh water. As he is busy doing this, Keene pulls Evans to the side for a private chat.

"Admiral, Billy doesn't look too good."

"Yeah, it was a rough night for him. Getting some food into him should help. It should help us all get a little strength back."

Keene's next words draw the admiral's full attention, "I saw what we needed at a small village where we got the corn. It is about two miles south and in a small inlet. There are fishing boats there. We can get out to sea on one of them."

Evans and Keene look at Warbuck. Evans speaks, "Two miles, eh? That could be tough."

"It is even tougher," Keene says. "The fishing boats are on one side of the dock. North Korean gunboats moor on the other side."

Evans exhales as he says, "I guess nothing good ever comes easy."

CHAPTER TWELVE

Major McWalters is glad she wore her flats to work this evening. It has made it much easier to quickly hustle down the miles and miles of Pentagon corridors. And tonight she feels like she has covered all of those miles. If she had worn her heels with her uniform the massive amount of walking she has done in a short time would have taken a toll on her tender arches.

In the past half-hour she has been to the Air Force side of the Pentagon and back to JCS three times. She has a large manila envelope under her arm as she passes through JCS security. She hurries to the NMCC briefing room. Senior officers are waiting for what she has retrieved.

Sitting at the head of the conference table is Secretary Verbel. To his right, leaning in to whisper to SECDEF is Bordon. Admiral Bella and General Adams have taken seats spaced separately from the two civilians.

McWalters is not a very good poker player. She always shows her feelings in her facial expression. Her professional demeanor tightens when she sees that SECDEF is in attendance at this briefing. When her eyes move to Bordon tenseness in her jaw is visible. She unconsciously moves to stand next to the Air Force general as she removes the contents of the large envelope and slides them across the table towards Verbel.

"Here are the satellite photos, sir. They were taken shortly after dawn in Korea; about two hours ago. Here are the enhancement shots of the two figures on the cliffs above the beach." McWalters moves to point to a large map of North Korea now posted on the wall, and continues, "Their location is five miles north of Kuum-Ni, the largest city on

208

that part of the coast. That places them eight miles north of the DMZ. These photos appear to show two men wearing flight suits heading north, away from the DMZ."

The four men closely study the photographs. Bella is the first to speak, "Julie, what is that they are carrying between them?"

"It looks like some sort of container, but we are not sure just what it is," McWalters answers, forgetting to add a "sir" to her comment because Bella is able to put her at ease.

Adams asks, "Are these the only photos that show these men?"

"There are no sightings of the men on subsequent satellite passes," McWalters answers. She answers confidently, having anticipated their questions. "These photos were possible because of a momentary break in the cloud cover. We are not sure why they are heading away from the DMZ."

Adams continues to study the enlargements with a small plastic magnifying glass he carries in his breast pocket for just such intelligence presented at these briefings. Then he asks, "Are we sure they are even our men?"

Julie McWalters takes a deep breath and silently exhales before she shares her personal opinion of the situation with these highest ranking members of the military establishment. Her voice steady and as emotionless as possible, she says, "It is a high probability that they are crew members of Tuna King. Their location is within the hypothecated area. They appear to be wearing flight suits." She points to the biggest enlargement with her mechanical pencil. "Especially this one on the left. There, you can see the outline of the pocket on his left calve as he steps forward."

"Maybe you can, major. It is not so clear to me," Adams says without looking up from his magnifying glass.

SECDEF now speaks. Verbel's question is directed to all in the room, "How can we be sure they are not just some

Korean sportsmen out digging for clams in the early morning?"

All the military members in the room cringe a little at the SECDEF asking such a naive question. Does he really think that there are any "sportsmen" in North Korea? There is a long pause before anyone speaks.

Bella breaks the silence and rather than address the SECDEF he looks at Bordon who has been strangely quiet up until now, "There is only way I know to find out, but I am not sure you at the White House want to hear how to do that."

Before Bordon can respond, Verbel blurts out, "Are you suggesting some sort of armed incursion on the sovereign territory of another country?"

Bella does not blink and maintains his stare at Bordon who remains looking at the photographs. Bella says, "Yesterday I ordered assets to move into position in case they might be needed. We could insert a SEAL team onto that beach after dark local time and recon the situation. If there are survivors we will bring them out. If these are pictures of fishermen, then we will know that too. There is only one way to get the truth. We must put men on the ground."

"But what if the team is detected?" Bordon responds as his head jerks up and his eyes lock with Bella's. "Or worse yet, they get caught? We can't afford to acknowledge Tuna King's presence by any men being taken alive. These are very grave risks for the President based on some fuzzy photographs and conjecture."

Bella has an answer, "I told you that you wouldn't like it. It is tough decision time for the Commander-in-Chief. Do we take a political and diplomatic risk to support men who have taken flesh and blood risks for their country?"

Bordon has caught the blatant sarcastic tone of the Admiral's comments and it makes him angry. He shoots back, "It is a little more risk than a possible drop in the polls, Admiral. If we get caught with our hands in the North

Korean cookie jar, the upcoming Chinese summit could fail to happen."

The room is beginning to grow smaller and hotter as Bella stands to reply, "Oh, yeah, that's right. We're close to negotiating opening more markets for our corporations. Gee, let's see, I guess the Chinese should be viewed as one billion potential new customers for McDonalds's burgers or Chevy Impalas. We wouldn't want to jeopardize those big campaign contributions with mid-term elections next year. Let's not risk that for the sake of saving the necks of aviators who risk their lives daily for their country. Let's see, how much is the potential contribution we put at risk by showing some balls?"

"Screw you, Bella," Bordon forces out through clenched teeth.

"No, I want to know. How much is a service member's life worth? A half million? Oh, I do hope it is at least a million, at least enough to cover the tax dollars spent to train a naval aviator. It costs more than a million dollars to make—."

Verbel interrupts, "That's enough, admiral."

But Bella is full of steam and it is full speed ahead. He continues, "Or maybe we can hire a South Korean mercenary to sneak in there and put bullets in any survivors' heads. That would clean up the mess real nice, plus save all those Black Jewel dollars, wouldn't it, Mr. Bordon?"

"Enough!" SECDEF shouts. Bella maintains his eye lock on Bordon and sits down. There is a long, tense silence. McWalters gives thought to advancing the discussion, but being, by far, the most junior person in the room, she correctly put that urge out of her mind.

Finally, Adams breaks the silence, "So what is the recommendation to the President?"

Bordon immediately responds, "I know what I will recommend."

It is silent again as Verbel re-examines the photographs very carefully. Then he tosses them on the table and sighs. He nods with resignation towards Bordon. At this, Admiral Bella snaps to his feet, shoving his chair to the rear and storms out.

* * * * *

It is 8:30 P.M. on Wednesday night, thirty hours since Joyce Keene was told she might be a widow. Since then she is running on instinct. She follows her nine-year old blonde-haired, blue-eyed daughter up the stairs to the child's bedroom. A mature nine-year old, Meredith ponders much in her developing mind. She can tell her mother is under great strain. Joyce is working hard to present a front of confidence and casual continuity to her younger children, but it is very shallow and her true anxiety shows through more often than she can control.

Joyce and Meredith know their respective parts in the bedtime ritual. Meredith reaches her bedroom and falls to her knees at the bedside. Joyce lowers herself next to her daughter. She listens to Meredith say her children's bedtime prayer. But Joyce did not hear anything the child said after, "Please bless daddy." Her mind was filled with a panic prayer of her own, "Yes, please dear God, send a legion of angels to protect and support Jim. Please bring him back to us. Please spare Meredith the pain of his loss. Spare me, Jesus, spare me, please, oh Lord, please."

Once her prayers are complete, Meredith moves to the next standard line that is repeated nightly during their bedtime routine, "Can I read a little before you turn out the light?"

"What are you reading tonight?"

"Another Baby Sitting Adventure," Meredith says as her mother pulls the covers back. Meredith climbs under the sheets and rests against the headboard as she adjusts her glasses with one hand and grabs a paperback book with the other.

"Okay," Joyce says as she tucks her only daughter in. "But try not to fall asleep with your glasses on tonight."

Meredith nods and there is a long silence as Joyce, still on her knees, pauses by the bedside and watches her innocent child start to escape into the fiction of her book. Joyce wants to escape too. Joyce wants to assure Meredith that her daddy will be back as scheduled. Almost without the ability to stop herself, Joyce kisses Meredith on the forehead as she rises and says, "I love you so much, darling."

Without her eyes leaving the page, Meredith smiles and says, "I love you too, Mommy."

Joyce turns to see little Sammy sleeping in the other bed. She envies him his peaceful sleep. He is so innocent and so full of tomorrow's bright potential when she can only see dark clouds and storms ahead.

Next she goes to Peter's room, knocks and then enters. He is at his desk, his back to the door, bent over his homework. He glances over his shoulder to acknowledge his mother, and then returns to his studies.

"Peter, how are you doing?"

His eyes remain on his work as he answers, "Fine, I guess."

"Got a lot of homework?" Joyce asks trying to avoid the true subject.

"Not really," Peter says as he turns his head to see her. "This report isn't due until next Friday."

The silence that follows is very heavy. Joyce wants to talk to her oldest son about her doubts and feelings but she hesitates because it just doesn't seem right to burden him. She starts to back out of the door, and Peter returns to his work. But then Joyce stops and blurts out, "Peter, can I ask you a question?"

Peter shrugs in reply.

She continues, "Do you still think Dad is alive?"

Peter stops his work, but keeps his back to his mother. He does not know how to answer such a tough question. Ever since he heard of his father's situation, he has been relatively successful in blocking it from his thoughts. Now his mother has made him focus on it directly. He responds like all teenagers. He says what he hopes his mother wants to hear, "Yeah, I guess so." Then he adds what he wants to know, "Do you?"

These two words give Joyce the chance to unload what she has been pondering non-stop since the day before, the day her life changed, "Honestly, yesterday I thought he probably wasn't. Then last night I began to wonder if perhaps he might still be alive somehow. Tonight, I truly believe he is alive. I don't know why. I just feel it, deep down. I just somehow know it."

Peter turns to face her. He has a confused expression on his face. It is obvious that he doesn't understand what his mother is feeling and saying. He struggles to find a comment that would fit the discussion, but all he can say is "Oh,. ..okay.."

Joyce sees his confusion and tries to better explain her premonition. "Remember last summer when your team was playing for the district soccer championship and I was sure you were going to win it all? And you did? Well, this feeling I have is even stronger than that, but..." Her voice trails into silence.

"But what?"

"But I'm still scared. What if I am wrong?" Without wanting to, Joyce starts to sob. Peter is extremely uncomfortable and unsure what to do. Finally, he stands and goes to her. He hugs his mother and whispers into her ear, "You're not wrong. Dad will come back."

As Peter reassures his mother he lifts his eyes to the bookcase behind her. There his vision rests on a picture taken last summer of his dad helping him raise the soccer championship trophy.

* * * * *

Jones is struggling with his survival knife as he uses its point as a toothpick. The corn is stuck in a large food trap between his molars.

"Look out, Jonesy," Keene says playfully. "You might slit your throat!"

Jones shakes his head and continues to try to clean his teeth. The ashes of a small fire and bare corn cobs litter the cave floor as each of the survivors has eaten his fill and now is reclining against the cave sides.

Keene continues, "I would hate to see you unable to take advantage of a new career opportunity. When we get back I am personally going to write a recommendation to the Chief of Naval Personnel that you be sent to the finest culinary institute in the nation. I have never tasted such exquisitely prepared hog slop in my entire life. You missed your calling. You could be one of the all-time greatest chefs."

Evans joins the scuttlebutt session, "And it will be my pleasure to favorably endorse the recommendation. Bravo Zulu, Petty Officer Jones. Well done indeed."

Warbuck holds his water bottle above his head as if examining it in the light and adds, "Yes, I think his choice of this clear, non-bubbly wine was the perfect accompaniment to the light vegetable taste of the entrée."

Jones takes the knife blade from his mouth and shakes his head at the good natured ribbing he is getting from all three officers. He hides a smile as he returns the knife to its sheath.

Keene turns from facing Jones to talk to his good friend, "I see a little food has put you back into good spirits, Mr. Warbuck."

"Yes, Mr. Keene, I am feeling a little less poorly."

"Billy," Keene says, "You think you're up to a little two-mile stroll come evening?"

Warbuck's smile disappears as he contemplates the pain that will accompany the efforts. He makes eye contact with his personal mentor and friend and nods slowly and says, "Do I really have a choice?"

Evans answers him, "Not if you want to get home."

"Honestly, Admiral," Warbuck says with exhausted eyes, "I'm not so sure home has that much attraction. But I do know I want to get out of here powerfully bad."

Jones now joins the conversation, "So what's the plan? What're we gonna do to get out of here?"

"What we need is back in that village," Keene responds. "If we can get one of those fishing boats and sneak out to sea, maybe we can get far enough out into the SOJ before the North Koreans come gunning for us."

"Nice idea, Boss," Jones says as he strokes the stubble on his face. "But how are we gonna do that?"

Keene surprises the senior petty officer with his response, "I've been thinking on that. So far nothing has quite clicked for me yet. You got any ideas?"

"Don't you think those gunboats will have a little to say about us going fishing?" Jones asks.

The admiral now adds his thoughts to the discussion, "You're right Petty Officer Jones. Maybe we shouldn't try to get to sea in a fishing boat. I mean, if we're going to steal a boat, maybe we should steal a fast boat."

Jones, Keene and Warbuck all exchange glances of incredibility. It takes a moment for the admiral's suggestion to sink in.

Jones, as usual, is the first to question his superior, "Admiral, are you suggesting we steal a gunboat? That's nuts!"

Keene adds, "Sir, I'm inclined to agree with Petty Officer Jones. Are you really suggesting we go after a gunboat armed with just survival knives?"

"Logically, I can see two compelling reasons to consider it," Evans explains in a flat, calm voice. "First, if we take a fishing boat we can expect the North Koreans to uncover our theft and come after us. We are going to be chased no matter what we steal. At least in a gunboat we should expect to match the speed of our pursuers."

Evans pauses to let the logic sink in with his sailors. Keene breaks the silence, "What's the second reason?"

The admiral smiles as he says, "It is bold. It is unexpected. It is daring. It is what Stephen Decatur would do to surprise and confuse the enemy."

Warbuck has an air of disbelief in his voice when he asks, "So, you're saying we should steal a gunboat because it is our heritage?"

"Yeah, I guess I am," Evans says with a sheepish grin.

Jones, Keene and Warbuck look at the admiral and each other, all of their mouths open in disbelief. These dumbfounded looks are soon replaced by smiles.

Warbuck sums it up for everyone, "Cool."

* * * * *

Lieutenant Commander Cantrell has been mulling over what he can expect when he lands back at Misawa. He's sure he will lose his PPC papers for busting the PARPRO boundaries. He expects that the North Koreans probably reported the ESM hit via channels and the skipper and wing personnel will be there to pull his papers when Crew Seven lands. He just hopes they don't pull his wings, because he figures his shot at being promoted to commander is now out the window, but he hopes to at least stay in a flying billet until he is forced to retire at twenty years.

The conversation in the cockpit has been minimal and solely business related for the entire flight home. The approach and landing are routine. As the lineman directs the aircraft into its parking spot, Master Chief Strait remains sitting silently on the radar cabinet.

After the engines are shut down and the checklist is complete, it is silent in the cockpit. As they slide out of their seats and exit the cockpit, the copilot and FE squeeze by the master chief who remains on the radar cabinet. Cantrell makes eye-contact with the Maintenance Master Chief as he climbs over the FE seat to leave. Strait reaches out his hand and stops the mission commander.

"Commander Cantrell, you did good, sir. We had to try and save our shipmates. We had to."

Cantrell nods in reply. The master chief's words make a great difference in his thoughts, "Yeah, he's right. We had to. No matter what the career cost."

Cantrell feels better as he climbs down the aircraft ladder to face the music for doing something he does not regret. To his pleasant surprise he is not met by the C.O. or anyone else higher in the chain of command. Yeoman First Class Mazurak is the only welcoming party at the foot of the ladder. Cantrell figures he has a message from the head-shed to report for his flogging in the afternoon. But when he reaches the sailor, Mazurak stands erect and reaches out his right hand and speaks as he shakes the commander's hand, "Thank you, sir." Then Mazurak turns and walks towards the barracks. Cantrell smiles, pauses, then proceeds to the hangar and Maintenance Control to complete the flight paperwork.

* * * * *

Jones slept well. He had been tired. Now it is late afternoon and he is anxious for the night to fall. The temporary euphoria that came with a full stomach and solid sleep has vanished. Now he just wants to go home. He looks at the three sleeping officers on "their" side of the cave and for the first time it hits him that he is the only enlisted crew member still alive. He thinks, "It figures that way. The officers always get the breaks. Always."

He stands to get his blood moving after hours of sleeping on solid rock. He checks his flight suit hanging on a rock. It is still damp, but not soaked like before. But he figures his boots won't be dry for another three weeks. He wishes he had worn more than boxers and a tee shirt under his bag for this flight. He promises to himself that he will never make that mistake again.

He leans against the cave wall and the cool stone causes a shiver down his back. As he pulls away he hears a small pebble fall to the cave floor. He bends over and examines the small rocks that lie near the cave walls. They are softer than he had previously noted. Jones reaches for his survival knife. He pulls it from its sheath and starts to poke at the cave wall with the tip. At last, something to do to pass the time.

CHAPTER THIRTEEN

Warbuck can barely breathe. It feels as if a 100-pound boulder has taken residence on his chest. The climb from the cave to the top of the cliff was torture. Even with the help of his three shipmates pulling and pushing him to the top, he became totally exhausted by the exertion. All four were temporarily spent when the climb was done, but Warbuck's breathing difficulties have yet to subside. It took nearly an hour for the band to travel a single mile towards their destination. They were paralleling the dirt road and trying to make headway through the brush. Keene took the lead, while the admiral and Jones each supported an arm of the TACCO. Warbuck barely managed two steps for every three of his shipmates'. They were carrying him more than he was advancing on his own efforts.

They had seen a truck pass them about twenty minutes previously. This had necessitated taking cover to avoid detection. The sailors remained in hiding for nearly a quarter-hour to gather their strength before pressing on. Now, after just a few minutes they are in need of yet another spell. Warbuck is not alone in needing this rest. The four sailors are sprawled out in a depression at the center of solid shrubbery.

Evans rises to one elbow from his reclined position and gets Keene's attention. "How often do those trucks come by?"

"Every twenty to thirty minutes."

Warbuck lifts his head at the sound of Keene's voice. The sight of Warbuck's tortured and gaunt face in the shadows of the moon light startles his friend and leader. Evans can see Keene's shock.

"Commander, then there should be a truck along anytime now. Let's just rest until it passes. We all need it. I know I do."

With the decision to take a long rest, Jones moves to Warbuck's side. He builds a bump in the dirt as a pillow for Warbuck. The TACCO smiles in appreciation. Jones whispers to him, "Looks like we can get a good spell for now, Lieutenant."

Evans asks, "How much farther to the village?"

Jones looks to Keene who then responds, "Maybe another mile, I guess?"

Jones nods.

Fifteen minutes later all are feeling stronger. Suddenly Jones jumps to his knees and looks north. He is the first to hear the rumble of a patrol truck approaching.

The slow moving truck seems to take forever to reach them, its searchlight sweeping each side of the road. The survivors stop breathing when the truck stops and the light beam hesitates above their heads. Slowly the truck and its light start to move on towards the south.

"Admiral," Keene says, "We should be good for the next twenty minutes or so. If we take to the road we can make better time and maybe make the village before the next patrol."

Evans looks at Warbuck and says, "I don't know about you young studs, but this rest was too short for me." He looks at his watch and continues, "Let's wait here until the next patrol passes, then we can use the road."

Jones thinks to himself, "Okay, so maybe this admiral is one of those who actually thinks about his men." Then he says aloud, "I may be a stud, Admiral, but I can use the rest too if we have the time."

"We have the time, sailor. It shouldn't be daylight for another couple of hours," Evans responds.

All four survivors lay on their backs and rest. Five minutes into their quiet time they all feel the earth vibrate.

Jones flips to his stomach and crawls to where he can see the road. Coming from the south is another truck. He speaks, "Good decision, Admiral. Here comes another truck. If we had moved out, we would have been caught in the open."

Warbuck remains on his back, staring into the black sky while concentrating on controlling his breathing. He works to keep his gasps quiet. The other two officers crawl next to Jones's position where they have a view of the road as well. They see the truck approaching and when it is fifty-yards away they lower their heads to avoid detection. But rather than the truck continuing north on patrol, the sailors hear brakes squeal. Fear boils to the surface of their thoughts, "How did they find us? What can we do? How can we run with Warbuck? Gotta move! Gotta do something! Now!" But each of them, without realizing it, instinctively reverts to their previous evasion training. All keep still. No one raises his head to see what is happening. That was drilled into them at SERE school. Movement draws attention. Freeze and there is a good chance no one is looking at you. Move and all eyes will turn towards the movement. Each expects to hear the sound of boots moving through the brush as soldiers approach his location. But the only sounds are those of truck doors opening and closing, followed by the noise of a tailgate slamming as it is dropped. Then the tinny sound of Korean music being played on a cheap portable radio is heard. Jones turns his head and makes eye contact with Keene. Both smile. Both know what is happening, again. Evans sees his shipmates smile and his face registers confusion.

"Coffee break," Jones whispers to Evans. The admiral nods and smiles in relief as well. Keene points to himself and then makes the sign with two fingers that he will take a peek. Evans nods. Keene raises his head and surveys the truck party resting on the side of the road. He sees three soldiers huddled around a lantern set on the ground in back of the truck. Each is squatting with their butt just a couple of inches above the Earth, and each is holding a cup in both hands. One of the Koreans is telling a story and his buddies are totally enthralled with the tale. Keene quickly lowers his head and nods towards the admiral and petty officer. Evans and Jones raise their heads and take in the situation.

Evans then crawls where his face is by Warbuck's ear. He motions for the other two to join them. All four heads are within a foot of each other when they start their tactical conference.

Evans speaks in a quiet voice, "Gentlemen, there's transportation over there. Are you up to taking it from the owners?"

Jones and Keene exchange nods over the top of Warbuck's chest. Jones responds, "Lead on, Admiral."

"The truck crew is skylarking and not expecting to be surprised," Evans says as he pulls his survival knife from his left calf pocket.

"Are we going to have to kill someone?" Keene asks a fleet sailor's question. Unless you're a SEAL, in the Navy you deliver death and destruction from a distance; from ship-to-ship via large guns, air-to-ground in aviation, or from a hidden submarine. Seeing an enemy's face when you take his life is what Marines and soldiers do. It is not something a fleet sailor has ever been trained to do.

Evans is not thinking about killing. He is thinking about solving the current problem. His answer is more analytical than emotional, "We just might. I hope not, but we're going home. Whatever it takes. We are going home."

Warbuck surprises his shipmates when he joins the conversation, "I've never killed anyone, but just stand me near where you need the job done and I will oblige. They've got it coming after what they did to Bobby."

The other three survivors are a little taken aback by the intensity of Warbuck's belligerence. The admiral responds, "Billy, you wait here. We will get the truck."

"Yeah, whatever it takes," Jones adds.

Jones and Evans crawl to where they can observe the truck crew. Keene remains behind to tell Warbuck, "Don't you go anywhere, killer. We'll be back in a little bit to get you."

"Just don't get yourself killed. This crater is not deep enough to be my grave."

Keene smiles at Warbuck and searches for his survival knife. He pulls it from its sheath and places it in his mouth as if he was a pirate. Warbuck smiles, and then waves his hand for his friend to get lost. Keene crawls to the admiral's side and asks, "What's the plan, sir?"

"Petty Officer Jones, you circle around to the left," Evans says in his standard order-giving voice, "Commander, you go to the right. I will give you each five minutes to get in position. I will then walk into the camp to draw their attention. Once I am within striking distance, you guys fall upon them simultaneously. "

Jones and Keene like the strength in the leader's voice, even if they are under-whelmed by the sophistication of his plan. But they are good sailors and can carry out orders. Together they automatically respond, "Aye aye, sir."

All three men check their watches. Jones departs first, with Keene leaving immediately after. As Jones lightly steps through the trees he keeps his eyes glued on the three Koreans passing the time around the lantern. Suddenly he trips over a fallen branch. He hits the dirt with a thud, his head barely missing a soft-ball sized rock protruding from the forest floor. Jones freezes and listens. The Korean conversation continues without interruption. The petty officer places his hand on the rock as he rises. His fingers remain fixed to the stone and he moves to his assigned position now armed with a caveman's original weapon.

Keene's stomach is turning. He is nervous and hesitant about what he has been ordered to accomplish. He has no desire to break the sixth commandment. For the first time in his career, his chosen profession has come directly into conflict with his Christian faith. As all men of conscience before him, he is conflicted about what his duty requires and his personal beliefs. And as nearly all of the men who have faced this dilemma have done, he pushes his personal beliefs far, far away. He focuses solely on his assigned mission. He thinks, "God help me. I will think about what happens only after it happens." He reaches a good attack position and covers his watch as he presses the stem to illuminate the face. He is there two minutes early.

For the next two minutes he refuses to think about morality or even home. He funnels all of his attention on where he expects to see the admiral appear. Once he sees the admiral make his attack move he will abandon all internal thought and plunge into the fight. What do they say in the TACAIR community? There are no points for second place? Winning is the only option. The next couple of minutes will define his life and he has very little time to prepare for it. He has one thought he repeats over and over in his mind, "Don't think, just do."

Admiral Evans checks his watch. It has been a little more than five minutes since his shipmates departed. He whispers to himself, "Here we go."

He rises and starts a slow, measured walk towards the three Koreans. He raises his arms over his head and moves forward. After closing to within fifteen yards, he notices that the Koreans are so intent on their discussion that his presence has not been detected. The admiral lowers his arms. He takes his knife from his pocket and slides it up his right flight suit sleeve. Quietly and steadily he advances towards the preoccupied enemy soldiers. He is only ten feet from the men when the sergeant looks up and is surprised by the American standing over the squatting Koreans. He yells and starts to un-sling his AK-47 from his shoulder as he quickly scrambles to his feet. Evans is overcome with adrenaline and takes one quick step then lunges over the backs of the other two Koreans and tackles the sergeant before the rifle can be made ready. The other two Koreans stand and struggle to get their weapons from behind their shoulders. Just as they reach their feet they become aware of a scream approaching from behind them. Jones is at full speed and smashes into the one on the left. The Korean careens off the other and all three men fall to the ground. Jones is on top of the nearest enemy. He raises his rock and smashes the skull of the Korean. The Korean doesn't move again, not even a quiver. The third Korean is struggling to regain his feet when he is struck on the head from behind. Keene has used the butt of his survival knife to hit the Korean right behind the left ear. The Asian falls to the dirt as if he had received a knock-out punch in the ring. He rises to his hands and knees and tries to regain his orientation. With one sweeping motion, the American snatches the AK-47 on the ground and points it at the Korean.

Jones rolls his victim over so that the Korean is facing the sky. Brains, bones and blood cover the rock, but Jones retains his death grip on his weapon. Seeing the condition of the Korean, he looks towards the fight going on between Evans and the Korean sergeant. Jones crawls the few feet to the two tussling enemies. The petty officer pulls the Korean off of the admiral. The Asian is on his back and under Jones, who raises his rock far above his head. But the American hesitates at the top of his swing. The Korean now realizes that the end has arrived. Quickly, the sergeant raises his hands over his face and waves, submitting to the American. Jones's blood is running too hot to stop his fighting passion. He arm comes down to slam the rock onto the enemy. At the last split-second he diverts his aim and smashes the rock next to the Korean's head so closely that it rips off the tip of his enemy's ear. The Korean is bleeding profusely from this wound but he is alive.

"Frisk them carefully!" Evans speaks the first words after the fight is over. Evans has found the sergeant's rifle and is pointing it at the bleeding Korean. Jones searches the sergeant and rolls him to his stomach, hands stretched to the side. Then the petty officer moves swiftly to the other living Korean and repeats the procedure. Jones hesitates, but then also searches the body of the enemy he killed.

Keene is standing over the Korean he had surprised. He is full of elation and relief until he looks over to the dead soldier. In the lantern flicker he can see the brains and blood oozing from the skull. His elation turns to sadness and a very queasy stomach. He looks back at this captive and keeps his vision on the living.

The admiral is still in his natural command mode and says, "Jones, go see if there is something in the truck we can use to tie up these guys." Jones does as he is ordered and returns with six straps off of three back packs. He goes right to work securely binding the captives.

Evans says, "Commander, help Jones tie those two to a tree back off of the road. Then drag the dead one someplace where he can't be seen."

Jones and Keene use the straps to tie the Koreans hands and feet. Keene looks in the bed of the truck and finds a headset with a long wire. He takes the wire and the sailors use it to tie the Koreans to a tree. Then Jones takes the coat off of the dead Korean and uses his knife to cut long strips from the side and sleeves. Keene and he use them to gag the Koreans.

Keene grabs one arm of the dead enemy. He forces himself not to think of this as a human being, but rather a burden that must be put out of sight. Jones grabs the dead man's other arm and they quickly hide the body.

While the Koreans are bound and hid, Admiral Evans searches the truck cab. The keys are still in the ignition. He attempts to start the truck but it fails to kick over. He tries again. Same result. The admiral slides from the truck cab and trots to Warbuck. The TACCO is relieved to see a friendly face.

"Okay, sailor, time for you to quit goldbricking and get in the fight. Let's go," the admiral says as he lifts Warbuck to his feet. It only takes a minute for the flag officer and injured junior officer to reach the truck. Having completed their task with the Koreans, Jones and Keene arrive in time to assist the admiral in lifting their hurt shipmate into the passenger side of the truck front seat. Evans runs to the driver's side and attempts once again to start the truck. Again, it cranks but does not start. Jones shuts the passenger side door and moves around to the admiral's side.

"Sir? Let me have a crack at that. I used to drive a school bus part-time and sometimes these diesels can be trouble to start," Jones says as he climbs onto the cab step. Evans slides to the middle of the bench seat and Jones gets behind the wheel. The petty officer adjusts a manual choke on the dash and pumps the accelerator three times. He turns the key and slowly depresses the gas pedal. The engine catches and struggles to life as Jones feeds the accelerator and closes the choke. The engine slowly works to a full roar. Big smiles grow on the three shipmates' faces.

Keene rushes to the rear of the truck and throws the AK-47s into the bed and climbs aboard as the truck moves forward. In the cab, Jones grinds the gears as he executes a three-point turn on the narrow dirt road. Soon he has the truck heading south towards the village. He drives with his left hand as he attempts to wipe the dead Korean's blood from his killing hand. Evans lifts the AK-47 from between the TACCO's legs. The admiral cycles the action and rests the butt of the weapon on his thigh.

Warbuck watches these warriors emotionally come down from the combat high that had filled their minds for the last ten minutes. It is in his sarcastic make-up to make a comment without thinking, "Well, that went well."

Jones and Evans recognize his sarcasm but are not appreciative of his humor under these circumstances. They frown.

* * * * *

The ocean sky is overcast near the beach. The sky is black; no stars, no moon, no human lights. The sea surface is relatively calm. The Sea of Japan is undisturbed; it is quiet and open. Until, out of the dark sea a periscope rises rapidly. There is only a very small feather of a wake. The submarine has bare steerage way on. The conning tower follows quickly, silently as the surfacing evolution rapidly transpires. Soon there is a blur of movement on deck as black-clad sailors inflate a commando raft under dim red floodlights. It is slipped over the side and tied to the sole stanchion erected on the nuclear submarine's topside. Four shadows climb into the raft and push off. They paddle with all their might, yet make minimal noise. They head due west, and do not turn around to see the large black ship fall back beneath the surface. In less than three minutes from when the periscope first broke the serenity of the ocean, the submarine has returned to its lair, swallowed by the security and comfort of submerged invincibility.

The SEALs work as a highly efficient unit. No effort is wasted on speech or indecision. After two-miles of constant rowing, they professionally guide their craft through the surf, using the sea's massive energy to place them perfectly on the beach. All four grab a corner of the raft and hustle to the rocks at the foot of the cliff across the narrow beach. The Lieutenant looks at his watch and holds up three fingers that he then folds into a fist. Then he points to the north and nods to the two sailors opposite him. That pair moves out, going up the beach. He then touches the petty officer next to him and moves at a fast trot to the south. The SEAL follows his leader, weapon held across his chest.

Soon the north pair reaches the path previously taken by Lieutenant McKay's band two days prior. They quickly climb to the top of the cliffs. Upon reaching the road that runs along the cliff the two special operatives grab night-vision goggles from their utility belts. They are pulling them on when a truck is heard approaching from the north. The SEALS hide themselves very effectively in the five-foot high grass. The truck passes, its search light off. Once it is clear, the sailors search the area for a direction to proceed using their night-vision goggles. By the pathway, one sees two spent shell casings. He grabs them and secures them in one of his leg pockets.

To the south, the Lieutenant and his companion have reached the rough surf crashing against the rocks at the foot of the survivors' cave. The officer climbs on the rocks in an attempt to continue beyond the point where the surf blocks the way south. He is able to reach a location where he has a view down the beach beyond the point. He puts on his night vision goggles and scans the empty beach to the south. He lifts his scan to the cliffs above him and spies the cave entrance.

The north team leader checks his watch. Their further search of the top of the cliff and road has uncovered an area of high grass that has been smashed down. They search the area and cut samples of the wide grass leaves. The leader believes the dark spots on the blades could be blood. He wraps his evidence in watertight bags. He checks his watch again and signals for his shipmate to head down the path to the beach. Their time is up.

To the south, the Lieutenant and petty officer crawl into the cave entrance. As are all SEALs, they are in terrific physical condition and being nourished and strong, the climb was easy for these warriors. Instinctively, they each take position against opposite cave walls at the opening. Both put their night-vision goggles on again and have their weapons in a ready position. They commence a search of the cave. As they proceed deeper into the cave the sound of crashing surf diminishes and the sounds of movement beyond the rocks ahead is heard. The petty officer raises his hand in a fist.

Both SEALs freeze. Their fingers slide inside the rifle trigger guard and slight pressure is applied. The Lieutenant steps forward and quickly moves beyond the rocks ahead. Immediately three frightened sea gulls flap their wings and escape the cave in a flurry. The SEALs jump, but maintain fire discipline as they hit the deck.

They examine what the seagulls had been eating. The SEALs kick around the residue left by the two-day stay of the Tuna King crew. Strewn around the remains of a small fire are bare corn cobs, an old can, unused sea dye markers and a Mae west life preserver. The Lieutenant checks his watch. It is time to move to the rendezvous with the other team element. Hopefully they have had better luck. As he turns to leave he notices something inscribed on the cave wall near the backside of one of the large boulders. At the base of the rock is a pile of small bits of sand stone, the result of a recent carving. Above the pile, at shoulder level are some markings. Even with night-vision goggles, the Lieutenant cannot read the message in the darkness. He removes his goggles and turns on his red-lens flashlight. He reads, "Crew Eleven was here. Gilroy sez hi."

The Lieutenant and petty officer are nearly sprinting to reach the raft rendezvous on time. There waiting for them are the other two seals. The Lieutenant grabs one side of the raft with one hand and checks his watch with the other. He looks at the north team leader and shakes his head. The SEAL replies to his officer with a similar shake of the head. The four move quickly and quietly towards the surf, the raft between them. There is no hesitation as they plunge into the cold water and penetrate the waves. Soon all four are straddling the raft sides and paddling in unison to make their pick-up on time.

Meeting a submarine in the open ocean is a tricky navigational problem, and a sub commanding officer will not put his vessel and entire crew at risk multiple times when inside the territorial waters of an unfriendly nation. The

Lieutenant knows this, but his superb training and confidence makes this remarkable evolution routine. The four SEALS make their pick-up precisely and without difficulty.

* * * * *

McWalters hurries down the Pentagon hallway. It is a true maze and very crowded at this time of day. After her years in the puzzle palace, Major McWalters is an expert at navigating the challenges very quickly. She arrives at the security entrance to the JCS spaces and gains easy entrance by showing her special identification badge. She repeats this process once more before arriving at the glass-enclosed briefing room. As she enters, Admiral Bella, General Adams, Assistant White House Counsel Bordon and Secretary Verbel are reading a printed message.

Adams turns to look at McWalters as she approaches the four men deep in thought. He updates her in one sentence, "Julie, the SEAL team has finished its job."

McWalters forces herself to ask the one question to which she fears the answer, "Any survivors?"

There is a pause before the general answers. McWalters is afraid the answer might be, "Not any more." She was not told, but she assumed that if there were survivors and they could not be safely evacuated, then the SEALs would terminate and bury any potential embarrassment for the nation. It pained her professionalism to think that such an order could or should be given. But she steels herself for such an answer.

Adams shakes his head as he responds, "None found. But they do report evidence of a small fire and G.I. issue survival items in a cave on the sea cliff just south of where your intel predicted."

"Oh, they found more than that, General," Bella joins the conversation. "They found proof that someone in Crew

Eleven survived. And that sailor kept their sense of humor about their situation."

"Admiral?" McWalters questions.

"Julie, they left their sarcastic message on the cave wall."

"What happened to them?" McWalters asks almost rhetorically. "Didn't the SEALs search for them?"

Bella responds, "No luck. They did find spent shell casings to the North which could indicate that they might be shot or captured. We just don't know."

"What do we do now?" McWalters says in a forceful voice. "We can't just write off the whole crew. Can we...sir?"

Adams and Bella shake their heads as they ponder the situation. Bordon now speaks, "We're open to any suggestions, Major."

McWalters pauses and measures her words. She is aware that what she is about to suggest can be a career ending moment if not handled correctly. For just a split-second she considers not responding and taking solace in the fact it is a decision way above her pay grade. Yet, her commitment to the air crew will not let her keep quiet. With her emotions in check, she speaks in a controlled monotone, "I still believe there are Tuna King survivors that are currently alive in North Korea. I do not know if they are hiding in the countryside or if they are prisoners of the North Koreans. But I do believe that some of that crew is alive. I suggest we notify our forces on the DMZ to be alert for any attempted crossings. We should concentrate all available resources on increased intelligence monitoring of the North Koreans. If they are prisoners we should expect a bump in traffic. But, sirs, we should do something. We should find someway to help these guys!"

The senior military and civilian officers look at each other. Major McWalters's words have vocalized what they were thinking. But solutions and next steps are tricky to identify. Adams is the first to respond, "The major has great faith. I'd like to believe that Admiral Evans and the crew are alive and well. But my faith isn't quite as strong as yours, Julie."

"Okay, let's get down to cases," the Secretary of Defense says as he is making up his mind on his next move. "The President over rode the NSC and me when he approved what could have been a one way mission if it had been necessary. We can't expect him to do more under the circumstances. I just don't think there is anything further we should do right now. Maybe something will develop soon, but we'll wait to react to that if it happens. We don't want to re-start the Korean War."

SECDEF gives the general and admiral a long stare. He slides his chair back and leaves the room without acknowledging the major. Bordon says nothing nor gives any indication what he is thinking. He just stands and exits the room. Once they have left, Bella stands to his feet and forcefully says, "You can be sure that we're not going to re-start the Korean War, but we're sure as hell not going to sit around and do nothing either!"

"What do you mean, Admiral?" McWalters asks.

Bella is standing erect now, his chest out and feeling the power of the stripes on his sleeve when he says, "We're going to put the fleet to sea and surround those bastard Commies with a wall of gray steel! If any member of that crew is alive and can get out to sea, I promise you he won't have to swim very far before he runs into something floating that is big and gray and has an American flag fluttering from its yardarm!"

"But what about SECDDEF? Doesn't he have to approve this?" the major asks.

The admiral is still puffed up, but now he has a sly smile coming over his face as he answers the field grade officer's question, "Julie, you have to understand how the game is played. We make the operational decisions and if it's a success, the politicians get the credit. If we fail, then nothing happened, no failures, no denials, just another boring military training exercise."

Adams now stands as well. With a twinkle is his eye, he joins in the Washington D.C. two-step, "You know, Norm, I think it is about time we hold a surprise readiness joint exercise in the Sea of Japan. Don't you?"

* * * * *

As the truck weaves its way through the forest, Keene sweeps the roadside with the search light in the same pattern he had noticed the Koreans doing. For just a fleeting second he smiles as he considers what he is attempting. A Naval historian, he is well aware that he is using the same technique that pirates utilized to close their enemy. He is trying to look like a friendly through deception. This prompts him to speak into the blowing wind, "Arggh, matey! Stand by to drop the ensign and raise the skull and cross bones!" No one can hear him say it, which makes it all the more funny to him. This is no time for laughing or smiling, but now that he is alone for the first time in days, Keene is finding a way to release the pressure and renew his spirits. A thought of how that dead Korean's life was preceding on one path and now it is over tries to surface, but the pilot has the learned capacity to shut it in a separate compartment and ignore it for now. He will only let himself consider the Korean's parents, wife, and perhaps even kids sometime later. Not now.

Behind the wheel, Jones is not thinking about anything but the curves in the road. He is waiting for the road to drop off into a steep decline just before they reach the village. Jones wants to get to the village and out to sea as quickly as possible. His focus is solitary and almost desperate. He wants to finish his escape, but the bad road keeps his speed to a minimum for now. He is unaware that he continually wipes his right hand on his flight suit pant leg. The wet blood was wiped clean the first couple of swipes. But he can still feel it on his skin.

Evans notices Jones right hand struggling to remove the stain of killing. The admiral ignores it and scans the road ahead. His blood pressure and respiration are controlled, a talent he developed when turning final to the boat on a moonless night in the Tonkin Gulf. His training has all of his attention funneled on what is ahead of him. The scan of his eyes rapidly sweeps the edge of what is illuminated by the truck headlights. This focus in interrupted by a thud to his right. Warbuck has passed out and his head hit the passenger door window. Evans returns his concentration to what is ahead while he takes his right arm and puts it around the TACCO's shoulders. The admiral pulls the junior officer towards him. Warbuck's head is supported by the admiral's shoulder, no longer bouncing against the glass.

The road straightens and the trees disappear from along its side. The truck headlights now illuminate the sky ahead. Suddenly the front wheels fall away and the vehicle is descending rapidly.

"Here we go, Admiral!" Jones says through clinched teeth. Keene loses his footing and falls to the truck bed as the descent accelerates. Jones instinctively hits the brakes to slow the fall, and when he does Keene slams against the back of the cab. The pilot maintains his grip on the automatic weapon throughout this tumbling.

By the time they reach the bottom of the hill, Jones has regained control of his speed. Upon slowing, Warbuck regains consciousness and cringes as he takes a deep breath. Evans removes his arm from around the lieutenant. At the edge of the village, Jones slows the truck to a mere crawl. Evans nods forward, indicating that Jones should proceed up the unlighted street. Jones sighs deeply and shifts into second and accelerates. Keene has regained his feet and now stops the searchlight scan. He keeps the beam pointing ahead of the truck, conscious that the light could awaken a sleeping villager if he illuminates a house.

Suddenly, two headlights flash on at the end of the street. Another truck is departing the compound and is starting its patrol. Jones starts to slow, but Evans speaks, "Press on, Petty Officer. But your headlights on bright beam. Maybe we can blind them as we pass."

Jones steps on the floor high beam switch. Keene sees the headlights brighten. He quickly grasps the intent and turns the search light beam to the cab of the on-coming truck. The approaching Korean truck responds by flashing its high beams. The Koreans' searchlight comes on and is pointed directly at Keene. He lowers his head to where he is nearly hidden by his own searchlight. The two trucks pass quickly, squeezing by each other on the narrow street in the center of the village. As the Koreans pass, the Americans hear angry shouts from the other truck. "Screw you!" can be understood in any language.

As the Americans approach the compound at the far end of the village, Evans reaches over and douses the headlights. Jones stops the truck and parks in the city square fifty yards from the compound gate. Keene shuts off the searchlight when he sees the headlights go out. Under two faint lights, one over the guard shack at the entrance gate and one on a pole at the head of the small pier, the evaders notice something obviously wrong.

"There are no patrol boats!" Jones says. "What do we do now, Admiral?"

Under his breath, Evans responds, "How should I know? Kill the engine." He wants time to think. There is only one situation that makes Evans mad. He has no problem in doing the right thing, even when it is difficult or dangerous. But he cannot tolerate a situation where the right thing is not known. Time to think is what he needs; time to determine the next right action.

Jones turns the key and the engine stops. It is a little more than an hour before dawn and all is quiet in the village. In the silence of the moment it is now possible to hear the faint whimpers coming from Warbuck with each breath he forces himself to take. Jones leans forward to observe the TACCO. Evans is focused on the problem and options, unaware of the condition of the officer next to him.

* * * * *

Commander Eric Roberts assumed command of the USS Schofield fourteen months ago. It is his first duty on this older class of guided missile frigate, but it is not his first command. He commanded an old minesweeper when he was a lieutenant commander. Other than those three years, his sea duty has been in the "greyhounds of the fleet." He is what was called in the old Navy, "a tin can sailor." And he is proud of it. Every man in the crew expects him to be selected for promotion to captain on the next selection board. Roberts's career is intact and progressing in a most usual manner; more sea duty than assignments ashore, post-graduate school as a lieutenant, a tour in the Pentagon, and command tours. If nothing happens in the next couple of months to derail it, he is a shoe-in for O-6. No tour with the JCS or at the White House, and no command of a new class of destroyer so his chances for making admiral are minimal, but making captain is practically a given.

Roberts is hunched over the Combat Information Center primary tactical station trying to read a flash message that was just handed to him by a radioman. At 44, Roberts has just recently had to start carrying reading glasses. He pulls them from his left chest pocket of his working khakis. Lieutenant Josh Brevins, the Tactical Action Officer, leans back to remove his shadow from the message. Roberts reads and re-reads the short message.

"TAO," Roberts speaks as he hands the lieutenant the message. "Set flight quarters and take us to the point noted in this."

Brevins quickly scans the message as he responds automatically, "Aye, aye Captain." The flash orders direct the Schofield to steam at best speed to a point just north of the Korean DMZ in the Sea of Japan. Once in the vicinity they are to join with other units moving rapidly to the rendezvous and conduct a training exercise named, "Operational Search Exercise 85-16." The TAO looks at the chart on the DRT and then keys the squawk box over his head and says, "Bridge, CIC. Come to course 300 and bring speed to flank." Brevins will refine the course in a minute, but 300 degrees will get the ship heading in roughly the right direction.

"Captain," Brevins addresses Roberts as the senior officer is starting to open the forward door of the CIC and head to the bridge. "I estimate reaching the rendezvous point in about four hours."

"Concur," Roberts says as he exits. He had done the math in his head already and had come up with about three hours forty-five minutes by his calculations. Roberts is pleased that the lieutenant had been that close with his estimate in such a short time. Now Roberts is thinking about contacting engineering and checking his fuel consumption at flank speed. Luckily the ship had just topped-off from the local SOJ oiler before dusk last night. Fuel should not be a problem.

CHAPTER FOURTEEN

It is late afternoon in Washington D.C., but Margie and her sister are asleep. The shades are drawn tightly and the room is dark. Their daily schedule has been turned topsy-turvy. They had decided to drive straight back from Savannah rather than spend more time away from Washington and possible news about Frederick. It was dawn when they pulled the shades and collapsed into bed.

They are both petite women and have excess space in the Evans's king sized bed. Far off in the distance, Barton hears something ringing. It rouses her to near consciousness. After a moment she determines that her sister's telephone is ringing on the night stand next to Margie's head.

"C'mon, sis," Barton says as she gently shoves her sister's shoulder, "Get the phone, dear, the phone." But Margie is so deeply asleep that she does not stir. Barton opens both her eyes and reaches over her sister and grabs the telephone.

"Hello?"

"Margie, this is Norm, I have an update for you," Admiral Bella states without waiting for a response. "We have evidence that some of the crew survived the crash and made it ashore." He waits for an expected reaction of hope.

"Wait," is all the officer hears. Barton sets the receiver on the night stand and gets on her knees. She shared a room growing up with her sister and Barton knows it can take a cannon blast to awaken Margie when she is dead to the world. "Wake up, sis! Wake up!" she shouts as she forcibly bounces Margie on the mattress. Barton now shouts a name that will be sure to rouse her sister, "Frederick! Frederick! News about Frederick!"

Both of Margie's eyes pop open. They are full of confusion, but her mind is quickly adjusting to being awake. "What? What about Frederick?" she says breathlessly.

Barton hands her the phone and says, "It is Admiral Bella."

"Norm! What about Frederick?" Margie blurts out even before she gets the receiver to her ear.

"Margie, as I promised, I have an update about the search. Don't ask me how we know, but we have evidence that at least some of the crew survived the crash and made it ashore."

"Where, Norm? Where?"

"No place good. But I cannot say where."

Even with her mind still a little hazy, Margie can put two and two together. North Korea. The rectum of the world. Commie North Korea. She responds, "Was Frederick with the survivors?"

"Don't know one way or the other," Bella says tenderly, but still with the unvarnished truth. He learned as a junior officer that honesty is the only proper way to address bad news. Covering it up or delaying it never makes it better.

Margie immediately looks at the half-full glass. "No positive evidence of his..." Margie lets her question trail off as she has trouble even saying the word .

"Nothing to confirm his status at all, Margie."

"What are you doing to get him, eh, them, back?"

"All we can, but that is very limited. Our options end at the territorial waters of a sovereign country," Bella says. He wants to assure this Navy wife that he has marshaled the entire strength of the Pacific Fleet to find her missing husband. But he cannot share his actions with a civilian with no security clearance.

"You do whatever it takes, Norm," Margie says then pauses before she adds, "I know you will. I trust you."

Bella is once again in awe of the strength of Navy wives. No ranting, no blaming, no expectations of the impossible.

241

But unfailing faith that her man will return to her is the order of the day.

"Thanks, Margie. I'll call when I find out anymore."

Margie hangs up without saying goodbye. She looks at her sister with telling eyes and then falls back down onto her pillow. She pulls the blanket under her chin and shuts her eyes. Barton tucks her in then rises to fix an early dinner.

* * * * *

The lone sentry at the guard shack by the compound gate notices the parked truck. It is unusual for the truck to stop short of the compound. He puts his AK-47 at the ready position. He peers into the darkness to determine why the strange goings-on. Obviously, this non-standard situation has him confused. Should he leave his post to investigate why the truck has parked? The guard starts to move towards the truck, his curiosity stronger than his assigned duty.

Keene cycles the action of his automatic weapon and takes aim over the truck cab. The Korean is centered over his metal sights. Keene is not sure what he will do, but his training dictates that he be ready. The Korean closes their position. Keene's finger makes contact with the trigger. With each hesitant step the Korean takes towards the truck, Keene's pressure on the trigger increases slightly.

At twenty-five yards, the Korean stops, turns and faces the pier. Keene raises his eyes from the end gun sight and looks to the pier. Around the jetty, a searchlight beam can be seen sweeping the small harbor entrance. Soon the sight and sound of a returning patrol boat jolts the still early morning as it closes the pier. The Korean looks towards the truck and back to the pier. He then hustles to the compound gate. He opens it, enters and then shuts the gate. He jogs to the pier. Upon reaching it, he slings his weapon over his shoulder and grabs for a mooring line tossed from a soldier on the boat bow. The guard ties the line to a cleat on the pier.

Jones and Evans smile at their good fortune. The admiral now knows the right course to take. Warbuck's eyes are closed, but the other two survivors intently watch as the patrol boat is tied to the pier. They see four crew men disembark and drag themselves to the billeting hut a hundred yards up a slight hill from the dock. They are bushed after an all-night patrol. On the boat, the engines are idling and the captain is reviewing orders with a junior officer on the open bridge.

Keene hangs his head over the left side of the truck and loudly whispers to Jones and Evans, "What's the plan? We go now?"

Evans looks around Jones and answers quickly, "You blind the sentry with the light and we plow through the gate and then take the boat."

Keene nods and resumes his position at the search light mounted on the cab roof. Jones sees four fresh crew men departing the billeting hut, slowly walking towards the idling patrol boat. "Look!" he says to Evans.

"We go now! Go! Go!" the Admiral nearly shouts.

"Aye, aye, sir," Jones responds as he goes through the truck starting procedure. He gets it running and slams it into gear. The truck lurches forward and Jones continues to build speed as he races to the compound gate. Just returning to his post, the sentry hears the on-coming speeding truck and raises his head. Suddenly his vision is lost in the intense spotlight focused on his face. The guard raises his hand to shield his eyes. Before he can react further the truck is upon him. Jumping to his left he barely misses being smashed by the heavy vehicle as it zooms by. The truck crashes through the chain-link gate, easily breaking the gate hinges. The gate flies off to the left. The new boat crew is stunned by the turn of unexpected events and stop in their tracks. Jones aims the truck towards the end of the pier. It is just seconds before he is rumbling down the wood structure that is swaying under the weight of the truck.

The boat captain and junior officer leap to the pier from the bridge. Each fumble to draw their side arms from tightly closed holsters. They position themselves in the middle of the narrow dock and open fire at the oncoming speeding truck. One shot flies by Keene's ear; another cracks the windshield just above Jones head. This makes Jones accelerate more. The two Korean officers leap into the water near the boat bow to avoid being hit. Upon reaching a position abeam of the brow, Jones slides the truck to an abrupt stop.

Out of the crew hut five more Koreans join the relief crew in running towards the truck. But these five are armed with automatic weapons. Bullets riddle the rear of the truck cab, but miraculously miss Keene. The pilot turns to face his attackers and opens fire with his AK-47, spraying rounds in the general direction of the approaching enemy. This causes them to stop temporarily, giving him time to scurry to the end of the truck bed and jump to the ground. He looks to his left and he sees the bow line. Keene fires with his right hand as he unties the rope with his other. In just a few seconds his magazine is empty. Throwing the weapon into the water, he now uses both hands to complete freeing the bow line. He is so focused on his task at hand, Keene does not notice the Korean captain treading water between the pier and the bow.

While Keene is fighting the approaching Koreans and freeing the bow line, Jones slides from the cab. He runs to the passenger side of the truck and grabs the handle. In one quick, continuous motion he grabs the machine gun between Warbuck's knees and the TACCO around the waist. Lifting the officer with just the strength of one arm augmented by pure adrenalin, Jones carries him up the short boat brow and drops him on the cockpit deck. Evans is right behind him. Without being directed, Jones runs aft to cast off the stern line. The admiral scans the bridge controls. Throttle, gear shift, light panel. It is not very complicated. A combat veteran, Evans is in his fighting mode and never notices the bullets starting to ping off of the bridge windshield.

Keene pushes the bow away from the pier and leaps to board the craft. His timing is off and he hits the gunnels with his stomach, grasping for a hand hold on the bow fittings, his legs dangling over the side. His feet are wet and his purchase insufficient to pull himself aboard immediately. His hands scramble to find something better to grasp. Suddenly he feels himself being pulled into the water. The pilot clamps his hands on a section of anchor tackle and a nearby cleat. He realizes that someone has hold of his legs. He kicks furiously, but the weight is still there. Now bullets start to slap against the hull around his legs. The on-coming Koreans have reached a closer firing position and their accuracy is improving. But still the bullets fail to reach their target.

Jones quickly finds and casts off the stern line. He waves to the admiral. Evans throws the gear lever forward, spins the wheel to the left and jams the throttle to the firewall. The patrol craft lurches and immediately picks up speed.

The strain this causes on Keene's grip is tremendous. He starts to slip, but just when he is about to be cast into the harbor, the weight pulling him down into the water vanishes. The rapid, swinging left turn has been too much for the Korean captain to withstand. He lost his grip on the American's legs and floated away from the turning craft. Keene is too weak to climb onto the bow, but now his hold is sufficient to keep him stable in his current position.

As the admiral gets the boat heading for the harbor entrance, Jones sees a red light coming from a hatch leading to the engine room. He enters the hatch and descends the steep, four-step ladder with his weapon pointed into the small compartment. There he finds a junior sailor staring at him. Jones can see the panic and doubt in the Korean's eyes. It is the first time the American has acknowledged to himself that he is fighting real persons, and not just "the enemy." Jones thinks to himself that the Korean's skin is pale and his black eyes slightly larger than necessary for the size of his flat face. "Odd," Jones thinks, "This guy is really strange looking."

Jones can hear the shots being fired at the bridge and bow. He doesn't have time to think anymore. He must get back into the fight. With an upward motion of his rifle, he indicates for the Korean to raise his hands. Then Jones backs out of the compartment, up the ladder with his gun pointed at his captive. The Korean follows slowly. As Jones's eyes reach a level above the deck he gives a quick glance towards the action at the front of the boat. When he does this, the Korean quickly grabs a nearby 12-inch screw driver and stuffs one end of it into his rear pocket. He has his hands back in the raised position before Jones looks back down at him.

On the bridge, Evans has completed the 180 degree turn and has the craft approaching the harbor entrance. Shots are still echoing from the pier, but few land near him. He throttles back and shifts the transmission into neutral. As the boat slows, the admiral scrambles to the bow and grabs Keene's arms. Once he has pulled Keene to a position where the officer can finish boarding the bow by himself, Admiral Evans rushes back to the cockpit. He shoves the transmission back into forward and opens the throttle wide.

The young Korean engineman reached the deck just as the boat lurches forward. He wobbles, but maintains his feet. Jones looks aft and can see flashes from the rifles firing on the pier. The American sailor raises the AK-47 to his shoulder and squeezes off a couple of rounds, his first of the fight. As he lowers the weapon, satisfied that he was able finally to shoot at something, a dull, terribly painful blow to his kidney area causes him to throw his head back. Instinctively, he wheels to his left, hitting the Korean behind him in the mouth with the butt of his rifle. The Korean flies overboard, but Jones cannot hear the soldier's splash in the

dark waters. The American sinks to his knees. He slowly
reaches for the screwdriver sticking out of his lower left
back, but he cannot reach it. All he can think about is the dull
pain in his back. No flashes of past experiences, no thoughts
of home, no last prayer on his lips, just a pain he cannot
reach. He falls forward onto the fantail deck. Petty Officer
First Class Ambrose Jones, United States Navy, takes two
more labored breaths, and then dies.

Keene has recovered his strength and now stands on the
boat bow.   He uses the mount for a fixed small caliber
automatic cannon on the deck to steady himself against the
rapid bouncing motion of the boat. He climbs back to the
bridge cockpit and as he enters he stumbles due to the rough
ride at full speed. Keene falls, smashing and bruising his
right knee cap when he hits the steel deck.

"Crap!" he shouts in pain. Now on his hands and knees,
Keene's face is near Warbuck's. The TACCO is barely
conscious, one eye closed and other just a slit with tears
slipping out of its side.

"Billy," Keene says in a voice loud enough to be heard
over the diesel engines at top speed. "How are you doing?"

Warbuck shakes his head. He doesn't even try to speak.
He slowly, very slowly fills his lung with air. Then just as
slowly he exhales. After a long pause, he musters enough
strength to repeat the exercise. His entire being has been
reduced to these singularly difficult and all-encompassing
two actions, inhale and exhale. Keene reaches out and places
his hand gently on his friend's shoulder and says, "Hang in
there shipmate. We're on our way home now."

Keene grabs his bloody and bruised knee as he rises to
his feet. He stands next to the admiral. Evans presses his
weight against the helm and tightly grips the steel wheel with
both hands. The boat has just exited the small harbor, the
man-made jetty passing to their port side. As they enter the
SOJ, the moon and stars disappear under the low overcast.
The way ahead is totally black. In his mind, Evans has

returned to the South China Sea in 1971, at the controls of an F-8 streaking into the light-less sky after catapulting from the deck of a carrier. He often thought then that if any civilian wanted to experience this sick feeling, he could paint his sports car windows black then stomp on the accelerator until maximum speed is reached. You are throwing yourself into the unknown with the only senses open to you being touch and faith; faith that what lies ahead is not the mouth of death opening to gobble up you and your craft; faith that you will be able to function as a blind man traveling at an uncontrollable speed.

Keene waits for the senior officer to acknowledge his presence. After a minute, Evans speaks, "Commander, how is Billy doing?"

Keene turns and looks at Warbuck before he answers, "Not good. Not sure how much longer he can last." Evans quickly glances over his shoulder at the injured sailor, and then nods.

"Can you take the wheel, Jim?" Evans asks as he releases his right hand from the helm. "Jones went aft and he hasn't come back up here yet. Thought I'd see what became of him." Keene slides to his left, favoring his right knee as he does so. He takes the wheel as he nods.

Evans first squats next to Warbuck and touches the injured sailor's forehead. He then checks the TACCO's pulse. The admiral looks aft and sees that the signal flags locker is directly behind the bridge. He pulls out the "Echo" and "Foxtrot" flags and uses them as blankets to tuck around Warbuck. He then moves along the narrow starboard catwalk that leads to the fantail. Upon reaching the aft deck, Evans can see Jones's body illuminated by the faint red light coming from the engine room. The admiral kneels over the petty officer and examines the body. Seeing the screwdriver sticking from the American's back, he pulls it out and tosses it into the water. Evans rolls Jones over and glides his fingers over the deceased's eyes, shutting them.

Then to himself, he says quietly, "Sorry, Petty Officer Jones. I am truly sorry."

Admiral Evans searches the aft engine room, but finds it deserted. He returns to the cockpit via the port, exterior catwalk. The senior office nods to the plane commander as he slips behind the wheel to resume steering the boat into the open, dark sea. Keene gratefully relinquishes the helm and slumps down onto a small steel seat built into the cockpit starboard bulkhead. His knee is swelling quickly and the pain is throbbing and distracting.

"Jones is dead," Evans says without taking his eyes off the darkness to the front. "Stabbed by a Korean aft. Can't find the S.O.B., so he probably went overboard."

Keene hears what his superior is saying, but he has trouble putting his thoughts around the concept that his shipmate could be dead.

Evans continues, "Take some of those flags back there and cover him up."

Upon hearing this, Keene has the thought of what a burial at sea was like. Without thinking he says, "Should we bury him at sea?"

"NO!" came the admiral's stern, loud and rapid reply, punctuated by Evans turning his face from forward to make eye contact with Keene. "I said he would not be buried in Korea. He will be buried in his hometown."

Keene nods and turns to do as he was ordered. When doing so he notices that Warbuck has opened his eyes and had heard the Admiral's declaration. Warbuck even manages to raise his eyebrows and force a reaction from his lips as he and his friend respond eye-to-eye to the admiral's leadership on this point. Keene grabs the "Zulu" and "November" flags from the signal locker and heads aft.

Upon reaching Jones, Keene forgets the pain in his right knee. There before him is the unshaven, tired looking face of a shipmate. A shipmate he had flown hundreds of hours with and observed his strengths and flaws. Sure, Jones was a pain in the butt at times, but he was also one of the best AQA-7 operators in the Pacific. Once he gained contact on a submarine, he could tell you the hull number and the Soviet commander's name and maybe even the OOD on watch based upon how the boat was handled. This may not have been true, but when Jones said he could, there was always a part of you that believed he was a good enough operator that it might be true.

Now he lays here still. His hands folded over his stomach and his eyes shut and still. Just still. Inside of Keene there is more than sadness and reflection. Inside of Keene is anger. And not just anger at the situation, but anger at the person who caused his shipmate's stillness. For just a moment, Keene understands the rage that had surfaced in Billy when the TACCO had offered to kill someone to get even for the death of a friend. Jones was not a friend; he was a shipmate, which is different. Shipmate is a status of trust and not necessarily friendship. Jones had trusted his pilot and Keene had trusted the professionalism of his Sensor One operator. This trust came with a strong bond, often times deeper and more important than friendship. And now someone has taken another shipmate from Keene. Anger simmers in the pilot as he makes his way forward to the bridge.

"You hungry?" Evans asks Keene as the PPC returns.

"Yes, sir, now that you mention it, I am hungry."

"Why don't you go below and see if there is anything to eat?" The admiral put his order into a polite question.

"Aye, aye, sir," Keene automatically responds, then adds, "and maybe I can find a chart as well."

He then slips down the short ladder leading from the bridge to the main forward cabin. As he reaches the bottom, his left hand slides over a light switch. He moves it down, expecting red-light night illumination which is a habit he had developed on U.S. ships. Surprisingly, it is the same on this North Korean vessel. As soon as the red lights come on,

Keene sees movement in a passageway that runs forward from the main cabin. The pilot reaches behind him and grabs the AK-47 lying on the bridge deck next to Evans feet. He cycles the action and freezes. "Maybe it was just a door swinging in the rocking motion of the sea," he thinks to himself. "Maybe, but Jones was killed by someone still on the boat, so better safe than sorry."

Keene has a clean vision line across the main cabin, and he is alone in this room. So he hobbles forward towards the passageway. At the entry, he pauses and listens. Hearing nothing but the ocean slapping against the hull, he squints into the dark corridor. There are three doors, two on the right and one centered to port. Keene takes a deep breath, puts his right forefinger on the rifle trigger and reaches across the face of the nearest door with his left hand. As soon as he moves the latch, the door flies right toward him. Its force hits his rifle muzzle, jamming his finger in the trigger guard. Keene loses his grip on the weapon and the AK-47 smashes to the deck.

A large North Korean is upon the American sailor in a split second. Both tumble into the main cabin. Keene grunts as his back is forced against a table that is bolted to the deck. He can smell the kimchi on the Korean's clothes and breath. A fist crashes into his left ear. This blow ignites in Keene a memory of second-class midshipmen boxing training at the Academy. As he pushes back against the Korean, Keene thinks, "I proved I could take a punch in boxing. This guy picked on the wrong opponent this time!"

Keene rolls to his left, clutching the Korean who is throwing rapid rabbit punches to the side of Keene's skull. The two sailors fall from the table to the deck, Keene landing on top. The American's blood is hot and the frustrations of the past days bubble to the surface. With all the strength he can muster, Keene raises his left knee into the groin of his enemy. But it doesn't have the desired effect he expected, so Keene slams his knee again and again into the groin.

The Korean gives a muffled yelp on the last kneeing, and goes limp for just a split second. Keene uses this second to push off the Korean and scramble for the rifle on the deck at their feet. He reaches the weapon and rolls over to his back just as the Korean gets to his feet and starts towards him. Keene pulls the trigger. The Korean grabs his testicles and falls to his knees. Keene's bullet had struck about five inches below the Korean's belt. The Korean throws his head back and screams. Keene rapidly struggles to a sitting position and raises the rifle to his right shoulder. He fires two more shots at point blank range into the Korean's chest. The enemy falls backward, awkwardly bent at the knees, arms spread and limp. He is dead.

It is over in a matter of seconds. Keene is in shock. He looks at the still Korean and then he looks down at the weapon in his hands. He opens his fists and lets the rifle fall to the deck. Covering his face with both hands, he drops his chin to his chest. Uncontrollable tears slide down his cheeks. He is stunned at how sad he feels. He has killed his first living creature, man or animal. It is the hollowness of guilt that comes with the first kill. Keene wants to pray for forgiveness, but God seems far, far away from this sin. Surely, God cannot be near something as dirty as killing.

CHAPTER FIFTEEN

Inside the Pentagon JCS situation room, Major McWalters is sitting at the main computer terminal. Standing behind her are Admiral Bella and General Adams. The first to speak is the general, "Look at all those red dots, will you?"

"It looks like the North Koreans have launched from five coastal air bases," McWalters says while moving the cursor over the screen. "They all seem to be heading for a position near the DMZ." Then she points with her manicured fingernail to the screen and adds, "Right about here."

Adams asks, "Anyone care to venture a guess what they're doing? Think it could be in response to our impromptu fleet and air exercises in the SOJ?"

Bella keeps his focus on the screen as he answers, "I don't think so. We've only had time to start these five ships moving to a rendezvous about here." He points to a spot off the coast of North Korea.

Suddenly a slew of yellow dots start appearing over South Korea and moving out to sea. Bella asks, "Uh-oh! What's that?"

McWalters answers, "Looks like the South Koreans have responded to the unusual air activity up north. I'd say they launched about four squadrons already."

"Oh great!" Adams interjects. "What? Are we watching a restarting of the Korean War?"

"This does look like it has the potential to get out of hand," the major responds, "What are those crazies up north doing? I don't think they are launching a real assault against the South or we would've had some intelligence chatter on their intent."

As the Air Force officers discuss the situation, the admiral is processing what he sees against what he knows about the Tuna King flight. He asks McWalters, "Julie, have you any information on small surface activity?"

"Nothing unusual we can pull out of the normal fishing fleets."

"What are you thinking, Norm?" Adams asks.

"Look, there is no air activity on the Korean west coast, but about every plane they have on their east coast seems to be heading out to sea just off the point where we believe the crew of the Tuna King went ashore. Maybe those naval aviators have made their way to where all good sailors go—to the sea!"

The two Air Force officers give the admiral an incredulous look. But Bella is smiling, personally satisfied that he has the answer to these events. Keeping his eyes on the computer screen he leans over and points to a green triangle nearest the DMZ latitude and asks, "What ship is that?"

McWalters clicks the mouse over the top of the triangle and the label, "Schofield/FFG" appears. Upon seeing this, Bella quickly moves across the room and picks up a red phone. Without identifying himself, he barks, "Patch me through to the C.O. of the Schofield. It's in the SOJ."

* * * * *

Admiral Evans keeps the patrol boat heading east to the open sea with the throttle full open, racing into the black night. It is a very rough ride, and Evans steers with one hand while keeping a tight hold on a stainless steel bar mounted on the cockpit bulkhead.

Keene appears from the hatch leading from the main cabin. He is clutching two oranges and a chunk of stale black bread in his left arm as he maintains his balance with his right hand.

Evans sees the pilot and says, "Good, you're back. No sign of anyone following us yet. I'm hoping this cloud cover keeps their air force grounded or at least blind until we can put some distance between us and the coast."

Keene takes the seat to Evans's right and uses his good leg to brace himself to where he can use both hands to start peeling one of the oranges. Keene says while he works on the orange, "Come sun up I figure they'll be on us."

"Yeah. Probably. Unless we can come up with a way out of this."

Keene hands the peeled orange to Evans. The admiral smashes the juicy treat nearly whole into his mouth. There is a long silence as these sailors mull over their situation and feelings. Finally, Keene speaks, "I killed a man below."

Evans stares at Keene, and then looks back over the bow, out to sea. He responds, "I heard the shots. We're going to make it, Jim. In a few days you'll be sleeping with your wife and playing with your kids. It will be all over and we can go on with our lives knowing we did what we had to do...we did our best."

"You ever kill a man up close?"

"Not up close. I just shot down an enemy airplane and bombed targets. Never wanted to think of them as people," Evans says with complete honesty. He doesn't want to diminish what he has done; he is just explaining how he has dealt with it in his life.

Keene says, "I watched his eyes. I made him die."

"It must hurt more. But—"

"Let's just finish this job," Keene sharply interrupts. "God will sort out the rest later."

Suddenly a dozen lights start popping up on the water's surface. The lights bounce up and down and extend from beam to beam. The Americans are surprised and confused by the darkness erupting so quickly with these lights. Keene grabs the nearby AK-47 and jumps to his feet, rifle at the ready and adrenaline blocking any pain from his injured knee.

Then Keene immediately recognizes the situation from his experience one night departing San Diego harbor when on the bridge of an LPD during midshipman cruise. He blurts out to Evans, "Admiral! They're fishing boats! We have run smack into a night fishing fleet. We're running right through their nets. Go to neutral before we foul the props!"

Just a few seconds after Evans shifts into neutral, a loud bang and scrapping sound starts at the bow and runs aft along the port side. They see the mast of a small boat sliding against the hull, quickly approaching the bridge area. Now they hear angry shouts followed by splashes in the water.

The patrol boat has driven into a formation of night fishing boats about a mile off shore. The fishermen lighted their single lantern in each boat when they heard the approaching patrol boat diesel. With no moon, stars or shore illumination and the patrol boat running in total darkness, the fishermen were unsure of which direction the danger approached. The unlucky fisherman and his teenage son were located on the western edge of the small night time flotilla. Their small open sailboat was hit on their starboard bow by the speeding power boat. If Evans had not shifted the transmission into neutral just seconds before slamming into the sailboat, the fisherman and his son would have been injured and the boat sunk. As it is, they are swimming unharmed to a nearby fishing boat and their craft is banging against the port hull of the patrol boat.

Keene moves quickly to the port side amidships while ignoring the pain in his knee. He grabs the mid-ship mooring line and jumps overboard. Evans sees his head disappear from view and wonders what the officer is doing. Soon Evans hears Keene shout, "Admiral! Go forward slowly, then go to neutral once we have way on!"

Evans does as directed. Then he leaves the controls and moves to the port side. There he sees Keene standing in the sailboat, tying the mooring line to the mast step. Once the line is secure, he looks up at Evans and says, "We might need this boat before morning."

Evans nods and then helps Keene climb back aboard the patrol boat.

* * * * *

Joyce Keene slowly opens her front door and enters her home. It has been an especially difficult day. She has managed to get home in time to start dinner. Most of the afternoon was spent visiting with other squadron wives. The support meeting was organized by Jessica Morse. The commanding officer's wife is the de facto leader of the squadron wives club. Jessica is nothing like her husband. Joyce has experienced the leadership of several C.O.'s wives, and Jessica is as good as any before. Jessica tries hard, but it is a very tough assignment when your husband is such an arbitrary jerk. Still, she has done a fine job mobilizing the wives club to reach out to every spouse, both officer and enlisted. Joyce appreciates Jessica's efforts. However, Joyce still feels terribly distant from the others. She has based her social life around church activities and not wardroom and squadron functions. In addition, although most of the other non-Crew Eleven wives are very tender, she feels that they cannot truly know the emptiness and misery Joyce and the other probable widows have right now.

Upon entering the front door, Joyce sees Peter sitting on the sofa, a game show on the television. Little Sammy is asleep on his older brother's lap. Joyce smiles at the scene. Peter looks up at his mother, but doesn't stir.

"He said he was tired," Peter offers.

Joyce nods as she smiles. "Where is your sister?"

Peter nods towards the kitchen. Joyce sets down her purse and locks the front door behind her. She goes into the tiny kitchen and Meredith is pouring cereal into a plastic bowl. Her daughter looks up and smiles with her lips but not her eyes.

"I'm fixing us dinner!"

"Thank you, Sweetheart," is all Joyce can muster. She goes to Sammy. He remains asleep as she lifts him from Peter's lap and carries him to the stairs. Joyce stops and turns to Peter before she starts upstairs. "This boy is just like his father. He can sleep through anything. What time is it in Japan right now?"

Peter is quick with the answer, "About 0700 tomorrow." Having lived on a military base for a couple of years, answering in military time is second nature to him.

"I pray he has had a restful night."

Peter knows his mother's thoughts have centered on his father for the past two days, so much so that most everything else has been pushed from her mind.

* * * * *

It is a Navy morning. Like a warship, the sky is haze gray. It is becoming lighter every minute as the sun rises. The patrol boat is now three miles beyond the small North Korean fishing flotilla, moving at ten knots with the small sailboat dragging to port. Admiral Evans sweeps the horizon with the binoculars he found on the bridge. He sees nothing to the east, looking into the sun, and it is still too dark to see far to the west. Evans turns and looks to Keene who is kneeling next to Warbuck. Evans speaks, "It looks like now would be a good time to make the transfer." Keene nods.

Evans shifts the transmission to neutral and idles the throttle. Then he disappears below decks. Meanwhile Keene leans next to Warbuck's ear, repeating words of encouragement, saying, "Billy, Billy. Come on, shipmate, we're going for a nice relaxing sail. Stay with us, Billy. We'll be through this soon. We're on our way home, Billy. Come home with us, Billy."

Keene pulls his TACCO to a position where he can slide both hands under the injured shipmate's shoulders. Carefully Keene helps Warbuck sit up. As soon as his chest reaches the vertical, the NFO wretches with a wicked cough. Blood oozes from the side of his mouth. Panic fills Warbuck's eyes as he throws his chin back in an attempt to fill his one good lung with air. He is sure that he is choking to death at this very moment. Keene sees the blood and quickly lowers him, laying Warbuck on his injured side. Keene is surprised just how much he remembers his Navy training. "Keep the good lung above the bad to prevent it from also filling with blood."

Evans returns, his arms full of provisions; food, containers of water, and loaded AK-47 magazines. He sees blood coming from Warbuck's mouth. He sees the fear in the TACCO's eyes as he struggles to survive. Then he notices the determination in Keene's eyes. It hadn't been there before, but now the pilot will not accept defeat. Keene has decided that his friend, his shipmate, is going to survive this ordeal whether he wants to or not. Evans quickly goes to the port side. He throws the supplies into the fishing boat and returns to help Keene.

"Grab his feet, sir, and we can get him comfortable in the boat where he can rest."

Evans moves to Warbuck's legs and lifts in unison with Keene. As gently as possible, they manage to load the dying man onto the small craft. Keene works to set Warbuck in a position that is easiest for breathing. Evans jumps back to the patrol boat and heads aft on the small cat walk. Upon reaching the fantail, he pauses as he kneels next to Jones's body. The admiral whispers to the corpse, "Petty Officer Jones, I promised you would not be buried in Korea. We'll take you home to your family, to your hometown to rest." Evans checks the ties holding the flags to the body and then lifts the corpse to his shoulder. It takes nearly all of his remaining strength to transport Jones along the narrow cat walk and reach the sailboat. Evans grabs Jones's feet and together with Keene they lower the body into the bottom of the boat.

Evans asks, "Can you raise the sails?"

"Aye, aye, sir."

"I need to do one more thing before we shove off," the admiral shouts as he returns to the bridge. There he opens a cabinet below the helm and rummages through a tool box. Using a pair of pliers and a small hammer he found, the admiral unbolts and frees the compass from its stand just ahead of the wheel. He hands the device to Keene. Then Evans returns to the bridge and takes two lanyards from the signal flags and ties them to each side of the helm. Then he shouts to Evans and Warbuck, "Hold fast, it's going to get rough for a second!"

Evans turns on the small transceiver located on the bridge. He turns the UHF radio to a frequency of 243.0 and then keys the microphone and jams it into a niche next to the radio. The mic remains keyed in this position. The admiral then places the transmission in forward and slowly advances the throttle. Soon he has enough forward motion to make the rudders functional. Evans turns the patrol boat due south and then ties off the helm to keep the rudders centered. The admiral then shoves the throttle full open and quickly leaps to the sailboat. He uses his survival knife to cut the tow line. The sailboat falls off to port as the patrol boat speeds south. Keene is sitting by the rudder and pushes it hard to starboard. The bow swings to the northeast. Just as Keene does this, Evans recalls his sailing instruction decades ago at the Academy. The admiral grabs the main and jib sheets and pulls them tight to catch the wind.

As the patrol boat speeds away it becomes quiet on the sailboat. Soon the primary sounds are the lapping of the sea against the hull and terrible coughs coming from the injured TACCO. The sailors begin to feel very small in a very small boat in a great big ocean. And they like it. The smaller the better. They want to be nothing but a speck in the sea when the enemy comes looking for them. The quiet also is calming. The natural way of crossing oceans, with wind power and sail can seem remarkable to modern sailors who have known nothing but big, complicated ships and aircraft driven by profanely loud, powerful engines. There is no sun beating down on them and the temperature is mild. The seas are nearly calm and the winds are steady at ten knots from the northwest. Things are looking good for the crew. Hope is rising in their hearts. For now.

* * * * *

Everyone on the bridge is using one hand to hold his balance and another to conduct his assigned duties as the Schofield plunges through the waves at flank speed. Commander Roberts notes a flashing amber light on the red phone located on the bulkhead just ahead of him. He slides down from his high bridge chair and grabs the handset and keys the secure R/T phone. He waits for the connection to "sync up" and then answers, "This is Schofield Charlie Oscar, over." The entire bridge team stops all chatter and listens to their captain's half of what is obviously an important conversation. But they hear very little, other than the skipper nodding as he listens and interjecting, a "yes sir" and an "aye, aye, sir" every now and then.

"I understand, Admiral." Roberts finally says a complete sentence. "Then I can expect verification of these directions from CTF 74, is that correct?...Aye, aye, sir...yes, sir...If they're in international waters, Admiral, we will get them...yes, sir. Schofield, out."

Roberts hangs up the receiver and punches a button on the squawk box next to it. He pulls down on the squawk box lever and says, "Combat, this is the captain. TAO give me a course to a point one-half mile outside the territorial waters of North Korea, directly east of Kuum-Ni." Roberts now moves to the navigation table at the rear of the small bridge and leans over the chart laid out on it. His elbow touches that of QM1 Phillips, the senior quartermaster in the crew. Phillips is a squared-away sailor and contributes much more than would be expected from his pay grade. Without being told, he is entering a new Omega fix of the Schofield's current position on the chart. Having overhead the directions to CIC, he locates Kuum-Ni and plots a new course with his standard level of precision.

"Course 282 true, Captain," Phillips says with pride that he beat CIC in computing the correct direction. Roberts nods and turns toward the OOD.

"OOD, come to course 282 immediately," Roberts orders. Just as the words leave his mouth the squawk box blares out, "Bridge, CIC, recommend course 283 to target point." Roberts and Phillips smile at each other.

Phillips looks down to his chart, uses a pair of dividers and scribbles a little math problem on his scratch pad. He looks up and says, "Captain, at flank speed I estimate we will arrive in a little under three hours, at 0953."

"Very well, navigator. Thank you." Whenever Roberts thinks it appropriate, he takes the opportunity to recognize the excellent work of Phillips by referring to him as "navigator." Technically the executive officer is the navigator and the signals division officer is the assistant navigator on this class of frigate. But QM1 Phillips does all the real navigation work; the officers are barely proficient at their collateral duties of navigating.

Roberts moves next to the OOD and says in a soft voice, "We will be going to general quarters right after I address the crew." Then he maneuvers across the pitching bridge to the 1MC station just aft of the helmsman. He says to the Boatswain Mate of the Watch, "Give me PA, including topside." The BM3 turns five switches vertically and pulls the bos'n pipe from his shirt pocket and places it in his mouth. The captain nods to him and the boatswain mate cups the pipe with his right hand and keys the microphone with his left. He blows two different, long blasts on the pipe signaling "attention" then hands the microphone to the captain.

Roberts keys the mic and says, "This is the captain speaking. We are at flank speed heading to a point just outside of North Korean waters. As soon as I finish this briefing we will go to general quarters because currently it appears that the entire North Korean air force is on its way to meet us there. We have no certainty what those crazy bastards are up to. But I just spoke with the Pentagon and they believe the North Koreans are responding to an escape of some very important persons. The Pentagon feels these V.I.P.s might have attempted to escape to Japan by sea. Our job is to find them and pick them up before the North Koreans can kill them. We will close the North Korean coast at our present speed and investigate all contacts heading easterly. LAMPS pilots report to CIC for mission brief on the double. Gentlemen, we're a good crew and fight a good ship. Now it is time to show it. Captain, out."

Roberts hands the microphone back to the BMOW. Then the captain nods to the OOD who announces in a loud command voice to the entire bridge team, "Set general quarters!"

The boatswain mate of the watch keys the microphone and announces, "Now set general quarters. General quarters. This is not a drill, set general quarters. Set Condition Zebra throughout the ship." He then turns the red painted, round switch to the right and the ship fills with the sound of running sailors and the clang of the alarm.

* * * * *

Admiral Evans sees the first jet before he hears it. Traveling at nearly 400 knots, the MIG is upon the small sailboat within seconds of Evans' sighting. He immediately throws the fishing net located at his feet over Jones's body and the TACCO. He is able to cover most of his body with the net as well before the jet races directly overhead at 200 feet.

Upon sighting the airborne intruder, Keene unzips and tugs at his flight suit arms. Quickly he has the top down around his hips, revealing a sweaty and dirty light blue tee-shirt. Then he hears the admiral shout to him, "Turn northwest! Make it look like we're heading in after a full night of fishing! We don't want him to think we are trying to escape." Keene throws the tiller to his right and swings the bow towards the northwest. Evans tends to the two sail sheets to keep the boat in trim. The jet makes a wide, looping turn to the east and rolls out on a heading to pass over the sailboat once again heading due south. His low altitude keeps him just below the overcast and this creates the illusion that he is moving even faster than he is.

Beneath the nets, Warbuck opens his eyes, but he does not move. He can hear the roar of the jet engine as it rushes right over their position. This development has temporarily removed the pain from his body as adrenaline pumps through his veins. In fact, the smell of rotten cork and old fish guts now captures his attention. He thinks to himself, "This is just great. My life is really screwed up. How did I ever end up in this situation?" And then he smiles to himself at the total absurdity of the situation; no fear, just exhaustion and pain tainted by irony.

Keene and Evans wave at the pilot, but receive no recognition from the North Korean that he is responding to their gesture. Because their focus is locked on the MIG, it is a loud surprise when two more North Korean jet interceptors roar overhead from the north. Buzzing past at very low altitude, the high decibel scream of the jet turbines pushing out maximum power seems to make the entire small craft shiver and the mast roll side to side. The jets race on and catch the first jet just before the flight of three disappears over the gray, southern horizon.

264

Keene speaks first, "Think they saw the patrol boat heading south?"

Evans shrugs and points for Keene to resume an easterly heading. He then scans the skies for any more unexpected guests. Seeing all is clear, he pulls the fishing net off Warbuck.

The TACCO cocks his head back to make eye contact with the flag officer sitting farther forward in the small craft. Warbuck asks, "We still alive?"

"So far, I guess. But I don't know what will be coming over the horizon next."

* * * * *

The aft door of the U.S.S Schofield's CIC swings open. Two pilots dressed in flight suits stumble in, having trouble keeping their balance due to the ship's flank speed advance and its accompanying rolls and pitches. The Schofield is a pretty ship and can ride nicely in most seas, but today's combination of long rolling swells and charging speed have combined to create a harmonic action that causes the ship to ride very roughly during this race to a helicopter launch location.

The first through the door is the HSL-35 Detachment 4 Officer-in-Charge, Lieutenant Commander "Frito" Lopez. A veteran light ASW helicopter pilot, this is his forth WESTPAC deployment onboard a frigate. However, this is his first time flying the Sea Sprite SH-2 Foxtrot model. Previously his many, many hours were flown in the SH-2 Delta version. The only difference between the two is the tail wheel. The Schofield is a Brooke class frigate and the fantail of the Garcia/Brooke class frigates is the smallest LAMPS flight deck in the fleet. The tail wheel on the H-2D had to be moved forward seven feet just so the helicopter's landing gear could all fit on the deck.

Behind Lopez is Lieutenant JG Tom Parker, call sign, "Colonel Tom" after Elvis's manager. A slightly built man, barely 5 foot 7 inches, and this being his very first deployment, he is having more trouble keeping and maintaining his balance. Parker hits the back of the ESM operators' chairs as he fumbles his way through this dark, often forgotten corner in CIC. Finally he is able to regain his footing and mumbles an apology to the sailors at their dimly lighted consoles. The sailors ignore him on the surface, but each is thinking, "Dumb S.O.B. pilots. Why do they have to take a shortcut through this space?"

The pilots reach the NC-1 plotting table and grab its edge to steady themselves. It is extremely crowded around the plot. The CO, TAO, two operators and two communicators jockey for the best position to do their respective jobs. Roberts looks up and makes eye contact with Lopez. "Frito, you guys are our best shot. This is our area of interest," the C.O. says as he points to a chart position just outside the territorial waters of North Korea, 100 miles to the Northwest. "When can you launch to give yourself at least forty-five minutes on station for a surface surveillance mission?"

Lopez puts on his "cheaters," reading glasses he was forced to get on his last birthday. He draws nearer to the chart until the numbers become clear. Checking the plotter scale he does a quick mental "aviation math" calculation. He points to a location along the charted route of the Schofield and says, "We can launch here and get at least three-quarters of an hour on station if you continue to close us at flank speed." He points to another position and continues, "Then we can recover here."

"Commander Lopez," Petty officer Dancer joins the conversation. Only a second class petty officer, he is still the best Anti-Submarine Air Controller, or ASAC, in the crew. As such, his GQ station is manning the SPS-10 surface search radar. The ASW helos fly so low they are controlled by surface search rather than air search radar. He continues, "I am afraid I cannot give any help when you first get on station. You'll be out of range of the 10."

Lopez and Roberts nod and then the senior pilot says, "We'll start a ladder search to the north from here. Just keep pinging the TACAN and we will be able to use it to keep us out of North Korean airspace. But, Captain, what are we searching for?"

"Investigate any craft large enough to hold thirteen people and is heading away from land. Once we find it, then rescue operations will be put into effect."

"Investigate? Roger, but it would sure help to know who we're looking for."

"Mr. Parker, you can go prepare to launch." Roberts says as he moves towards the forward CIC door. "Frito, you come with me." Parker follows the two officers out of CIC. He heads down the ladder to go aft and the flight deck. Lopez follows Roberts up three steps to the bridge, and then to the starboard bridge wing. They must break the water-tight door to gain privacy out in the small open air space. Both lean over the high railing and face the sea.

Roberts scans behind them and satisfied that no one can hear, he says, "A couple of days ago, Patrol Squadron Forty out of Misawa lost a P-3 off the North Korean coast. You might be looking for survivors who have escaped the North Koreans and made it to sea in some sort of boat. This is classified and just the two of us on this ship know it and it will remain that way. Understand?"

Lopez nods and asks, "How do we know this?"

"You be on your best and most vigilant behavior out there, Frito. We know the plane is missing and as I told the crew, all the planes the North Koreans appear to be headed out to sea in a panic search. So don't expect to be alone out there. You be safe, but you find them before those bastards do."

Lopez nods and turns to head down the bridge wing ladder aft, but he remembers something and then stops and turns to face Roberts. "Did you say PATRON Forty? Did they mention the plane commander's name?"

"I believe they said it was Beam or Keene or something like that."

Lopez's eyes grow larger and he shakes his head as he mumbles excitedly to himself, "Wow! Talk about a small Navy! Jim Keene! Wow!"

"You know this officer?" Roberts asks.

"If it's Jim Keene, I do. He's a classmate and he lived two doors down the hall in Thirty-First Company."

Roberts responds, "Well, COMFAIRWESTPAC is with him and eleven other naval aviators, so try not to leave them behind if you classmates have a reunion out there."

"Aye, aye, sir. We'll bring them all back."

CHAPTER SIXTEEN

Lopez keys his mic and transmits, "Tango Charlie, Seasnake One, over."

"Tango Charlie reads you five by five, out," the ASAC completes the airborne radio check.

Lopez is in the right seat, where the helicopter commander sits in the U.S. Navy, and his co-pilot Parker is in the left seat. In the rear is the third crewman, Petty Officer Third Class Tony Grabo, the sensor operator and rescue swimmer. As is his preference in the Sea of Japan, he is riding with the sliding cabin door open. All speed is relative and at fifty feet the water appears to be racing by even though the helicopter is barely doing 110 knots. Grabo enjoys the wind and noise. It is much better than all the time he has spent in shore-based trainers learning to operate his equipment, prior to this, his first deployment.

Grabo's moment of pleasure is interrupted by the sound of Lopez's voice in his helmet, "We will proceed out to a point thirty miles from the ship, and then start a ladder search to the north. Grabs, don't radiate the radar until I tell you. Let's keep quiet until we reach the A.O.P. proper."

"Aye, aye, sir," Grabo responds. "Can you tell me what we are looking for?"

"Any surface craft that can hold up to thirteen men," Lopez answers.

Grabo starts to ask another question, but the ASAC's voice comes over the radio before he can speak. "Seasnake One, Tango Charlie. We have an ESM cut at freq two-forty-three bearing three-one-niner your present posit. Suggest you turn to new heading three-one-niner to investigate."

Frito answers, "Seasnake One, roger, three-one-niner."

"Seasnake One, Tango Charlie has lost radar contact. Please commence posit reports on the quarter hour," the ASAC notifies the aircrew.

"Rog," Lopez replies in improper surface navy radio-telephone procedures, but the most common phrase in "nasal-radiator slang."

Parker turns the helicopter to a new heading of 319. As he does so, Lopez points up and shows two fingers. Parker nods and starts a climb to two hundred feet.

Just a few seconds later the excited voice of the ASAC pierces their ear phones, "Seasnake One, Tango Charlie— Bogies! Multiple bogies your twelve o'clock! They're closing you fast—and I mean really fast! They must be low; I have them on the surface search."

Tom and Frito squint into the clouds and across the horizon ahead of them. They can see nothing but the gray morning sky and the gray sea. Lopez keys his mic, "Tango Charlie this is One, No joy on bogies. Say again how many."

"Okay, one, you must have climbed; I have radar contact again. On your eleven o'clock I count three...four...six, that's six bogies! Three miles and closing rapidly!"

Lopez shoots a confused look to Colonel Tom and responds over the radio, "Tango Charlie, One, they must be above the overcast because I have no joy on any...Wait! Tally ho! Tally ho on two MIG nineteens!" Lopez points to the incoming aircraft. Tom follows the commander's point to see the enemy aircraft. Immediately upon sighting them, he hears Lopez's voice shouting and giving directions without the use of the ICS, "Down, Tom! Take us down now! They're coming right at us"

Parker shoves the stick forward and the helicopter nose dives for the surface of the ocean. Immediately after departing their altitude, two jets fill the airspace they had just vacated. The helo shutters as some of its lift is sucked up by the low passing MIGs.

"I've got the aircraft," Lopez says in his best Chuck Yeager voice and grabs his stick and collective. "You take the radios, Tom. I'm gonna suck some salt spray and continue out that last ESM bearing."

Tom nods and keys his radio, "Tango Charlie, this is One. Do you still have us on radar?"

"You're in and out. Out right now. My last was two-eight-niner at twenty-four. Say altitude." Petty Officer Dancer has earned his reputation as an excellent ASAC, a shipmate that aircrews have learned to trust with their lives. He is always on-top of any situation and is not afraid to drive the problem.

Tom replies, "Well, the skies are a little crowded today. So we're so low, we're going to have to climb to recover on your deck. Where you got the bogies?"

"My best guess would be at your four o'clock, if you're where I think you are."

Lopez pulls his mic switch to ask a question pressing on his mind, "Tango Charlie, One, How far from my last posit until I bust North Korean airspace?"

"Estimate maybe twenty miles."

"Rog."

Lopez keeps changing heading every five seconds in random fashion as he works his way to the northwest. He shouts to his co-pilot, "Got a TACAN fix on Tango Charlie?"

Parker uses the ICS to respond, "Naw, we're too low."

Lopez next asks Grabo, "Sensor, flight. Turn on the radar and let me know if you see land."

"Aye, aye, sir." Grabo flips three switches, fires up the radar and expands his scope to its farthest setting. He then responds, "No land and no contacts on the first three sweeps."

"Rog," says Frito, "Keep it up and give me a detailed ladder search with five mile legs centered on that ESM cut."

"Bogie! Four o'clock high!" Grabo shouts over the ICS as he looks to his right out the open door. "He's diving right at us!"

Immediately Lopez banks the aircraft hard right and turns into the oncoming jet. He is nearly done with his hard turn when the MIG zooms by spitting out cannon shot. At this wave-top altitude, the crew sees the ocean splashes as the fire straddles both sides of the helo. Lopez keeps his turn rapidly swinging to his right and continues until he is nearly on his original heading. He is instinctively using his training to close the fast-mover to shorten the time the MIG has to target and shoot during the engagement. He continues his turn to keep sight of the jet. While yanking and banking as quickly as he can maneuver this small helicopter, Lopez transmits on the radio, "Tango Charlie, One is being fired upon by North Korean MIG 19. We're taking evasive action."

On the Schofield bridge, Roberts is sitting in his elevated captain's chair with his feet resting on the bridge window ledge ahead of him. Externally he appears calm and in command. He wears a command face very well. Inside, his mind is racing through possible scenarios and his options on what his next steps might be. In the background of his thoughts he has one ear tuned to the ASAC controlling frequency dialed into the radio speaker near his chair. Upon hearing the initial hostile report from Lopez, his feet drop to the floor and he pops out of the chair, standing in one rapid motion. Along with multiple considerations about how best to fight his ship, he is surprised that one of his first thoughts is about the tenor of Frito's voice. It came across in the standard aviator "No problems" tone. It is the verbal expression of the naval aviator's code. "Can't sweat the small stuff and it is all small stuff. Whatever happens is just the breaks of Navy Air." His next thought is more true to his nature, "Childish aviators. Never take anything seriously."

Rather than relay directions through the squawk box, Roberts bounds through the aft bridge door and down the three steps to CIC. As he enters he is barking orders to the GQ team, "ASAC, have Seasnake One clear to the southeast and to standby. TAO, if the MIGS close enough to enter missile range you have weapons free to engage." Roberts pushes a button on the squawk box mounted over the NC-1 table and continues with his orders, "Radio, this is the captain. Send a flash OPREP-Three immediately stating that our LAMPS helicopter has been fired upon by North Korean MIGs. No casualties, yet." The captain now looks over to the AN/SPS-40 air search radar operator and loudly asks, "Do you have tracks on the MIGs?"

"In and out, Cap'n," the operator answers. "They are very low and we lose contact often. Best guess is that six is a good count. None closing us yet that we can see."

Dancer is quick to follow the skipper's direction. He transmits, "Seasnake One, Tango Charlie, Charlie Oscar directs you to clear rapidly to the southeast." Then Dancer breaks the professional demeanor he maintains in his relationship with pilots he controls and adds, "Commander, come back behind us and we can protect you with our missiles."

Frito looks quickly at Tom and it is immediately understood that the senior pilot will respond to this radio call, "Thanks. Wait, out."

Frito now keys the ICS and says, "Anyone see where he went?"

"He must have climbed," Tom responds. "I hope he follows us back and the ship slashes that S.O.B."

"Hey guys, it sure went from peace time to war real fast, didn't it?" Lopez says.

As the commander continues his random evasive turns, Grabo's voice comes into his helmet, "Flight, sensor has a small, intermittent radar contact along that previous ESM cut. About ten miles out."

273

Lopez swings the nose of the helo to the northeast and then says, "Let's take a look. Grabs give me vectors until we get a visual."

"Tango Charlie this is Seasnake One," Frito calls the ship. "We have a skunk at ten miles along the ESM cut. We're closing to investigate."

Roberts reaches across the SPS-10 radar repeater in CIC and puts his hand up in front of Dancer's face. With his other hand he pulls down an R/T handset that is tuned to the ASAC frequency. The commanding officer wants to respond to this latest helo transmission personally. "Seasnake One, this is Tango Charlie, Charlie Oscar. That's a negative. Abort your mission and clear to the southeast immediately."

"Roger, you are garbled. This is Seasnake One closing to investigate," Lopez transmits. Then he looks at Parker and says through a mischievous smile, "Young lieutenant, that really drives those ship drivers mad when you ignore them, and there is nothing they can do about it!" They both laugh.

Back on the Schofield, Roberts hates being ignored. He shares his frustrations with the watch team by saying loud enough for nearly all to hear, "God save us from naval aviators. TAO, weapons tight. We won't be able to do anything until these cowboys get out of the way."

* * * * *

Admiral Bella is in civilian clothes, in fact rather formal attire. He shows his identification to the Marines as he rushes into the Pentagon JCS suite. Soon he arrives at the NMCC briefing room. Waiting for him is Major McWalters, her uniform still sharp even after her sixteen-hour day in these window-less spaces. The senior naval officer blurts out his immediate question before he has even fully entered the room, "They were really shot upon?"

McWalters nods. She moves across the room and hands the flag officer the OPREP-3 message from the Schofield.

She adds, "We received this a minute before I called your beeper. That was fifteen minutes ago and no amplifying information has been received." She notes to herself how distinguished this gray-haired, mature gentleman looks in dinner dress. It is the first time she has ever seen him in something other than a naval uniform. She offers, "I am sorry to have to disturb you when you had other plans this evening."

"You did right, Julie. In fact, it was one of those mandatory political events at the White House. It was just winding down when you contacted me," he says as he lifts the OPREP message a little higher. "The Schofield is required to submit further information within thirty minutes of this, right?"

McWalters nods.

"Then I will give them another ten minutes before I advise the NSC and the President." He then moves to the computer plot to see the latitude and longitude noted in the message. He notices the symbol for another Navy unit just to the south of the incident site. He points to it and asks, "Who is that?"

McWalters highlights the symbol and then turns to the admiral, "It is the USS Harold E. Holt, a ten-fifty-two class frigate."

"Relay this OPREP to them and order them to close the position at flank speed. Have them launch their helicopter at maximum range and let's hope to God it is not to search for Schofield survivors."

"Aye, aye, sir," Julie responds, surprising herself that she used a naval expression. She wonders, "Where did that come from?" She figures it must be from working so closely with sailors and focusing so much on the Navy the last couple of days. She smiles upon realizing that she had said it for the very first time.

"Very well, major," Bella responds with the same surprised smile.

* * * * *

Onboard the Harold E. Holt, the crew has just set flight quarters. In less than ten minutes their LAMPS helicopter is airborne and speeding northerly towards the Schofield. As is Seasnake One, this helo is from HSL-35 out of North Island; its call sign, "Seasnake Four." The Det O-in-C and aircraft commander is Lieutenant Dirk Riley, a seasoned pilot on his second sea tour flying the Sea Sprite. The rookie next to him is Lieutenant J.G. Evan Goldsmith. In the rear is Petty Officer Profitt, a first class with three deployments under his belt. He has enjoyed these first two months of this deployment because the Harold E. Holt actually does live up to its nickname of "Happy Harry." Good leadership, good crew, good food and good flying. Yes, it has been a good detachment so far.

Goldsmith is at the controls and once established at three hundred feet, he starts to slow down to best cruise speed. As he does this, Riley shakes his head and adds power to increase to maximum speed. He shouts over the air rushing in from the open side doors and loud engine noise, "Buster it, Evan. We'll top off to replace the fuel once we reach Schofield." Riley is not sure that Schofield's deck is clear and that the ship can refuel them onboard. Regardless, a week earlier he had been able to complete a Helicopter In-Flight Refueling evolution from the fantail of Schofield. Seasnake One was down for maintenance so the deck was not available to them. Riley is confident that the Schofield's HIFR gear is operational and he can fuel there one way or the other. Provided, of course, the ship is still afloat when they arrive.

* * * * *

Tom Parker points and shouts "Look! At ten o'clock, more MIGs!"

"Yeah. It looks like they are attacking someone else," Frito replies. "Let's go see what they are diving on."

"Are you crazy, commander?" Parker wants to know. "We can't even shoot back. No North Korean commie VIP is worth getting killed over."

"You're right." Lopez now keys his ICS mic so Grabo can hear what he says next, "But just supposin' I said we might be risking our lives to rescue some fellow American Naval aviators?"

Grabo responds first, "Is that the truth, sir?"

"That's what the captain told me. But he swore me to secrecy because I guess these guys from a P-3 crew flew where they shouldn't of."

Tom shakes his head and says, "Man, I'm gonna hate to die on account of some P-3 pukes."

Knowing that the brotherhood of aircrew meant that they were not going to turn back, Grabo says, "I'll get my wetsuit on."

"Commander, did the ol' man really say we were looking for downed aircrew or are you just playing with our heads again?" Tom asks. Frito Lopez has a reputation as a "steamer" when he hits the beach and as a practical joker in the wardroom. Parker figures it is always better to call him on things that sound fishy, than later find out that Frito had "stretched the truth" again.

"Truth," the senior pilot responds. "It's the honest truth and he said no one else on the ship could know."

"Then why are you telling us?"

"Because we are not on the ship now," Lopez says with a smile.

The senior pilot is flying totally by outside reference. He has the helicopter at top speed and zigzagging as he approaches the skunk, now only five miles away.

Parker leans far forward in his seat, his harness unlocked. He speaks, "I've got a tally on the MIGs' target. Twelve o'clock. See it?"

Lopez responds, "Yeah, I got it now. Some sort of small combatant."

"Bogie—I mean bandit! Three o'clock and closing! Here they come again!" Grabo spits out quickly over the ICS.

Frito yanks the aircraft to his right again and climbs quickly to charge the MIG head-on. In a matter of just a couple seconds the jet has passed, its cannon walking a line through the ocean as it dives at the small target before it. As it passes overhead, Lopez wheels the helo ninety degrees to the left to once again close the surface contact.

"We might as well get a close look at what they don't want us to see. There isn't much more they can do to us they haven't already tried. I'm taking us right over the skunk. You guys give a good look for any Americans," Lopez tells his crew.

A little feeling deep within Parker is screaming for attention. He can hear it yell, "This is stupid! This man is trying to get you killed! This is stupid!" But Parker ignores the voice and nods at Frito in agreement with the plan.

Lieutenant Commander "Frito" Lopez may have a reputation as a steamer ashore and a jokester in the wardroom, but he is also recognized throughout the HSL community as a great stick. He further enhances that reputation now. The main rotors are nearly chopping the tops of the waves as he has the helicopter's nose down to achieve maximum speed. As he speeds over the water's surface, Lopez is rolling and banking in aggressive evasive maneuvers. The next two minutes seem to last a life time for Parker and Grabo. Lopez closes the small surface craft like a sailboat tacking up wind. When he is a mile away, Parker points to the sky and says, "Bandits diving from right to left, one o'clock. Looks like they're strafing the boat."

In the rear compartment Grabo has fought the violent maneuvers to complete the donning of his wetsuit. Now he is kneeling in the main cabin door so he can scan the sea and sky better, his harness and headphone cord being his only attachment to the aircraft. The severity of twists and turns being employed by the pilot has knocked the sensor operator back and forth in the main cabin. But he has kept his vision on what is outside the aircraft. It pays off now. He keys the ICS and says, "Not all of them. Not the one coming up our tail, level!"

This time Lopez banks left. The jet passes over head and disappears to the west so quickly that Lopez can continue his turn for 360 degrees. It positions him for a rigging run on the boat on a southerly heading, from stern to bow. He is just seconds away from the boat when another jet strafes the water craft. Once this MIG passes, the helo quickly moves down the port side of the patrol boat. Frito has just passed amidships when the next MIG arrives from the west and fires on the boat and helo. The North Koreans have set up a daisy chain of jet after jet making west to east passes on the target. The MIGs are not very accurate with their cannon and so far have made just a couple of non-critical hits on their target. This is because their tactical employment of their weapons is fundamentally unsound. They are attempting to hit a moving target across its narrowest point rather than run up the stern of the patrol boat with less relative motion and a longer target to hit.

At the bow of the boat, Frito spins his helo and drops his speed to a near hover. He reverses his course, making another pass going down the boat's starboard side. Being occupied with flying the aircraft, Lopez cannot examine the boat as well as Grabo who is leaning out the cabin door. Parker is scanning the skies to the west looking for the next MIG to appear from on high and make its pass.

"Frito," Parker speaks steadily, "Our friend is back. Diving from nine o'clock at maybe two miles. And he is coming like a bat out of hell. I'm beginning to think these guys don't like us much."

Lopez answers over the ICS while keeping his eyes on the water and the boat, "I'm beginning to think they were too cheap or in too much of a hurry to bring any missiles along."

"Either that or they are really insulting us by using only their cannon."

"Look!" Grabo shouts over the intercom, "The wheel is tied off on that boat! It's on autopilot! There's no one on deck!" He is interrupted by the loud thud of a cannon shot penetrating the helo fuselage.

"We've been hit!" Parker shouts. Lopez immediately starts a slight left turn to open the distance from the boat that is nearly under him. Immediately after the turn takes effect, the patrol boat explodes. The passing MIG has hit the fuel tank on this pass and the nearly empty tanks were full of fuel vapor. It ignites and throws large chunks of aluminum a hundred feet in the air. It is accompanied by a hundred-foot high red and black fireball. Lopez feels the helo jump up and veer to the left. He also feels heat on his neck and jaw, his only skin not covered by his flight suit, gloves and helmet.

The explosion knocks Grabo backward and slams him against the port bulkhead of the helo. Grabo's chin and neck are burned and he suffers a terrible bruise on his lower back caused by landing on the fire extinguisher mounted to the bulkhead. But his helmet and wet suit have prevented him from receiving any serious injury.

Lopez smoothly and delicately responds to the foreign forces being applied to the controls. Both hands and both feet quickly and gently, but with authority, rapidly maneuver in coordinated efforts to regain control. This response is automatic and the natural extension of the pilot after thousands of hours at the controls. This is flying. Without thinking about it, everything previously learned and experienced is being funneled into these seven seconds. No time to think; just do what is natural; just fight it until you win or lose, but never give up. The belly of the SH-2 kisses the surface. It goes airborne again. It dips to the left and spins left. The belly touches the surface again. But Frito will not let this bull throw him. He will ride it until the rodeo horn blows. The spin stops, the rotor blades level; the helo climbs to fifty feet and stabilizes. Lieutenant Commander "Frito" Lopez has added another chapter to his reputation as a "good stick."

Frito keys his mic, "Everyone all right?"

"Yes, sir," Grabo responds as he rubs his back.

Parker nods.

Lopez speaks to Parker, "Tom, we should get a report out to the Schofield."

Parker is a little confused by this statement. He was on the radio with the ship during the last pass of the patrol boat. "I sent a mayday saying we had been hit and an estimate of our position already."

Lopez does not doubt what his copilot is saying, but he cannot remember hearing the transmission. Frito was so focused on flying that his other senses were temporarily shut down. But he is impressed by the ability of Parker to do his assignment in such extreme conditions. "Tom, good on ya shipmate. I was a little busy back there to think of that."

Parker nods as he keeps his scan outside looking for more MIGs in the area.

Lopez gingerly moves his collective, stick and rudder petals in all directions, then says, "I think any damage we got was cosmetic because she seems to be flying okay. Let's go land and check it out."

Grabo is looking out the cabin door again and says, "I can't see any jets. They must have left once the boat exploded."

* * * * *

281

Both Keene and Evans have kept their scan of the horizon centered to the south. While sailing on an easterly heading, they keep an eye out towards the starboard side. The jets that had buzzed them a half-hour ago disappeared in that direction. Suddenly, just beyond the horizon an orange glow rises. Its colors are reflected off the low gray overcast. No sound has reached the survivors but it is easily identified as an explosion.

"Gentlemen," the admiral says, "I think we just saw ourselves die."

Warbuck sucks in a half a breath and exhales just one word, "Cool."

For the first time since finishing their meal of corn on the cob, Keene feels his spirits rise. He cannot help smiling as he looks at his good friend and says, "Another few hours heading east, and then we should be far enough from the coast to turn south and make for South Korea. One more day, Billy. One more day and we'll be out of kimchi and into roses!"

All three sailors smile. For the first time in a long time they can taste freedom again.

* * * * *

All personnel in the Schofield CIC are stunned into silence. A normally very noisy environment is unusually quiet. Everyone in this dark room is a peace-time sailor. Shipmates have been lost to accidents and drug overdoses, but never to hostile fire. Although some are Vietnam veterans, they served in the destroyer community and never came under enemy fire. Now it is personal. LCDR Lopez, LT (j.g.) Parker and Petty Officer Grabo were alive and onboard the ship just an hour ago, sailing in peace-time waters. Now, just seconds ago, the ASAC speakers had crackled with Parker's voice saying, "Mayday! Mayday! Seasnake One has been hit and is out of control! Position about thirty-six miles on the 320 radial Tango Charlie! Mayday! Mayday!"

For the next ten seconds all in CIC and on the bridge listen rather than talk. Their eyes all fixed on the speakers tuned to the ASAC frequency. Dancer starts to squeeze his microphone trigger to call the stricken aircraft when sound comes over the speaker.

It is Lopez once again sounding like Chuck Yeager after breaking the sound barrier, "Tango Charlie, this is Seasnake One, over."

Every sailor in CIC and the bridge exhales and starts to breathe again as relief floods the control spaces.

Dancer responds, "Roger, this is Tango Charlie, over."

"One is R.T.B.," Lopez transmits, "Have unknown damage from MIG cannon and possible fragging from explosion of a gunboat. Request immediate green deck. ETA Tango Charlie about twenty minutes, over."

"One, Tango Charlie, copy all. Will have crash crews and deck ready when you get here," Dancer replies using the formal R/T procedures that are second nature to military controllers. He next asks the standard tactical question, "What state One? Over."

"One has zero plus four-zero hours left, no arms, no buoys and three souls on board. Over"

Roberts is relieved that he has not lost a helicopter, but his primary concern now is the safety of his ship. He holds up his hand to Dancer and grabs a headset to join the conversation, "Frito, this is Charlie Oscar. We have no joy on air search radar. What's the latest on the bandits?"

"I believe the ones we were playing with went home after the gunboat went up," Lopez answers, surprised by the informality of the normally stiff Roberts.

Grabo interrupts Lopez over the ICS, "Sir, I think I saw one splash after flying through the fireball."

Lopez continues his radio transmission, "Correction, believe one may have splashed after explosion. No sight of any right now."

Roberts answers, "One, Data Link shows that the sky is still full of North Koreans to the north of your posit. Seasnake Four has arrived from the Holt to assist. We will finish his refueling and have the deck clear by the time you arrive. Hurry back."

"Wilco, out," Lopez says. In the cockpit Parker points to the TACAN and gives a thumbs up gesture. Frito sees they have a lock-on and alters course to close the Schofield directly.

CHAPTER SEVENTEEN

McWalters feels her heart has dropped to her stomach. No matter how many times she reads the message, the news remains bleak. So much was done, so much was fitting into place, so much hope in her heart, and now it is all gone. It was all for nothing.

She offers the message to Admiral Bella. He takes it and is interrupted from reading it completely by the arrival of General Adams. The general smiles as he enters the NMCC operations room. Then he makes eye contact with Julie who is about to give in to her emotions after such a long stretch with minimal rest, fatigue making her susceptible to the one emotion that female military officers must never display, tears. Adams drops his smile upon sensing the intense feelings in the room. Bella nods towards his Air Force counterpart and hands the message to the general. As the general reads the message, Bella goes to the rear door of the room and sticks his head out to tell his aide something.

"Well, that's it then," Adams speaks, "This report from Schofield ends it. If they made it on to that boat, they're lost now."

Bella is back in the room and responds, "What is this about Seasnake One's report that the helm was tied off, that the patrol boat was on autopilot?"

McWalters, who had been hiding her eyes by looking down at the Data Link screen, raises her head and speaks with hope restored to her voice. She had not considered that there might be another possible outcome. "Yes, sir, you're right! That could mean they had abandoned the boat before it was attacked and had sent it off as a decoy or something."

But Adams throws water on the idea, "Or it meant they had tied off the wheel to get below decks for cover and to minimize their exposure to the strafing."

"Could be, Norm," Bella says, "but wouldn't you think they would man the guns to defend themselves?"

"Against jets? Against cannon?" Adams asks a question he feels has an obvious answer.

McWalters returns her attention to the computer plot, Adams having sunk her last buoy of hope that had just surfaced. She returns to her professional briefing mode and says with an even voice, "The North Koreans must think they solved their problem. It looks like they have started to recall a lot of their aircraft. Most are returning to base."

All three officers are crowded around the computer screen when the back door opens and Admiral Bella's aide enters. He is also dressed in a civilian tuxedo and almost silently moves to the phone bank next to the computer terminal. He pushes two buttons and they start to flash. He gently taps his admiral on the shoulder and uses a very soft voice to say, "Per your request Admiral, line four is the White House, line five is Mrs. Evans."

Bella nods and the aide retreats to the back of the room. True to his previous orders from Margie, he punches her line first.

"Margie, we have news but it isn't good. I can't discuss it over this un-secure line, but some action has taken place in the area." Bella is trying to be gentle and prepare Margie for the worst possible scenario but he is being pestered by General Adams who is trying to get his attention. "Just one second, Margie," Bella covers the receiver and gives an exasperated look at the general.

"The President is leaving for the west coast right after tonight's White House affair finally ends. I think we might be able to get her on Air Force One. Regardless of whether they are alive or dead, she will need to get to the west coast and perhaps even Japan before this is all settled."

Bella responds to Adams, "I take back all those nasty things I've thought about you Air Force types. You're okay, after all." Then he returns to his conversation with Margie. He makes arrangements for her to be driven to Bolling Air Force Base within the hour.

He hangs up and pauses before he pushes the flashing light with the White House call. Bella takes a deep breath and is about to punch the secure voice communications link with the NSC when McWalters speaks, "Admiral Bella, it is still too overcast to get any satellite pictures of the area where the patrol boat went down. But the Schofield is still in the area and could commence a visual search for any survivors."

Bella nods in agreement and then connects with the NSC to give an update and explain why United States ships and aircraft were in the area. Once again, this is a case where his belief that "bad news doesn't get any better with age" guides him to be pro-active.

* * * * *

Onboard the U.S.S. Schofield, Seasnake One's rotors are gliding to a halt. Grabo jumps to the deck, a feeling of momentary relief sweeping over his entire being. This frigate may only be a little over 400 feet long, but its steel decks make it feel like solid land after being bounced through the sky in a flimsy, thin-skinned twisting and damaged helicopter. However, his feelings of relief pass quickly and his weak knees grow steady without giving a hint of his emotional confusion. He is joined by the pilots who have climbed out of the cockpit side doors. The three aircrew members are immediately joined by most of the ship's flight deck personnel as they examine the fuselage behind the main cabin. Two three-inch holes enter on one side of the airframe and exit with roughly the same size on the opposite side of the tail boom. Smaller slits of frag damage are peppered over the entire starboard side and belly.

The group is silent at first, but then sailors start to verbally express their wonderment in typical sailor fashion. Lopez and Parker do not realize it, but both are slowing shaking their heads in perfect unison. Suddenly, the group gaggle grows silent and parts like the Red Sea for the arrival of Master Chief Roy Pimaloy. Although a member of the LAMPS detachment, Pimaloy has established himself as the Bull Goose Looney of the crew in his few months aboard. Only one of two E-9s in the Chiefs' Mess, his competition for top leader is a weak sonar man who acts as the Command Master Chief, spending most of his time with the officers.

Pimaloy is a personality, a force not to be ignored or trifled with. His "skunk eye" look is nothing any sailor, enlisted or officer, wants to endure. He makes you want to do your best. However, with all his leadership talent and seniority, he pulled assignment on this small-boy detachment as a sort of punishment for getting in the face of both the squadron maintenance officer and operations officer back at North Island. But Pimaloy wears his exile with pride. In his heart he will remain convinced that these two lieutenant commanders had it coming to them. They were wrong and he wasn't going to let them pretend they were right. Okay, maybe his approach could have been a little less arrogant, but it is hard to remain respectful to officers who haven't earned that honor. And besides, what is another six months afloat? He is a sailor with an independent wife and no kids. Going to sea is never a punishment to him. More than half of his thirty years in uniform has been spent floating on the ocean; mainly on carriers as an aviation metalsmith, but also a couple of dets on frigates. And, let's face it, he is the de facto "King of the Deck" on this tub. Not bad duty. The pond is smaller than he is used to, but he is definitely the big fish in it.

"Okay sailors," Pimaloy says with authority but without barking, "Let's get back to our jobs." The group moves away from the aircraft and most pretend to be doing other duties while still looking at the damaged helicopter from a short distance.

Frito trusts his life and that of his crew to the judgment of this grizzled old veteran maintenance master chief. He asks, "Master Chief, is there any internal damage or did these shots pass straight through?"

Pimaloy likes this officer; more than that, he respects this officer. Commander Lopez is a talented pilot and he listens, but more importantly, he doesn't take himself so bleedin' serious. Pimaloy has his ever present flashlight off its belt loop snap and is using it to examine the interior of the tail using the cannon holes as access panels. "Commander, you're lucky you made it back on deck. One of these shots nicked your tail rotor control cable. If it had given out, you three would be SOJ shark bait right now."

"We want to be ready to go up again ASAP," Lopez states flatly. The next question he asks is that of a pilot who has tasted combat and wants to return to do it over, feeling he could have done better. "Can you fix it quickly?"

"Do you want a by-the-MIMS-manual proper permanent fix," the master chief says just as flatly, and then pauses before he finishes his question, "or do you want a battle repair to get airborne with risk?"

Frito knows his answer, but he doesn't fly alone. He shoots a questioning look at both Parker and Grabo. The petty officer nods right away, but the officer is giving it careful consideration. After a moment, Parker shrugs his shoulders, faintly nods and says, "As you said before commander, it sure goes from peace time to war real fast."

Frito does not feel it is appropriate to smile at this attempt to make light of a very important decision. But he does roll his lower lip under the top one and nods knowingly. Despite what Commander Roberts thinks, aviators do not court danger and treat every assignment with a cavalier's attitude. However, the very nature of their primary duty means they must accept risk with every mission. It is always just a matter of judgment on how much risk is acceptable on each flight.

Lopez turns to make eye contact with Pimaloy and says, "Okay then, Master Chief we want to be airborne in twenty minutes."

"Commander, I will have you spotted for take-off in fifteen," Pimaloy promises. He feels that "his" pilot has not let him down. Yes, Lopez is a good stick and an even better officer but, more importantly, he is proving to be a warrior; like those the master chief worked with on the flight deck of the old Oriskany off of North Vietnam in that war.

Lopez lays his hand on the back of Pimaloy's shoulder as he passes the master chief. "I gotta report to the skipper," Frito says and then glances as his fellow aircrew men and adds, "You better hit the head and grab a sandwich."

Pimaloy shouts across the flight deck to three members of the LAMPS Det he sees walking in the hangar, "All right then! Come on sailors! Let's get this bird ready to fly again, right now! Look lively, shipmates!" The sailors double-time it towards the aircraft. Pimaloy grabs Grabo's arm as the sensor operator walks by and says to him, "Just a minute Tony. You tired of getting shot at without shooting back?"

Grabo just replies with an inquisitive look. Pimaloy doesn't notice; he has his eye on a chief petty officer sipping coffee near the hangar door, just aft of his GQ station at the small arms locker.

"Say, Gunner! Come here chief," Pimaloy shouts as he motions for the gunners mate chief to approach. The chief draws close quickly without spilling a drop of his coffee. Pimaloy continues, "Gunner, these boys want to go back up there and maybe duke it out with the bad guys again. You got anything in that small arms locker we could rig as a door gun so they might get in a few licks?"

This is where the involved leadership of the master chief and the respect he has shown for the professional competence of his fellow chiefs pay off. With a wide smile, the gunner responds, "If you want it master chief, we'll get it."

* * * * *

Lieutenant Riley has completed the first leg of his screening pass. He has had to remain close to the Schofield with Seasnake Four to fulfill his assigned anti-ship missile defense mission. It is the one mission that no LAMPS crew ever volunteers to do. In fact, they like to pretend that ASMD is not actually in their mission profile. But it is and it sucks. The LAMPS helicopter is to hover near the ship and blip enhance any targeting radar from an inbound missile. Once the missile locks on the helo, the pilot will slowly move away from the ship to have the streaking stream of fire and death that is racing towards them move to destroy the three man aircrew instead of the couple hundred souls on the ship. In theory, the missile will hopefully just miss or hit the helo. In theory. More than one LAMPS pilot has joked that if they were ever launched with an ASMD mission, they would be about thirty miles away in total emission silence when the ship was hit. The ship's wardroom laughs, but they are never sure if the pilots are joking or not. Even for black shoe officers, it is hard to imagine that an American tactical doctrine included the planned sacrifice of sailors to save a ship.

On his second close aboard screening pass, Dancer calls Riley, "Seasnake Four, Charlie Tango. We have orders to search for survivors where the patrol boat was sunk. Turn to two-eight-three true for vectors to datum."

All three aircrew smile and the pilots exchange pleased looks as Goldsmith keys his mic, "Rog, Four to two-eight-three at cherubs two."

"I'll get my wetsuit on," Profitt says over the intercom.

Riley calls Dancer and asks, "Tango Charlie you got a TACAN posit from Tango Charlie for centering the datum?"

"Best guess is two-seven-two at thirty-one miles. Recommend cherubs three to maintain TACAN at that range."

"Rog," Riley responds, "Any other air traffic out here?"

"Fast movers to the north at about eighty miles tracking to the west. They should be opening your posit," Dancer says as he looks up to check the latest on the AAW grease board. "But be aware of intermittent air contacts about fifty miles to our north. Could be unknown helicopters. They are low and bouncing in and out of our air search."

"Rog," Riley says without realizing he has responded. His focus is the weather just ahead. A heavy rain shower is blocking his path. It is isolated and he decides to swing to the right a mile to avoid the gray, stove pipe column connecting the low clouds with the sea surface. Dirk keys his intercom and calls Profitt, "You dressed back there yet?"

"Yes, sir. What do you need?"

"Throw a point on your scope for the estimated center of the search area and be ready to get me to it. Looks like we will be dodging heavy showers and taking a rather circuitous route there."

"Aye, aye, sir." Profitt chuckles out loud. Riley is a good officer but sometimes his choice of words reveals his silver-spoon upbringing. "Circuitous," not the "long way" or "crooked path."

* * * * *

It is quiet on the sailboat. The wind has kicked up a little and the sea state has grown slightly choppy. Keene remains at the helm, slightly amused that he has re-acquired the feel for steering a sailboat. He hasn't been at a tiller since senior year at the Academy. The admiral is resting near the mast on the port side and Warbuck is lying between the two pilots, his head near Evans's feet. All three are wet. They continue to sail through short, but intense rain showers. It is quiet because all are too exhausted to engage in conversation. Keene and Evans continually scan the horizon, seriously hoping not to see anything. The TACCO winces with every roll of the boat. He struggles for every breath he can suck in.

Finally the thirty minutes of silence is broken by the admiral, "Looks like the weather might get worse before it gets better. Maybe we should try to eat something before it grows rougher."

Keene nods. Warbuck is in his own world, focusing only on capturing air in his one good lung. Evans opens the sack they had brought from the patrol boat. He removes wet bread and passes chunks of it to his shipmates. Keene reaches forward and takes his. Warbuck just shakes his head when he becomes aware of the bread waving in front of his mouth. Evans next reaches into his flight suit left arm pocket and pulls out a small folding can opener. He looks at the bare steel can he has pulled from the sack. There is Korean writing stamped on the top and no other indication what food stuff might be preserved in the can. Evans has difficulty getting his little can opener to puncture the all-steel can lid. It has been decades since he has seen real steel, and the thought crosses his mind that the North Koreans must be short of aluminum. He is only a quarter of the way around the top of this mystery food stuff when he hears something. He turns his head aft, towards the west and raises his hand to cup his ear. Keene now hears it as well. It could be an engine noise thinks Warbuck as he picks up the faint, distant hum. The injured man attempts to raise his head to give both his ears a chance to discern the sound source. But immediately, his head falls back onto the stinking fishing net.

Keene speaks first, "Multi-engine prop. Maybe above the overcast." He points to the west, and then continues, "That direction, I think. Wish it was a P-3, but it sounds more like a twin recip."

Evans nods and makes eye contact with the TACCO. With a look of regret, he pulls the net over Warbuck to cover him completely. Next he crawls under the net to his own neck as well.

The noise grows louder, and then suddenly a North Korean twin-engine patrol plane zooms out of the clouds just aft of the sailboat. It makes a straight line for the boat, and quickly passes directly overhead. Keene gives some thought to turning North or west from their current easterly heading. But noticing that the patrol plane does not seem to be armed, he decides to maintain his course. The plane makes a shallow, long turn to the right, staying below the clouds. Soon it is approaching the sailors from the south. The Korean passes overhead again. Keene waves to him with a big smile. The plane starts a smooth, wide left turn upon passing the boat. The plane establishes a horizontal figure-eight pattern centered on the sailboat.

"This guy seems interested. What's he up to?" asks Evans.

"I imagine he is probably wondering what we are doing this far out. If he would stop making overhead passes, slows down and rig us like a professional he might get a good look at us. Enough to know we are not Korean, anyway."

Evans points just off the starboard bow and says, "Head into that rain squall. No sense making his job easy."

Keene pulls the tiller slightly towards his belly. The admiral tends the sheets and the speed increases a little as the vessel pulls closer into the wind.

"No doubt he has made us," Keene comments. "At least we have a head start on any boat they send after us. We must be making near eight knots so the relative closing speed should give us some time."

Evans responds, "Unless they send a plane that can shoot."

"I was trying not to think of that."

"Damn." Warbuck joins the conversation. "And we were so close."

* * * * *

The lift-off was a little more dicey than normal. The ship's "repel boarders" .50 caliber attached to the winch in Grabo's door has moved Seasnake One's center of gravity a few inches to the right. This became apparent as soon as Frito got daylight under his main mounts. But he cleared the top of the hangar with one foot to spare. And any naval aviator will tell you that an inch is as good as a mile as long as you don't touch.

The ASAC frequency is now a party line. Both helicopters and Petty Officer Dancer are up. What is about to happen is equivalent to a "Vulcan mind-meld." The professionalism of these helicopter pilots and their controller will permit them to conduct a rather complicated and sophisticated evolution with only a couple of transmissions.

"Four, this is Seasnake One. Airborne. Enroute to Black sector at cherubs two, say border, over."

"Roger one. Four is a quarter ways through red pattern centered on true north through datum at cherubs three. No joy yet."

Dancer listens and thinks nothing of letting the two helicopters directly coordinate their own safety of flight. With more than one helo on-station, a good ASAC will sit back and monitor the aircraft but not interrupt; he is a good ASAC. The TAO reaches over and taps Dancer on the shoulder. The officer points to the NC-1 plot. Another watch stander has just drawn a line from the ship's cursor on a bearing of 355 degrees true. The line is labeled, "ESM, NK A/C comm." Dancer nods and keys his mic, "All traffic, Tango Charlie. ESM hit, possible North Korean aircraft radio freq, bearing three-five-five true Tango Charlie."

"One, rog."

"Four, rog."

On board Schofield the Data Link operator scribbles a quick position on the plotter. He labels it "Skunk M." The position is near the ESM bearing. There are no other unknown surface contacts reported in that area.

Dancer sees the latest and transmits to his birds in the air, "All traffic, Tango Charlie. Satellite hit on Skunk Mike. One it should be on your two o'clock at thirty miles."

"Charlie Tango, Seasnake one, roger," Lopez responds using proper R/T procedures to ensure the ship knows he is on it. He then pushes his ICS button, "Grabs, anything on radar?"

"Negative."

"Let me know when you do."

"Tango Charlie, One is proceeding to investigate. But we have squat for visibility currently due to rain and low clouds."

* * * * *

"Here comes our friend again, port side, wave top height this time," Keene shouts over the falling rain and quickening wind.

Evans has to twist in his seat to look behind him. He sees the North Korean patrol plane coming in for another pass. The admiral is tired, no, he is exhausted, and his patience is at an end. The warrior inside him has finally broken the civilized chains that have kept it in check for the past days. He blurts out, "Screw this!"

Evans throws off the fishing net covering most of him. He reaches for the assault weapon at his feet, but it is tangled in the net. He furiously struggles to get it free. By the time he can raise it to his shoulder the plane has buzzed the sailboat and is heading away. The admiral is mad. He stands in the boat, barely balancing himself as he tries to get a shot at the patrol plane but it is out of range and the sail is blocking his view. "Damn that peckerwood!" he shouts, "If that S.O.B makes another pass he is going to taste my extreme displeasure!"

The North Korean pilot starts a slow turn towards the west. Keene notes that the airplane does not continue its turn, but disappears to the south west of their location. Then Jim speaks, "Guess you scared him away, admiral."

"Yeah," Warbuck adds through clinched teeth and much pain, "They don't want to mess with Admiral Rambo Evans." This brings a chuckle to Keene and his TACCO. Evans realizes for the first time that he is standing in the small boat shaking the AK-47 at the sky. He quickly flops back down to his seat. Then even he smiles at what he had just done.

"Crap!" Keene says in an alarmed and angry complete one word sentence. He looks astern and asks, "You hear that?"

Evans and Keene simultaneously realize why the patrol plane has departed. Coming up from behind, bouncing and tumbling on the wave tops at maximum speed is a North Korean coastal patrol boat. "Not good," Evans says in a flat tone. Warbuck has removed the net from around his head and tries to rise to an elbow while asking, "What is it?"

"Billy, I think we're screwed after all," Keene shares with his friend. "It's a patrol boat closing fast."

"Where's a squall when you need one?" Evans rhetorically asks. "Gentlemen, I am too tired and in too sour a disposition to be taken captive by a bunch of goofy wanna-be sailors."

Warbuck nods and adds, "Screw 'em all. Hand me that other 47, boss." Evans hands the main sheet to Keene and then cycles the action of the assault rifle. He hands it to Warbuck. The admiral digs out the other AK-47 and then ensures it is ready to fire as well. Warbuck crawls to where he can just see over the gunnels. Propping the rifle barrel on the edge of the boat, he has assumed a one-armed firing position. Keene kicks around the supplies at his feet and pulls a knapsack from under the pile of items. He gently tosses the bag to the admiral. Evans opens it and counts seven loaded ammunition magazines. Then he assumes a firing position similar to Warbuck's.

Keene is looking at the North Korean boat when he sees a puff of white smoke. Immediately following he hears a loud clap, followed by a visible splash about one hundred yards aft of the sailboat. "That's not good," he says aloud what he is thinking.

As the words cross his lips he sees another puff of white smoke and hears another clap. Before the shell arrives, Keene pulls the tiller into his belly and changes course. But he is not the best sailor and he moves too far from the wind direction. The jib and mainsail began to flutter. The sailboat loses speed rapidly. Panic erupts in the pilot who fears he has made a terrible error. Instinctively he reacts to the situation and shoves the tiller away from him. The boat still has enough way on that the rudder responds to the violent maneuvering. The sails fill with wind and the boat starts to accelerate. Evans gives Keene a steely look and Keene shakes his head to indicate he knows he screwed up. However, Keene's moderate course change has caught the wind better than before and the boat's speed is increasing as it heads more northwesterly. But this puts the gunboat on the port quarter, an improved target solution for them.

Splash! No sound, just splash! The cannon shot is not big and neither is the height of the water it kicks up. But when it lands close aboard the port side, the splash throws water onto the Americans. The North Koreans are closing fast and have now officially reached a point where the sailboat is in range of the bow-mounted deck cannon.

Their ranging shots complete, next the Koreans send a flight of four rapid fire pops down range. Splash! Splash! Splash! Crack! The fourth round hits the bow sprint. The old wooden spar snaps off and with it goes the lower end of the jib. The force of it flying to starboard snaps the forward stay connection at the top of the mast. The jib sail is now dragging along the starboard bow connected to the craft by its halyard, acting like a sea anchor. Evans reaches into his flight suit right calf pocket and pulls out his survival knife. He reaches towards the foot of the mast. He verifies that he has the jib halyard and cuts it with one angry pull of his knife. The jib halyard races through the rigging and the boat is free of the jib. Even with the bow sprint shot away, the integrity of the bow is still solid. Speed has been reduced, but the Americans are still moving, Keene steering an erratic course in an attempt to avoid further hits.

"Billy, I think they are still way out of range, but go ahead and squeeze off a round and I'll try to see where it splashes," Evans directs. Warbuck takes aim and fires. Simultaneous with the report of his rifle, a cannon shell flies through the sail. A five-inch hole almost dead center is torn in the old, soiled cotton fabric.

"Couldn't see it land," the admiral says as he ducks his head below the gunnels. "Maybe in another minute or so we can start to fight back."

With the forward mast stay gone, the mast has stayed upright because the wind is from the beam allowing the port stay to take the primary strain. However now the crew's bad luck turns worse. The wind veers forward and as it moves to the bow, the mast falls aft and over the starboard stern quarter. The boat starts to take water over the starboard side. Keene is thrown from the stern into the water. He maintains his grip on the main sheet and uses it to pull himself back into the slowly sinking boat.

The three man gun crew on the bow of the Koran boat is joined by a fourth armed with an old Chinese rifle. This Korean gets into the action and pops off shots at the helpless boat.

Between raking shots by the cannon, Evans notices the pesky ping of small arms fire. He peeks over the raised port side and estimates that the Koreans are only two-hundred yards away and closing fast. For some strange reason, Evans feels relief upon ascertaining that the boat has closed to small arms range. Now maybe he can go down fighting. He was worried about losing without firing a shot. If he is going out, it will be swinging for the fence and not on a called strike. The sailboat is at a twenty-five degree list to starboard which allows him to nearly stand upright with his feet on the starboard bench seat to gain a firing position over the port gunnels. The admiral takes aim and squeezes off a short three-round burst. He sees he is low. He raises his aim slightly and fires off another burst. It rakes the patrol boat bow. One of the gun crew falls to the deck holding his leg. Evans smiles. He knows it was a lucky shot, but any honest fighter pilot will admit that being lucky is as important as skill in battle.

Warbuck pulls himself to a firing position. Once again, the adrenaline pumping through his system blocks his pain and he is able to join the fight. His aim is erratic, but it causes the helmsman of the North Korean craft to start taking evasive action. Not well versed in the use of automatic weapons, Billy goes "Hollywood" with his firing. In just two short bursts he has emptied his magazine. He reaches into the bag and grabs a new magazine and is surprised how simple the AK-47 is to reload. He now makes a conscious effort to be more sparing with his ammunition use. Rat-a-tat, re-aim, rat-a-tat. Still, even with this fire discipline, he is out of rounds in a very short time.

Evans has reloaded twice himself. Why not? He figures the enemy will be upon them in just a minute or so. No sense being taken down with ammo still in the bag. The cannon fire is getting more accurate now. The sailboat's hull splinters upon receipt of a well placed round at the stern. Warbuck gives a quick glance at where the tiller had been. He expects to see his plane commander and close friend blown apart. But there is no sign of Keene. Then the TACCO feels a tug on his leg. He looks down and a soaking wet Keene is holding a new magazine. Warbuck smiles at his shipmate. Keene is too exhausted to smile back. But he does ask, "Billy, this one is mine. Let me have a turn before we sink." Warbuck fires off the last of his current magazine and then rolls over to his back and hands his assault rifle to Keene. The pilot loads the weapon and rises over the port gunnels to take aim. He is shocked by how close the Koreans are. They couldn't be more than one hundred yards.

After being surprised by receiving return fire from what they thought was their toothless prey, the patrol boat skipper had slowed their speed. A hundred yards is a long distance for an assault rifle, especially in the hands of inexperienced sailors, but it is very close range for a 20-mm cannon. Cannon shells are falling all around the stationary, slowly sinking target, but the sailboat has yet to receive the deciding kill shot.

Evans wants to get lucky again and hit the man in the shoulder crutches firing the cannon. He takes careful aim and squeezes his trigger for what he is confident is an accurate shot. But nothing happens. "Damn," he mumbles to himself as he reaches into the knapsack for another magazine. When he cannot lay his hands on one, he looks into the bag. It is empty. "Damn...DAMN!" he utters and looks at Keene. Just then the chatter of Keene's weapon stops. The two pilots make eye contact and both shrug in their acknowledgement that all the ammunition is gone. The pilots slump into the bottom of the listing craft, joining Warbuck in a place of imaginary safety.

Warbuck reaches into his flight suit pocket and pulls out his survival knife. This results in a loud laugh from Evans, but it is a laugh that demonstrates his pride in his fellow officer's statement and understanding of the comic element in this futile action. The admiral pulls out his survival knife and unsheathes it. He waves it like a sword, still smiling. Keene shakes his head and sneaks a peek over the port side at their soon-to-be-victorious enemies. The sound of the cannon is now very loud and its rapid fire mode has covered the patrol boat bow in white smoke. Keene feels more like a spectator now and finds the view rather fascinating.

Suddenly, through the smoke shrouding the patrol boat, he sees the cannon loader fall to the deck and large holes peppering the forward cabin. Then he hears it. The unmistakable wop-wop-wop of a helo. Looking up, just sliding over the sailboat bow from the southwest is the sight of a green angel with "U.S. Navy" painted on its side.

"Pour it onto them Grabo!" Parker shouts without using the ICS, "That's it! Whack those commie bastards!" He is stretching his neck to look across Lopez to see the gunboat on their right side.

"Grabs, continue to concentrate on the bow," Lopez calmly directs over the ICS. "I will hold it here in a hover to make it a little easier on you." Then he shoots a quick glance at his co-pilot and mouths, "Get help."

Parker nods, and keys his mic, transmitting, "Seasnake Four, this is One. We're in a fire fight with some commies on a boat trying to kill some sinking Americans. We need help getting them out of the water. Location is last posit provided by Tango Charlie earlier. Need assistance *now!*"

Before Riley can even respond to Parker, Profitt comes over the ICS and says, "I got 'em on radar. Go zero-zero-four." This senior petty officer learned how to keep the big picture in focus years ago. In this critical moment, no time will be lost because his crew had to go looking to find its squadron sister.

Riley quickly spins his helo to the new heading and pushes the aircraft up to full speed. He calls Parker, "One, Four is on the way. ETA about five minutes."

"Make that two minutes or you'll miss the dance."

Lopez is amazed at the unusual forces the large caliber machine gun puts on this small helicopter. Years of flying experience and natural skill are being put to the test in trying to hold a stable platform for Grabo. Frito is even more amazed by the accuracy of his sensor operator. Granted, the range is less than a hundred yards and he is spraying shot in rapid fashion everywhere, but hitting a moving target from a helicopter using a jury rigged gun is no easy task; especially for an amateur.

The gun operator on the Korean vessel has been moved aside and a loader has taken his place on the controls. Soon the boat is directing all of its fire on the hovering helo just ahead. Lopez can feel every hit made on his airframe. Thud-thud-thud. Those three were the worst. But his controls remain effective. Smash! The wind screen by his ankle is hit. But he feels no pain and the aircraft is still responding to all inputs. So far so good. The loud clatter of Grabo's machine gun continuing to pour rounds into the boat tells Frito that he must hold his position, no matter how hot it is getting. But it can't last forever, so Frito transmits, "Tango Charlie, One, any word on CAP support? We need help out here now!"

Dancer can only relay what he has been told and it makes him feel helpless, "They were told to scramble from Osan. I estimate they should be here in just a couple more minutes, but no contact with them yet."

When Frito keys his mic to answer the helo takes another hit, slicing open a foot wide gash just below his seat. He keeps his mic keyed while he interrupts his communicating to aviate. While he has his mic active, all of the Schofield CIC and bridge team can hear the chatter of Grabo's .50 cal and the hit on the aircraft from the boat's cannon. It sounds like war. It fascinates and also scares every member of the ship watch team, especially Dancer. Lopez now has the time to respond to the last transmission, "It had better be sooner than later. Close us fast. We're losing up here."

Grabo is totally focused on his task at hand. His biggest challenge is keeping his footing. The spent .50 cal casings are large and underfoot. Most slide right out the open cabin door, but some rattle around the floor of the compartment.

The Gunner Chief had rigged his gun with it supported by the in-door hoist and pulled back to Grabo by two lanyards attached to each side of the door. It gives Grabo just enough slack to aim at targets below him and nearly abeam. Grabo keeps both thumbs pressed on the trigger and moves the barrel slightly left and right, raking the bow of the gunboat. Many rounds splash around his target, but one in every ten is effectively keeping the boat's gun crew preoccupied sufficiently to prevent them from accurately aiming their cannon. Suddenly his gun goes silent. The magazine is empty. Grabo struggles to replace it with the only reload he has. It takes nearly twenty seconds to get another round into the barrel. It is the longest twenty seconds in the lives of Frito, Tom and Tony.

Parker has ceased to look across Lopez to watch the fire fight. Now that it is one-sided, he pretends that if he can't see the boat, then the danger isn't real. He keeps his eyes on the instruments in front of him and on the sailboat sinking below him. His thoughts are confused and rushed. What is the plan? What should we be doing next? Where is our help? Just then Grabo's machine gun starts to bang away again. This clears Parker's thoughts enough to respond to a voice in his headset.

"One, this is Four. We have a tally on you. In bound. We'll be there in thirty seconds," Goldsmith calmly advises his squadron's sister bird.

Parker is back in the problem now and responds, "Roger, complete personnel pick-up from sailboat just below us." Parker then taps Lopez's left shoulder. Frito has his eyes centered on the slowly approaching patrol boat while attempting to maintain a firing position for Grabo. He turns his head quickly to glance at Tom. The co-pilot has his horizontal flat hand at shoulder level. He slowly slides it to the right. Lopez nods and adjusts his hover to close the patrol boat slightly. Seasnake One opens the air space above the sinking boat to permit the other helo to enter a hover right over the survivors.

While Grabo and his pilots provide cover for Seasnake Four to approach a pick-up hover, the survivors' situation is growing more desperate. The stern is now under water, and the mast is lying over the starboard side with fouled lines and stays. The damaged bow is the only part of the stricken vessel still bobbing above the surface. Keene is clutching the port bow gunnels with one hand and Warbuck with the other. Evans is next to him, doing the same with Jones's body.

In a flash these struggling shipmates are engulfed in a swarm of a million needles striking their faces. It becomes difficult to breathe as the rotor down wash of Seasnake Four centers over them. Their own private little typhoon has arrived to make things even more difficult to survive.

Profitt very calmly and professionally talks over the ICS, directing his pilot to a low rescue hover. Riley makes his approach from the west so the hoist and open cabin door will be opposite the firing gunboat for the rescue. He slides into a position just twenty feet above his target. Goldsmith's safety of flight scan dances rapidly between the radar altimeter, vertical speed indicator and Seasnake One which is very close on his left. Profitt's next call over the ICS is, "That's it lieutenant. I'm lowering the hoist." Profitt is ready to enter the water as a rescue swimmer if he has to, but he prefers to stay at his post to best guide the pilot and operate the hoist. From his vantage point, he sees both Evans and Keene moving well and taking care of two wounded men.

Keene watches as the horse collar survival device is lowered right above his head. But he does not reach out to grab it just yet. He thinks, "It is amazing at what you remember from your training even in times of maximum duress." He waits until the horse collar touches the water and discharges all the static electricity built up while being lowered. He has been through too much today to get zapped with a jolt now. It won't kill you, but it stings something fierce.

The nice quiet sail of just an hour ago is now a storm of water, wind, noise and fear. Two helicopters in a hover in close proximity, the constant popping of the .50 cal and the cannon explosions have made this small bit of the sea a miniature hell. Despite the situation, Evans and Keene know what they want to accomplish. Both are exhausted and operating on the very last ounces of their remaining strength. Keene snatches the end of the horse collar floating in the water within arms reach. He hears Warbuck scream in pain as he places the collar under the TACCO's arms and clips the free end to the hoist. "Just keep your hands by your side, Billy!" Jim yells above the massive din of the battle. Warbuck is near passing out. His body hurts so much that he is crying. However no tears come out because he is so far beyond exhaustion. Keene raises his right arm and gives a thumbs-up signal. Profitt hits the switch and Warbuck starts his ascent. The rotor wash is stinging their eyes, but Keene and Evans try to watch as the TACCO is pulled up, both thinking the same thing, "I hope he can stay conscious long enough, because it's taking forever for him to reach the helo."

Now the two pilots turn their attention to Jones. They unwrap their dead shipmate from the signal flags and each hold him by a shoulder with their free hand and to the bobbing boat with their other. They keep their eyes down and nearly closed fighting the terrible storm generated by the big whirling blades just a few yards above them. Soon Evans sees the horse collar being dragged across the water five feet from him. He reaches for it but misses. He releases his grip from the body and boat and lunges for it. His leap is successful. With the horse collar in one hand, he swims back to Keene. Together they put Jones's body into the harness facing backwards. They pull both of the corpse's wrists together in front of the body. Evans grabs one of the floating signal flags nearby and uses it to wrap together Jones's wrists. Up goes Keene arm again with the thumbs-up. Profitt hits his switch and Jones is hoisted from the water. The noise level suddenly drops. Grabo's machine gun is quiet again. Parker looks over his right shoulder and makes eye contact with the enlisted crew member. Grabo raises his empty hands and shrugs. The helicopter is no longer a gunship. It is out of ammunition. It is merely a target again.

At this exact moment a strange voice is heard on the radio, "Seasnakes, please hold your position while we make a pass."

Lopez looks at Parker; Riley looks at Goldsmith. Four confused faces. Then breaking under the overcast comes two United States Air Force F-4s screaming directly over the patrol boat at three-hundred knots, heading from west to east. After passing, the jets make a low wide left turn. The patrol boat throws its rudder hard over and jams its throttle to maximum speed. But their attempt to escape is futile. The F-4s complete a 180 degree turn and this time when they approach the target they expertly and accurately fire their internal cannons. The gunboat explodes immediately.

Lopez and Riley are too busy and Keene and Evans too exhausted to cheer. But Grabo, Parker and Goldsmith let out shouts of joy and relief. It is the most beautiful sight in their entire lives.

Profitt pulls Jones into the cabin and examines the body. He interrupts Goldsmith's celebration, "The first survivor is severely injured. This second sailor is dead."

In Seasnake One, Parker keys his ICS and says, "Wow! Was that ever a pretty sight! You okay back there Grabo?"

"Yeah, I'm okay, but the master chief is going to have a coronary when he sees all the holes in this bird!"

Lopez joins the conversation, "We seem to be flying okay." Now he transmits on the radio to his friend in Seasnake Four, "Dirk, you got everyone out of the water?"

"No. We got two and we're full. There are two left and they are sinking fast."

"Roger. Four you return to Tango Charlie. We'll snatch the other two," Lopez responds.

Dirk breaks his hover and looks at Seasnake One for the first time since they arrived. He is shocked by the condition of that bird. He is truly surprised that an SH-2 can take that kind of damage and remain airborne. "Frito, you look like a flying Swiss cheese. How you gonna go that?"

"Shhh," Frito transmits, "She's a good bird and she doesn't know she can't do it. You go back and deliver your packages. We'll be okay, just be sure you clear the deck before we arrive."

Grabo listens to this chatter while he is removing the machine gun lanyards and lowering the hoist to pull the large gun into the cabin. He unhooks the machine gun and is about to request permission to jettison it to make room for the survivors. But then he burns his hand on the hot barrel while trying to maneuver it. "Screw this!" he thinks. "What are they going to say if I ask permission? No?" He kicks the gun over the side and reaches for the horse collar to attach the sling to the hoist cable.

Lopez feels the aircraft jump a little when the heavy machine gun is jettisoned. He doesn't say anything, or ask what happened. He does smile with pride at the initiative and anticipation of the young petty officer who is coming of age as an American sailor.

Keene and Evans are waiting for the rescue collar to be lowered again when they feel the blast from above become even stronger. Then it disappears as Seasnake Four accelerates away from them and climbs. This does not cause immediate concern because Seasnake One is still in a hover thirty yards away. But when that helicopter breaks hover and heads to the west, the two survivors can feel their anxiety climb even higher. Are they leaving us? Don't they know we are here?

Lopez has climbed to fifty feet and opened datum. The wind is from the northwest and he wants to approach his pick-up from the southeast. At one-half mile he turns to start his inbound run. Upon seeing the helicopter start its turn and descent, Evans and Keene smile and become almost giddy. Can it be? Are we going to make it? They think that just maybe they are actually going to make it home.

The first in the collar is Keene. The admiral insists he will be the last one pulled from the water. It is what a leader does. He takes care of his sailors.

Ten minutes later Evans is pulled into the hovering Seasnake One. Grabo removes the horse collar from this last survivor and when he does it exposes Evans's name tag. Upon seeing the word "admiral," Grabo's eyes widen. He has never been this close to an admiral before and he reverts to a Boot Camp mentality. For just a second, he forgets the battle, aircraft damage and the danger. Here is a real life admiral in my cabin! The junior petty officer keys his ICS and says, "Commander Lopez, we just pulled an admiral out of the water, sir."

Frito smiles at the sudden innocence and astonishment of this sailor who seconds before was pouring a stream of lead on a gunboat trying to kill him. "Yeah, I know," he responds, "Who is the other guy?"

"Looks like a lieutenant commander."

"Ask him his name."

Grabo gets right into Keene's face and shouts over the engine and wind noise, "Your name, sir?" Keene turns so Grabo can see his nametag. Grabo relays it to Lopez. Upon hearing the pilot's response, Grabo leans into Keene's face again and shouts "Are you Lieutenant Commander James Keene, Class of Seventy-three?"

Keene nods. Next Grabo pulls his helmet off and hands it to the survivor yelling, "Someone wants to talk to you."

Keene pulls on the helmet. A voice comes through the earphones, "Say, Jim, what you been up to lately?"

Keene does not associate the voice with anyone he knows. He looks forward to the cockpit, but all he sees is the back of two helmets. He says, "I don't know who you are, but that was both the bravest and dumbest exhibition of flying I ever saw. Thank you."

Lopez turns to show his face to the passengers in the aft cabin. He slides up his tinted wind screen on his helmet. With a big smile he says, "Well, nobody messes with a member of seventy-three without they take on the whole class."

It takes a second, but he Academy reference answers the mystery in Keene's mind. He smiles even bigger and says, "Frito! Thanks, classmate."

Lopez responds with a thumbs-up and returns to the flying problem at hand. Evans has watched the exchange without hearing a word, but he recognizes a reunion of classmates. He smiles and shuts his eyes, enjoying being airborne once again.

CHAPTER EIGHTEEN

Epilogue

Julie McWalters is too tired to be demonstrative. Her feelings are bittersweet but she is satisfied her hard work was not totally for naught. Upon hearing of the three Crew Eleven survivors being pulled from the Sea of Japan she was elated. Soon after, upon receiving the follow-up OPREP that told of the deaths of the ten sailors who were not saved, she was angry and confused by the actions of the North Koreans. And she was sad. Who can ever understand that society, those people? Why would they do that to non-threatening crash survivors washed up on their beach? No matter how much study she does, an understanding of "those people" will remain beyond her grasp. When she took the rag and started erasing the names of the dead from her grease board she felt a personal loss for each sailor. They had ceased to be names to her. They had become shipmates that she had never met.

The traffic is very light on the Arlington roads as she leaves the Pentagon to drive home. Having spent nearly all of the past four days and nights inside the five-sided complex, she has forgotten that it is early Friday morning when she finally sees the sky again. Upon arriving at her small apartment, she has no interest in eating or trying to unwind. She skips her normal, detailed pre-bed routine this morning. It is 7 A.M. and she just scrubs her face, strips out of her uniform, throwing it over a bedroom chair and climbs between her cool, clean satin sheets. Her last thought before succumbing to a deep sleep is a famous line from her favorite movie, "I will think about that tomorrow."

311

＊ ＊ ＊ ＊ ＊

No guide is necessary. Both Admiral Bella and General Adams are extremely familiar with the way to the NSC compound in the White House basement. As they enter the conference room, Secretary Verbel and Assistant Counsel Bordon are seated on one side. The president's chief of staff, his assistant and the Chairman of the Joint Chiefs are all sitting around the table. Neither the admiral nor general wait to be asked to sit down. Both take seats at the end of the wide table.

Verbel speaks first, "This is serious, admiral. I am considering asking you to retire immediately. What did you think you were doing? I thought I had made myself very clear on what I wanted."

Bella may have spent his entire adult life in Navy blue, but he has learned what is central to every politician, and it is not doing what is right. He looks to his boss before he responds and receives a slight nod from the Chairman. Having received non-verbal permission to say what needs to be said, Bella calmly responds to the secretary.

"So you are upset that we saved three brave servicemen? I thought you would be mad at those commie bastards who murdered five of our sailors." Having re-framed the situation, he pauses to let the politicians reflect on the new picture. Then he changes their perspective once again, "And I am not sure what exactly I did that displeased you or violated your direction. You said I was not to re-start the Korean War and no divisions are rushing south across the DMZ last I heard." Now Bella turns his gaze to the chief of staff, "The next choice is the President's. He can tell the public that the North Koreans killed Americans and it took force to save the last three they were trying to murder, or we can announce that the fleet found three survivors of a plane crash that had gone down while in international waters. Either way, I think the voters will view it as a proud day in American history.

312

Either we stood up to tyranny or we celebrate the courage and abilities of three sailors who braved the harsh elements to remain alive despite all odds. It is an uptick in the polls no matter what."

The politicians around the table start a quiet conversation amongst themselves, completely ignoring the three military professionals at the table. Adams looks at Bella. He is having trouble keeping his knowing smile from being seen. Adams knows that the problem has been bumped to a higher pay grade and he and the admiral are untouchable. Success covers a multitude of sins, especially if politicians come out looking good.

* * * * *

The Schofield sickbay is crammed full of crew members. In fact, the passageway outside of this small medical office is also jammed with sailors trying to be close to the action. Inside, Hospital Corpsman First Class "Doc" Gillen is checking the IV in Warbuck's arm. All three survivors are clean shaven; Evans and Keene wear borrowed khakis and Warbuck is in bed wearing a hospital gown. Keene sits in one of the two racks with ice packed around his elevated injured knee. Roberts, Lopez and Parker stand next to the flag officer and the P-3 pilot. The captain offers any assistance to Evans while Frito and Jim catch up on classmate news. It is a few minutes before Roberts notices the fatigue wash over the faces of the survivors. Obviously, the adrenaline high has run its course and both Evans and Keene are about to fall asleep where they sit.

"Okay, sailors. Let's clear sickbay so these gentlemen can start their recovery now," the captain orders as he gently starts pushing the well-wishers through the hatch.

Soon the only door to sickbay is closed and the passageway outside cleared. Only the corpsmen and Roberts remain. Evans says, "Thank you, Captain. I think we could use a little sleep now."

Keene joins the conversation, "Captain, how soon before Billy can get to a surgeon?"

"Doc Gillen has been in radio contact with doctors on the Kitty Hawk and they have Lieutenant Warbuck stabilized now. We'll be within range of the Shasta's H-46 in about four hours. It will take all of you back to the Shasta. A quick turnaround refuel there and then they can reach the Kitty Hawk. The carrier has the surgery suite standing by. The plan is to have your friend in recovery, feeling better within twelve hours."

Keene turns to a quiet Warbuck and says softly to him, "Billy, thanks for sticking around and making the trip with us."

Evans takes the lieutenant's hand and squeezes it as he says, "There's a lot more to go home to than a seventy-eight Volare."

There is a tear running down the side of Warbuck's face when he says, "Don't I know it, admiral. Thanks shipmates. Thanks."

* * * * *

On the Schofield's flight deck Grabo is examining Seasnake One. It is one beat-up helicopter. Master Chief Pimaloy walks up behind him, and then stops next to him. Both continue to examine the damage in silence. After a long minute, the master chief speaks, "Tony, you did good shipmate."

Grabo keeps his eyes fixed on the massive damage covering so much of the aircraft. A significant memory rushes over his emotions upon hearing the "old salt's" words. It is the same feeling he first had in his life at boot camp graduation. It is the same feeling that will keep him in the Navy for thirty years. It is pride in doing something worthy of his very best efforts, something important in life, and the satisfaction in being recognized for doing it well. He never felt this same pride, this same feeling in civilian life. He will remember this moment and this feeling a couple of decades later when he will say the same thing to a young petty officer. It is this two-hundred years of tradition that makes regular guys into sailors. Grabo feels all of this, but he can only say, "Thanks, Master Chief."

Pimaloy slaps Grabo's back to punctuate his gratitude in seeing a young man uphold the "finest traditions of the Naval Service." Nothing more needs be said, so the master chief turns and returns to duties in the hangar.

* * * * *

Captain Carter throws a file on the desk in front of Colonel Milkus. The Marine opens it without looking up. He sees two letters, one clipped to each side of the folder. He reads the left one first. It is a formal request to immediately retire signed by Carter. Still keeping his eyes lowered and on the documents, Milkus reads the letter on the right. It is dated today and it is addressed to all members of the Senate and House Intelligence Committees with courtesy copies to members of the JCS and the President's Chief of Staff. In four short paragraphs it outlines the Gamma Three development plans leaked to the Chinese. It is signed by Carter with a blank signature space above Milkus's typed name.

Milkus reaches into his top desk drawer and pulls out a red folder. It is stamped in large letters "TOP SECRET." Inside is his own request to retire. He takes Carter's two letters and inserts them into his red folder. The colonel pulls a large rubber stamp and pad from his top drawer. He stamps the letter to the legislators with "TOP SECRET" in several places. Then for the first time he looks up at Carter. Their eyes meet and Carter can see that Milkus is near tears. Both feel terribly empty inside. Both have taken pride in their profession for their entire adult lives. It is this pride that is forcing them to do what they perceive is their duty. It is especially sad for Milkus. His entire being is totally defined by his place in the Marine Corps; no family left, no outside interests, only the Corps. His choices in life have shown that he loves the Corps more than wife and home. Now he must leave his Corps family. But without any further hesitation he grabs the pen from its holder above his blotter. He quickly signs his retirement request and then he carefully and deliberately scrolls his name on the letter to the Intelligence Committee members.

Together, Carter and Milkus personally make copies of the pages and prepare to hand-carry them to the Hill. Neither looks back as they march out of the JCS spaces, and neither turns around for one last look at the Pentagon as they walk to Carter's car.

* * * * *

Along with Warbuck, Evans and Keene were hoisted into the H-46 and flown to the U.S.S. Shasta, a large supply ship. They remained aboard the aircraft as it was quickly refueled and then immediately lifted off to rush to the Kitty Hawk. While Warbuck was in surgery, a COD took the admiral and patrol pilot to Atsugi Naval Air Station. At Atsugi they walked across the flight line to a waiting VP-40 P-3. Onboard the aircraft was the squadron CO and Master Chief Strait and Intelligence officers from Evans's headquarters. Two civilian members of the Intel community were also onboard. During the ensuing flight a complete debriefing was done. Now, less than twenty-four hours from being plucked from a sinking sailboat in the Sea of Japan, Evans and Keene are sitting in the dinette of the P-3 as it turns onto its final approach to Barbers Point Naval Air Station on Oahu.

After landing, the aircraft taxies to the front of base operations. The main cabin door opens and the ladder is lowered. Evans is the first to step out of the airplane. He sees a red carpet at the foot of the ladder with gleaming silver 6-inch gun rounds bordering it. A band strikes up Anchor's Away. Standing at the opposite end of the red carpet is the SECDEF and Bordon, each with an eye on the reporters and photographers off to their right. It is so very hard for these politicians not to be obvious as they jockey for the best photo op positions. They feel it is important for them to be in these shots after they made the 4,000 mile trip to meet the "heroes." Crowding behind the politicians are the base commanding officer and hundreds of sailors from this P-3 base.

Evans takes one step down the ladder and waits for Keene to step out of the airplane behind him. The admiral turns his head to speak to his fellow survivor, "Oh great, a real circus."

"Over there, by the front of base ops!" Keene whispers into Evans's ear. The admiral scans to the right and sees them. Off to the side, segregated by yellow tape from the pubic welcome he sees Margie and Keene's family.

"That your wife and kids?" he asks.

"Yes, sir."

"Then screw this official stuff and follow me!" the admiral says as he quickly starts moving down the ladder.

"Aye, Aye, sir!"

Upon reaching the red carpet the two pilots smile at the official welcoming party and then, rather than cross the carpet to be met by the dignitaries, they turn right and rush across the tarmac on a bee line for their loved ones, Keene hobbling to keep up on his swollen knee. Meredith Keene is the first to slip underneath the yellow tape and run towards her father. Keene kneels and she embraces him in a joyous hug. He sweeps her up and squeezes her. Soon he is surrounded by his wife and sons, all hugging and pressing against one another in a scene so familiar to all veterans returning from war. Joyce Keene is crying and laughing. She rocks her head back and looks up to heaven and mouths, "Thank you, thank you, thank you."

Admiral Evans goes from a jog to a full run. Margie has time just to slip under the yellow tape before her athletic husband has closed the distance between them. This is the first time he has returned from war or a deployment when she was there waiting for him. He could care less about proper flag decorum or the crowd of reporters and spectators. He embraces his wife and they kiss. It feels so wonderful to have her arms around him and to smell her hair and feel her body pressed against him again. He is a truly happy man at this moment. Seeing her is a real surprise which makes it even sweeter. He says, "They didn't tell us you'd be here. We expected you in California. How did you get here?"

Margie points over her shoulder to Air Force One parked behind the base operations building, and says, "You made your Commander-in-Chief a hero for a day. So, he lent us his wings."

Evans's smile grows even wider and he says, "Now that is traveling in style! The food any good?"

"Depends on what you order."

"All I want is a burnt Porterhouse steak."

*****

Forty-five days later, a small memorial service was held at the Franklyn Family Funeral Parlor in Manchester Center, Vermont. In attendance were two high school buddies of Ambrose Jones, twenty-one VP-40 shipmates who flew in a P-3 to Albany, New York then hired a bus to drive the one hour to Manchester Center, and one admiral accompanied by his wife, Margie. As Petty Officer Jones had no relatives in attendance, Admiral Evans placed the Silver Star awarded Jones on the hero's casket.

The last to leave the graveside service at Factory Point Cemetery was Admiral Evans. He had lingered after all left to talk with Jones privately. His last words before he saluted and turned to join Margie at the waiting car were simple but satisfying. "Promise kept, shipmate."

ABOUT THE AUTHOR

Commander Bartron is a retired Navy pilot and education administrator. During his 25 years on active duty, he survived one aircraft crash and five emergency forced landings including one where the aircraft was on fire, while accumulating over 5,000 hours in the air. He earned his Bachelor's degree (*History*) from the U.S. Naval Academy (Class of 1973) and his Masters *(Film)* from Empire State College, State University, New York. Bartron and his wife have been together for 50 years and have three grown children and seven grandchildren. Commander Bartron and his wife live in Sacramento, CA.